L3X1

R.C. Grabowski

Rustwerks Publishing

Published by Rustwerks Publishing
United States of America
www.RustwerksPublishing.com
rustwerkspublishing@gmail.com

ISBNs
979-8-9999961-0-7 (Hardcover)
979-8-9999961-1-4 (Paperback)
979-8-9999961-2-1 (E-Book – EPUB)
979-8-9999961-3-8 (L3X1 – Collector's Edition, Rustwerks Author Release)

Cover design by Marina_Lexa (via Fiverr) & Rustwerks Publishing
Interior design by Atticus & Rustwerks Publishing

This is a work of fiction. Names, characters, places, events, and incidents are products of the author's imagination or are used fictitiously. Any resemblance to actual persons, living or dead, or actual events is purely coincidental.

First Edition: 2025
Printed and/or distributed on demand

Collector's Edition
Signed and authenticated by the author.
Packaged and distributed exclusively through Rustwerks Publishing.

CHAP_00.exe - Prologue

Verellii is a planet that seceded from Earth after a catastrophic conflict known as the Great War. The war began when Earth sought control, clashing with Verellii's fierce determination to remain independent.

Earth had devolved into a dystopian wasteland ruled by governmental tyranny. Citizens faced crushing taxes of up to 80%, stripped of their rights and left to endure spiraling crime, poverty, and urban decay. The air was toxic in many regions; clean water became a privilege, not a right. Mandatory surveillance suffocated personal freedoms. Earth's leaders governed through fear and propaganda, while its people survived through submission.

In stark contrast, Verellii was a scorched, volatile frontier—harsh, but alive with freedom. Its deserts demanded resilience, yet they stripped away the oppressive order of Earth. Here, risk was currency, and those willing to gamble could forge their own destinies.

Victory in the Great War came at a steep cost. Earth's retreat was vindictive: engineers were executed, spacefaring technology vaporized, and faster-than-light research erased. Even Verellii's moons—Bretyl and Yesh—were cut off, leaving millions stranded beyond reach.

During the war, Earth deployed its first Infiltrators—augmented assassins tasked with eliminating Verelliian leaders. One such Infiltrator, designated A1AN/A, was killed in a failed operation. Her remains were recovered and reverse-engineered, forming the blueprint for Verellii's own Infiltrator program. In the same campaign, an Enforcer—Earth's power-armored infantry—malfunctioned when its self-destruct sequence failed. Verellii salvaged the disabled unit, integrating its armor and systems into the first generation of their own Enforcers.

Yet the war's most enduring legacy wasn't the weapons or Verellii's defiance—it was the metal beneath its surface: Verelliian Steel. Thin, flexible, nearly indestructible, it can be reshaped, remember its form, and convert other metals into its elemental structure. The government hoards what little is known to exist; civilians are forbidden to possess it. And Earth will come for it again.

Whispers persist of a hidden vault—an unlimited reserve of Verelliian Steel—buried deep and sealed since the war. No one knows if it's real. But everyone knows that if it is, whoever controls it will shape Verellii's future.

Today, Verellii remains cut off from the stars—isolated and wary. Though advanced, the planet is still recovering: its systems fragile, its people scarred. The shadow of Earth still looms.

For now, Verellii rebuilds—free, but never safe.

CHAP_01.exe – Initialization

Darkness.

Cold water rained down, plastering her hair to her face as hands forced her to the ground. Her knees slammed into the soaked asphalt, pain flaring sharp with every movement. She thrashed against the grip on her arms, her body twisting as she cried out, but their hold only tightened.

Neon-pink light spilled across the wet pavement, painting her silhouette in fractured color. Tears blurred everything.

A gun cocked, its barrel lifting to her right eye. Water bounced off the blued steel, sliding down its length in tiny streams.

A voice from the shadows, low and venomous:

 "Stupid robot bitch."

The gunshot split the night.

Lexi jolted awake, heart pounding, the phantom echo of the shot still burning in her skull.

***

"Good morning, ladies and gentlemen—it's another scorcher today!" the announcer's voice chirped, all forced cheer and syrupy brightness. "With a high of 130 degrees and a low of 120, remember to stay hydrated with Hydropure—synthetic water infused with electrolytes!"

The holoprojector's feed cut out with a static-filled hiss as the screen sputtered and died.

She yawned and rose from the couch, stretching overhead before rubbing her eyes. She crossed the room and smacked the flickering unit with the heel of her hand.

"Why do all these holos keep dying?" Lexi muttered, looking at the black screen. "It lasted three fucking weeks!"

With a sigh, she tossed the remote onto the couch. "Guess it doesn't matter. I've got to head to work soon anyway."

For a moment, she lingered in front of the screen, eyes adjusting to the intense light streaming in through the windows. Her toes curled into the plush carpet beneath her feet—a stark contrast to her apartment in the Central District Nexus, where most amenities were cold, metallic, and utilitarian.

She walked through the hallway, passing two doors on her right. The apartment's modest charm clashed with its age. The first led to a room she never used, its walls peeling with ancient mint-green paint. The second opened into her sanctuary—her bedroom—painted in her favorite color: pink. Bright, unapologetic, and alive. Unlike the rest of the apartment, it was immaculately kept, complete with a private bathroom, a rare privilege in her building.

She stepped into the bathroom and pulled her shirt over her head, catching her reflection in the mirror. Pale skin met her blue and pink eyes, marked with faint seams where augmentations met synthetic flesh—subtle, barely visible unless you knew where to look. Tattoos in vivid pink and black traced along her arms and legs, sharp-edged and puzzling. She had no memory of choosing them. They were simply part of her now—just like the steel beneath her skin. Letting out a slow breath, she turned on the shower.

Steam filled the space as warm, sugary Hydropure sprayed down. As the water flowed, Lexi's thoughts drifted toward Lyria.

"Are you going to work already?" Lyria called, her voice teasing and soft from the kitchen. "You're going to be really early."

"Yeah, babe," Lexi replied over the sound of the water. "That new holo already died. Can you believe it? Third one this year."

Lyria laughed. "If you didn't sleep on the couch with the holo on all night and smack it every time it glitched, maybe your electronics would last longer," she teased.

Lexi chuckled, letting the heat work into her muscles. After rinsing off, she stepped from the shower, grabbed a towel, and dried herself quickly.

***

Lyria was waiting in the bedroom, leaning against the dresser, emerald eyes dancing with mischief. Lexi moved to the drawer and retrieved a pair of black lace panties—thin, barely there, faint floral patterns stitched into the fabric. She slid them up slowly, savoring the silky pull against her hips. Lyria watched every movement.

"Those are my favorite on you," Lyria purred, stepping forward. Her hand traced the curve of Lexi's waist before delivering a playful smack to her rear, fingers lingering just long enough to make Lexi shiver.

Lexi smirked, unfazed by Lyria's boldness. She grabbed a pair of blue jean capris and worked her way into them, the fabric clinging snugly. Tight, but practical. Worn-in and built for movement.

She slipped on her pristine white athletic shoes and laced them tight.

Then came the jacket.

Black leather, short-sleeved, standard-issue for Infiltrators, though customized to fit her frame. It sealed with a soft click, the internal cooling system humming to life. Open at the front to vent heat from her chest, it handled temperature control, radiation protection, boosted comms, and a magnetic seal so it never shifted. Pure utility.

She grabbed her headset from the nightstand and placed it over her ears. A small antenna extended from the top of the right speaker as it synced.

"RAPID headquarters, do you copy?" Lexi asked.

A burst of static, then a crisp reply: "We read you, Lieutenant Hayes. All systems are operational on our end."

Lexi nodded to herself and turned toward her weapons case. Her eyes scanned her gear: her shoto, 9 mm pistol, and katana, each perfectly positioned. She put each into its place with calm precision, their magnets pulling them snug against their ports along her thighs and back.

The final piece was a silver dome pulsing with faint blue light, her Temporal Displacement Beacon Unit, or TDB Unit. A short-range device, it allowed her to "blip" a few seconds forward in time—just enough to dodge a bullet or escape a kill zone.

She strapped it onto her left bicep and checked the charge.

"A full charge? That's new."

Lyria stood in the doorway, watching her with a mix of hunger and pride. "You look so damn sexy and dangerous when you're geared up like that. It's unfair, really."

Lexi smirked. "Dangerous, maybe. Sexy? That's all you, babe."

Lyria rolled her eyes, stepping closer and placing a hand on Lexi's chest. "Just make sure you come back in one piece. I kind of like you the way you are."

Lexi placed her hand over Lyria's. "I will. I promise."

Before Lexi could step back, Lyria cupped her face and kissed her—slowly, deeply. Their lips met in a warmth that left no doubt. When they finally parted, a faint thread of breath hung between them—not obscene or dramatic, just quietly, unmistakably human.

"I'll be waiting," Lyria whispered, her forehead resting lightly against Lexi's.

Lexi's heart thudded against her ribs. She gently pulled away, hand trailing down Lyria's side.

"Don't keep me waiting too long," Lyria added with a smile. "We've still got tonight, remember? Just you and me."

"We'll go to Level 2," Lexi replied, a faint smirk tugging at her lips. "You'll fit right in down there."

***

Lexi stepped out of her apartment into a furnace of dust, radiation, and sweat—the hum of her jacket shifting to compensate. As she descended the concrete steps leading down to the street, tiny lights embedded in the edges of each stair flickered on—just bright enough to see by at night, barely visible in the harsh morning sun.

Heat shimmered across cracked pavement. Cars powered by sand whooshed past in robotic whirs, their exhausts leaving glowing particulates in their wake above sun-bleached concrete. Governmental and corporate buildings rose nearby, facades austere, solar glass drinking in the light, metal sigils glinting in the sun. Security in matte uniforms clustered at entrances, scanning the crowds.

People stepped aside as she hit the walkway—some casting sidelong glances at the gear on her hip, others simply sensing her presence. Lexi didn't slow or dodge; the city flowed around her.

Across the avenue, storefronts of polished glass and sharp neon beckoned: high-end tech boutiques, a tailor's shop with mannequins in expensive suits, the shimmering front of a hydration parlor—its fans pulling precious moisture from the air, turning it into clean water sold at a premium. Synthetic grass and plastic-leafed trees lined the walkway, a manufactured oasis of green set against the desert's yellows, oranges, and tans.

Somewhere overhead, delivery drones sped past, their shadows slicing across the plaza. Next to a set of Hydropure fountains, Rex had run his old coffee cart here for years before trading it in for the four crumbling walls now known as the Golden Grill. She'd be back for her usual, and Rex would have it waiting, like he always did.

As she passed a group of workers unloading crates from a rusted cargo truck, a few of them paused, their dirt-streaked faces twisting into leers.

"Damn, those jeans are painted on," one said, loud enough to be heard.

"Look at those hips—she could strangle a man without trying," another added.

A third scoffed. "Forget that—check the tits. Bet she paid for those."

Before the fourth could laugh, his eyes narrowed.

"Shut the hell up, you guys," he muttered. "That's an Infiltrator. You don't want her to hear you."

Lexi didn't flinch.

They didn't know what they were looking at. To them, she was just a woman, a body to fantasize about. Not the Infiltrator who could kill them before their next breath.

She kept walking.

Let them bark and posture like animals, trying to impress one another.

They didn't matter. Not one of them.

Her thoughts wandered to Lyria. Despite the occasional rough edges of their relationship, something always sparked between them.

She remembered the night they met. A call had come in for a low-end club where a cybernetically enhanced brute was tearing the place apart, throwing tables, chairs, and people across the room. He had been massive, far beyond her weight class, and every blow shook the walls. Lexi was first on the scene. She was smaller, quicker, forced to fight with precision and acrobatics until she finally brought him down hard enough for the enforcers to swarm in and drag him away.

That was when Lyria stepped out of the shaken crowd—composed, smiling just enough to mask the chaos around her. "You saved me back there... let me at least buy you dinner."

The way Lyria looked at her... it wasn't just desire. It was understanding. That kiss earlier—it had weight. More than heat. More than routine.

Lexi exhaled slowly and pushed it down.

***

Twenty minutes passed. R.A.P.I.D. headquarters rose above the skyline—white marble and mirrored glass catching the brutal sun. Across its face, a golden insignia: Robotic Augmented Police Intervention Department. A beacon of hope in a dying city.

Lexi eyed the tower. "Guess subtlety didn't make the final budget," she said, just loud enough to be heard.

A voice answered from behind her.

***

"What was that, Lieutenant Hayes?"

Lexi didn't move, but her posture straightened.

Captain Cybrix Thorne stood behind her; his power armor made him nearly eight feet tall, and as he stepped closer, he blocked out the sun, casting a wide shadow over the area. It wasn't just his size; it was the precision, the silence, the way the air itself seemed to wait for his permission to move.

Lexi turned smoothly and replied, "Nothing, sir."

Thorne's face was just as Lexi remembered: angular, military, locked in a state of permanent seriousness. A full, regulation-trimmed beard. A tight fade that hadn't changed in years. Neon-orange lines traced his joints like restrained energy, pulsing faintly beneath the dense, gloss-black plating. Two stars gleamed from his chest plate, symmetrical, spotless, regulation. He didn't flaunt his rank. He maintained it. Every detail on his armor, from the polished plates to the exact positioning of his insignia, was by the book. Because to Thorne, the book wasn't a guideline—it was law.

His green eyes locked onto her—not with emotion, but with evaluation, and he studied her like a report that had gone slightly off-format.

Then, a curt nod.

"You're early. Good," Thorne said, pausing before continuing, "Public conduct reflects leadership. Carry yourself accordingly."

"Understood," Lexi said evenly as she turned to walk into HQ. She could still feel his presence behind her—steady, precise, unbending.

"And Lieutenant," he called, just loud enough to be heard.

"Perception is policy. If they question your discipline, they'll question your entire corps."

Lexi didn't answer. She didn't have to. She just kept walking.

CHAP_02.exe - Integration

As Lexi crossed the entrance into the atrium, the temperature dropped instantly. The air carried faint scents of electronics, floor polish, and disinfectant. Cries for help echoed from civilians at reinforced booths, where exhausted administrators struggled behind bulletproof glass. Cylindrical tube lights descended from the ceiling. Security drones hovered between them, their hum a constant reminder of surveillance as they watched the chaos below.

Infiltrators, some adjusting jackets or securing weapons, moved with instinctive precision toward their assignments. Their synthetic skin shimmered beneath the atrium lights, metallic muscles flexing in mechanical readiness. Hulking Enforcers—imposing even without armor—stood in formation or marched to debriefings, their presence radiating authority. The air thrummed with movement, terse exchanges, and mission chatter barely audible above the building's mechanical hum.

Criminals were dispatched with clinical ease. At the far end of the atrium, a man shouted, swinging at a security officer—but before he could land the blow, an Enforcer slammed him down, driving his face into the polished onyx floor. Two security drones dropped in, gun ports exposed, hovering close around the suspect like vultures.

Lexi didn't react. Scenes like this were routine in RAPID.

***

She walked up to a turret built into the back wall next to a security barrier, its barrel tracking her briefly before retracting. It presented a glowing laser grid in front of her as she raised her right arm and scanned the barcode embedded in her wrist with a flick. The blue-hued barrier hissed open in response, granting her access.

The Eraway stretched ahead—a broad corridor connecting every major department on the ground floor, buzzing with activity. Operatives pored over mission data, techs performed maintenance on robotics, and admins dashed between departments, clutching files as if their lives depended on it. As Lexi moved through the crowd by the armory, a pair of Enforcers stood at attention as she passed. She acknowledged them with a brief glance—just as a young admin, eyes glued to his datapad, collided with her shoulder. Lexi pivoted, fixing him with a cold, steady glare. The admin went wide-eyed, put his palms up in apology, and stammered, "Sorry—sorry." She turned away, refocused, and moved on, catching the sound of the Enforcers snickering at the exchange behind her.

Her gaze landed on a group of female recruits, their anxious energy practically radiating as they gripped their issued gear. These weren't the wide-eyed rookies still fumbling through the baby-step program. No—they were bound for CRIS—Critical Response and Infiltration Skills—the crucible that stripped candidates to their bones and rebuilt them into something colder, harder, less human. Years of relentless drills, brutal tests, and simulations meant to break even the strongest, even before augmentations were added. Lexi tried to recall life before CRIS, but nothing surfaced, only fragments: pain, screams, and the endless grind of training.

Her mentor, Lena Boma, once a Captain for the Corps, had shaped her into what she was now: honed, precise, and dangerous.

As she neared the Infiltrator Corps section, familiar shouting spilled into the hallway.

"¡Carajo! ¿Qué hicieron con esto?" The words cut through the air like a whip, harsh and sharp.

Lexi's headset kicked in automatically, filtering the outburst with a soft chime:

"Fuck! What did you do with this?"

Sergeant Isabella Rojas was in full form.

Lexi leaned against the doorframe, a quiet smirk tugging at her lips. Not at the recruits—at the memory of being one.

There was no hiding Rojas' temper—it was practically a force of nature. Another string of rapid-fire Spanish followed, and Lexi's interface translated in real time:

"I can't trust you with anything. If you can't even handle basic equipment, how do you expect to survive a mission?"

After a few more heated commands, Lexi stepped inside. Her presence shifted the room's energy like a ripple through water.

"What happened here?" she asked, raising an eyebrow.

Isabella turned, still breathing hard, her expression locked in irritation. But she straightened when she saw Lexi.

"These idiotas broke the damn comms equipment again," she grumbled, shaking her head. "They touch everything like it's made of sand. Dios mío."

She exhaled hard. "I'm teaching them pre-CRIS skills, but they act like this is a daycare. Out there? One mistake, and they're not coming back."

Lexi nodded in acknowledgment before shifting her attention. Commands and directives filled her vision. She raised her left wrist—a light blue glow illuminating under the skin of her forearm, her comm suite coming alive.

"Senior Operative Debra Sinclair," she said, her voice even and commanding.

The square pulsed once, then a voice responded crisply: "Yes, commander?"

"Report to the office immediately. You've been tasked."

"Yes, ma'am. En route. ETA five minutes."

Lexi's focus went back to the recruits, watching Rojas shift back into instruction mode. She still had the bite, but it was now tempered with control. Lexi folded her arms, silently approving.

The door hissed open behind her.

Debra Sinclair entered, tall and composed, her jet-black hair pulled into a tight ponytail. A dark green headset wrapped around both ears, framing a face marked by intensity and clarity. Her eyes swept the room—both brown, but her right had a faint red hue beneath the surface.

Debra didn't flinch at the tension and didn't speak until she was close.

"What's the assignment today, boss? Another Kurogane mark?" she asked, voice low and confident.

"No. Unfortunately not. Even though every one of them deserves to burn." Lexi responded coldly.

She swiped two fingers across her left wrist, sending a data file to Debra's comms. Debra's red-hued eye lit up, glowing bright as it accepted the incoming intel.

"You're headed to the Union District," Lexi continued. "Reports say miners have been luring Enforcers underwater and stripping them for parts."

Debra's eye dimmed as the scan completed. She nodded once, already forming her response.

 "Are they even killing them before the scavenging?" she asked. "Because pulling parts off an active Enforcer sounds like suicide."

Lexi shook her head. "I don't have that detail. That's why you're going in. We can't afford to lose any more of them."

"Copy that, boss. I'm on it," Debra said, turning to grab her gear.

She reached for her weapon on the bench nearby—an old Relay pistol. The casing was matte black and scuffed but clearly maintained with care. She snapped it to its port on her right leg with practiced ease.

Lexi raised an eyebrow. "You still carry that relic?"

"It's old school," Debra said with a small shrug. "People see an Infiltrator with one, they know exactly what I'm about. No explanations. No warnings."

 She gave a faint grin.

 "Need a gun? Get your message relayed, with a Relay!"

Lexi chuckled. "That commercial was terrible."

"Yeah," Debra said. "That's why I love it."

"I'm out," she continued. "I'll see you tomorrow—hopefully with good news."

***

Soon after Debra left, a desk phone rang—sharp and sudden.

 "Lieutenant Lexi Hayes, Commander, RAPID Infiltrator Corps," she answered, her words calm and precise. "State your purpose."

"You are a Lieutenant now, ehh? Thatssss goood," came the voice on the other end. It was raspy, slow, and tinged with an unnatural hiss.

"Who is this?" Lexi asked, her posture stiffening.

"Good, good, good," the voice continued, unfazed. "I know where a shipment of beamers is... just came off a truck too... yesssss, hurry, hurry, HURRY!"

Lexi narrowed her eyes. "Location. Now."

A pause. Faint whispering echoed behind the speaker, too distant to catch. Then:

"Neuron Energy shipping yard. Port District. Cargo container Z4762. Fresh off the truck. Ready to disappear."

"The Port District is massive. What building number?" she demanded.

"Building 177. Tick-tock, Lieutenant. Tick-tock." Then the line went dead.

Lexi lowered the handset slowly. *"Yeah, that's definitely a trap,"* she said sarcastically.

She remembered briefs where Kurogane Syndicate members had been reported at multiple Neuron Energy locations in the past few weeks. So, if laser weaponry was present at one of their warehouses, there was a good chance the syndicate would be there too.

She walked into her office—stone and reinforced glass. A panel behind her desk hissed open and recessed into the wall, revealing a stainless-steel weapons cabinet. The slots were mostly empty.

She never trusted the armory's DNA locks—too easy to spoof. Usually, most of her gear stayed with her. The remaining loadout was minimal: flashbangs, extra magazines, and her recon drone.

Reaching for the drone, she paused. Its chromatic black casing reflected the overhead lights, but the indicator blinked red—a charge failure.

"Great. I'm flying blind," she muttered, snatching extra mags before stepping out.

As she exited, Isabella met her in the hall. "Who was on the phone, mami?"

Lexi smirked, slipping into a mock rasp. "A guy about a shipment of beamersssssss."

Isabella didn't smile. "Laser weapons? That's serious. Call if you need anything."

Lexi nodded. "I will."

***

She exited the office, cutting left down the Eraway, weaving through the crowd until she reached the lift at the far end, ascending to the top floor of RAPID HQ. A massive metallic door awaited her. As she approached, a facial scanner activated, emitting a high-frequency ping.

"Lieutenant Lexi Hayes, entry authorized," said a flat synthetic voice.

The door slid open without sound. Lexi stepped into a circular chamber beneath a smooth white dome. The room gleamed with surgical precision. On the far wall, a cylindrical track extended out of the building like the bore of a railgun.

To the right, a series of transparent spheres sat in charging cradles above magnetic rails. From the ceiling, a gloss-black cube matching the polished surfaces around it descended with a soft hiss and floated in front of her.

"INPUT AUTHORIZATION," the cube stated, its tone cold and robotic.

Lexi lifted her right wrist, presenting her ingrained barcode as it neared the cube's sensor. The machine scanned it before emitting a high-pitched chirp.

"VERIFIED. TRANSMIT DESTINATION."

"Port District. Neuron Energy. Building 177."

"COORDINATES ACCEPTED."

One of the clear spheres unlocked, dropping out of its pod and down onto the track before diverting onto the central rail and lighting up. A hatch spiraled open. Lexi stepped in without hesitation. The seat inside folded from the floor, conforming to her body.

"SEALING. LAUNCH SEQUENCE INITIATED."

Lightning arced around the chamber as energy built. The sphere vibrated as the rail aligned with the elongated tunnel.

"LAUNCH IN 3...2...1."

The world exploded into motion. The sphere fired from the rail like a bullet, the city outside a blur of lights and structures. Lexi remained still as the scenery shifted—from the crisp greens and metallic silvers of the Central District Nexus to the muted tans and wreckage of the outskirts.

Craters. Twisted mech frames. Ruins of old conflicts.

Then the seat folded away as Lexi crouched on the floor.

"EJECTION IN 3...2...1. EJECT."

Lexi kicked off the floor as the sphere burst open, launching her into freefall. Wind tore past her ears. Her body tucked tight, arms at her sides. Asphalt rushed to meet her.

She twisted midair, landing in a crouch that cratered the ground. A shockwave of dust and shattered concrete rippled outward from her point of impact.

She stood slowly, her shoes cracking through debris, her knee dripping green coolant.

The mechanic's gonna kill me, she thought, brushing grit from her jacket with a crooked grin.

***

Lexi studied the shipping building: an unsettling quiet draped over it. *Why so empty? No guards, not even at ten on a weekday? No customers, no vehicles—nothing.* Her eyes narrowed, suspicion growing.

She surveyed the perimeter: a massive gate and reinforced brick walls, far too secure for a shipping yard. The walls loomed high, blocking any escape. Excessive—but Lexi shoved the suspicion aside. Mission first, questions later.

She sprinted toward the gate, instantly closing the distance and examining the lock. *Child's play*, she thought, switching to X-ray optics. She saw through the lock's internal mechanics as she pulled out a set of lockpicking tools and deftly unlocked the gate...

"Shit," she whispered. A faint click from the door frame made Lexi freeze. Her enhanced vision picked out the outline of a pressure switch, its spring-loaded arm held down by the closed door. If that arm released, it would trigger whatever lay connected beyond.

"Cute," she muttered, drawing her shoto. With careful precision, she wedged the blade into the gap, holding the switch arm down. She inched the door open just enough to slip through, then pulled the door shut behind her. Only after the latch clicked did she withdraw her blade, allowing the arm to extend—rearming the trap for anyone who might follow.

The lock sealed with a metal click, and Lexi pulled her shoto free.

She smirked, sliding the blade back into place on her thigh. "Your problem now."

As she slipped into the outer yard, the silence was overwhelming; the only movement was the wind brushing against the dead grass scattered across the yard, a reminder of the desolation around her. She took in the surroundings, her trained eyes scanning for any signs of danger. She noticed wiring going from the door switch to several explosive charges along the wall and to strategically placed concrete cylinders around the yard.

Lexi knew these were not just structural remnants of the yard's design. They were high-powered turrets, positioned to guard the building. There was no way she could take them on in direct combat. The thought crossed her mind for only a moment before she dismissed it—her only option was through the front door of the building.

She caught a flash of something buried beneath the yard's surface. Landmines. They were carefully hidden, their sensors nearly invisible. They were sporadically placed and numerous. She'd have to rely on agility to cross the yard without triggering the mines.

Adjusting her stance, she prepared for a silent, acrobatic dash across the yard. Staying low, she moved with precise, fluid motions, keeping out of the turrets' line of sight. Each step was calculated as she navigated landmines and ducked behind scattered concrete, using every scrap of cover to mask her approach.

Finally, she reached the front door and grabbed the pistol on her hip. An electrified snap filled the air as the magnetic lock disengaged, echoing before it faded. She carefully unlocked the door, the faint sound of metal sliding into place as she entered the building.

***

As she stepped inside, the dim and dusty lobby offered no sign of activity. No lights, no sounds. The place felt abandoned. Lexi moved cautiously through one of the many dark hallways, her pistol at the ready; the only light coming in was from the open windows. She surveyed each attached room as she passed, clearing them with methodical precision, making sure no hostiles were hidden within.

As she neared the shipping area door, a sudden bolt of yellow light slammed into Lexi's left shoulder. Instantly, skin bubbled and peeled away, punching a hole through her metallic muscle. Pain detonated—sharp, hot, and electric. Lexi gritted her teeth and exploded into motion, vaulting over boxes and debris, ricocheting off walls—a blur, unpredictable and impossible to track.

The assailant fired a flurry of laser shots. Lexi darted sideways, pushing off the wall with one hand, sliding behind cover, never slowing.

She closed the gap fast. As she neared, she snapped her pistol up and scanned him.

"Tajiro Yoshimaru, you've been found guilty of attacking a RAPID Infiltrator. Punishment is death," she said, voice flat and cold.

Lexi's finger tightened on the trigger. The firearm came to life.

"Ballistic rounds. 12 plus 1 available." A mechanical voice emanated from her pistol, its front light shifting into a faint yellow glow.

Lexi fired. The 9 mm round punched through Tajiro's forehead. He crumpled, motionless.

***

Lexi advanced toward the main shipping room, paranoia seeping in as she inspected her surroundings for further signs of movement. As she approached two rusted metal doors, she heard shouting, the sound of machinery, and a beeping noise.

She peered through the small, reinforced glass windows, preparing herself for whatever came next.

She counted at least twenty hostiles in the room. Some guarded a large crate; others directed a box truck that had just pulled in. It was already reversing—too clean, too timed. This wasn't routine loading. This was an exit strategy.

"Buckshot," Lexi commanded. The gun's small light flashed green.

She slammed her foot into the double doors, kicking them clean off their hinges. Metal shrieked across the floor, sparking as it skidded.

Running into the room, she fired. A hailstorm of pellets erupted from the barrel, tearing through three men. They collapsed in a heap, their clothing shredded and blood pooling across the floor. Shots rained down from the catwalk above. She didn't hesitate. Sprinting toward the stairwell, she caught sight of a man leaning from the corner, guarding the stairs.

As she approached him, Lexi angled her pistol up and fired a single buckshot blast toward the catwalk. The blast ripped through the railing, sending sparks and debris flying. Several men dropped out of view, scrambling for cover.

Gunfire erupted in retaliation—rounds slammed into the floor and ricocheted off the walls. Lexi stayed low and fast, moving without hesitation.

"KOUFUKU, KOUFUKU!" the shooter peeking from around the corner screamed.

Her headset translated: "SURRENDER, SURRENDER!"

"Yeah, no," Lexi snapped, leveling her pistol. She pulled the trigger. Buckshot tore through the concrete corner, shredding the man's skull—blood and bone sprayed across the wall.

"Fuck, forgot to change configs."

"Zero mag," the pistol said, ejecting the spent magazine. Smoke trailed as it clattered to the floor.

Lexi cursed under her breath but wasted no time. She quickly slammed a new mag into the pistol, snapping it into place.

"Ballistic," she commanded again as the light on the gun flashed yellow.

"12 plus 1 available," the pistol announced.

Lexi ran up the stairwell; eyes locked on the catwalk above. Below, the truck finished backing up to the container. Four men rushed out, scrambling to load it while she was distracted by the shooters overhead.

"Lexi! The truck!" HQ commanded, "Turn around!"

Without hesitation, Lexi pressed her TDB Unit on her damaged left arm. She flashed forward in time, instantly appearing at the truck. She took out the four men with deadly precision, each man shot cleanly in the head with her pistol, the rounds fired so quickly they barely had time to react.

As laser bolts seemed to fire endlessly at her, Lexi crouched between the crate and the truck, savoring what little cover she had. *Fuck*, she thought, as she was pinned down by a relentless rainstorm of gunfire. She peeked out from behind cover, seeing men coming down from the catwalk, and fired a precise bullet to burst a pipe; steam poured out, burning three men. They collapsed to the floor, screaming, clutching their scorched faces.

One man yelled in Japanese, "HIROGERU!"

"Expand," her headset translated as she saw the men scatter in different directions.

"Fuck, man. You guys are really pissing me off!" Lexi growled, frustration rising as she spotted four men hiding behind the other side of the container with her X-ray.

Lexi jumped up, kicked off the crate with both feet, sending it skidding toward the men, crushing them as it slid across the floor, leaving a thick trail of blood behind. She flipped midair and landed smoothly on her feet.

As she landed, a laser bolt struck her leg. The pain was immediate. Her skin bubbled and smoked as the injury seared into her. Kneeling, she gritted her teeth, feeling the excruciating burn.

The man giving orders approached her, lifting her chin. "Anata wa subarashii senshi de, utsukushiku, soshite chimeiteki desu. Demo kyou, anata ga shinu no wa anata jishin desu," he said calmly, his voice almost serene.

Her headset replied: "You are a great warrior, beautiful, and deadly. But today, you will be the one who dies."

Lexi's eyes widened—Lyria flashed in her mind, the future she still hoped for, and the promise she'd made. Rage and instinct flooded her veins. Lexi surged upward, snarling, and gripped the man's jaw with brutal force. Her fingers dug into his flesh, and with a savage wrench, she yanked downward. Tendons stretched like wet cords, then tore free with a sickening snap. His scream gurgled in his throat as his jaw tore free, hanging by a ragged strip of skin before falling to the floor with a wet slap.

Blood poured from his face as he collapsed to his knees, gurgling incoherently—unable to scream, unable to beg. Lexi watched him, the man's blood dripping from her fingers, her chest heaving—not fear, but fury. She forced herself to steady her breath. This was survival.

"I won't be the one who dies today," she growled, voice razor-sharp and cold. "And I promise you—I will kill every Kurogane Syndicate member I come across."

She raised her gun and fired a single, precise bullet between his eyes. His body went limp and fell to the floor.

***

The other men, who witnessed her brutal move, scattered in fear, abandoning their positions. In their panic, several tripped over hidden landmines—sharp metallic clicks followed by violent eruptions that shook the walls. One of the survivors, wild-eyed, sprinted for the outer perimeter door. When he yanked it open, the pressure switch arm extended, and the explosion was immediate, tearing the entrance apart in a fireball of brick and flame. Lexi flinched, then allowed herself a grim smile. "Fucking idiots."

She lowered her pistol, arcs of electricity sparking off her thigh as the weapon attempted to lock onto its port. Before holstering it, Lexi swept the area, her eye flaring red as she scanned the building's corridors, slicing through the structure for any movement. After she confirmed the area was clear, she let the pistol snap to her thigh.

Lexi then started rummaging through the man's pockets, searching for anything useful. Her fingers brushed against a rectangular shape in his coat's breast pocket. "A slate! Fuck yes," she exclaimed, a victorious smile tugging at her lips. "This will definitely be useful," she said as she tucked the slate into her own jacket pocket.

"Let's see what they're hiding in this shipment and what they were so eager to protect." Lexi walked over to the crate that had slid more than 100 feet and lifted it up to expose the red gore that used to be human beings. She ripped off the lock and opened the doors to reveal over 50 illegal laser rifles, 100 thermite grenades, and some very rare laser-edged swords. Lexi took pictures with her eye and uploaded them to command.

"Your orders?" she asked, her voice steady.

"Lieutenant, orders are to destroy everything; leave nothing salvageable!" the voice from command responded.

Lexi ran back, putting distance between her and her target, and took aim with her pistol. "Explosive," she commanded.

The pistol responded, "Unable to use explosive—requires more rounds."

Frustrated, Lexi rolled her eyes and replaced the used mag with a fresh one, the light on the pistol turning orange. "Explosive configuration chosen," the pistol said.

She shot the container and watched as the payload exploded, the thermite grenades disintegrating everything in their wake. "If this shipment made it to the streets... we wouldn't stand a chance," Lexi muttered under her breath, her gaze fixed on the inferno.

***

After the fire fizzled out, she turned her focus, digging through the remaining shipments, looking for any information about who sent them—or who was supposed to receive them. But no further clues surfaced. Her gaze moved over the corpses scattered around her.

Her internal database flared, and she logged the Kurogane officers involved with this Neuron Energy location and the weapons she'd destroyed.

Unfortunately for RAPID, Neuron Energy was the only company on Verellii capable of creating these weapons. With Syndicate ties, this could end very badly. Lexi smirked through the pain. *"But not if I burn them down first."*

CHAP_03.exe - R3c0ver

As Lexi limped out the door, the turrets—armed by one man's failed escape through the gate—came online. One locked onto her, spitting high-caliber rounds that tore into the structure, a severed arm tangled across its barrel. She dove back inside, heart pounding.

Her voice cracked as she scrambled for comms.

"HQ! HQ, come in! Requesting extraction and fire support! Landing zone is heavily guarded!"

The turret's barrage drew others, all locking onto her position. Infiltrators could shrug off certain calibers, but these munitions were far beyond what Lexi's augmented frame could withstand.

Rounds chewed through the walls. The building groaned, then collapsed, slamming down on her with brutal force and pinning her to the floor. Darkness pressed in as her frame creaked under the crushing weight, a bone-deep ache radiating through her body.

***

Gritting her teeth, Lexi dug her palms into the debris and forced herself upward. Her augmented muscles screamed, lifting the weight inch by inch before a burst of gunfire shredded a support beam overhead. The beam snapped, crashing down across her back and driving her flat again.

"Bitch!" she roared, fury bleeding through the strain as the molten glow of the beams around her flared brighter as the rounds tore closer.

Helpless now, she listened to the distant roar of a Skyreaper-class gunship overhead. The craft strafed the battlefield, launching missiles from its wings and spitting 50 mm fire from its nose gun. The turrets switched targets as two Enforcers dropped from the gunship, their heavy frames slamming into the earth nearby. The Enforcers steadied themselves, servos whining as they rose to full height. Above, the gunship's engines shifted pitch, the roar fading as it swept the perimeter in a wide circle before pulling away.

"Did you see that shit?" one of the Enforcers laughed, as bullets ricocheted off his armor.

"See what?" the other one asked.

"I landed right on that turret and blew the bitch up!" the first Enforcer grinned.

"That's because you're a fat ass, Blackwood," the other soldier teased.

As the Enforcers eliminated the remaining turrets and secured the area, they began lifting the wreckage off Lexi.

"Holy shit," one of them muttered. Lexi caught the soldier's identification: Corporal Zalok Kalani. "You're still alive, Lieutenant. You Infiltrators are some tough bitches; I'll give you that."

"Watch your mouth, Corporal," Lexi said, wincing but managing a smirk despite her pain.

"Big talk from a small girl who needed saving... by me," Kalani laughed, hauling her up.

"Take that suit off, and we'll see who the little girl is that needs saving," Lexi shot back with a grin.

As they stepped into the open, a deep mechanical roar split the air—the Skyreaper descending through smoke like a hunter. Its flat-gray hull shimmered with heat, nose angled like a spear, wings swept outward in a predator's glide.

Twin engines in the wings rotated downward with a thunderous hiss, kicking up clouds of dust and debris. Missile pods retracted into the wings, while armored panels folded down from each wingtip and emitted a dull blue shield to protect the side doors.

Under the nose, the 50 mm cannon swiveled, tracking for targets. Dual thrusters flared near the tail, guiding the gunship into a hard, deliberate landing. Landmines popped beneath its frame like fire-crackers—barely scratching the armor.

As the landing gear struck, both side doors dropped open. Twin 20 mm miniguns spun up with a low, hungry whine—scanning for hostiles, covering the extraction as Kalani and Blackwood moved Lexi toward the waiting beast.

"All personnel aboard Skyreaper One," Blackwood called out as he and the team stepped aboard the craft.

"Copy that, lifting off," came the reply.

As the wings of the gunship folded up, the massive, mechanized bird soared into the sky, its engines roaring as it took flight.

Inside the gunship, Kalani laid Lexi on a medical bed. The soft hum of the interior contrasted with the chaos they'd just escaped. Diagnostic tools whirred to life, scanning her for injuries. Kalani steadied her before turning to Blackwood.

"She one tough wahine, bruddah—no lie," he said, giving Lexi a look that was both admiring and relieved.

Lexi, holding her shoulder, smirked. "I've got more where that came from."

***

The gunship rocketed through the sky, landing at RAPID HQ beside other Skyreaper-class ships. As the landing gear thudded down, medics rushed to retrieve Lexi. Her skin wounds were already knitting back together—a testament to her enhancements—but the deeper damage in her joints would take far longer to self-heal. If she wanted to be combat-ready today, she'd need immediate care.

"Must be awesome to have those powers," Blackwood said, watching as Lexi sat up slowly, wincing slightly as her skin closed over the wounds.

"Yeah, but if you had this and power armor, your ego wouldn't fit through the hatch," Lexi teased, her eyes sparkling with humor.

Kalani chuckled, slapping Blackwood's chest plate as they laughed. Lexi let out a tired smirk.

"But seriously—thanks for today," she said, her tone shifting.

Kalani bumped her fist, then flashed a quick shaka, his grin steady.

"Anytime, ma'am. You're one of us."

"Hayes, get that damage fixed," a voice crackled over her comms. "You did a good job today, but you were sloppy."

"Chief Graevos?" Lexi asked, surprised by the voice.

"Yes, Lieutenant," came the authoritative response. "Tomorrow, I want you in my office first thing. Is that understood?"

"Yes, sir," Lexi replied confidently, though the lump in her throat hinted at the weight of the conversation to come.

Lexi returned to HQ for the second time that day—this time on a gurney. The building was eerily quiet, not a soul in sight. They wheeled her straight to the Mechanic's workshop.

***

"Put her on the table," a voice ordered—low, direct, unfamiliar.

Lexi turned her head. "Who are you?"

"I'm the new wrench. The last doc rotated out." He didn't look up. "Sit back and relax—we'll be done soon."

She narrowed her eyes but didn't argue.

The Mechanic scanned her right wrist. As a console lit up behind him, his posture stiffened as he examined the screen, muttering under his breath.

"Well, Ms. Hayes, you've got a few coolant ruptures, some damaged strands... but nothing unrepairable."

He activated a laser-edged scalpel. It gave a soft whine as its edge glowed faintly, slicing into her damaged leg and shoulder. Lexi didn't react—until the blade nicked bone.

"Ow, what the fuck," she snapped.

The Mechanic smirked faintly, eyes never leaving his work.

"You know, Ms. Hayes... you Infiltrators and Enforcers always come back broken and ruptured—but somehow, your foul mouth is the one thing that never breaks."

Lexi's eyes dropped. Her voice was softer now.

"Not everyone comes back."

Lena never came back. No upgrades. No rebuild. Just silence.

Her gaze snapped back to him. "Wait—how do you know that about me?"

The Mechanic jerked his chin toward the console. "Your file. Says you've got a knack for cursing." He returned to his work without another word.

Lexi watched with detached fascination as he pressed on, green coolant spilling from her synthetic muscle. She didn't flinch—just another reminder of how far from human she'd become.

Minutes later, the whine faded into silence.

"You okay, Doc?" she asked.

No answer.

He tapped a few commands into the console. A file flashed open—too fast for her to read—before he muttered again and shut off the screen. He crossed to a bin labeled SCRAP and pulled out a rusted hunk of metal, corroded and flaking with age. He hesitated a moment before pressing it into her damaged leg joint.

The effect was immediate. Rust hissed into steam. The scrap glowed, folding inward until it fused seamlessly with her metallic strands, vanishing into her like it had always belonged.

The Mechanic froze, eyes wide.

"As I live and breathe... I never thought I'd see it."

Lexi frowned. "See what?"

But he didn't answer, his gaze fixed on her leg like he'd just witnessed the impossible.

He grabbed a sleek, twin-barreled device and sprayed a fine mist over her torn skin, cells regenerating in its wake. Tattoos of pink and black reappeared exactly as they had before. No overlays. No data input. Just back, like memory stitched into her DNA.

***

His hands hovered above his tools before he hastily scribbled something on a pad, shielding it from her.

"Everything good?" Lexi asked.

"Yeah. You're stable. I'll need to order more strands. Now go—I've got work to do."

He ushered her toward the exit, too quickly.

"Thanks, Doc. You never gave me your name."

"I don't have one. Now go!" he snapped.

As she passed his desk, Lexi glimpsed a file on the console's screen before it vanished. The heading at the top read: CLASSIFIED: L3X1

Lexi froze. "Is that my name?"

"Yes," he muttered, shoving her through the door.

"But why is it spelled so—"

SLAM. The door shut in her face.

"That was weird," Lexi muttered as she walked away.

***

She made her way to the Infiltrator Department. Once inside her office, the panel on the back wall slid open.

Lexi removed her swords and TDB Unit, reloaded her gun, and hung everything on the wall. The TDB Unit's dome flashed, signaling that it was charging, while her recon drone glowed a neon orange.

"I really hope this shit actually charges tonight," Lexi muttered, watching as an overhead light flickered and buzzed.

Once she finished with her weapons, Lexi turned to her locker. She removed the slate from her pocket and placed it on the desk before taking off her jacket. The office windows responded by shifting to an impenetrable black as her door closed automatically. She shoved the damaged jacket into a chute, grabbed a new one from the locker, and put it on. It sealed to her frame, and the windows reverted to transparent.

She sat at her desk, logged onto her computer, and completed a requisition order for a new pair of pants. The system assured her they'd arrive at her door by midnight.

Standing up, Lexi rotated her shoulder, feeling the repair adjust to her movements. *I need a drink*, she thought, excited to go out with Lyria tonight.

CHAP_04.exe - Masquerade

...error//data_corrupt ...applying_pΔtch.exe

Lexi left the RAPID complex and began the walk back home, glancing up at Verellii's twin moons—Bretyl and Yesh—etched into a star-scattered sky.

Bretyl glowed green, blanketed with forests and pleasant weather. Yesh brooded under dense, fluorescent yellow poison fog—beautiful, dangerous, deadly.

Before the Great War, both moons were colonized and heavily mined to supply Verellii with resources.

Spaceflight died with the Great War. No one had left Verellii since.

Sometimes Lexi wondered what escape to another planet would be like—if a ship launched tomorrow, she'd volunteer without hesitation. The thought filled her with longing and a sharp ache, making her painfully aware of how trapped she felt on Verellii.

Lost in daydreams of space travel, Lexi tripped on the sidewalk. She looked down. A relatively plain woman lay lifeless on the concrete. Lexi's eye flickered, scanning.

"Elsa Smith," she muttered, reading the identification log. "Even the name is boring."

"Damn. Am I really so cold that I don't care about a corpse?" she wondered aloud, a mix of guilt and numbness making her voice waver, her words lingering uncomfortably over the body.

***

Lexi called it in, knowing no one would bother with a case where the victim was already dead. Crime had spiked 250% over the past year, leaving the Norms—her word for unaugmented Verellii Public Service Department (VPSD) officers—buried in active cases. No augmentations, no power armor. *Where's the fun in that?* she thought with a smirk.

She remembered the stares, the whispered comments, the hands that got too bold—that is, until she'd snapped a VPSD officer's wrist in front of everyone. The memory tugged a smile from her, recalling the awe and fear that followed.

As Lexi neared her apartment, excitement and nerves tangled in her chest. The thought of spending the night with Lyria made her heart race. She shouldered through the apartment's front door.

"Lyria! I'm home. Still want to go out?" she called, trying to catch her breath.

No answer. "Lyria?" Lexi called again, walking through the empty apartment. The silence felt wrong—a sharp contrast to her earlier excitement. As she moved down the hallway, anticipation soured into disappointment. Was something wrong? Why isn't she home?

Just as Lexi began to feel a pang of worry, she froze. The robotic whir of an engine cut through the silence.

A car pulled up outside the apartment. Heart quickening, she rushed to the window and caught the silhouette of a man in the driver's seat.

Then the passenger door opened as Lyria stepped out.

"I'll see you later, my love," Lyria said, her voice smooth as silk as she leaned into the car window.

Lexi tried to scan the man, but with the wrong angle and light, her scan returned with no ID. Who the hell was this?

The sight hit Lexi as a hot rush of anger, confusion, and hurt surged through her, mixing so fast she almost trembled. Shock held her, then suspicion crept in. *What's going on?*

And why was Lyria calling him "love"? Lexi watched Lyria ascend the steps, jealousy rising. Heart pounding, she forced herself to focus, pushing aside gut accusations. She'd get answers before confronting Lyria. After all, they were happy, weren't they?

***

"We are... right?" Lexi whispered to herself as the front door swung open and Lyria walked in.

"Babe! You're home early!" Lyria exclaimed.

"I am, but more importantly... who was that in the car—the man you called 'Love'?" Lexi asked, her tone calm but sharp.

Lexi saw panic in Lyria's eyes, the hesitation in her expression as she scrambled for an answer.

"He's... uh, Burton Marx. Kind of a wellness consultant," Lyria said quickly. "He's been helping me with some recovery work in the gym, and we've crossed paths a few times."

Lexi's pink iris flared red—public records scrolling across her HUD.

"Burton Marx. Age: 55. Occupation: Head of the Bioengineering Research and Development Department of the Union. Ten years in current position. Former lead researcher for the genetically modified food sector. No criminal records or flagged affiliations," her headset reported.

Lexi frowned. "Be careful around him. The Union's been targeting augmented personnel. I don't want you caught in anything. But seriously... 'Love?'"

Lyria shrugged, playful. "You know me—I flirt to get what I want. Doesn't mean anything. Actually, since we're going out tonight, we should give it a try. Free drinks!"

Lyria took Lexi's hand and guided her toward the bathroom.

"I almost didn't make it today," Lexi murmured, her voice quieter than usual.

Lyria paused, searching her face. Lexi didn't offer more—just looked at her, like she was the only anchor in a world pulling her apart.

***

Then Lexi leaned in, kissing her—slow and hungry. She tugged Lyria's sports bra over her head and tossed it aside, her fingers already sliding into the waistband of her yoga pants. They slipped down with ease, revealing a black thong.

Lexi pressed a kiss to her collarbone, then another down her chest. Her hand slid upward, fingers teasing until Lyria moaned.

Lyria stepped back, eyes playful. "Get the water hot. I'm not doing anything cold tonight."

Lexi smirked and turned on the shower, waiting as the sludge cleared and Hydropure poured through. Steam filled the room quickly.

She returned to Lyria, sliding her thong down like it was the easiest decision she'd made all day, fingertips lingering on every inch of skin.

As Lexi traced her curves, savoring every detail, Lyria unbuttoned Lexi's pants and slipped off her jacket.

Lyria stepped beneath the spray as Lexi shed the rest of her clothing, following her in.

Water slicked down Lyria's caramel skin, highlighting every curve of her body. Lexi's eyes drank in the sight—strong, soft, devastatingly gorgeous.

Their mouths met again, wetter, needier. Lyria gasped as Lexi's fingers gripped her hips and pulled her closer.

Without a word, Lyria's hand trailed up Lexi's torso, cupping one breast. Her thumb flicked across Lexi's nipple, coaxing a sharp gasp. Then her hand slid lower—gripping Lexi's ass with possessive hunger, fingers pressing deep like she owned it.

Lexi shuddered, a low hum escaping her throat.

Then Lyria's hand moved lower, trailing between Lexi's thighs, her fingers rubbing in slow, deliberate circles—drawing pleasure from the center of her. Lexi's lips parted in a soft moan, her breath catching as her body melted into Lyria's touch.

Lyria grinned and sank to her knees.

The water poured over her as she kissed her way up Lexi's inner thigh, tongue flicking before sliding into a rhythm that made Lexi tremble.

Lexi braced herself on the wall, threading her fingers through Lyria's dark curls, hips twitching toward her with every pulse of pleasure.

"Don't stop," she moaned.

Lyria's fingers joined her mouth, teasing and claiming every inch of Lexi's body. The pleasure burned through her, raw and unstoppable, dragging her to the edge.

Lexi's breath caught, her body arching. "Fuck, babe... yes... don't stop!"

The orgasm tore through her in a violent shudder; her cry muffled by her forearm as her body convulsed under the wash of ecstasy. For all the steel and code inside her, it was Lyria's touch that made her feel human—achingly, breathlessly alive.

Water poured down, steam swirling in time with her heartbeat.

When she finally opened her eyes, Lyria stood over her with a cocky smirk. "You were saying something about not leaving the house?"

Lexi leaned back, heart still hammering. The tile cooled her spine, but it was Lyria's touch she felt—branding her in the best way. She let the silence linger, drawing a breath that was more than relief—it was gratitude.

Then she grinned. "You're dangerous."

"Damn right," Lyria replied. Her smile softened, then turned wicked. "You still owe me a night out. So towel off before I drag you out dripping."

"Shit… after that, I'm staying in," Lexi said breathlessly as she leaned against the shower wall.

"Oh no, you don't!" Lyria shot back with a smirk. "You promised me a night together—we're going out for drinks!"

Lexi chuckled, steam curling around her as she fought to steady her breathing. "Yeah, yeah… give me a minute. I almost died today, remember?"

Lyria kissed her again—just a brush of lips this time, gentle and grounding. "Exactly. Which is why tonight, we celebrate."

Lexi groaned as she stepped out of the shower, grabbing a towel and dragging it over her shoulders. "Still think staying in sounds better," she muttered, the words half-lost in the hiss of the water. She wiped the steam from the mirror as she dried off, catching Lyria's reflection.

Minutes later, the heat of the bathroom gave way to the scents of perfume, fabric, and the sharp clatter of heels on tile.

Lexi lay sprawled on the bed, a towel still wrapped around her. As Lyria entered, her black curls bounced as she revealed herself in a tight black dress and sparkling silver sequin heels. The light caught the scales like fire. "I love these shoes," she beamed. "They're perfect for me… but I don't wear them enough."

"You look good in everything," Lexi muttered, pushing herself up and tugging on a tight white tee. "I prefer things that are more… functional."

Lyria's eyes flicked over, amused. The shirt wasn't sheer, but it didn't have to be—the fabric stretched tight, her nipples peeking through with unmistakable intent. Her abs still glistened with heat, and her jeans clung like paint as she forced them into place. Scuffed, blood-streaked white shoes finished the look.

"How is that functional?" Lyria smirked.

Lexi waved her hands and kicked a leg up. "I can move really well...
see?"

They both burst into laughter.

A horn blared outside.

"Honk, honk!"

"Let's go party!" Lyria grinned, extending her hand.

***

They slid into the back seat of the waiting cab.

The cab was a battered yellow beast, its chipped body dulled by years
of sand-blasted storms and poor maintenance. A checkered pattern of
faded neon lights traced the perimeter of its frame—pulsing unevenly
like it could short out any second. From the exhaust, thick black
chunks of burnt carbon spit out in coughing bursts, each one flaring
with tiny sparks like the cab was on its final ride.

The tires had no tread, just smooth rubber and a lot of hope.

Inside, the air reeked of stale sweat and scorched circuitry. The front
dash held three flickering screens: one displaying a jittery GPS, one
running up a toll cost, and the third scanning the passengers—green
bars confirming Lexi and Lyria's IDs while also flashing the cab
driver's name and photo in the corner: S. KORSAN — Verified Transit
Operator.

The driver looked like the cab felt: half-functional, one foot from
collapse. His stained white shirt clung to his gut, and his khaki cargo
shorts were tattered and sun-faded. A crooked hat hid greasy, un-
kempt hair, and his thick mustache twitched with every chew of his
lower lip.

"Where to?" he grunted, eyes never leaving the center screen.

"Level 2, Neon District. The Void," Lexi replied.

He glanced back just long enough to eye Lyria's bare legs in the backseat. "You two sure you can handle yourselves down there?"

"We've got it handled. Drive." Lexi's voice was sharp enough to cut steel.

The cab veered off the main road and dropped into a tunnel, zig-zagging through angled ramps and deep service roads. Rusted catwalks crisscrossed overhead. Streetlights buzzed weakly against concrete walls streaked with exhaust and graffiti. Neon ads bled color across the glass—pink, teal, yellow—while blue and red service signs pulsed faintly between them. Half the signage glitched in frozen loops, the rest sputtered in and out of static before blinking out.

The deeper they went, the more it felt like the planet was swallowing them whole.

Lexi leaned back. Level 2 wasn't far, but it always felt like falling into another world.

A track kicked on—"Neon Dreamscape."

Both girls lit up.

"This is our song!" Lyria squealed.

Lexi cranked the volume.

Together they sang:

 "Snort the Blaze, feel the bass,

 Lose your mind, forget your face.

 You're already late—

 For the Neon Dreamscape."

The driver muttered something under his breath and rolled his eyes.

***

Then...

Level 2 exploded around them. It was chaos wrapped in light.

Holographic signs flickered above rusted awnings, glitching in and out of legibility. Animated ads pitched everything from massages to mindless pleasure tabs. Street callers shouted over one another—promising credits, intimacy, euphoria, salvation. A woman in a cracked gold visor whispered about full-body sex spas while slipping vials into the hands of passing addicts.

Strip clubs and bars lined both sides of the street. Some looked like high-end lounges, all polished chrome and velvet drapes. Others were nothing more than open concrete boxes with strobing lights and half-naked dancers grinding against chain link railings.

A towering casino loomed to their left—the Yugen Club—styled with vertical red and white paper lantern cylinders glowing softly in the haze. Untranslated Japanese banners fluttered above the entrance in bold and ceremonial writing. Two massive holographic dragons circled the building's roof—one made entirely of brilliant gold, the other a deep, violent red. One chased the other endlessly, as if fortune itself was just out of reach.

To their right was SynthSkin. The soft pink exterior glowed beneath layered neon strips, every edge of the building traced in sharp, electric pink light. Massive photos of dancers—male and female—posed across the outer walls in full seductive display. Two massive bouncers stood silently at the entrance, their eyes replaced with bulky, metallic sensors that scanned each passerby with a low, mechanical hum. The club's logo hovered above in soft, bubbly white letters outlined in pink—glowing like a whisper of comfort in a place that promised anything but. Lexi didn't look directly at the entrance. Something about the place made her skin crawl, though she couldn't say why.

The cab jerked to a stop at the curb, the brakes hissing under the weight of heat and grime. Lexi and Lyria climbed out, the thick air of Level 2 slamming into them like a wall. The bass from nearby clubs vibrated through the pavement, and the smell of synthetic smoke and sweat was impossible to miss.

A street caller in a glowing vest locked onto them instantly, grinning wide as he waved a flickering holo-coupon.

"Ladies! Half-off drinks at the Yugen Club tonight—special deal, just for the pair!" he shouted over the bass.

Lyria didn't even slow. She shoved the coupon back at his chest with a sharp laugh.

"That watered-down shit? No thanks."

The caller smirked, already turning to chase his next marks.

Lyria glanced around as they started forward. A guy stood against the wall, pissing openly while chugging a warm can of beer. Steam drifted from the overhead pipes, and sparks spat from shorting neon signs and frayed wiring above. The air carried the scent of fried grease from a food stall and the heavy musk of too many bodies pressed into too little space. Empty bottles and crushed cans littered the ground, kicked aside by the crowd as they moved through the chaos.

Lyria took a deep breath, grinning. "Smells like trouble."

Lexi rolled her eyes, already regretting this.

They headed straight for The Void, laughing and weaving through the crowd, when a paint vendor came into view beneath a magenta canopy. Buckets of glowing paint surrounded him, neon streaks already smeared across half-covered bodies. He twirled glowing brushes in the air, shouting prices over the noise.

Lyria's eyes lit up like fireworks. "Paint booth! Yes!" she shouted, yanking Lexi toward the stand.

"Wait—what the fuck?" Lexi muttered, staring at the sudden splash of color.

She lifted a brow. "We're not—"

"Oh, we absolutely are," Lyria cut in, tugging harder on her arm.

Before she could protest, Lyria had already dragged her into the magenta-lit space. The vendor, a wiry man with a grin full of metal teeth, shoved a dripping brush toward them and barked, "Ten credits for a color! Twenty for full-body—Want your face looking like a rave threw up on it? That'll cost extra!"

"C'mon," Lyria said, eyes glittering. "Let me paint you."

Lexi folded her arms. "I'm not—"

"Lift your shirt, or I swear, I'll embarrass you in front of everyone."

Lexi glanced around. A few guys were already eyeing them. She sighed. "You're the worst."

"Wrong," Lyria grinned, dipping her fingers into a pot of wild pink. "I'm the most fun."

Lexi reluctantly lifted her shirt halfway. Lyria immediately ran her paint-covered hands across her abs, leaving chaotic, electric pink streaks in their wake.

Cheers erupted from a group nearby. Lexi flushed, mortified.

"She's not done!" Lyria shouted, turning back to Lexi with a grin full of trouble. "What, you scared now? Come on, you got the whole street's attention. Give 'em a real show."

Lexi hesitated, her fingers gripping the edge of her shirt. The crowd was watching, hollering, already halfway there.

Lyria leaned in close, teasing in her voice. "Do it, nerd. Flash 'em. I dare you."

Lexi closed her eyes for a moment, heart thudding. She let out a shaky breath and muttered, "Fuck it," more anxious than bold, and pulled her shirt up all the way.

The crowd howled. Lyria dove in, shoving her paint-covered face between Lexi's tits like she was claiming a prize. The cheers turned feral.

Lexi laughed, breathless, her face burning with embarrassment, and yanked her shirt back down just as someone from the crowd tossed a set of glowing beads at her. They bounced off her shoulder and hit the pavement with a clatter.

"You earned those!" someone shouted, followed by another yelling, "Welcome to Level 2!" followed by more cheers.

"Lyria, you're a bad influence," she muttered, still red-faced, slipping the glowing beads around her neck with a defeated little shake of her head.

They walked on, grinning like lunatics.

The noise shifted as they neared The Void.

The main road ended at a four-story monolith of black steel, sunk into the ground and massive enough to feel claustrophobic even from the outside. Above the entrance, a black circle—the mark of Verellii's black sun, Anthrallii—pulsed in a yellow-white rhythm, a beacon for the mayhem and sound within. Bass thumped hard enough to rattle the pavement.

Cages flanked the front, dancers grinding under strobing lights. Between them, two massive white-marbled doors loomed like the gates of a holy temple to sin.

And at the right cage—chaos.

A nude man spun inside, his oiled body rippling under the lights. A red-faced bride in glowing heels had climbed onto the bars, cackling as she jerked him off through the grate. Her bridesmaids screamed and hurled credits, phones out, recording it all like a memory they'd never forget.

"Verellii's finest," Lexi muttered.

Lyria laughed so hard she nearly tripped. "If we don't top that tonight, I'll be disappointed."

Inside, the air pulsed. Bass vibrated through the walls. Painted bodies swayed under strobing light.

Lyria grabbed Lexi's hand. "Let's burn the night down."

They made their way to the bar.

The bartender—shirtless and half-metal—grinned. "Welcome to the Void. What'll it be?"

Lexi wiped sweat from her neck. Her shirt clung to her chest, the paint beneath glowing bright pink under the blacklight.

"What are your specials?" she asked.

He listed them with a smirk, eyes locked shamelessly on Lexi's painted tits: "Cybernetic Cooler, Quantum Quencher, Nebula Nectar, Time Warp Tonic..."

Lyria leaned on the counter. "Time Warp Tonic!"

"What's in it?" Lexi asked.

"Mandarin gin, tonic, and a splash of Blaze."

Lexi frowned. "Blaze is illegal."

The bartender shrugged. "So is flashing a crowd of strangers. Yet... here you are."

Lyria laughed. "Two, please. One for me, one for my nerdy girlfriend."

She poked Lexi's nose, leaving a little dot of paint behind.

Lexi sighed, but her smile betrayed her.

They made their way to a booth—low seats, glowing cushions, holographic fire licking at the tinted walls.

Lyria curled up on Lexi's lap, clinking glasses.

"To chaos," she said.

Lexi raised hers. "To temporary mistakes."

They drank.

Then, without warning, a figure rose from behind the couch—Burton Marx.

His arms slid around both of them, his head pushing between theirs like a sweaty, grinning serpent. "There you are," he breathed. "Been hunting all night for you two."

Lexi flinched. Lyria froze—just for a second. "Hey, B," she said, smile flicking on.

Burton leaned in. His fingers brushed the rim of Lexi's glass and then—a pill slipped under the drink with a hiss of bubbles.

Lyria's smile froze for a breath. Her eyes darted—first to Burton's hand, then to Lexi.

Lexi caught it. "What was that?"

Lyria's smile faltered. "What was what?" she shot back, too fast.

Lexi's eyes narrowed. "You looked at my drink. Then me. Why?"

"You're reading into something that's not there," Lyria said, recovering quickly.

Lexi didn't respond. She just stared at Lyria for a moment, watching for any subtle change in her demeanor—then took a sip.

Lyria tugged her by the belt loop onto the dance floor, pulling them flush, her hands roaming Lexi's body.

For a moment, Lexi let go. She traced her face, lips, breasts, and torso with her fingers, sweat building as her hips swayed with the beat. Neon washed her in pink, then blue, then pink again.

Lexi turned—and Lyria had vanished.

Then the high went sideways.

Heat coiled in her chest, spreading fast. The bass hit different now—muffled, as if underwater. The club warped in her vision, colors bleeding at the edges. Every sound distorted, slurred into itself. The strobes pulsed slower and heavier.

Lexi blinked hard, trying to focus. Everything shifted as she pushed through the crowd toward their booth.

Empty.

Lyria wasn't there.

She blinked again, longer this time, and her stomach dropped.

Lyria was straddling Burton. Her dress was pushed down, tits out, body moving in rhythm. Burton's hands were on her ass. His face buried in her chest.

Lexi's mouth opened, but no words followed.

She stumbled forward, disoriented. Her hand slapped a mirror.

A face appeared.

A woman with painted lips, glitter around her eyes, and bright blue hair approached her—or at least, Lexi thought she saw a woman.

"Oh my god. Pixie?!"

Lexi's brow furrowed. Pixie? The name didn't register. It bounced around in her foggy head with no anchor, no memory to cling to.

"It's really you! From SynthSkin! You just disappeared one night—where the hell did you go?"

Lexi opened her mouth. Her lips moved, but the words stuck in her throat, thick and slow.

"I'm not—Pixie."

***

Then the ground gave out, and her world slipped into darkness.

CHAP_05.exe - De$ync

...patch.exe → failure...system_errOr//

Lexi's eyes cracked open, and she immediately winced. Something hard and plastic was wedged between her lips. She gagged, spitting it out with a groggy mutter.

"What the fuck…"

The beads tumbled onto her chest, still loosely hanging around her neck—sticky with saliva and tangled in her hair.

The air was thick and stale. Sweat covered her skin, sheets soaked, heat oppressive.

Sun blazed through the blinds, casting harsh white stripes across the room. Her AC was dead—again—and the rising temperature had finally forced her awake.

Her head throbbed—a steady, pulsing ache, a shrill ring cutting through her ears.

She sat up too fast—immediately dizzy, heart pounding.

Her eyes darted to the digital clock blinking on the nightstand: 06:50.

"Shit. Shit, shit, shit."

She scrambled out of bed, tripping over a small package on the floor—the requisitioned pants from the night before. Her shirt clung like glue—dried with sweat, paint, and whatever else she'd soaked in last night. Jeans twisted around one ankle, and she nearly ate shit against the bathroom doorframe, catching herself with a muttered curse.

"Fuck you bitch!" Lexi said, kicking her jeans off. Her heart thundered in her chest.

She'd never been late. Not once. Not in her entire career.

She yanked the beads off her neck and tossed them aside as they clattered against the wall. She peeled off her shirt and threw it in a corner. Still dizzy, she gripped the doorframe to steady herself, then stumbled into the bathroom. *Cold water. No time to think. No time to breathe.*

Paint and grime swirled down the drain. Her hands shook as she scrubbed her skin raw. In under two minutes, she was out.

She ripped the package open and yanked on the fresh pair of jeans, shoved her feet into her blood-stained white shoes, and threw on her black leather jacket. Magnets snapped into place; the cooling unit came alive.

Headset—where the fuck—there. She snatched it up and slapped it on. "Comm check. Lieutenant Hayes. Anyone on?"

A pause. Then a voice crackled back, crisp: "Loud and clear, Lieutenant. You're good to go."

Lexi exhaled, breath shaking. "Lyria, are you here?" she shouted.

Silence.

She checked the kitchen. The couch.

Nothing.

Lyria was gone.

And the ringing in her head still wouldn't stop.

***

Lexi bolted out the door. No thoughts, no plan—just speed. Every synthetic fiber in her metallic muscles screamed as she pushed them faster, beyond calibration limits. Her cooling system howled in protest, condensation slicking across the leather, beading and dripping like rain. Heat bled from her chest until the lines beneath her skin glowed faint red, casting an angry shimmer as she tore through the streets toward HQ.

As Lexi stepped through the doors of RAPID headquarters, the weight of the coming conversation hung over her like a storm cloud. She moved quickly through the Eraway, footsteps silent against the chaos around her. The wall clock read 07:10. Heat radiated from her chest, her jacket's cooling system slowing as it lowered her core temperature.

She could almost hear Lena's voice beside her:

"Chin up. Walk faster. Control your breathing."

But Lena wasn't here anymore.

Her comms buzzed to life.

"Lieutenant Hayes," Graevos's voice cut in, clipped and commanding. "Change of plan. Report to your office. Now."

Lexi entered her office to find Graevos already seated behind her desk, a scowl hardening his severe features. Files glowed across her terminal as if it were his own. He didn't rise, simply gestured toward one of the wooden seats she usually reserved for dressing down her own people.

"Lieutenant Hayes," he began, voice low and cutting. Lexi instinctively stood straighter before sitting.

"I know why I'm here, sir."

Graevos narrowed his eyes. "Last night was a mess, and I know you know that. You're not a rookie. You're in command of the Infiltrators now. That means setting the example, even when things go sideways."

Lexi said nothing.

Graevos's tone stayed level but firm. "You're lucky it didn't end worse. Lena isn't here to hold your hand anymore. You're one of my best, Lexi—but even the best lose their way if they stop checking their footing. As a lieutenant of the Infiltrator Corps, I expect precision, stealth, and accuracy...not luck."

"I understand, sir."

After a long pause, Graevos pushed back from the desk and stood. Lexi snapped to attention, spine rigid.

"I'm not looking to replace you, Hayes. I'm looking to see you rise to what I know you're capable of."

Lexi's jaw flexed, but she nodded. "Thank you, sir."

He walked to the door. Outside, a pair of fresh recruits caught sight of him and instantly stood at attention, their movements sharp but nervous.

Graevos left without another word. The office door hissed shut behind him with a finality that echoed down the hall.

Only then did the recruits let out their breath, their postures relaxing.

***

Lexi exhaled and crossed to her side of the desk. She lowered herself into her chair, the familiar weight grounding her. Her mind drifted back to last night; Lyria straddling Burton in front of the entire club, his face buried in her chest as she laughed like it was all some sick joke. Lexi blinked, and the memory hit harder.

The sweat on Burton's face. His hands gripping Lyria like she was a trophy.

Then the girl's voice: "Oh my god. Pixie?!"

That name echoed like a bullet in her skull.

Pixie?

Reality slammed back into her, and she noticed something that didn't belong on her desk.

The slate.

She stared at it. The device she'd pulled from the Kurogane officer in the Port District. The one she'd meant to decrypt this morning.

Still powered. Still locked.

Lexi muttered, "Fucking Burton..." her mind still circling back to Lyria and Burton last night.

The slate blinked. A soft chirp. A red file icon pulsed to life.

VOICE PRINT MISMATCH — LOCK ENGAGED

Her stomach dropped.

She barely had time to react. Her headset lit up, sync chimes in her ear, directorate updates flooding in as her systems linked. Red-tinged files shimmered into view as her right eye flickered.

As she headed into the briefing area, the Infiltrator office door opened.

Debra, Amber, and Elise stepped in, excited and ready for the day. They formed a tight line in front of their commander as Isabella took her spot next to Lexi.

"Ladies," Lexi said sharply, "Let's debrief. Izzy, you're senior—start us off."

"Yes, mami... uhh, ma'am. We have updated and repaired all communication equipment. Planetwide communications within the team are possible again."

"Great work," Lexi said proudly.

"Sergeant, you're on the baby-step program again. Keep the pre-CRIS kids alive long enough to learn machine repair. Electronics, mechanics, discipline—the basics. You've made good progress with them."

Lexi smirked, knowing Isabella would rather do combat operations instead of babysitting.

"Copy," Isabella said, voice low as she headed into the adjoining office. Through the glass wall, a group of wide-eyed recruits sat up-right, already waiting.

"Debra, you're up," Lexi said confidently.

"Yes, ma'am." Debra nodded. "In the Union District, I found that in fact, workers were using water-filled ditches to strip Enforcers for parts. They rigged an electromagnetic crane to hoist the bodies. I neutralized the team responsible. Saved four out of five. The survivors return to duty tomorrow after a psych exam."

"And the last?" Lexi asked.

"We have a scout team looking for him now," Debra replied.

"Good work." Lexi nodded. "Amber. Elise?"

Amber stepped forward. "We tracked a narcotics shipment to a ware-house on Level 3. As soon as we entered, they opened fire. We elimi-nated the hostiles and destroyed the goods. No records on any of them, but they all had a mark."

She turned her head slightly, miming the gesture. "Back of the neck. A broken line. Letters above it: T, N, O."

Lexi's expression darkened. "A broken line...? What the hell is T.N.O .?"

Elise answered softly, "No intel found, ma'am. Nothing in their gear or data files."

Lexi was quiet for just a second. Then: "Debra—go with Amber. Stake out the warehouse. If anyone shows up looking for the shipment, take them in. Call for an Enforcer if needed."

"Copy that, Lieutenant. Amber, let's go!" Debra said eagerly.

Lexi turned to Elise.

"You're with me today."

Elise hesitated. "Yes, ma'am."

Lexi's tone softened just a hair. "You'll be fine. Follow my lead."

Elise gave a quick nod and stepped towards her locker to prep.

Lexi returned to her office, the wall panel sliding open to reveal her gear and weapons. Her TDB Unit and recon drone sat fully charged, the air buzzing with a low hum of static.

She placed her swords into their ports—across her back and left thigh. The pistol snapped effortlessly to her right; TDB Unit locked onto her arm. Last was the drone, clipped to her waistband. She cast one final glance at the blinking slate.

"I'll deal with you later," she muttered.

She stepped out of the department and called over her shoulder, "Elise, let's move. We're heading upstairs."

The Eraway echoed under Lexi's mission-focused footsteps. Elise caught up beside her, voice low. "I've never used the spheres before."

Lexi smirked. "You will today."

They reached the elevator at the end of the hall, where Debra and Amber were already waiting.

Elise tensed. Debra gave her a calm, warming look. "You've come a long way, rook. Keep your head down, eyes sharp, and don't freeze. You're with the boss—nothing's touching you."

Elise nodded, her nervous expression shifting to one of focus, like a soldier trying to make her instructor proud.

The group stepped inside the lift. Its walls were smooth alloy, the faint hum of magnetic drives rising as it carried them upward through the spine of RAPID HQ. Lexi leaned back against the wall and put a foot up, arms crossed over her chest. She looked untouchable. Elise snuck a glance at her, trying to calm her nerves. Debra squeezed Elise's shoulder once, firm and grounding. "You'll be fine."

Seconds later, the doors slid open to reveal the launch chamber, and after Debra and Amber fired out of the tube in their spheres, Lexi scanned her barcode and requested two spheres to the Mining District.

"The Mining District?!" Elise exclaimed. "Isn't that area incredibly dangerous?"

Lexi nodded, her voice low and serious. "It's part of the Union District, but it's a subsection—separate, but still heavily controlled. Dangerous territory, but that's why we're going. They need us down there." Lexi's eyes flashed with intensity. "Listen, if you worry, you'll die. If you hesitate, you'll die. You're an Infiltrator now. Start acting like one."

Elise looked confused, taken aback. Lexi had never scolded or yelled at anyone before, and this harsh tone was a jarring shift.

The room rotated, and two spheres rolled down from the rack, replacing the ones Debra and Amber had just used. They rolled into position before Lexi and Elise.

"I've never used mine before," Elise nervously repeated.

"You'll feel it the second we launch—like your guts get yanked through your spine," Lexi said. "The sphere gives a countdown before ejection. Listen for it. You need to jump when it says eject, or it'll blip back to HQ and leave you falling."

"Got it," Elise replied, her voice full of determination, but still a little unsure.

The two climbed into their spheres, electricity sparking around the room as they prepared to launch. Elise looked around nervously as arcs of electricity snapped across her sphere. Her eyes widened, and she gripped the edges of the transparent shell tightly.

The launch was instantaneous. Her body slammed into the seat as the world outside blurred into streaks of light.

As the spheres neared the Union District, Elise glanced at Lexi, who clutched her head, lost in her thoughts.

I wonder what's wrong with her today, Elise thought to herself, watching Lexi's tense, troubled expression.

As the spheres got closer, Lexi prepared herself for the descent.

"3...2...1... EJECT!" the sphere called out.

Lexi moved like a seasoned veteran, her motion smooth and practiced.

Beside her, Elise hesitated—just a second too long—and the sphere vanished from under her with a flash of light. She tumbled in a wild, uncontrolled spin, the ground surging up with terrifying speed.

"God damn it, Elise," Lexi muttered, adjusting her descent.

She tucked her arms in and gained momentum to catch her.

Lexi caught up and wrapped herself around Elise. As the ground rushed closer, she smacked her TDB Unit. A faint blue glow flared—and in the next instant, Elise was locked in her arms as Lexi slammed into Verellii's tough crust, her body taking the full force of the impact.

"Oh, thank you!" Elise exclaimed. Lexi let her go.

Lexi put a finger to her lips. "Quiet! Don't say anything. They've probably already been alerted."

Who? Elise wondered, confused.

She looked around and saw no one—just massive mining equipment, scaffolding, and large piles of rocks. After a moment of personal investigation, she spotted the mouth of a tunnel. Looking up, Elise realized they were about 500 feet underground.

Lexi rose out of her self-made crater. Rocks fell from her knee as she drew her pistol. "Loadout," she whispered.

"Ballistic, 12 plus 1," the pistol whispered back, the light on its front turning to a soft yellow hue.

Elise, wasting no time, unfolded a stick with a handle and ignited a blue barrier, transforming it into a riot shield. She pulled out her own pistol and set it to buckshot.

"Here's the plan," Lexi whispered. "We're here for two things: One—investigate who ordered the harvesting of Enforcers. And two—Extract them if possible. Kill them if not. Keep the shield hidden for now. We'll use it only if we need it."

Elise nodded, understanding the mission parameters, and turned off the shield, attaching it to its port on her left thigh.

As the two moved stealthily through the tunnel, aware of every sound and mindful of the noise their footsteps made, they came to a fork. Three dark tunnels branched out in different directions.

"Shit," Lexi muttered. "We'll use night-vision, split up. Use your re-con drone and explore different tunnels. If you find anything, don't engage—come back here and meet at this junction."

"Y-Yes, ma'am," Elise stammered. Her hands were steady, but her voice wasn't.

With her pistol held outward, her eye glowing green, she disappeared down the left tunnel.

Lexi surveyed the last two tunnels. The middle one seemed unused, but the right one had electrical cables and tubing running through its depths.

"Right, it is," Lexi muttered, heading toward the right tunnel.

Lexi crouched low as the corridor descended. The tunnel no longer felt like it belonged to the Mining District. The industrial texture gave way to something older—crafted. Snake-like vines twisted up towering black columns, carved directly into the rock, each one re-sembling a twisted spire reaching upward. The walls had the coldness of a mountain, the ruin of a factory, and the reverence of a cathedral.

Irradiated veins pulsed red through the stone, casting a soft, unholy light. The color wasn't just light—it was presence, crawling up Lexi's spine with every step. The air vibrated with it, like the entire cavern was alive.

The corridor ended at an overlook. Lexi crouched and peered over the railing into a deep chasm carved into the stone. The blackness below offered no clues—just silence.

Two paths split off from the overlook. Lexi pulled her recon drone from its housing and flung it down the left hallway, keeping low to avoid detection.

She moved slowly down the right. Her hands trembled slightly. Something about this place was... off.

As she reached the end of the hallway, it curved into a pitch-black spiral staircase.

"Stealth," she whispered.

The weapon's info light blinked out. Her ammo count floated in her eye as her iris shifted green—night vision on.

She inhaled slowly, controlling her breath. Every step was deliberate, silent—a tiger in the forest.

An audible switch snapped her attention back. The drone returned to its housing.

Nothing down the left path. No people. No rooms.

Strange. Lexi thought.

The staircase opened into a courtyard made of stone—massive, polished, and seemingly complete. Arches lined the perimeter. Sculpted pillars stretched upward like ancient watchtowers.

But it was a dead end.

No exits. No sound.

Then the lights came on.

The sudden brightness stung her eyes. She darted behind the stairs and crouched—waiting.

No footsteps. No alarms.

She flipped off night vision and crept forward again.

Where the hell is everyone? She thought.

Activating X-ray, her eye shifted to a red hue. The walls bled with hidden structure.

Five doors.

She passed three standard-looking hallways behind synthetic rock—easily masked, easily bypassed. But the fourth...

Lexi paused.

The scan returned nothing. No clues. No heat. Just a long, flat void.

It wasn't empty—it was absent. Like something had carved the data out of it.

She frowned.

Something was in there, not trapped. Just... watching.

Her jaw clenched. *Not now.*

She turned toward the fifth door—this one had a key slot.

Lexi punched through the false wall. Synthetic rock crumbled, revealing metal. She slipped her pick into the slot and twisted.

Click.

A faint blue glow lit the panel.

Lexi pressed it.

The door slid back and up, vanishing into the ceiling. Red light spilled out like blood, bathing the floor.

"Someone's bound to hear that," she muttered, stepping inside.

As Lexi moved forward, the sound began—distant at first. A low rumble, then a chant. Muffled, rhythmic. Growing.

Voices. Hundreds of them. Thousands.

Lexi's steps slowed as the tunnel opened.

And then she saw it.

A vast, carved grand hall unfolded beneath her—so massive her eye had to recalibrate its depth markers. The ceiling disappeared into darkness above, supported by towering pillars carved with more snake-vine designs. Irradiated rock veins glowed red throughout the chamber, painting the thousands of bodies below in warped firelight.

Lexi turned off X-ray, just to be sure. The scene didn't change.

The people crowded ledges, scaffolds, benches—any surface that gave them a view of the central stage.

And on that stage...

He paced.

A hulking man—cybernetically monstrous. He was more machine than flesh. His spine glowed faintly. His feet clanked with every step, the sound echoing through the rock like distant gunfire. His eyes burned a fiery orange, sweeping over the crowd with inhuman clarity.

Lexi crouched deeper, analyzing the scene.

She narrowed her eyes, and her scan flickered.

Cybernetic readout: ACTIVE.

Dense plating. Internal reinforcement. Hydraulic spine. 50 Caliber minimum penetration.

None of her current rounds would make a difference.

At the center of the stage, bound and kneeling, was an Infiltrator—synthetic skin split and her muscles bleeding green. Her limbs hung loose—dislocated, bruised, and broken. Her hands were tied behind her back. She was naked, humiliated, and completely exposed beneath the Union flag that hung behind them.

Lexi rose slightly, just enough to attempt a scan—but the hall was too large.

Out of range.

Her gut twisted.

Then she noticed something else.

To the left, behind a low barrier of steel, hung something suspended in the shadows.

An Enforcer.

The missing one.

Stripped. Nude. His armor had been cut away. His body was hooked by the spine, shoulders, and thighs. Still alive.

His limbs were partially dismembered—one arm missing, a leg severed at the knee. His skin was red, purple, beaten to pulp. Blood dripped steadily into a catch pit beneath him. His neural uplink still blinked softly, trying to connect to a suit that no longer existed.

People in the crowd jeered, mocked, and threw things at him. One man poked a jagged rod into his side. Another pressed a white-hot branding tool against his hip.

The Enforcer groaned—a raw, wet sound, barely human.

Lexi's teeth clenched.

They didn't kill him.

They displayed him.

She forced her gaze away from him and toward the edges of the room—that's when she saw them.

Cages.

Dozens of them. Welded shut. Lined against the far walls, tucked in shadow. Inside were augmented civilians—not agents, not Enforcers. Just people. Some wore work uniforms. Others had damaged implants, twitching prosthetics, or light-sensitive eyes that flared under the red glow.

A child with half a mechanical arm whimpered into her knees. An older man sat slumped against the bars, his breathing shallow and labored. None resisted. None spoke.

Lexi's chest tightened.

They thought they were one of us. So they locked them up like animals.

***

Then the man on stage raised a hand.

The chamber erupted in rage.

"KILL THEM ALL! KILL THEM ALL!"

Lexi flinched, every part of her body tensing. She watched him stalk across the stage with terrifying calm.

"Today," he called, voice amplified and guttural, "we send a message to the tyrants above!"

Roars echoed from every direction.

"We give them our metal. Our crops. Our labor. And they give us surveillance. Debt. Upgrades for their weapons while our children starve!"

The crowd howled.

"And here—" he gestured toward the Infiltrator, "is another one of their monsters."

He circled her.

"She came to spy. To kill. To wipe us out, one by one, and bury what we've built. And tomorrow they will expect more!"

Boos. Screams. Fists in the air.

"But we built this world. Not them. Not him—" he pointed at the Enforcer—"and not her."

He crouched beside the captive.

"What's your name, beautiful?"

The Infiltrator lifted her battered head—teeth missing, one eye disfigured.

"Fuck you," she said—and spat green fluid at his face.

The man froze—then smiled.

"Defiant," he said. "Just like the rest of your kind."

The crowd exploded again.

He stood and picked up a mining laser.

"What will you do now, Lexi?" he called.

A spotlight snapped on, illuminating her fully as the crowd turned. For a breath, silence—thousands of eyes locked on her, unblinking.

Lexi's pistol snapped up, aimed at his skull.

People began to move toward her—slowly, like zombies stalking prey. *Not just angry. Unhinged. Deranged.*

She looked at the woman again.

Lexi's breath caught. She wanted to save her. She wanted to do something.

But she wouldn't make it ten feet.

Her pistol stayed up—but she didn't pull the trigger.

She turned and ran.

The spotlight swung wildly. Behind her, the door began to seal.

"Fuck. Fuck. Fuck!"

She was out of time.

She hit her TDB.

Blip.

CHAP_06.exe - Collaps3

Lexi reappeared mid-sprint, tennis shoes slapping stone. Momentum hurled her forward—she stumbled, caught herself, and skidded to a stop. Behind her, the door sealed with a heavy metallic slam, severing her from the grand hall.

She was out—but not safe.

She closed her eyes for just a moment. Her breath caught. Her body trembled; fingers curled into fists as she hunched against the wall, forcing air into her lungs. The weight of what she'd just seen clung to her like a toxin—thick with evil, poisoning her thoughts, movements, and control.

Then the walls groaned.

A mechanical grinding echoed through the space as all five doors began to move. Dust and debris fell around her as shafts of firelight, flashlights, and floodlamps cut through the dark.

And then came the voices.

Thousands. Chanting. Rising.

Lexi's eyes snapped open. She surged forward.

She ran. Up the spiral staircase—legs burning, arms pumping. The echo of chanting flooded up the walls behind her, growing louder with every step. More lights flared to life—chasing her up the stone like the fires of hell itself had been set loose.

Then she heard it. A sound that didn't belong in any cave, or world, or memory. A shriek—not human, not even animal—ripped through the air, high and warping, as if it came from the void itself.

The chanting fractured. Then turned to screams.

Lexi didn't dare look back. Terror was coming. And it was faster than she was.

Lexi reached the top of the stairwell, lungs burning. She tapped her left wrist. Her comms suite lit up—red. No signal.

Chanting still echoed below. The inhuman shriek. The screams. The chaos. And the lights—still climbing, chasing her.

She sprinted through the narrow tunnel that led back to the intersection, the heat in her chest building fast. Her core temperature was spiking—deep, internal heat flooding her limbs, the kind that only came when her body was pushed too far, too fast.

Up ahead—a figure, standing near the tunnel entrance she had explored earlier.

Lexi didn't slow.

She magnetized her pistol to its port, reached over her shoulder, and drew her katana with a metallic schwing. The blade gleamed as she charged, instincts screaming.

The figure blurred—blipping behind her.

Lexi reacted instantly. She spun, her katana already in motion, slicing through the air with growing speed. Just as the blade reached its target, it stopped, slamming against a shimmering blue wall that lit up in front of it.

Lexi's eyes snapped up. The blue light illuminated a familiar, wide-eyed face.

"Elise."

"Ma'am—we have to get out of here," Elise panted, words tumbling over each other. "I found a section—they were harvesting people—just civilians—ripping out parts—these people are insane!"

Lexi's jaw clenched. "We've got more problems than that."

The lights behind them grew louder, brighter. "We need to call for extraction."

"I did!" Elise yelled, almost laughing. Her eyes were wild. "I called it in, ma'am—I swear! Let's just make sure they get a good lock on us!"

They turned and sprinted toward the cave entrance, still hundreds of feet ahead. Lexi magnetized the katana to her back, the lock clicking into place. Elise deactivated her riot shield, magnetizing it to her thigh.

They both drew their pistols.

And then as they exited the cave—

Lexi heard it.

"LEXI!" A voice bellowed from the mouth of the cave.

She didn't want to look. She knew better. But then—

"LEXIIIIIII! YOU'RE GONNA WANT TO SEE THIS!"

***

Lexi turned.

She shouldn't have.

The augmented man stood at the center of the cave mouth, with a countless number of soldiers at his back. A mining laser hissed in one hand. The other was hidden behind his back.

He grinned.

And then, slowly, he pulled his arm forward—holding Debra Sinclair by the hair.

Her body was limp. Beaten. Battered. Broken.

"Hahaha..." The man's laugh was a twisted, breathless rasp—manic and vile.

Then he drove her head into the cave wall—hard, fast, and without pause. Bone met stone in a sickening rhythm, each impact tearing her further apart.

Synthetic skin split.

Green fluid streaked across the rock—her body breaking down with every blow.

He let her drop, as she crumpled against the stone, her body twisting unnaturally as it hit.

Lexi had sent her here for this mission.

And now she was watching her die.

He lifted one heavy foot, mechanical joints clicking. Four talons snapped out with a sharp metallic clatter.

Then he slammed it down onto her skull, bone crunching beneath the weight, twisting her head toward Lexi.

Lexi froze, powerless.

"Hold her," the man said.

Two soldiers stepped forward and pinned Debra's spasming limbs to the floor.

The mining laser whirred to life—a rising screech that shook the air.

And then it began. The beam carved through her—synthetic skin first, then muscle, then deep into what was still human inside.

That's when it came. A single tear, sliding over coolant and grime clinging to Debra's cheek.

Her mouth moved. No words came. Just fear.

Her glowing red eye flickered—as if it was still trying to capture the moment. Still doing its job. Even now.

Then she screamed.

A scream that split the air and shattered something inside Lexi.

For a heartbeat, the chamber itself seemed to hold its breath.

Then the light in Debra's eye went out.

Lexi cried.

***

She couldn't stop it. All she could do was listen as the sound of Debra dying shredded her from the inside out.

Then—just as fast as it had started—the air went still. No movement. No voices. Not even the echo of pain.

Lexi looked up.

The man was staring at her. Debra's body lay smoking at his feet.

He raised his arm—the one that once held Debra—and pointed it at Lexi.

"Get them."

Hundreds of people began charging toward Lexi and Elise as they sprinted further into the open, searching for cover. They settled on an old excavator—rusted, massive, and thick enough to soak up gunfire.

Both Infiltrators turned and raised their pistols. Anyone unlucky enough to be at the business end of an Infiltrator's weapon didn't last long.

Then, out of nowhere—

From the sky.

A Skyreaper-class gunship descended into the quarry, dodging scaffolding and mangled machinery as the air crackled with energy.

The nose-mounted 50 mm cannon roared to life, unleashing devastation through the cave mouth like thunder from the gods. Each round slammed into the tunnel, shattering stone and vaporizing flesh, the ground shaking under the barrage.

The front line of miners never had a chance. They were shredded instantly—limbs blown apart, torsos inverted, bodies hurled back against the rock like butchered meat. Shrapnel screamed through the air, the stench of scorched earth and blood flooding Lexi's lungs as she ducked behind the excavator. "Thank Anthrallii!" she panted, fighting for breath.

The ground rattled beneath her feet as massive shell casings clattered across the quarry floor. Above, the gunship's side-mounted 20 mm miniguns spun up, its roar joining the thunder of the 50 mm—a symphony of carnage.

Missile ports snapped open under the wings. Warheads streaked into the tunnel, erupting in fire that lit the passage like daylight. Explosions tore through bodies and gouged the walls, leaving the cavern scorched and trembling.

Lexi peeked out, pistol raised, picking off anyone who slipped through the wall of lead, her shots punching clean through the chaos.

To her left, Elise was locked in as well—her hands shaking, but her aim solid. Her pistol bucked in her grip as she took down target after target.

One miner broke through the suppressive fire—rushing Lexi from the right, weapon raised.

Elise turned and dropped him in a flash.

"I've got your six, ma'am!" Elise yelled.

Lexi glanced at her—and gave an approving nod.

Suddenly, two loud metallic thuds echoed on either side of the gunship.

Lexi looked.

Enforcers.

Corporal Zalok Kalani and Private Ethan Blackwood dropped in, power armor slamming into the rock. They immediately took up defensive positions, weapons roaring to life.

Kalani's rotary cannon spun with a high-pitched whine, spitting hot metal death. Shell casings piled around his boots, crushed flat beneath his armored weight.

Next to him, Blackwood's flamethrower surged—a roaring stream of fire that cut down waves of miners in seconds. Screams turned to smoke.

"Welcome back, ma'am," Kalani snickered through his helmet, voice steady in the storm, his gun shredding through the attackers.

Blackwood laughed, completely unfazed by the carnage.

"She just can't get enough of our sparkling personalities, huh, sir?"

"Eh, leave the cool shit to me, bruddah," he shot back with a grin. "Now, ma'am—pardon my language—but get the fuck in the gunship!"

The gunship extended its wing, folding downward to form its deployable shield, deflecting incoming fire.

***

Lexi and Elise ran—full sprint—leaping into the open bay, pistols blazing as they fired at the remaining miners chasing them.

The Enforcers didn't stop shooting—their covering fire was brutal, relentless, and lethal. No one got close.

The gunship's engines screamed, dust and smoke blasting outward as the remaining enemy forces began to retreat—trampling Debra's broken body on the way back into the cave.

Kalani and Blackwood fell back slowly, guns still hot, unloading every round they had left.

They both jumped onto the edge of the gunship's side door, weapons smoking.

Blackwood pounded his fist once against the inner hull—

The pilot turned, nodded once—

Then the gunship lifted, engines roaring, climbing away from the cratered battlefield below.

"Skyreaper Nine, leaving the hostile zone," the pilot called out, banking hard as the craft rose, weaving between scaffolding and fractured steel.

Inside the gunship, Elise clung to a handhold, chest heaving, hands trembling. She didn't speak for a few seconds. Then, quietly: "Tell me this doesn't happen every mission..."

Lexi looked at her. For a moment, she said nothing. Then, just soft enough to be heard over the engines: "Sometimes better. Sometimes worse."

Elise blinked, surprised. Lexi looked away, back out at the cratered battlefield.

As the gunship ascended, Elise sat near Lexi at the door, still panting. "What was that shit? Are those guys crazy?" she managed.

"It was an uprising," Lexi replied coldly. "We have a powerful, new enemy."

Lexi glanced at Elise—still catching her breath, flushed, eyes wide. Her voice softened as she set her hands on Elise's shoulders and met her gaze. "Even though you started as a pain in my ass... you held your own back there. Good job, Elise."

Elise's lips curled into a shaky smile, pride blooming across her face.

A blinding lance of yellow light split the air. Lexi's expression froze. Elise's eyes rolled back, the smile still on her lips as a smoking hole bored through her head. Her body slumped, lifeless—and before Lexi could react, Elise tumbled backward out of the gunship, vanishing into the smoke and chaos below.

Lexi's arms were still outstretched, fingers reaching for someone who wasn't there. "No—no, no, no!" she shouted, scrambling to the edge. "Put the gunship down! We have to get her!"

"The landing area is a warzone!" the pilot snapped.

Blackwood muttered, "Ma'am, that's suicide."

Kalani locked a new belt into place. "Not if we're the ones doing the killing. I ride with the L.T.—all the way."

Lexi's fists clenched, voice sharp and unyielding. "We're going back. That's an order. Gear up."

Blackwood started reloading, the two Enforcers quickly checking their gear as the gunship dipped back into the chasm. Lasers streaked the hull, burning new scars into already maimed armor.

Below, Elise's body lay exposed. Deranged miners were already swarming, closing in with scavengers' hunger, eager to strip her for parts.

As the pilot dropped the gunship into the fray, its weapons unleashed a full barrage. "Kalani! Blackwood! Covering fire—I'm going!" Lexi barked.

The Enforcers and gunship rained hell on the mob, clearing a path as Lexi sprinted into the open. She weaved between hostiles, katana flashing in tight arcs—decapitating and maiming with brutal preci- sion. Reaching Elise's body, she slung it over her shoulder, magnetized it to her back, and drew her shoto—carving her way back with swift, efficient strikes.

Then the ground trembled beneath her shoes.

The miners stopped, fleeing for the cave—only to be shredded under Kalani and Blackwood's merciless assault.

Lexi vaulted into the gunship and hit the deck, lying back with Elise in her arms.

The ground split. Then erupted.

A massive creature tore upward from the dirt—a pitch-black, scaled monstrosity with finned claws and slit-lined teeth that spread open like jagged fans when it roared.

Blackwood paled as he looked up. "It's a fucking Slitfang!"

The beast lunged and clamped onto the gunship's landing gear with its maw.

Kalani dropped his weapon and ran straight at it. He gripped the Slitfang's lower jaw and forced it wide open. The beast thrashed violently, screeching as its claws shredded the metal. Kalani's arm bled as one fang punctured through his armor.

Blackwood tried to get a lock with his sidearm but couldn't fire—the Slitfang was too erratic, flinging Kalani in all directions.

Kalani roared, drove his fist through the creature's mouth, and ripped out one of its flared teeth.

Then he stabbed it—again and again—driving the jagged tooth into its skull until the Slitfang's head was a twitching pulp.

Blue blood splattered everywhere.

Kalani staggered back—one arm soaked in red, the other in blue ichor. He jogged toward the gunship, laughing, fang still in hand.

"Holy shit!" he bellowed, tossing the tooth at Blackwood. "Ho, brud-dah—you see dat?! Hah!"

Lexi let out a shaky breath. Relief hit her like a wave as Kalani neared the gunship, Blackwood catching the bloodied tooth.

Then—a blinding bolt split the still air, punching clean through Kalani's helmet.

He froze mid-stride, arms still outstretched from the throw. Smoke curled from the neat hole in the center of his head before he dropped to his knees.

Lexi's heart broke.

At the cave's mouth, the augmented man lowered his heavy laser rifle, smoke still wafting from the barrel, and grinned—wide, victorious, and sick. With deliberate care, he dragged a fresh tally mark into the rifle's blackened stock.

Kalani's suit began to beep.

A slow, rising whine.

Lexi jumped to her feet.

"No!"

"Ma'am, I need you to sit down!" the pilot barked. "He just flat-lined—Kalani's suit is registering self-destruct! He's too heavy to lift—we need to go, now!"

The gunship lurched upward just as Kalani's body exploded in a thunderous shockwave. The force rocked the gunship, vaporizing what remained of him.

Silence followed.

No fire. No movement.

Only the hum of the engines.

Lexi sat in the corner, blood and coolant smeared across her. Elise's body rested in her lap. Lexi's hand stroked Elise's hair as quiet sobs escaped, tears dripping onto Elise's scorched face.

After several minutes of silence, Blackwood slammed his fist against the wall, denting the gunship.

"What the fuck, Lieutenant?" he snapped. "We lost Elise! And instead of letting go, you got Kalani killed. You wanna go down and pick up the pieces of him, too?! Maybe get me killed?!"

"Sit down, Private," the pilot cut in sharply. "I'm in command of this vessel. Sit, or so help me, I will bury you up to your neck in paperwork. Haven't we all had enough violence for one day?"

Lexi didn't respond.

She didn't look up.

Blackwood's voice came again—lower, but bitter.

"Two. Two people... because you went back for a corpse."

Lexi didn't move. She didn't answer.

She just stared down at Elise.

The pilot spoke into comms.

"HQ, this is Skyreaper Nine."

"Go ahead, Nine."

"Two confirmed KIA. One evac. The other... abandoned. We're coming in hot."

"Copy that, Nine. Medbay's standing by."

The gunship landed with a hard metallic grind against the platform. The hissing release of pressure drowned out the hum of the engines. Lexi sat on the edge of the open bay door, her arms wrapped around Elise's limp body, her synthetic frame still warm from the battle.

A group of medics sprinted to meet them with a stretcher. One of them stepped forward. "Ma'am, we need to—"

Lexi didn't move.

"Ma'am, please."

They reached for Elise, but Lexi's grip tightened. Her arms locked around the body like steel. It took three of them to gently pry her off. Even then, her fingers lingered on Elise's hair and face, as if letting go would make her vanish forever.

She watched as the medics hurried Elise away.

***

"Lieutenant Hayes," came a calm, commanding voice.

She turned.

Chief Graevos stood at the edge of the platform, black and gold armor gleaming in the sunlight. Captain Thorne stood beside him, unreadable.

"My office. Ten minutes," Graevos said, voice low. "Clean yourself up."

"Yes, sir."

***

Thorne looked at Blackwood and gave a single nod. "Private. With me."

Blackwood hesitated only for a moment before following Thorne, leaving Lexi alone on the pad.

79

CHAP_07.exe - Fracture

...system_stability: CR1TICAL ...attempting_auto_recover
...FATAL_ERROR// CHAP_07.exe — Critical_Failure

In the high command restrooms, she rinsed the last of the green coolant and blood from her palms and stared at herself in the mirror—eyes red and tired from crying. She looked down as Elise's muscular fluid circled the drain, her lips quivering—until the door opened. Then she straightened up and stepped into the corridor.

The second floor of HQ felt colder than downstairs. Unlike the chaotic hum of the lower levels, this hall was silent—heavy with history. The walls were dark stone, lit only by recessed floor lights, casting a golden sheen up the sides. On the left wall, the names of Infiltrators lost in the line of duty were carved into black stone. On the right, Enforcers—etched in the same sharp, respectful script.

Three new names were being added even now.

Senior Operative Debra Sinclair.

Recruit Elise Beaumont.

Corporal Zalok Kalani.

The quiet chip-chip-chip of chisels echoed faintly—one on each wall—as two individuals, dressed in ceremonial gray, etched the names in real time.

Lexi paused, breath catching in her throat.

Then she moved forward.

At the end of the corridor stood a broad set of double doors, framed by two black stone pillars. They were sleek, dark, and engraved across the center in brilliant gold:

CHIEF RHYDIAN GRAEVOS HIGH COMMANDER, RAPID DIVISION

She adjusted her stance and knocked once—precise, controlled.

"Enter," came his voice from within.

The office smelled of coffee, aged leather, and lingering cigars. The walls were paneled in dark wood, the lighting low and golden.

A large painting caught Lexi's eye—an older man with a proud beard, dressed in a full military uniform.

Graevos followed her gaze.

"General Pike. A fine man. He ended the Great War, you know." Graevos paused. "I have a paper copy if you would like to read about it?"

"Yes, sir. I'll read about it," Lexi said faintly.

"His file predates our digital records. I like to keep a hard copy. I'll get it for you in a second," Graevos said.

She gave a quiet nod, then let her eyes trail upward to the insignia on the wall behind his desk. A single shield, bordered in silver, dominated the space. In the lower left sat a black circle with a diagonal ring—Verellii. The upper right held a black star—Anthrallii. Next to the Verellii circle, two small black dots represented Bretyl and Yesh. Below the emblem, mounted in bold relief, were two stars of command.

Lexi found herself in awe—this one man, standing at the helm of so much power and responsibility. A single individual—Chief Rhydian Graevos—ran the most dangerous unit on the planet, a mixture of Infiltrators and Enforcers.

Graevos gestured firmly toward the chair across from his desk. His tone left no room for choice.

"Sit."

Lexi obeyed, posture stiff.

He crossed the office to a small bar in the corner of the room, poured two glasses of whiskey, and returned with measured steps. Setting one down, he slid it across the desk until it rested within her reach.

"To the fallen," Graevos said, lifting his own glass.

Lexi met his eyes, raised hers, and clinked it against his.

They drank.

A pause.

Graevos set the glass down and leaned forward, elbows on the desk. "Talk to me. What happened?"

Lexi's jaw tightened. Her voice trembled, but her face remained still.

"I... I don't even know where to start, sir. First Debra. Then Elise. Kalani. The mission was a disaster from the moment we hit the ground. And... there's something else."

Graevos watched her closely, saying nothing.

Lexi rubbed her temples. "I went to a club last night. With my girl-friend, Lyria. We were drinking. I think something was slipped in my drink."

Graevos' brow creased. "What kind of something?"

"I'm not sure. But I started seeing things, like hallucinations. I saw Lyria... with a man."

"Who?"

"I don't know. Some guy named Burton."

Graevos didn't flinch at the name, but his gaze sharpened.

She looked down at the glass in her hands. "Then Lyria was gone this morning. And I haven't heard from her."

Graevos leaned back slowly, weighing her words.

"You're overwhelmed. And I can see the toll. You came in today not entirely yourself—whether it was the lingering effects of the night before, emotional exhaustion, or whatever drugs may still be in your system—I don't know. But it's not like you." He paused. "So, I'm relieving you of duty. Temporarily."

Lexi's head snapped up. "Am I being suspended, sir?"

"No. You're being protected."

He stood and walked around the desk, extending his hand. "Your sidearm."

Lexi hesitated, then handed it over. "Sir, the lock—it's still bound to my imprint. It could stun—"

Graevos accepted the weapon with calm precision and gave the grip a firm squeeze. "Disable weapon."

The pistol gave a soft whir and went silent.

"As Chief, I have override capabilities," he said evenly. "Every weapon issued under my command includes a failsafe."

She gave a stiff nod.

"Sergeant Isabella Rojas will take command of your unit while you're out. She's already been briefed."

Lexi stared at the floor. "Understood."

She stood to leave.

"Lieutenant Hayes," Graevos called.

She turned.

He walked to a nearby cabinet and pulled out a thick paper file. "That file you asked about. General Pike. I'd read it—holds some good information."

She stepped forward and took the file in both hands. "Thank you, sir."

"Get some rest, Lexi," he said. "And when you're ready—come back swinging."

She nodded once, file tucked under her arm, then turned and walked out.

***

Lexi walked slowly down the stairs of HQ, her shoes squeaking faintly against the polished onyx floor. Amber stood near the entrance, posture stiff, eyes locking onto Lexi's approach.

"Lieutenant... a moment?" Amber said, her voice low.

"Go ahead," Lexi replied, pausing.

Amber stepped closer. "I just wanted to say... if you need anything while you're on leave—call me. Seriously. Anything."

Lexi looked at her for a moment. Amber's hand rested lightly on her upper arm.

Lexi gave a faint smile. "Thanks."

Amber's fingers trailed down her arm before she turned and walked off.

Lexi stood there for a second longer, the file under one arm, her shoes still wet with blood and ash.

Then she turned and walked out of HQ.

Into the heat. Into the silence. Into whatever came next.

***

Lexi began walking toward her apartment, her mind filled with questions, confusion, and anger. She had lost two Infiltrators—Debra and

Elise—and a good Enforcer, Zalok Kalani. The weight of it all pressed down on her like a mountain.

She arrived at her apartment, still in disarray and empty. Lyria wasn't home, and her calls went straight to voicemail. Frustration bubbled up inside her. *This isn't like Lyria*, she thought. *What the hell happened?*

She kicked off her shoes and stripped off her sweaty clothes and attached weapons, throwing them into a pile in the living room, walking freely into the bathroom.

She quickly jumped in the shower, washing off the dust, gunpowder, and blood from the day's events. She let the water run over her as steam filled the room, her mind trying to unwind from everything she'd endured.

Later, she changed into soft pajamas and began tidying up the apartment. Music pulsed from the speakers as Lexi moved through the room in a steady rhythm, trying to force some order into the chaos. She grabbed a laundry basket and began tossing in the scattered clothes, determined to clear her mind.

As she worked, the familiar low growl of a car rolling to a halt outside made her stop in her tracks.

"No fucking way," Lexi hissed, rushing to the window. Lyria was getting out of the same car she'd seen the other day.

Blood boiling, Lexi stormed out the door.

"Hey, babe!" Lyria greeted her, standing beside Burton's car.

"Don't you fucking babe me," Lexi spat. "Tell me where the hell you've been—or I'll drag it out of him."

"Oh, Bertie and I were shopping in Level 2," Lyria replied, her tone oddly chipper—but her eyes avoided Lexi's. Her hands trembled slightly.

"What exactly is your relationship with 'Bertie'?" Lexi's voice was laced with sarcasm and betrayal.

Lyria glanced at the car, where Burton sat confidently. "You might as well tell her," Burton said softly, his tone just a little too calm.

Lyria faced Lexi, her voice distant, "You've been busy. Bertie hasn't. We've been seeing each other for a while now."

Lexi's heart shattered. A hollow ache took its place, spreading through her chest as she tried to make sense of it all.

She ran back into the apartment. Without thinking, she started throwing Lyria's things into the street—clothes, pictures, trinkets—everything went flying, landing in a heap on the lawn.

Neighbors gathered; their curious gazes fixed on her outburst. Lexi stopped herself from destroying Burton's car, but couldn't shake the urge.

Lyria stood off to the side, emotionless, her jaw clenched, arms folded tightly—as if she were trying to hold herself together. Lexi's anger boiled, confusion and rage consuming her.

The neighbors called the police, and as the sirens neared, Lyria ran to their cruisers.

As the officers stepped out of their cars, Lexi realized her muscles were tense, her body coiled with anger. She took a deep breath, trying to calm herself.

"Thank god you're here!" Lyria exclaimed, pointing to Lexi. "I came to get my things," Lyria said coolly. "She lost it and started hurling them into the street."

She motioned to the front lawn as Lexi stood still, heart sinking, unable to process the coldness of it all.

Lexi stared at Lyria, her heart cracking further with every second. The person she had trusted, the one who held her at night, had been with someone else for months.

Lexi's gaze shifted to Burton, still sitting in his car. Too calm. Just watching.

"Ma'am, can we talk to you over here?" one officer asked.

"Sure," Lexi replied, seething, her steps heavy as she moved toward the designated area.

"We just need a statement, and we'll be on our way. We know you're with RAPID," the officer said reassuringly.

Lexi took a breath, her voice low and steady. She recounted the last two days—missions gone sideways, unexpected losses, and a betrayal she hadn't seen coming. A stranger had called her something she didn't recognize. And now, she was on temporary leave. Each word dragged heavier than the last. The officer didn't interrupt, his expression shifting as the full weight of it settled in.

"I'm so sorry," he said, his tone sympathetic. "Are you going to be okay on your own tonight?"

"I'll be fine," Lexi answered with defiance. "Just get that bitch out of my face," she added, pointing to Lyria.

Lyria, with her defenses up, gathered her things and loaded them into Burton's car. As she climbed in, she looked back at Lexi—just for a second. Her expression unreadable. Whatever was behind those eyes, Lexi couldn't tell.

As the car pulled away and the police cruisers faded into the distance, Lexi felt an overwhelming sense of emptiness. For the first time in a long while, she realized how utterly alone she was.

Inside her apartment, Lexi let the tears fall freely, looking around at the space she and Lyria had built together. Every memory—the love, the fights, the laughter—now felt like it belonged to someone else. She stepped into the shower, water soaking through her clothes. She collapsed down, pulling her knees to her chest and wrapping her arms around herself. Her head dropped between her arms as she wept quietly, hidden from the world.

***

Hours later, the sound of Hydropure sputtering to a stop pulled Lexi from her thoughts. She glanced at the water meter blinking red, signaling an empty tank. Slowly, she stood and walked out of the bathroom, her wet clothes leaving trails on the carpet. Standing before the full-length mirror, Lexi barely recognized herself. The woman in the reflection was a hollow version of the fierce woman she used to be. Anger replaced heartache as she stormed back to the living room, leaving wet footprints behind.

Lexi dug into the laundry basket, fingers closing around the shoto's grip, fury and pain sharpening her focus. Without flinching, she walked back to the bathroom, raising the blade to her hair and slicing through in one clean stroke. Blonde strands hit the tile floor in silence, until only a pixie cut remained. The doorbell rang, but Lexi ignored it, staring at the fierce rage that stared back at her in the mirror, too consumed with reclaiming control over something, anything, in her life.

The bell rang again.

And again.

Lexi stormed toward the door. "SHUT THE FUCK UP!" she yelled.

She swung the door open aggressively, the hinges squeaking in unison.

CHAP_08.exe - Reb00t

...fatal_err0r → contained   ...system_diagnostics: PASS
...restart_complete

"Hello, ma'am," Amber said softly, offering a small wave.

Lexi narrowed her eyes, tone sharp and weary. "What are you doing here?"

"The officer who responded called in to HQ and told them someone should check on you. Isabella asked for a volunteer. I... I said I would check in on you. See if you were fine."

"And? Do I look fine?" Lexi retorted sarcastically.

Amber, momentarily flustered, stammered, "Well... even with everything going on, you clearly have good taste in hairstyles," she added, glancing at Lexi's newly cut hair.

"What else do you want?" Lexi demanded, frustration bubbling over.

Amber, undeterred, offered a half-smile. "I want to help. Do you want to talk, grab something to eat, or... I don't know, just get out of here for a while?" She gave a nervous chuckle, trying to cut the tension.

Lexi didn't hesitate. "No! I don't!" she barked—and slammed the door in Amber's face. The frame rattled. She stood there, jaw tight, pulse hammering. A moment passed, and she cursed under her breath before she ripped the door back open.

Amber gave her a comforting smile. "Still here!"

Lexi threw her head back, groaning. "God, I could go for some tacos and drink until I can't feel anything anymore."

"I can make that happen! I've got a car, and I'll cover everything," Amber said, her enthusiasm brightening the mood. "But first, maybe change into something a little less... soggy. I know a really fancy place we could go."

Lexi opened the door wider and gestured to the couch. "...Gimme a second," she murmured.

Amber stepped inside, taking a seat as Lexi disappeared down the hall and into her bedroom.

***

Ten minutes later, the sound of heels echoed through the apartment. Amber turned—then froze.

Lexi stood in the doorway in a red dress, black high heels, and that sharp pixie cut—utterly stunning.

***

Amber's face flushed bright red, unable to hide her appreciation.

Lexi tilted her head slightly, eyeing Amber with tired confusion. "Why are you turning red?"

Amber stumbled over her words. "Umm... you're just so pretty."

"Okay... let's go then," Lexi said. "You said you'd help me have a good night. You've got your work cut out for you—are you up for it?"

Amber straightened to attention, giving a mock salute. "Yes, ma'am!"

Lexi gave Amber a hollow smile as they headed out the door. Amber led the way, running to the car and opening the passenger door for Lexi.

"For you, ma'am," Amber said with a smile.

"Thank you?" Lexi asked, confused.

As she lowered herself into the car, a strange scent filled her nose.

"What's that smell?" Lexi asked, furrowing her brow.

"It's pine. Do you like it?" Amber replied.

"What the fuck is a pine?" Lexi said, clearly puzzled.

Amber laughed. "It's from Earth, I think. It used to be a type of tree. I found this air freshener in a scrapper shop. Smells nice, right?"

"It reminds me of Central District Nexus in the spring," Lexi said, a hint of nostalgia in her voice.

"THAT'S EXACTLY WHAT I THOUGHT WHEN I BOUGHT IT!" Amber exclaimed, her excitement infectious.

The car pulled away from Lexi's house, heading toward an unknown destination. Lexi gazed out the window, her mind swirling with thoughts of everything that had led her here. She sniffed, trying to hold back tears, and noticed Amber watching her.

"Is the air freshener bothering you?" Amber asked gently.

"No," Lexi replied quietly. "It's nothing."

"You can talk to me," Amber said, sincere.

Lexi hesitated before speaking. "I lost some really good people under my command today."

Amber listened, then responded confidently, "Elise was new. She was timid, scared... she shouldn't have been on that mission, but she was an Infiltrator and knew the risks. As for Lyria, if what the report says is true, maybe it's better she left. She didn't seem happy, and clearly, she didn't care enough about you. Kalani, though... that was a big loss. His records were solid. He was well-liked, a great field commander. Debra—we'll talk about that later."

"They were all good," Lexi replied softly.

As the car approached the edge of the Central District Nexus, Lexi noticed a large, tarnished building with a disheveled red sign with bold yellow letters reading just one word: Tacos.

"I feel like I'm overdressed," Lexi said, eyeing the place.

"Wait 'til you see inside," Amber said, excited. She winked. "Trust me."

They walked through a dim, unimpressive entrance, and Lexi's initial excitement faded as she began to feel disappointed. Amber asked the hostess to let them into the back-room, and the woman guided them through a maze of hallways, pushing aside bead curtains to reveal something unexpected.

Lexi stepped inside, her hands covering her mouth in awe. She took in a massive aquarium filled with fish, eels, and sharks, along with small, adorable creatures...

"Seahorses!" Amber said with a grin.

"They don't look anything like horses," Lexi remarked, still amazed.

***

"I know, isn't it incredible?" Amber replied. She gazed into Lexi's eyes. "I asked about the creatures when I found this place. Apparently, it's been here, untouched, since before the Great War."

A sealed, pre-War closed-loop kept the water cycling—priceless and self-contained. Imported Earth stock, preserved since before the War, drifted past like living relics.

"That's amazing," Lexi said, feeling a sense of peace she hadn't felt in a while. "Thank you for bringing me here."

The hostess led them farther into the back-room, through an elegant archway decorated with vines, into a secluded area of the aquarium. A soft, ambient light filtered through the water, casting a mesmerizing glow on the walls. Large tanks, filled with a variety of sea creatures, created an ethereal atmosphere. Schools of shimmering fish swam lazily by, their movements almost hypnotic. The calmness of the space wrapped around them like a comforting embrace, the gentle sounds of bubbling water and distant chimes creating an almost surreal feeling of serenity.

They were seated at a corner booth, with a perfect view of the vast aquarium. Lexi looked around, taking in the beauty of the space—a rare moment of tranquility after everything she'd endured.

As the hostess left them to enjoy the view, Lexi turned to Amber, her voice softer now. "How did Debra get caught by the Union, but you didn't?"

Amber hesitated, choking up before she could speak. "It was crazy. We were staking out the warehouse and tracked some guys to a mine. When we went in, they ambushed us. Debra had burned all her blips on fancy moves, so she was an easy target."

She paused, pulling herself together. "This big guy—scarred, all messed up—grabbed her. I charged with my sword, but he snapped it like it was nothing. Then he slammed me into the wall. His people pinned me there while he beat Debra."

***

Amber's hands curled into fists. Her voice dropped to a whisper. "He raped her. Right there in front of me. She fought until her body gave out—screamed, clawed, bit. He laughed through all of it. Like it was a game."

Lexi didn't say a word. She just listened, the tank's glow rippling faint light across her face. Her jaw clenched, eyes fixed ahead. Amber saw it—how hard Lexi was holding back. Despite everything, Lexi was shaken.

"She fought him. I've never seen anything like it." Amber's lip quivered. "And that sick fuck just smiled—like it was fun for him."

A tear slid down her cheek. "Two of them had me pinned. Debra drew her old Relay and shot the one on my right. The other hesitated, and I stabbed him with my shoto."

Her voice faltered, hollow now. "Debra turned on the bastard raping her. Emptied the entire clip into his face."

Amber swallowed hard.

"He didn't even blink. Just... kept going. Like it didn't matter."

She buried her head in her hands, trembling. "I ran. I ran because my sidearm was useless. Because she gave me the opening, and I didn't know what else to do. I left her there. I left her."

Lexi reached out, her hand resting gently on Amber's. "You didn't leave her," she said softly. "She made sure you got out. You didn't run from her. You ran because of her."

Amber looked up, eyes red and raw. "I'm a coward."

Lexi leaned in, her tone calm but unwavering. "No. You froze, then calculated. And then you acted. You lived, Amber. That's not cowardice—it's survival. Debra made her choice. She wanted you to live, and you did."

Amber swallowed hard, her lips pressed into a trembling line. "Thank you, ma'am."

"Lexi," she corrected gently. "Call me Lexi."

"Thank you, Lexi," Amber repeated, voice barely holding together.

Lexi leaned back in her chair, stretching her arms above her head, and let out a deep sigh, closing her eyes for a moment. "What the fuck do we do now?"

As she asked the question, she felt a soft touch on her lips. Opening her eyes, she saw Amber's face inches away, eyes closed, lips brushing against hers. For a brief moment, Lexi pulled back in surprise, but before she could say anything, Amber smiled and pulled away.

"How about we just... enjoy some tacos and drinks first?" Amber suggested, attempting to lighten the mood.

They waved the waiter over and ordered without holding back—loaded tacos, crispy empanadas, sweet fried plantains, and a steaming dish of mofongo packed with garlic and chicharrón. Amber added margaritas to the order. Lexi asked for a beer. Then a second.

When the food arrived, it barely fit on the table.

They dug in without shame—chewing, sipping, laughing between bites. The salt, the spice, the grease—it all grounded them, anchoring them to the present like a lifeline.

Between mouthfuls, they talked. About the mission. About the ones they lost. About the guilt they hadn't outrun. But under the low lights and the bubbling of the aquarium tanks, it all felt... manageable.

For the first time in a while, they just were—two people, full plates, and the silence between them no longer felt like a weight.

Lexi leaned back, wiping her mouth with a napkin, her eyes tracing the soft edge of Amber's smile.

She shouldn't say it. Not with Lyria still echoing in her chest.

But the words came anyway. "Do you want to come home with me?"

Amber didn't answer at first. She simply reached for her credits, tossing a few small metal bars on the table, and stood. "Yes," she said.

***

The ride home was quiet. The city passed by in soft glows of yellow and blue, streetlights blurring against the windows.

When they reached Lexi's place, the couple walked up to the door. Lexi stopped, her hand hovering near the lock.

"Before we go in..." she said quietly. "I need to be honest with you."

Amber looked at her, unsure.

"I can't give you what you want tonight," Lexi said. "Not like that. Not after everything."

Amber didn't pull away. She just nodded.

"I wasn't expecting anything," she replied. "I just didn't want you to be alone."

Lexi exhaled, then unlocked the door and let them in. The apartment was dark and quiet.

"I'll get you something comfy to wear," she said.

Amber nodded, trailing after her down the hall. They changed into loose shirts and soft shorts.

They ended up on the bed, not from desire, but from the need to breathe. Amber curled on her side, facing the wall. Lexi slid in behind her, wrapping an arm carefully around her waist.

Amber exhaled—a small sound of relief—and sank into the warmth.

"You're warm," she whispered.

Lexi smiled as her lips brushing the back of Amber's neck.

Amber's eyes fluttered shut. Lexi's did too, her breath softening as the weight of the day slowly melted away.

She didn't know what tomorrow would bring. But tonight, with Amber in her arms, she let herself believe she'd survive it.

CHAP_09.exe - Parallax

Morning came, and Lexi was the first to wake, her arm tucked under Amber's neck, their bodies pressed together. She eased her arm free and headed into the kitchen, a clump of blonde hair sticking straight up. Rubbing her face, she went for the fridge.

She opened it to find an open container of sour cream and a plastic container of—

"What the fuck is that?" Lexi said, wholly grossed out.

She opened the container and sniffed, gagging as she threw it into the garbage. After confirming the fridge held nothing but biohazards, she returned to the bedroom, where Amber still slept. She sat on the edge of the bed and gave her a gentle nudge.

"Amber," she whispered. "Wanna get something to eat?"

Amber stirred with a groggy sound. "Mmm... you were warm. Why'd you leave?"

Lexi smiled, brushing a strand of hair from Amber's face.

"Only if you promise there's coffee," Amber mumbled, still half-asleep.

She finally pushed herself upright, stretching as Lexi slipped off the bed and headed for the bathroom. The hiss of sputtering Hydropure followed a moment later as Lexi stepped into the shower.

"I have no clothes!" Amber called down the hall.

"Wear whatever you want of mine," Lexi called back with a smirk. "Though your boobs might not fit in my tank tops."

Amber laughed from the bedroom. "Your tops better learn to handle stress. My girls don't compromise."

When they were finally dressed and ready, they stepped out the front door, heading for the corner diner. There was a silence between them—worn thin by loss, softened by comfort. It wasn't happiness exactly… but it was something.

They walked a few blocks before Lexi suddenly stopped in her tracks.

"SynthSkin."

Amber blinked. "Come again?"

Lexi turned to her, animated. "We have to go to a strip club."

"I'm sorry, did you just say we have to go to a strip club?" Amber asked, raising a brow.

"Not like that," Lexi said, already laughing. "When I was out with Lyria that night—drunk, drugged, whatever—a girl came up to me and said she knew me. Said I used to work at a place called SynthSkin."

Amber's eyes widened, then she grinned. "Okay, this just got really interesting. Can we still get coffee before this adventure?"

Lexi gave a small nod. "Yeah. Coffee first. Then I'll tell you everything."

She hesitated, her voice dropping. "You might regret asking."

The heat outside was relentless, rising off the pavement in shimmering waves. The synthetic grass and trees along the sidewalk looked wilted, almost melted under the sun. On the corner, the Golden Grill sat weathered, surrounded by polished storefronts, its flickering sign the last whisper of an old city.

Inside, the air was thick with the smell of old grease and burnt coffee, clinging to cracked leather booths that had seen better days. Rex gave a tired smile and wave, already prepping Lexi's usual.

"Can I get a pumpkin-paste and caramel iced coffee, please?" Amber asked.

Rex rasped as he held Amber's cup in hand, squinting at her through a curl of smoke drifting from the cigarette between his lips. "Cockroach caramel, or that cloned honey trash? Union says they're both safe. I say bullshit."

"Uhh… cockroach caramel," Amber said.

Rex grunted and set to work while Lexi started, filling Amber in on all the details in a low, steady tone. Her hands moved occasionally as Amber listened. Slowly, Amber's grin faded as the story unfolded. She didn't interrupt.

Rex slid the coffees across the counter. "No charge for you, sweetheart," he rasped.

"Thanks, Rex," Lexi said, giving him a wink.

"You! That'll be fifty credits. CARAMEL AIN'T CHEAP!" Rex barked at Amber.

"Damn, that's steep," Amber muttered, dropping credits on the counter.

They left with coffee in hand and headed down the street to Amber's car—carrying more than just caffeine now. Moments later, the engine turned over, and they rolled toward Level 2.

By daylight, Level 2 looked nothing like the chaos of the night before. The music, the neon, the bodies packed shoulder to shoulder—all of it gone, burned away under Verellii's star. Anthrallii beat down through the retracted panels overhead, flooding the streets in merciless light. The air shimmered with heat, stripping away the glamour and leaving only silence.

They pulled up outside SynthSkin, a once-glowing beacon of temptation.

In the sun, it seemed smaller. Exposed. The pink facade was sun-bleached and cracked, its neon trim barely visible. Massive posters of dancers still clung to the walls, but without the haze and shadows, they felt more desperate than alluring. Above it all, the once-bubbly sign sputtered faintly—its charm gone, its glow no match for the star overhead.

Lexi didn't look at it long. Something about the place still made her stomach twist.

Two massive bouncers flanked the entrance, their optical sensors humming softly, tracking every step as Lexi and Amber drew near.

Amber fanned herself with her hand. "Why is Level 2 even open in this heat?"

Lexi offered a small, dry laugh. "Let's just get inside."

As they stepped up to the entrance, one of the bouncers held out a hand. "Hundred credits... each."

Amber rolled her eyes. "Seriously?"

"We are RAPID Infiltrators, here for information," Lexi said, steady and confident.

"Can't party without the cash," the bouncer said as he looked Lexi up and down. "I can never tell the difference between Infiltrators and our sluts," he muttered.

Lexi didn't flinch, but something in her jaw tightened.

Amber stepped between them.

Her voice was calm. Cold. "Watch your tone, or we're going to have a problem."

The first bouncer straightened, sensing the shift. The second one didn't back off.

Amber's eye flickered red. "Let's see here, Luther. You've got several warrants out for your arrest. Should I notify the VPSD?" She tilted her head slightly. "You think SynthSkin's gonna protect you?"

The bouncer scowled, lips curling, but stepped aside.

"Welcome to SynthSkin," he muttered. "Enjoy yourselves."

The doors slid open.

Beyond them was a softly lit hallway—pink, white, and gold lights washed over the silk drapes hanging in soft folds from the ceiling. Each set of fabric framed a slow-turning holographic display of a nude dancer, their bodies moving in graceful loops, glowing with a dreamlike sheen.

The music built with every step, the bass growing heavier, more present—until it began to reverberate through their chests, pulling them forward toward the main floor.

At the far end of the hall, a glowing doorway waited—spotlights angled to shine directly at anyone approaching. Lexi shielded her eyes as they walked forward, blinking against the sudden brightness.

Then they stepped through.

And there it was.

SynthSkin dropped ten stories below them—layered, alive, and dizzying.

Every race, sex, fetish, and fantasy was playing out across the endless levels. White, pink, and gold lighting washed over the walls, dancers spinning on platforms as patrons threw tokens. Some patrons were pulled into back-rooms, chasing some brief version of love they'd forget by later that night.

Lexi stood frozen at the edge, staring down.

She didn't say a word.

Amber's gaze flicked to the dancers before she turned to Lexi. "What are those?" she asked, voice soft, curiosity replacing the earlier frustration.

"Transfer tokens," Lexi said, eyes scanning the crowd—looking for glitter, painted lips, or a flash of bright blue hair. "They make sure credits go to the right person, kind of like a temporary credit card. Physical chits linked to a throwaway wallet—burned after payout."

Amber nodded. "Now what?"

"Now, we take it all in," Lexi said, still searching, trying to match the blur in her memory to a face on stage. "I need to see if I remember her face. She said she knew me."

After a while, an announcement blared over the speakers. "Ladies and Gentlemen! We welcome to the stage the sexy, fiery, and mysterious Mia!"

The crowd cheered as a slender Asian woman with delicate features stepped onto the stage, dressed only in heels.

"That's her!" Lexi said.

She moved to a man seated at a desk beside a row of curtained rooms.

"I'd like a private dance with her," Lexi said, pointing at Mia.

"You like Asians, huh? Me too. Hundred credits," the man grunted.

Lexi transferred the credits, and the man whispered into an earpiece before opening Curtain Three.

"In you go. Don't be inappropriate with the girls, or you'll be dealing with me," he said, flexing his arm to show off a little muscle.

"Oh, fuck!" Lexi said, sarcasm dripping. "You're certainly a man not to be trifled with. How would I, a tiny Infiltrator, ever take down such a man?" She rolled her eyes. "Get the fuck out of here."

Defeated, he backed out of the room and yanked the curtain closed behind him.

After the song ended, the curtain flew open, and Mia stepped in—still wearing her heels, but now wrapped in a silk kimono that kept sliding off her shoulders. One of her tits popped out almost immediately, but she didn't seem to notice—or care.

"Oh my god! Pixie! You were so fucked up the other day, I wasn't sure if you'd even remember me! How've you been? Besides getting shot in the face, you look great!" Mia said, practically vibrating with excitement.

Amber opened her mouth to speak, her eyes darting to Mia's exposed breast. "Uh, hey, your—"

"I'm sorry, I don't know you," Lexi cut in, her voice flat, ignoring the exposure.

"What? Oh! Right, I've seen this thing on the holo where people get shot in the face and don't remember shit..."

As Mia kept talking, the kimono slipped off her other shoulder. Her other boob joined the conversation.

Amber lifted a hand, clearly uncomfortable. "You're kinda—"

"Something about a lobby, lopey, lobo, lob thing in your brain. If that gets shot, you just become, like, stupid. Are you like stupid now or somethin'? Nah, you're still the same ol' Pixie. Did you come here to get your job back? Oh my god, Mia, of course she did. Why else would she be here, duh? Well, we can talk to Marco, the new manager. He's gonna want to take you for a spin. Not the worst lay I've had, but he..."

Lexi started rubbing her temples as Mia went on, the words piling over each other in a dizzying mess of details and tangents.

"MIA, MIA, STOP!" Lexi snapped, cutting her off. "I'm not here to get my job back, I'm not stupid, and I'm not fucking Marco. I need to know what I did before I got shot and how I ended up in my current situation."

Mia smiled brightly, blowing a bubble with her gum. "Oh, that's easy, baby doll. You was a stripper."

Lexi stared, waiting for more.

"Oh, right," Mia added. "You was dancing one night, and this guy, he seemed real into you. You went for a private dance, but he got real aggressive."

"Okay, and?" Lexi asked, impatient.

"So, dude gets bounced, but he really liked you," Mia said, popping her gum. "He was waitin' outside all soaked from some pipe or somethin' leakin' I guess, just waitin' for you. You come out, his boys hold you down, you were on your knees, beggin' for your life, gettin' soaked, makeup all smeared, and then he says, 'The Natural Order sends their regards, stupid robot bitch,' and blows your face off."

Lexi's jaw tightened. She'd heard those words before, whispered in the dark of her own mind. *Not a nightmare*, she realized. *A memory.* And it left her wondering—*how many of her dreams were only dreams, and how many were pieces of her stolen past?* She shook the thought off, forcing her focus back to Mia.

"The Natural Order? What's that?" Lexi asked, confused.

"Yeah, them weirdos who kill people with cybernetics. Don't like people bein' unnatural," Mia said, chomping on her gum.

"What cybernetics did I have?" Lexi asked.

"Oh, baby! You had one of those chips that swipes credits from customers without them knowin'. You was makin' bank!" Mia said, jealousy edging her voice.

"What happened after that?" Lexi pressed.

"We called the cops," Mia said with a shrug as her kimono slid off and pooled on the floor.

"What exactly happened, Mia?" Lexi said, frustration peeking through.

"Well, me and the other strippers just watched from the doorway. They already killed Vince and Bear. You got blasted, slumped over, then they cut you open, pulled out the chip, and crushed it. Then they got in their car and left you there bleeding, like it was nothin'. But look at you now, you're fine, looks like you got patched up," Mia said, placing her hand on Lexi's left hip.

Amber picked up the kimono and tried to hand it to her, but Mia didn't even glance her way.

"Then, okay, get ready, this part," Mia continued. "The cops never came. These guys in black showed up in a huge black truck, one of those big six-wheeled armored things. Pixie, picture it: I'm you now, right? You look up, and the thing just keeps goin' up. Pixie! You're not liftin' your head."

Lexi sighed and lifted her head slowly.

Amber glanced up, her eyes glazed over from the whirlwind of words.

"Up, up, up. STOP! That high, right? Crazy! Saw government bar-codes, so I thought it was legit. They scooped you up, threw you in the truck, and drove off," Mia finished.

"Thank you, Mia," Lexi said, her voice heavy with exhaustion.

The song ended. Mia stood and gave Lexi a tight hug.

"Pixie, it was awesome seeing you again, but I gotta go make that money. Not everyone's got a credit-swiping chip, ha ha ha. Okay, Mia, let's go."

Mia pulled the curtain open and disappeared down a hallway and behind a stage, forgetting her kimono. The crowd went wild as she reemerged.

Lexi stepped out of the private room, more confused than ever—but at least now she had some answers.

***

Amber was waiting just outside, eyes wide with concern.

"You good?" she asked softly.

Lexi gave a small nod. "Yeah. Just need to find out who took me."

They left the club and climbed into Amber's car. The doors creaked shut as the AC kicked in. The air was blissfully cooler—maybe ninety degrees, but it felt like paradise.

As they drove, Lexi and Amber talked about what Mia had said.

"The Natural Order? You mean, like T.N.O.?" Amber asked.

Lexi looked at her, surprised. "You're a genius, Amber!"

Amber blushed but smiled, clearly pleased. "Just trying to help."

They pulled up outside Lexi's apartment. Inside, the two collapsed on the couch. The silence stretched for a moment.

"Do we use black transports for anything?" Lexi asked suddenly.

"Nope," Amber said. "Everything else is white and blue, except for gunships that are dark gray. Why?"

Lexi leaned back. "Mia said a black vehicle with a government barcode picked me up after... after I got shot."

Amber frowned. "That's not right. Those don't exist. Not officially."

"Black, six-wheeled, barcode but no registry—off the books," Lexi said, jaw set. "So who the hell took me?"

***

"Well, we have two weeks to figure it out!" Amber said, trying for cheerful.

Lexi blinked. "Why two weeks?"

Amber sighed. "Sergeant Rojas gave me a temporary leave. Said I needed time. After what happened in the mines."

Lexi's expression shifted—understanding, guilt, and something else. "Right... you saw Debra. That's a good call from Rojas."

Amber nodded. "It's just two weeks, and I was going to use it to find a new place to live. My landlord jacked up the rent again, and... I can't afford it anymore. So technically, I'll be homeless soon."

"So you're dealing with trauma, rent hikes, and still helping me?" Lexi said. She didn't think—she just acted, like always. "Then stay here. Seriously. The green room's yours."

Amber looked surprised. "Are you serious?"

"Yeah. You're a damn good Infiltrator, I trust you, and honestly... if our friendship keeps growing like it has the past day, you'll be here all the time anyway."

Amber beamed. "Thank you! I promise I won't be a burden!"

She ran outside, jumped in her car, and tore down the road like her life depended on it.

Lexi laughed. That girl was all sunshine. So different from Lyria—who had secrets and chaos. Amber, though... Amber protected her, made her feel seen and wanted.

Hours passed. Lexi cleaned the place, ran laundry, and tried not to overthink everything. Eventually, Amber's car rushed into the driveway. She kicked open the front door, arms full of clothes and boxes, grinning like a kid on her birthday.

"This will do nicely," Amber said, walking into the mint-green room.

"Sorry about the paint," Lexi replied, leaning against the doorframe.

"Are you kidding? I love old things, and my favorite color's green. Thanks again, Lex," Amber said gratefully. She walked up to Lexi and softly kissed her lips.

"Um, you're welcome," Lexi said, slowly falling for the girl who'd crashed into her life.

"Want to watch a movie and eat some ice cream? I can have it delivered," Lexi asked.

"Only if we snuggle under a blanket," Amber called out, digging through a garbage bag of clothes.

"Fuck, forgot the holo's broken. Guess no movie tonight," Lexi said begrudgingly.

"No worries," Amber replied. "I brought mine."

Lexi grinned. "Well then, I've got the blanket, and I'll cool down the apartment."

She went over to the thermostat and turned the temperature as low as it would go, the air conditioner groaning to keep up with her demand.

After the ice cream was delivered and the movie ended, Lexi asked, "How's Izzy holding up with the recruits?" Outside, Verellii's sun dipped below the horizon.

"Sergeant Isabella is amazing," Amber said. "Hard exterior, but I think she truly cares for them... and us. She even called me today to ask how I was doing."

Izzy's one of the best, Lexi thought.

"Sergeant Izzy also said they brought in a new Infiltrator to help with the office. But weirdly, she has no record—like she popped out of nowhere. I think her name's Elsa," Amber said, trying to keep ice cream from spilling.

"We don't have anyone named Elsa. Where would she have come from? How new is she? Did she just get back from CRIS?" Lexi asked, concern edging into her voice.

"Umm, I don't know. She's only been there a couple of days, since you left, actually. They've just got her babysitting the office while the Sergeant focuses on the recruits and missions," Amber replied.

"Something's not right. I know every Infiltrator that is in—and is coming in. I'm checking this out," Lexi said, suddenly standing.

"Take the car," Amber offered, shoveling more ice cream into her mouth.

"Thank you!" Lexi said, turning back to Amber before she bolted out the door.

***

She started Amber's car, and as it sputtered to life, an uneasy feeling settled in her stomach. She drove as fast as she could to HQ, parked, and rushed up the steps, through the atrium, the Eraway, and into the Infiltrator division.

"Hi! Can I help you?" a woman behind one of the desks asked.

Lexi froze, her pink eye turning a deep red as she scanned the woman.

"No. It can't be. How are you here?" she said, terrified.

"Oh, you must be Lieutenant Hayes! It's a pleasure to meet you! I'm Admin Elsa Smith!" the woman said eagerly, snapping to attention.

"I asked you a question. How the fuck did you get here?" Lexi demanded, voice sharp.

"I got a call a couple of days ago, and they asked me to come in and help Sergeant Rojas," Elsa replied, confused by the tension.

"What do you remember about being an Infiltrator?" Lexi pressed, panic rising.

"Well, that's a sad story. The medical examiner said I was on a mission when I got hurt. They repaired my cybernetics and got me back up and running—pretty lucky, huh? I don't remember anything about the mission... or anything before it, actually," Elsa said, trying to offer clarity.

Lexi stepped back, her legs giving out beneath her. She leaned against the entrance to the division, panic intensifying. Elsa rushed over to help.

"Don't fucking touch me!" Lexi yelled, breath quickening. "Don't touch me!"

Elsa opened her mouth but couldn't find the words as she backed away from the shaken lieutenant.

Lexi's chest heaved, her pink iris burned hot. She ripped a sidearm from a locker, grip trembling. Her voice came out cracked but sharp: "Lieutenant Lexi Hayes, Commander, RAPID Infiltrator Corps—override: ballistic."

The unbound pistol chirped: "Override authorized."

Its light turned yellow as she leveled it at Elsa's head.

"Wait, no! What did I do?" Elsa pleaded.

Isabella, hearing the commotion, rushed out of the communication room. Seeing Lexi aiming the gun at Elsa, she shouted, "¡No, mami! ¿Qué estás haciendo? ¡Baja la pistola y hablemos de lo que está pasando!"

Lexi, not wearing her headset, didn't understand Isabella's words but saw her rushing toward Elsa, clearly focused on protecting her.

Lexi pulled the trigger. The bullet struck Elsa's skull, but like any Infiltrator, it ricocheted off, leaving only a minor cut in her synthetic skin.

"So, they got you too," she muttered, realization heavy.

She dropped the gun. It slipped from her fingers and hit the floor with a lifeless clatter as she squatted down, her body giving in.

***

"I saw you dead," she whispered.

"You… saw me dead? What does that mean?" Elsa asked, confused.

"I was walking home, and you were on the ground. I scanned you and reported your death to the police. I never thought I'd see you again… *not in a million years.*" Lexi paused, eyes welling. "Do you remember anything about the medical person who worked on you?"

Elsa's eyes widened. "Yeah! I saw him in this building. He's really quiet. After he fixed me, he said I had amnesia and that I was supposed to report to Sergeant Rojas before moving to the southern hemisphere branch."

"There is no southern hemisphere branch—never has been," Lexi snapped back.

Lexi processed everything Elsa, Mia, and Amber had said, piecing it together. The mechanic was the key—the one who could explain what was going on inside the Infiltrator program.

Isabella, worried about her lieutenant, knelt beside Lexi and pulled her into a close embrace. Resting her head on Lexi's blonde hair, she spoke in a caring voice, "Lieutenant, go home. Get some rest. You've had some rough days. I've got this."

"I need to confirm something," Lexi muttered.

She stood and turned on her heel, pace urgent, leaving Elsa and Isabella speechless.

Lexi pushed into the mechanic's office first; it was dark and empty. No tools running, no chatter, not even a datapad left glowing on standby. The chair sat pushed back, abandoned.

Her unease deepened.

She stepped back into the corridor—silent, deserted. Not even a janitor. Something was wrong.

Opening her onboard database, she pulled up her files—only for a NOT AUTHORIZED warning to flash across her vision.

She didn't hesitate. Moving quickly to the stairwell, she descended to the basement level, where old paper records were kept for emergencies.

***

At the terminal, she scanned her wrist. Credentials failed. Lockout. The system wasn't broken.

Someone was watching.

CHAP_10.exe - Subjugate

Having no other options, she forced the records room door open, the old mechanical lock giving way with a loud snap. But before she could take a single step inside, something slammed into the side of her head.

Lexi hit the ground, her vision blurred.

A shadow loomed over her.

"You have been identified as an enemy of the state, a traitor, and you will be eliminated," the voice declared.

As her sight focused, Lexi saw an Enforcer standing over her, his visor glowing orange. His rank and name were now visible on his chest.

"Stand down, Sergeant Vorn," Lexi commanded.

"Order not authorized," the Enforcer replied coldly.

"I'm Lieutenant Lexi Hayes, Commander of the Infiltrator Corps, here on official business. Return to your post, and there'll be no retaliation," she said, trying to reason with the seemingly entranced Enforcer as she slowly stood.

"Termination imminent," the Enforcer replied, advancing with deadly intent.

Enforcers, with their nearly indestructible armor, immense strength, and resistance to poison, fire, and asphyxiation, are formidable foes. They cannot be intimidated or interrogated, and their invulnerability when in armor makes them a brutal force to reckon with. However, Enforcers have one glaring weakness: Infiltrators. Lexi knows firsthand that Infiltrators are uniquely equipped to deal with unruly

Enforcers. Fortunately, she has passed this test with a perfect score every year during her annual exams.

Her left hand warmed as a blue light began to glow under her skin. As the Enforcer swung at her, Lexi sprang backward, flipping in midair to evade. The Enforcer swung again, and this time, Lexi jumped forward, landing and sprinting up his arm. The blue light under her skin intensified, blindingly bright.

With a forceful punch to the Enforcer's head, she released an electrical surge that shattered every lightbulb around them and knocked the Enforcer unconscious while incapacitating his armor. Lexi landed on her feet, her left arm smoldering. She watched as the skin blackened before it burned away, revealing the metal-muscle shell beneath—extending from fingertip to shoulder.

She flexed her arm, marveling at its strength as the strands moved and flexed under her control. Still high on adrenaline, she punched through the door, sending it flying off its hinges.

With the door out of the way, she stepped into the files and documentation room. Something yanked her hair—HARD. In an instant, she was airborne, flung across the room. She hit the wall with a thunderous crack, concrete buckling under the impact. For just a moment, she hung there—then slumped forward and dropped to the floor.

Concrete rained around her as she hit the ground, dazed.

"Fuck, that hurt," Lexi grunted, dragging herself up and waving her hand, trying to coax her Shockwave Inhibitor back online—cooldown warnings flashing in her vision. The blue glow beneath her skin flickered, then faded. Another Enforcer emerged, visor glowing.

"You have been identified as an enemy of the state, a traitor. You will be eliminated." Word for word—an echo. Programmed. Mindless. A wall of armor and orders.

"Yeah, yeah, elimination, got it," Lexi muttered dismissively.

She ran down the hallway, the Enforcer pursuing her. Finding an electrical control box, she waited, letting the Enforcer close in.

"This is going to hurt," she muttered to herself, then punched the control box. Electricity surged through her metallic muscles, making her skin smoke as she prepared for the Enforcer's approach.

"Come get me, bitch," Lexi growled, her anger flaring.

The Enforcer swung at her, and Lexi grabbed his arm, sending an electrical shock through his suit. Unfazed, the Enforcer grabbed her by the hair and slammed her head into the control box over and over. The relentless blows, coupled with the surging electrical pulses, left Lexi with no other choice but to black out.

***

When Lexi woke, she found herself within a cell in an unfamiliar place. This wasn't like any police or governmental station she'd seen before. The walls were lined with red energy shields, not bars, and there were at least fifty cells, though only a few were occupied.

"Where are we?!" Lexi yelled to a man in a nearby cell.

"Shhh, don't talk," he whispered, fear evident in his voice.

"WHY?!" Lexi yelled in frustration, and as if on cue, bolts of lightning surged through each of the cells.

Electricity tore through Lexi's body, dropping her to her knees. She looked down—her synthetic skin was gone, replaced by scorched metal plating. As her vision blurred, she heard the screech of a door opening somewhere in the distance.

Definitely steel. Reinforced, she thought, her mind foggy as shadowy figures advanced.

"Who's the newest?" one of the masked figures asked.

"Lexi Hayes. Lieutenant and Commander of the RAPID Infiltrator Corps," another replied.

"A live Infiltrator?" The first figure sounded surprised. "And a lieutenant, no less? Well, today just got interesting."

They approached her cell, studying a datapad.

"Who is this?" the leader demanded.

"It's Lieutenant Lexi Hayes, sir," the assistant said.

The boss jabbed at the screen. A photo appeared. "This is Lexi Hayes? That's a robot." He pointed at her through the shielding.

"We found her at RAPID HQ, collapsed on the floor," the assistant said quietly. "Her skin burned away after she tried to take down an Enforcer with an electrical control box."

"She didn't use her Shockwave Inhibitor?" the boss asked.

"She did, sir—but on a different Enforcer."

The boss laughed, loud and disbelieving. "Ha! She took on two Enforcers and lived?" His grin darkened. "She must've died at some point. Our Enforcer program doesn't stop until the target is dead."

He keyed in more commands. The reinforced door hissed open again, revealing figures in full hazmat gear. As they approached, another surge of electricity crackled through the cell. Lexi collapsed.

The boss entered a final sequence. A second jolt ripped through the room, and Lexi's world went black.

***

She awoke to the soft cling of an elegant white dress against her body. Her synthetic skin, tattoos, and dermal markings were whole again, the fabric flattering every line of her form.

Only then did the room come into focus: a finely crafted wooden table before her, velvet-lined chairs encircling it, chandeliers glittering overhead. Paintings and gilded trinkets crowded the walls; wealth pressed into every surface.

The sense of luxury faltered when she felt a sharp pinch at her neck. Her hand found a cold, metallic collar. A warning beep answered her touch.

"I wouldn't touch that, or move too much, Ms. Hayes," a man's voice said from behind her.

"What is this place? What do you want with me?" Lexi whispered, careful not to trigger the collar.

The voice was calm, razor-edged.

"You are becoming a thorn in my side. Asking questions, digging where you shouldn't put your nose. I've spent years perfecting Infiltrators and Enforcers—let's just say, for personal purposes—and I'm not about to let one Infiltrator ruin what I've built."

Lexi clenched her fists at her sides. "I don't understand your meaning," she said.

"The Enforcers are simple," the voice continued. "Mindless brutes. A cube in their heads, and they obey with a flick of a switch. Infiltrators were harder to augment, but still manageable. Every repair cycle, every upgrade, we fitted them with control cubes—one by one, a leash drilled straight into their skulls. When the order comes, they will all move as one."

Lexi forced her voice steady. "That's a lie. I've never had one of your cubes."

A soft chuckle brushed her ear, close enough to feel the breath.

"Oh, but you did. Or rather—we tried. You, Lieutenant Hayes, or should I say L-3-X-1. You're an experiment, meant to be the best servant Earth ever created. Your self-repair treated the cube as an infection, broke it down before it ever rooted. *You didn't even know.*"

Her throat tightened against the collar. She wanted to fire back, but the certainty in his tone curdled her gut.

"And you're not the only complication," he said, pacing slow circles behind her. "There is also a rare I5 model. A unit coded with Modules Eleven and Thirteen—memory anchoring and regeneration. Together, they mimic your X1 resistance. *Another liability. Another problem I intend to correct."*

Lexi's stomach knotted.

The voice leaned closer—she could feel his skin against the back of her neck.

"The cubes make them slaves. You and the glitch are different. But you'll still serve a purpose eventually. Because the Verelliian Steel Vault is real, Lieutenant. Buried deep. Hidden so well it became a myth."

Lexi snorted, her voice sharp despite the collar biting her neck. "*That's just a fairy tale we tell children."*

His voice curved darker, almost amused. "Then let's pray you never learn how much truth sleeps inside your bedtime stories."

His tone hardened. "Earth wants that vault, and I will claim it. When I send the leashed ones into the dark, you will lead me to it—whether you want to or not. And if you resist, I have fail-safes."

"What kind of fail-safes?" Lexi asked cautiously.

His voice curled with amusement. "Remember that girl you found dead in the street? Elsa. She was my assistant. She grew a con-science—thought about warning you. I ended that foolish idea. Now she's mine, remade into a weapon where you'd least expect it. *You'll find out soon enough.* How many others will oppose you, I wonder, Ms. Hayes?"

Lexi's frustration grew. "So, what now?"

The man's voice hardened. "While you've been sitting here, I've been waiting for the cube we implanted while you were unconscious to take root. It hasn't. So, I'll move on to other avenues. And now—you die. If I can't control you, I'll eradicate you."

He turned toward the door. "Send Thorne in."

Expecting Captain Cybrix Thorne, Lexi's heart skipped when she saw his son, Recruit Gavin Thorne, enter instead. His eyes were ablaze with orange.

He lifted a laser rifle and pressed it to her forehead. Before he could pull the trigger, a bolt of energy streaked through the window, hitting Gavin in the leg.

"Son of a bitch!" he yelled, the orange light vanishing from his eyes.

"What—what the hell am I doing here?" Gavin stammered, staring at the rifle in his hands. His eyes darted to Lexi, then to the smoking hole in his armor. "Lieutenant... what happened? I—I was going to shoot you, wasn't I?" His voice cracked. "What the fuck is wrong with me?"

"You were about to kill me when a shot came through the window. I don't know what it was, but it snapped you out of whatever control you were under," Lexi whispered urgently. "Can you get this collar off me?"

Thorne limped to her side and, without hesitation, tore the collar free. It clattered to the ground, wires spitting sparks.

"Down!" Lexi barked, dragging Gavin with her as another bolt scorched the wall where she'd been sitting. They dropped low, Thorne flipping the ornate table into cover as shards of wood and glass rained around them.

Gavin grimaced, clutching his leg. "Who the hell is shooting at us?"

Lexi glanced over the table, lips curling. "Good thing whoever it is can't shoot straight."

Blood trickled from the smoking hole in his armor as Gavin shoved a laser rifle toward her. "Do you know how to use this?"

"No. Laser weapons are illegal," she shot back, crouched low.

"RAPID Enforcer Mandate Directive 14-7—exigent use of non-standard or illegal weaponry is authorized when standard kit is unavailable. We destroy it after." He tapped his wrist screen. "Confirm file sync."

"I accept," Lexi said. Her eye flared red, white lines flooding through it as the data streamed.

"Now you've got the information. Put it to good use. I'll make sure the Chief writes you up later for using an illegal firearm."

"You're an asshole," Lexi muttered, checking the rifle.

"Yeah. But I'm the asshole bleeding for you. By the way. You look ridiculous in that dress."

As they sat behind cover, Gavin pulled out his sidearm, chambering a round. Lexi grabbed the train of the dress, ripping it off to expose her long legs, letting out a relieved sigh. "Ahhhh, much better."

The window groaned. Glass shattered inward as a shadow climbed through.

Lexi peeked over their cover, rifle steady in her hands. "Elsa...?"

The echo of the man's voice lingered in Lexi's head—*a weapon where you'd least expect it.*

Her office assistant dropped into the room, eyes blazing orange, rifle aimed squarely at them.

"You have been identified as enemies of the state," Elsa said, voice cold. "Protocol Terra is active."

Elsa's finger tightened on the trigger—

—Thorne lunged, vaulting himself over the overturned table, crushing her head with his suit-enhanced strength. Her body dropped lifelessly to the ground.

***

"Thank you for the intervention," Lexi said, breathless. "I've lost too many good Infiltrators the past few days. I don't think I could've put one down myself."

"Don't mention it. I'm guessing that's the eye thing you were talking about?" Thorne asked. "Let's get out of here, shall we?"

The pair moved toward a door, entering a mahogany-adorned hallway filled with expensive furniture. Suddenly, a bullet whizzed into Lexi's arm, peeling away her newly regenerated skin.

"Fuck, I just got that skin too," she joked, trying to keep things light as bullets and laser fire began to tear through the furniture.

"Take cover!" Lexi shouted.

They quickly dived behind whatever cover they could find, the projectiles flying in from rooms branching off the hallway.

"We can't stay here!" Lexi said.

Thorne punched through one of the walls, creating an opening. "Lieutenant, go around! I'll draw their fire!"

Lexi nodded and rushed toward the room, moving to intercept the hostiles.

A man with a rifle opened fire, the bullets doing little but irritating Lexi. With precision, she aimed her gun as it charged, preparing to take her shot.

This thing charges so fucking slow, Lexi thought as she threw the rifle at the man's head, splitting his skull open. The man, the gun, and a splatter of blood hit the ground.

Lexi took a sharp left into the next room, punching a man so hard he flew down the hallway, crashing into the ongoing firefight between Thorne and the aggressors. The man hit the wall, his face caved in from the impact.

Fueled by rage, Lexi picked up a rifle with twenty rounds left.

"That should be plenty," she muttered, starting to execute the assailants one by one with deadly precision.

The firing stopped once the bullets ran dry. Lexi slammed the rifle's barrel into a man's skull, pinning him to the wall.

The remaining aggressors, outmatched by the blood-soaked Infiltrator and the Enforcer at the end of the hall, fled—realizing they were marked for death if they stayed.

Lexi caught her breath as she heard voices coming from the next room. She signaled Thorne to the door with a quick hand motion.

Thorne nodded and moved in, flanking the opposite side of the doorway from Lexi.

"Before we go in, take this," Thorne said, tossing Lexi a pistol he found on the ground.

Lexi quickly scanned the pistol, loading its configuration into her memory banks. "Thanks," she said, relieved to have a weapon she could handle with ease.

Lexi cocked her leg back and burst through the door, splintered wood flying across the room. She surveyed the space—it's large, with bookshelves lining the walls and a beautiful desk in the center, the chair facing away from them.

"Much faster than I expected," a voice said from behind the chair.

Lexi froze, recognizing the voice as the man who spoke to her in the dining room—and the one in charge down in the cells.

"Turn around," Lexi commanded. "You're under arrest."

"Now, why would I be under arrest?" the man responded, not turning. "I still have the upper hand."

The chair swiveled. Burton Marx sat there, calm smirk in place.

"What—why—how?" Lexi stammered, her confusion evident.

"You really want to know?" Burton said, his tone mocking. "Well, who am I to deny a dying woman her last wish?"

Burton's smile was thin, his eyes cold and calculating.

"The Union Bioengineering Division—Verellii's pride, its lifeline. On paper, I was its Director, trusted to push the division further, faster, stronger. In truth, I was Earth's man. Every time Verellii reached too high, every whisper of spacefaring ambition—I made sure it collapsed. Space was to remain out of reach. That was my mission."

He sat calmly, too comfortable with the situation. His voice was steady, almost clinical.

"But sabotage wasn't enough. The coroners—those who handled every ruined Enforcer, every shattered Infiltrator—they became my hands. We placed cubes in their skulls, one by one. A leash no one could see. And when the order came, Verellii's strongest would go exactly where I wanted them—digging, searching, marching toward the Vault."

A smirk cut across his face.

"RAPID was always to be a double-edged sword. Outwardly, RAPID's elite. Ultimately, my creations—built to dig for what Verellii buried, and to fracture the Union from within. Let them feud, bleed, and hate while the government feigned ignorance. A divided Verellii is easier to conquer after all."

His expression hardened, voice dropping colder.

"And through it all, I drained the Union dry. I ordered resources in excess, demanded more, pushed harder. Eighteen-hour shifts. Starving workers. A machine that would consume lives until nothing remained. Verellii never knew, and its citizens never cared. They took, and took, and left the Union to rot."

Burton's eyes gleamed as he straightened.

"The uprising is coming—and it will be forged by my hands."

He lifted the Kurogane slate with a cruel smirk. "This was never supposed to be in your hands, but luckily, Elsa is proving extremely useful in her new role. Lena will have to make more versions like her."

"Elsa was easy work. She won't be helping you anymore," Thorne said coldly.

"Lena, who?" Lexi asked, her gaze hardening as she stared into his cold eyes.

Burton's smile turned even more sinister. "Come on, Lexi. You're smarter than this. You know exactly who Lena is."

"Lena... Boma?" Lexi asked, her blood running cold as the name struck her.

"That's right," Burton said, his tone laced with disdain. "An L3 model, like you—albeit brutal, ruthless, psychotic. She never cared for you, Lexi. To her, you were just another machine—a prototype to sharpen and discard. Those hissing messages, the marks, Building 177... all just experiments to watch how you evolved."

"You were supposed to be the perfect Infiltrator—flawless, obedient. But you are flawed, with your sickening, irritating, and relentless free will."

He smirked, his voice cold as ice. "Once she's done fulfilling her purpose, I'll end her, just like I'll end you."

His eyes shifted from Lexi over to the wall. "*Do what you must, my dear.*"

Lexi's grip tightened on her gun as a high-pitched ringing built behind her ears. Heat swelled through her head, warping the edges of her vision.

Thorne's voice pierced the haze—frantic, distant.

The world tilted. Lexi staggered, then collapsed.

Blackness crept in, swallowing sound and light.

A figure loomed in the fog, rifle still smoking.

Lyria.

CHAP_11.exe - Breakpoint

"Wake up, Lieutenant Hayes!" Thorne commanded, his voice breaking through the blackness.

Lexi's blue and pink eyes fluttered open, her surroundings a blur. Above her, the sky shifted through shades of pink, red, and orange.

"Holy shit, you're one tough son of a bitch," Thorne said, a mix of pride and disbelief in his voice as he leaned over her.

"Ugh... wha hap penned? I was gon choot Burt. Gun was up.. . then—nothing. Just black..." Lexi struggled to speak; her words were slurred.

Thorne hesitated, then said, "Yeah... Lyria shot you in the head with a laser rifle."

Lexi's expression slackened in confusion.

"Would it make you feel better if I told you I ripped her head and spine out together?" Thorne asked with a laugh. "It's actually harder than it looks."

"Wha we gon' do now?" Lexi sputtered.

"Umm, oh! I called in a gunship. We're getting you back to HQ. Amber should be meeting us there. I saw her address change, so I assumed you two had gotten closer," Thorne assured her.

"Nuh-uh. *No H que. Donn trust it.* Go... somewhere else."

"Copy that. We have a safe house in Level 3. Can we go there?" Thorne asked.

"Uh-huh," Lexi responded.

Lexi nodded as she drifted back into unconsciousness.

***

She woke up in a dirty room, her head wrapped in gauze. She was lying on a makeshift medical bed. Amber rested on her torso, quietly staring at the ceiling.

"Amber?" Lexi whispered.

"Lex, you're okay!" Amber squealed, her voice breaking into a smile.

Gavin Thorne entered—no longer stomping in power armor. He wore a black T-shirt, olive green cargo pants, and combat boots.

"Hayes, we've got a mechanic coming to patch you up. In the meantime, stay here. You'll be safe," he said, concern etched into his voice.

"No. I don't trust anyone from HQ. When he arrives, I want one of you to do the exam," Lexi insisted, her voice weak. She slowly raised a trembling hand to point at the back of her head.

"Plus, I'm already starting to heal... see?"

A deep hole in her skull revealed small hexagonal cells forming and knitting into synthetic tissue.

"Lieutenant... we need you now, and neither of us is qualif—" Thorne started.

"I am," Amber cut in. "Rojas made me take the field-medic track last year. I just... didn't know Infiltrators could self-heal."

"Not all of us," Lexi smiled faintly. "And unfortunately, I can only heal slowly."

A loud bang came from the front door. The mechanic entered, but Thorne intercepted him immediately—still imposing, even without his armor.

"That's as far as you go. Give me the bag," Thorne commanded, extending his hand.

Without a word, the mechanic handed over a satchel. Thorne dug through it: muscle strands, a strange flashing cube, and a light blue-and-orange skin sealing gun. Thorne then held the cube up near the mechanic's face.

"What is this?" he growled.

"It's a new upgrade. Rapid auto-healing module. I was instructed to install it," the mechanic said—nervous but rehearsed.

"She already has auto-healing. Who told you to install it?"

"It will allow her to heal in combat. As for my directives, I'm not at liberty to disclose that, Enforcer. It's above your pay grade," the mechanic said with a shaky laugh.

Thorne grabbed him by the neck and slammed him against the concrete wall.

"You know how easy it is for me to rip your limbs off one by one?" Thorne hissed. "I'll cauterize the wounds and keep you alive the whole time, you piece of shit. Now—answer the question."

"Yes, yes, yes... I'm aware of your abilities, Enforcer," the mechanic wheezed, a grin creeping across his lips. "Your serum makes you a bit hostile."

"I asked you a question!" Thorne snapped, increasing his grip around the mechanic's neck.

"You... don't... hold... any... power... over me."

The mechanic tapped a glowing panel on his wrist unit.

Thorne's eyes flashed bright orange. His grip loosened. He stumbled back, clutching his head.

"What... is going on?!" he yelled, staggering.

The mechanic laughed, picking up the satchel and placing the cube inside.

Amber burst through the doorway. She saw Thorne hunched over, clutching his head. The mechanic's wrist unit glowed with streaming code, as the cube inside the bag flickered violently—orange light spilling out.

Then Amber felt something crawling beneath her skin. A pulse. A charge. Her arms trembled uncontrollably.

She didn't waste any time.

She fired a single shot from her pistol. The bullet tore through the mechanic's head, dropping him instantly, painting the wall with spattered blood.

***

Thorne collapsed to the floor, groaning. Amber rushed to him with steadying calm. He waved her off—dazed but alive.

She walked over to the mechanic, removing his wrist unit. Then headed towards a mirror.

"Let's see what this does." She pressed the button. Her eyes started to glow orange as she stared at her reflection. Her body twitched.

"Shit—no—" she muttered, trying to gain control.

Thorne, staggering upright, smacked the unit from her hand. It clattered to the floor and went dim; he smashed it with a thunderous crunch.

"Fuck... this is bad," Amber breathed, stepping over the mechanic's body as she headed upstairs.

Thorne stayed behind, catching his breath before kneeling beside the corpse. He rifled through the mechanic's pockets, turning up only the usual restricted access cards—standard issue for non-augmented staff at RAPID.

Finding nothing else of value, he headed upstairs.

He reached the top to find Lexi and Amber locked in a weighty conversation.

"I have bad news," Thorne said, his tone serious.

"She told me," Lexi muttered. "Guess I know why you and Elsa turned on me. But that's weird... when Lyria shot me, her eyes weren't orange."

Thorne held up the cube. "This means I already have one of these in me," he said, disgusted. "Amber, you probably do too. We need them out. Now."

L-3 models, Lexi thought as Amber and Thorne's conversation drifted into background noise. Burton had spat the words like a curse. Her. Lena. Both stamped with the same designation—but twisted in different directions.

"Thorne... what happened to Lyria? And Burton?" Lexi asked.

"I already told you, but you were pretty fucked up." His voice hardened. "Lyria shot you. I ripped her spine and head out before she could finish the job. Burton escaped while I was dragging you out. That sick bastard is still out there."

Amber retrieved the medical gear and began working on Lexi's heavily augmented head, inspecting the neural ports that traced every inch of her skull.

"Is there any of you left?" Amber asked, marveling at the tech.

"Yeah," Lexi said quietly, leaning forward. "*I'm still in there.*"

"So, what's next?" Amber asked.

Lexi sighed. "*We've got too many fires, and no idea where to start.* You got any ideas?"

Thorne didn't hesitate.

"Everything's connected—Infiltrators, Enforcers, the Union, the Mechanics, and Burton Marx. It starts with him. He's controlling people; we just don't know how many. *Finding Burton Marx must be our priority.*"

"I agree," Lexi nodded. "But how do we find him? And don't forget, you and Amber are still threats."

"Luckily, we outrank the VPSD. I'll have them issue an all-points bulletin for Burton Marx. We'll flush him out. In the meantime, we find a way to *cut this shit out of our heads*."

Amber smiled. "All done, Lex. Just hold still—I'm going to hit you with the regrowth gun."

Lexi raised an eyebrow.

"For your hair," Amber added with a grin. "Didn't want it growing back all patchy."

Thorne walked out of the room, and Lexi could hear him making a call. She quickly pulled Amber so that she was straddling her. Amber lifted her shirt slowly, her eyes locked on Lexi's with a shy, nervous smile.

"I want you to see me," she said softly.

Lexi's breath caught. Her eyes wandered, taking in Amber's curves—letting her gaze linger on Amber's full breasts.

She leaned in and kissed Amber deeply, then trailed her lips down to her neck, dragging a breath across her skin before biting gently.

Amber exhaled, her hair slipping over Lexi's shoulder like silk.

The door creaked open.

Lexi didn't stop. Her mouth stayed on Amber's neck as she lifted one hand and gave a casual wave, fingers flicking dismissively through Amber's long, straight hair.

Thorne paused, saw Amber's bare back straddling Lexi, and smirked.

He backed out and quietly shut the door.

***

The following day, Lexi woke up to Amber softly kissing her stomach and breasts.

"Hello, beautiful," Lexi said, smiling as she stroked Amber's hair.

"How are you feeling?" Amber asked.

"In general, or about last night?" Lexi said flirtatiously.

"In general. I know how last night was—from all your moaning," Amber said mischievously.

"Much better. You did a great job on my head. I can't even feel where the hole was. My hair's growing well, too. Thank you... truly, for everything," Lexi said before softly kissing Amber.

When the girls heard a knock at the door, they quickly ducked under the blankets, hiding their bare bodies from the intrusion.

"Are you guys up? Good. You kept me up all night with your 'activities,' but it's good to see you doing better, Lexi. Anyway, you two need to get dressed. The police found Burton," Thorne said, clearly eager.

Thorne tossed two duffel bags into the room before leaving.

Lexi and Amber opened them, each revealing black leather jackets, blue jean capris, a pair of athletic shoes, and fully charged recon drones.

"I don't want to get up," Amber said as she flicked Lexi's nipple with her tongue.

"Stop! You're tickling me," Lexi laughed aloud, smacking Amber's head with a pillow. "We will be together later."

The girls got dressed before heading downstairs and outside, revealing Level 3, dark, and only lit by flickering streetlights.

"It's cold down here," Amber said while shivering.

"It's 70 degrees," a VPSD officer yelled from the driver's seat of his cruiser.

"Lieutenant, if it's okay with you, you and Officer Densler are going to talk to Burton in custody. Amber and I will figure out how to solve our cube problem," Thorne suggested.

"If you were a woman, I'd recruit you for the Infiltrator Corps right now," Lexi said with conviction.

"Thank you?" Thorne replied, clearly confused.

Lexi got into the cruiser, and it sped away, rushing to Level 1. The coldness of Level 3 disappeared as they climbed to the planet's surface, which averaged 150 degrees today.

"Holy fuck, it's a hot one today," Lexi said as sweat beaded on her chest, her jacket whirring to life, trying to keep her augmentations cool.

The officer stared at Lexi and almost crashed into oncoming traffic, mesmerized by the Infiltrator's beauty.

"Eyes on the road, Densler," Lexi demanded.

"Have you ever been..." he started to say before he was interrupted.

"Been with an officer I'm about to kill if he doesn't keep his eyes on the road? No, I can't say that I have," she said, agitated.

The officer snapped his head back to the road and looked out the window for another five minutes before placing a courageous hand on Lexi's leg.

"Remove your hand," Lexi warned, frustrated.

"Come on, I won't bite. You may like it," he said as his hand moved up Lexi's leg, increasingly by the second.

Lexi grabbed his hand with outrageous speed as he panicked.

"Let's play a game. You drive, and I'm going to give you the experience of me holding your hand. Be careful about the bumps—I don't want to 'accidentally' break your hand," she said with a devilish grin.

As the cruiser came to a stop in front of the district's precinct, Lexi looked into Officer Densler's eyes.

"Now, what to do with you?" she said, still holding the scared officer's hand.

He looked at the dangerous woman before him and then down at his hand.

"I can tell the others not to touch you when we get inside," he offered.

"I think we'll hold hands like this until I reach the cells. If anyone touches me, it'll be your hand that breaks. Are you ready to go?" Lexi smiled.

As Officer Densler and Lexi walked in, the whistles, jokes, and cat-calling began.

"YEAH, DENSLER, YOU'RE THE MAN!" one officer yelled.

Another officer approached, looking at Lexi.

"Hey, baby doll, want to go on a date with me?" he said.

"Excuse me," Lexi asked politely, trying to get through the crowded hallway.

"I asked you a question, bitch," he responded, grabbing her arm as she tried to push past him.

Lexi looked at him, still holding Densler's hand.

"Sorry, Densler," she said.

With an effortless snap, Lexi broke Densler's hand, his screams echoing through the quiet corridor. She let go of his hand, and he curled up in pain by the wall, clutching his wrist. Chairs creaked as officers backed up; a coffee cup shattered. Silence filled the space—except for a snicker from a female officer and Densler's weeping. Everyone stepped aside, clearing the path to the cells.

"About time he got what he deserved," the female officer murmured.

Lexi smiled, exaggerating her hip movements as she walked down the hallway, the screams of her vanquished opponent fading behind her.

She walked down a stairwell to a very pristine prison section of the precinct. Its walls were painted utilitarian white; the dividers were clear ballistic plastics, allowing no privacy between cells.

"Hello, Lexi," Burton Marx said as soon as he saw her. He sat cuffed to a table that was bolted to the floor in a small cell, watched by cameras.

"Hello, Burtie." Lexi smirked. "Enjoying your stay?"

"You are a hard person to kill, Lexi Hayes. Hard to kill, indeed. So, what do I owe the pleasure of your visit?" His tone was cocky.

"I want to know what's going on. You're going to die anyway, so you might as well tell me what I need to know," she teased.

"You can't do a damn thing!" he hissed.

"I have the authority as an Infiltrator to end your life for all the crimes you've committed. So, here's the question, Burtie: Do you want this to go down slow, painful, and full of suffering—or fast and painless?" Lexi asked.

"I'm not telling you a goddamn thing," Burton mumbled.

Lexi glanced over at a nervous guard sitting behind a desk. "Open this cell for me, please. Then leave the room," she said confidently, her tone commanding. "Oh, and leave your knife on the table. Thanks."

The officer obeyed without question. "I... I have to tell my supervisor about this," he stuttered.

"Please do." Lexi watched as the officer ran up the stairs.

Burton filled with panic when his cell opened, and Lexi walked over to the abandoned desk; she picked up the knife. A devilish smile crossed her face as she approached him.

"So, which one is it... Burtie?" she said, setting the knife on the table.

"Fuck you!" Burton screamed, spit flying at her face.

Lexi wiped it off and picked up the knife again. She pricked her finger on the edge to test the sharpness.

"You know what's so good about a sharp knife?" Lexi asked. "The dull ones take too long to kill anything. You have to hack and hack, and then all you do is make a mess. But the sharp ones—the sharp ones—you can get creative."

Lexi dragged the knife across Burton's arm, his hair rising.

"Still not talking, huh?... That's fine," she said coyly.

She took the knife, accurately jamming it into Burton's left index finger, and pushed the blade through the table. Burton's screams filled the station as the officers upstairs sat wide-eyed, listening to the chaos.

"So, Burtie. What will it be?" Lexi asked, slightly twisting the knife.

Burton moaned and wriggled in his chair from the immense pain. He took a deep breath.

"Okay, okay, okay, okay, okay—I'll tell you what you want to know, just ask."

"See? Isn't that easier?" Lexi said as she pulled the knife out of his finger and sat across from him.

"Lyria. What was Lyria's part in all this?" Lexi asked as she picked crud from under her nails with the bloodied blade.

"Lyria was a necessity. I had no plans for you. Your modifications didn't allow for a cube, so I had to watch you somehow. I needed someone to spy on you and find your weaknesses. She had no choice. I took her husband and children and threatened to kill them if she didn't comply."

Burton smiled cockily as tears streamed down his face.

"Lyria was married. And had children?" Lexi's voice shook, the blade twitching in her hand. "What did you do with them, you sick fuck?"

"She *was* married. After that monster Thorne ripped her head off, I left and flipped their collars. The collars had explosives built in—none of her family lived," he said, scared of the knife in his face.

"So, she never truly loved me? We were together for so long," Lexi mumbled.

Her chest tightened. Amber's smile, her touch, her voice—they felt real. But so had Lyria's. And now Lexi couldn't tell the difference.

"It was all a facade. I regularly gave her mind-wiping drugs to take her edge off, so it came off as genuine, like she wasn't scared for her family. She would literally do anything I said... Remember the club? I fucked her so good that night. You dumb bitch, you never even knew? HA HA HA! Even a stripper believes the act was love! The irony!"

Lexi stood up, her eyes becoming glossy. She took the knife and stabbed another one of his fingers.

"AHH YOU BITCH!!!" Burton screamed in agony. "FUCK YOU!!!"

Lexi walked over to the chair she had been sitting in, pulled it out further, sat down, and kicked her feet up on the table. She turned to wipe tears onto her jacket's sleeve.

"Okay. What about the slate? What's on it?" Lexi asked, sniffling a bit.

"The slate is a drop-off point for weapons. Even if I tell you where it is, you'll never get in or out of there alive."

"What is at the site, Burton?"

"I've never been to that one, so I couldn't tell you. Just heard it's used to fund an Earth victory when they return."

"When they return?" Lexi asked, fear creeping into her voice.

"Of course, you stupid girl. You think Earth isn't going to come back for a priceless alloy? I'm going to find it, and I'll be giving it to Earth's president," Burton said with a coy smile.

"How many Earth sites are there? And how did you get the Mechanics to betray the government?" Lexi, intrigued by the conversation, asked.

"Money rules the world. I quadrupled the coroners', or as you know them, the mechanics' salaries, and gave them the parts Kurogane supplied. As for the Earth's sites, I don't know the exact number," Burton exclaimed, watching his blood drip onto the floor.

Lexi pressed the knife to his skin. "Who's your Kurogane contact?"

"I don't know!" Burton's voice cracked, panic rising.

"LIAR!!!" Lexi yelled as she jammed the knife into his next finger. "Give me a fucking name!"

"I swe—I swea—I swear," Burton gasped, writhing in pain.

Lexi pulled the knife from his hand, the table covered and smeared in blood.

"Who are the Coroners?" Lexi asked calmly.

"Th... the... They are a group that takes deceased people of interest or ones you send to CRIS training and turns them into Infiltrators. Each one of you is different in little ways," Burton started to explain, before passing out from blood loss.

Lexi walked over and slapped him repeatedly until he woke up.

"No, you don't, you bitch. I'm not done with you," she said angrily. *"You ruined everything I loved*, tore it from me, drove me crazy—all for some fucking information. Well, Mr. Marx, I have some information for you. You fucking piece of shit."

Lexi started crying, tears streaming down her face as she thought about the lives Burton had destroyed—her love for Lyria, the agony he caused by tearing her away, and the lives that could be lost from this psychopath's plans.

She ripped the cuffs loose from the bolts holding them to the table, stood Burton against a wall, and drove the knife through his arm, forcing him to stay upright.

Lexi punched his torso over and over again, tears streaming down her face as his skin split and bones broke. His screams echoed through the corridors—until they didn't.

Lexi, covered in blood spatters, stepped back and looked at the gore-covered corpse in front of her. Her breaths were shallow as she fought to fill her lungs.

***

She walked through the corridor of the police station without interference. Everyone stepped away from her. Lexi slicked her hair back, streaks of red running through her blonde strands.

She looked over and saw medics tending to Densler, still weeping.

"Where are Burton Marx's things?" she asked, rolling her eyes at the sight of the man who had been so confident before.

A nearby female officer quickly handed her a briefcase.

"This is all?" Lexi asked.

The officer nodded.

"Good." Lexi exhaled slowly. "Can you give me a ride to Level 3?"

"Y-yes, ma'am," the officer stammered.

As they walked toward the patrol car, a sharp voice cut through the quiet.

"Stop right there!" the chief of the station yelled.

Lexi turned to face him, her expression calm.

"Sir. How can I help you?" she asked.

"You tortured and killed a man in custody. You assaulted an officer. I'm placing you under arrest."

"Actually… you're not." Lexi didn't flinch. "Densler sexually harassed me in his patrol car. His sentence was carried out. I'm assuming your department has a zero-tolerance policy for sexual harassment? The prisoner in your custody, Mr. Burton Marx, mutilated and killed multiple people—either directly or by coercion. His sentence was death."

She paused, then added, "The torture may have looked excessive. I'll admit that. But it was sanctioned. RAPID Infiltrator Mandate,

Directive 22B-11 states that any Infiltrator is within their right to serve justice at their discretion, as long as the sentence isn't excessive for the crime committed."

The chief stared at her, mouth slightly open. "Well... yes. I suppose so. But your leadership will hear about this."

Lexi said nothing more. She climbed into the cruiser with the officer, and as they drove, Lexi broke the lock on the briefcase and saw one item... the slate.

"Police override," Lexi said.

"VOICE PRINT MISMATCH — LOCK ENGAGED," the slate said robotically.

Lexi let out a sigh and tucked the slate into her jacket pocket.

***

As the vehicle pulled up to the Enforcer safehouse, Amber ran out to meet them, grinning.

"Lexi! Thorne said we could go into HQ and talk to the Mechanics! He told the Chief what we figured out, and the Chief gave us an all-access pass to HQ to help uncover how deep the corruption goes!" She beamed, bouncing on her toes.

"Isn't that great? Level 1 access! We just have to go see the Chief first!"

"Wow! That is great news," Lexi said. "I'm going to head there right away. Are you coming with me?"

"Of course," Amber replied. "Our adventure continues."

Lexi rolled her eyes as she let out a small smirk. Then she turned her gaze to the officer in the cruiser.

"Can you give us a ride to RAPID HQ?"

"Of course, hop in, ma'am," the officer responded.

Once in the car, Lexi started asking questions about what they found.

"Where is Thorne?"

"He went to HQ ahead of us to give an update to his dad about the situation. He found out that the mechanic he killed was Mack, and the one at HQ right now is Mel. Those are their code names. I just wanted to wait for you so we could unravel this together," Amber said from the back seat.

"At least it's some sort of lead," Lexi responded.

Amber wasn't the sort to be quiet for too long. After a few minutes had passed, Lexi got a strange feeling.

She turned around and looked at Amber from the front seat. Seeing Lexi looking at her, Amber quickly turned her head to face out the window.

"Amber, let me see your eyes," Lexi said cautiously.

"Why? You've seen them a lot," she snapped back.

"Amber, turn so I can see your eyes," Lexi repeated, more commanding.

Amber turned her head slowly toward Lexi, her eyes ablaze with orange, a wicked grin spreading across her face.

"You thought you stopped us just because you killed Marx? You haven't even scraped the surface!" Amber said in a raspy voice, which was not her own.

Lexi's stomach sank. Whoever she was staring at—it wasn't Amber anymore.

Amber lunged forward between the front seats, her legs pushing off the back. She reached over and snapped the officer's neck; the officer slumped over, her foot pressing harder on the gas.

Amber purposely steered into oncoming traffic as the cruiser's robotic whir became louder with increasing speed.

Seeing the oncoming traffic, Lexi grabbed the steering wheel and fought Amber for control. The cruiser swerved, narrowly missing cars and pedestrians through the ascent to Level 1.

Lexi straightened the car out momentarily before placing her back against the passenger door and unbuckling her seatbelt.

She kicked Amber in the head. The passenger door tore off its hinges, Lexi riding it as Amber's skull smashed through the driver's glass.

The door—and Lexi—hit the ground, sparks flying and metal screeching as the door dragged on dry asphalt with Lexi on top of it. Ahead, the police cruiser slammed into a fuel truck, causing a massive fiery explosion.

Amber's eyes, still aglow with orange, emerged from the flames; her clothes and skin singed and flaking off, until only her metallic shell remained, with someone else in control of her thoughts and actions.

Lexi slammed her hand into the ground to slow her slide, her skin ripping away from her metallic grip. She grabbed the door, jumped, flipped forward, then hurled it at Amber, hoping to disrupt the signal—just like with Thorne in the mansion.

Amber jumped, grabbed the door midair, and threw it back at Lexi. Lexi sidestepped and waited patiently, backing slowly to the wall behind her as cars stopped in both directions from the raging inferno in the distance.

Amber closed in fast. Lexi waited until Amber was within striking distance before jumping back, bouncing off the wall, and bringing her leg down like a hammer into Amber's head, smashing it into the ground.

As Amber lay face down in the cracked and cratered asphalt, Lexi approached, flipped her over, fist clenched, ready to strike, but stopped when she saw Amber's eyes closed and her breathing slowed.

Lexi carefully opened Amber's metallic eyelids, revealing a faint green hue.

"Oh, thank God," she breathed, pulling Amber's head tightly to her chest.

The impact had damaged Amber's metallic muscles, now leaking precious cooling fluid that kept her body within allowable limits.

She didn't wait. Lexi surged to her feet, lifting Amber over her shoulder.

She ran.

Her muscles flexed with every stride, straining at full capacity, metallic fibers taut beneath her skin. Core temperature spiked—150°F... 200°F... 250°F. Warnings screamed across her HUD.

The radiator in her chest turned bright red, a pulsing glow bleeding through her skin. The synthetic layer couldn't keep up—it blackened, cracked, and began to peel. The air stank of scorched polymer.

She didn't stop. Amber's green coolant was still pouring from her body.

If she slowed, Amber would die.

"We'll figure this out. Just hang in there," Lexi murmured.

Focused and unwavering, Lexi reluctantly headed to HQ, knowing only a mechanic could fix Amber now. She stopped for nothing—*her mission was clear: fix Amber and handle the "cube" situation.*

CHAP_12.exe - Thresh0ld

Once in HQ—and more importantly, the Infiltrator Corps office—she entered the back panel and grabbed her swords and TDB Unit.

"Izzy! Where the fuck is that gun?" Lexi called out.

Isabella, confused from a back desk, answered, "What gun?"

Lexi sighed in frustration. "The gun I shot Elsa with... where is it?"

Isabella slid open a drawer and handed it to Lexi. "It's right here. Estás en serios problemas, mami."

"What?" Lexi said, quickly counting the rounds.

"You're in serious trouble," Isabella repeated in English.

"All thirteen?" she asked, balancing Amber on her shoulder.

"Um, yeah, I filled it after you left," Isabella said, worry creeping over her. "What's going on, and is that Amber?"

Without answering, Lexi magnetized the weapon to her right thigh and headed down the hallway to the mechanic's office. She threw open the door.

The mechanic didn't look up. "An 'excuse me' would be nice."

Lexi slammed Amber onto the operating table, clearly agitated.

"Was that really necessary?" the mechanic grumbled, still scribbling.

"Hey, Mel..." Lexi's voice cut sharp as ever.

"Where did you hear that name?" The mechanic looked up, freezing as Lexi pressed a gun to his forehead.

"Doesn't matter. What matters, Mel, is that I've had a hell of a day. I'm beat up, dirty, tired, and done with everyone's shit. You're going to open that girl's head, take the control cube out, fix her up, and put her back together. Then maybe—maybe—I won't blow your fucking brains out."

Her tone dropped to a growl. "Now... take a seat."

Lexi watched him work, finger steady on the trigger.

A metallic clang echoed as Mel dropped the cube into a surgical tray, slick with green fluid, lights still blinking.

"Now put her back together," Lexi ordered.

Mel stitched her piece by piece—plating sealed, rips closed, synthetic skin and hair restored. Each second dragged. Each breath from Amber came shallow and uneven. Only when Mel finally stepped back, tools down, did Lexi let herself breathe.

She moved closer, scanning Amber's face. No movement yet—but she was breathing. That was enough. For now.

"It'll be a coupl—" Mel began, before the pistol whipped across his jaw.

Lexi stood over him, gun pointed at the unconscious mechanic, unsure of what to do with him. A camera in the corner of the office turned, lens locking onto her.

The door slammed open. Two Enforcers stormed in, seizing her arms as she let the gun clatter to the floor.

"The Chief wants to see you immediately," one of the Enforcers said, surprisingly calm.

Lexi entered the same office she once visited as a guest but now wondered how the Chief would treat her after everything that had transpired. The Enforcers released her and exited, closing the door behind them.

The Chief stood with his hands folded behind his back, looking out the window.

"One dead Enforcer. One—one assaulted with a Shockwave Inhibitor. Three dead Infiltrators."

"Sir, I—"

"I'M NOT FINISHED, LIEUTENANT HAYES!" Chief Graevos bellowed. "Burton Marx—butchered, in police custody! One officer's wrist broken, another killed in a collision—and now a mechanic's been assaulted!"

He slowly turned to face her, voice breaking with rage.

"You think I'm supposed to be proud of this?"

Lexi stayed silent.

"You were put on leave for a reason, Lieutenant! Told not to stir the pot! But you—you went and kicked the whole thing over and—and then—" he slammed a fist against his desk, words catching in his throat. "Then you had the audacity to blow it up! *You're a fucking wrecking ball, Hayes!*"

She opened her mouth, but he cut her off with a raised hand.

"Then, as if that wasn't enough! You broke into the documentation room and started destroying the place. What the fuck is wrong with you, Hayes? I want an explanation, NOW!"

"I was attacked by two Enforcers with orange eyes. The damage you see is from me defending myself after they attacked me," Lexi calmly stated, standing her ground.

Graevos' chest heaved, his face red with heat. He snatched the glass off his desk, took a long sip of water, and dabbed his forehead with the back of his hand. When he looked at her again, the fire hadn't gone—it had just cooled into something sharper.

"Our footage doesn't show any Enforcers—just you. Jumping and running around, causing damage. Discharging your Shockwave Inhibitor. Throwing yourself through walls." He sat down, leaning back slightly, voice measured now. "This is intriguing. Go on."

"I spoke with Burton Marx after I was knocked out by one of the Enforcers. He explained that I'm a special model of Infiltrator. Lyria was only with me to gather information on how to take me out, or Marx would kill her family."

Graevos blinked, the anger in his eyes dimming. His voice dropped low, steady now.

"She had a family?" He shook his head, a weary breath escaping. "Damn... tough break."

Her throat tightened, and the word slipped out like a confession.

"*She did.*" Lexi looked down, disappointment and grief washing over her.

"Burton told me the Coroners—or mechanics—implanted command cubes in every Infiltrator and Enforcer to control us, except for me and an I5 model. He was working with the Kurogane Syndicate to obtain laser weapons intended to destroy the government and help Earth retake Verellii. I destroyed those weapons."

"Did he say who the contact at the Kurogane Syndicate was?"

"No, sir."

"Too bad." The Chief sighed. "What about Lyria's family?"

"Burton killed them with explosive collars." Lexi's voice cracked. "Lyria died too. He killed them all."

The Chief was silent for a moment, his expression grim.

"Do you have proof of these command cubes?"

"Yes, sir. I knocked out Mel the mechanic after he took Amber's cube out. On our way here, she killed the officer who was driving, causing the collision, then proceeded to attack me—her eyes were orange, and the words she said weren't hers. Recruit Gavin Thorne also attacked me—his eyes were orange too, and he was following Burton's orders."

"Now what's this about Earth?"

"Burton said the slate I have ties to a weapons drop, maybe even something bigger—he mentioned that the location is being used to fund Earth's return. That's all I got out of him. The thing's locked, so I don't know if he was lying or not."

The Chief didn't respond immediately. His silence stretched until it became uncomfortable.

"All right," he finally said. "Let's say I believe you. Then, I suppose it's time to shed some light on certain things. The Coroners are—or were—a sanctioned branch of the Verellii Protectorate. Based on this new information, it seems their role was broader than most of us realized.

Officially, they were the ones who repaired us—every shattered Enforcer, every broken Infiltrator that came limping back.

But they are more than mechanics. They also run the CRIS program. Women who volunteer are scored, measured, pushed until their limits are shown—and then the Coroners rebuild them into Infiltrators, each augmentation chosen to match their CRIS profile. And when the dead have value—when a woman's strength, intellect, or skills were too rare to waste—the Coroners brought her back as well. *Rebuilt. Reforged. Given another chance to serve... like you.*

They also hold the keys to the Enforcers. The Coroners dose them with serum—increasing muscle density, sharpening reflexes, and driving them to be bigger, stronger, and faster. Without armor, they are weaker than Infiltrators but still far beyond any normal person's capabilities; once inside their suits, however, they vastly surpass even the strongest Infiltrator.

That much I knew. But this business with cubes..." He shook his head. "I had no knowledge of that until now. If Marx was right, then the

Coroners weren't just rebuilding—they are leashing us. And that's a very different story."

Lexi nodded slowly, absorbing everything the Chief had said.

"By the way, did you read the file about General Pike?"

"No, sir. I haven't had the chance."

"General Pike... ended the Great War with a brilliant and unconventional strategy. He used misdirection and guerrilla tactics to turn Earth's forces against themselves. Pike recognized that Earth's forces were dependent on centralized command hubs. He outsmarted them by drawing their forces out, overwhelming their command centers and turning Earth's soldiers against one another. It was his ability to think outside the box that drove Earth's forces from Verellii, though at great cost—lost cities, devastated infrastructure."

He pauses, then looks at Lexi, a more solemn look in his eyes.

"You've made calls like Pike did—risky, brutal, necessary. You're the closest thing we've had to him since the war. The difference is, you're still alive, and you've got the chance to change things—to take down the corruption that's rotting this place from the inside. *You might be our only hope, Lexi. Just like Pike was Verellii's.*"

She wasn't sure if he meant to crush her or crown her. His words swung between damnation and praise, and she couldn't tell which weighed more.

The Chief sighs.

"Maybe we need someone like you. Someone who doesn't give a damn about appearances, protocol, or the old way of doing things. Because if corruption seeped in this deep while we played by the rules... maybe it's time someone broke them."

The Chief opened his desk drawer and took out a red card marked with three gold lines. One button press brought up a holographic computer, its surface glitching as it whirred to life. He entered a sequence, and a slot opened; he slipped the card in, followed by additional commands. A sharp beep confirmed the process before the screen flickered out. The Chief tucked the card back into the drawer.

Across from him, Lexi's eye glowed purple as streams of data raced past her vision.

"Sir, what is this?" Lexi asked, surprised.

"It's permanent Level 1 access," the Chief explained. "I'm granting it to you based on glowing reviews from your peers, especially Captain Cybrix Thorne. He believes you'd make an excellent Chief one day."

He pauses, then continues. "However, this access comes with a non-disclosure clause. You cannot speak about anything related to that level of clearance. Understood?"

"Yes, sir!" Lexi exclaims happily.

"Good. The Files and Documentation room is open to you. I suggest you go to the door at the far left corner, scan your barcode, and enter. Take the elevator to the only level it will go. Then go down the halls to section 11.12 and find the file labeled L3X1. I think you'll want that information before continuing your investigation," the Chief adds with a smile.

Lexi begins to leave, but then hears the Chief speak again.

"Did you say something, sir?"

"I just said, good luck, Captain," the Chief responds, sliding her pistol toward her.

"*Captain?*" Lexi asks.

"Yes, Captain...Welcome back. But Lexi..."

"Yes, Chief?" Lexi says.

"No more fuckups. I can't have a loose cannon on my team. I need someone like you—but more restrained."

"Yes, sir," Lexi says solemnly as she takes her gun, its barrel weathered, its grip perfectly conformed to her hand.

The Chief smirks. "You've proven to be a valuable asset, even in the face of adversity and personal struggle. You get results, even though you use unconventional and sometimes brutal tactics that I may not always approve of. In this world, results are key. Just don't lose sight of who you are. Understood, Captain?"

Lexi snapped a crisp salute, then turned and strode down the hallway.

Her patch shimmered into code, data lines streaking as it updated in real time. Verellii's circle glowed bold and unmistakable, the thin ring orbiting it like a halo. The black star of Anthrallii stayed in the upper right, watchful as ever. Then, with a final pixelated flicker, two new black dots appeared beside Verellii—Bretyl and Yesh. Moons that hadn't been touched since the Great War.

No ceremony. No announcement.

Lexi's breath caught. *Captain.* The word burned in her mind like an aftershock, heavy and unshakable.

She shook her head, muttering under her breath, *"The ass chewing of a lifetime... and then a promotion. What the fuck just happened?"*

A few minutes later, Lexi reached the now-repaired door of the Files and Documentation room, which opened automatically. She walked through the doorway, weaving through stacks of old, dust-covered papers. The room extended down several hallways. Files lined the walls and flooded the shelves, piled almost to the ceiling. As she passed the halls, she wondered why this room even existed anymore. After what seemed like an eternity, she reached a heavily reinforced door. As she neared it, a small scanner extended.

"Too new, too advanced in this old room," Lexi said to herself as she held her right wrist up, and the machine scanned her barcode.

"Captain Lexi Hayes..." the door acknowledged quietly.

"APPROVED, LEVEL 1 CLEARANCE DETECTED!" the door announced as the locks disengaged, and the large steel doors revealed a decrepit-looking elevator.

She entered the dingy steel lift, dust covering almost every surface. The light above her head flickered as if it hadn't been repaired or maintained for some time. Lexi looked at the control panel.

"A single button?" She said cautiously before pressing it.

The elevator groaned, every part of it straining, protesting against the movement. After a long descent that felt like hours, the elevator stopped. Lexi squinted as the elevator doors creaked open, expecting another dusty corridor. Instead, she was met with the opposite. Marble. Gold. Pristine statues. No dust. No decay.

The hallway was well lit—white marble with gold trim. Statues adorned the sides of the hallway on pedestals, each one displaying a name and rank. All of them different in their own way, minus one line: Aegis Titan. Lexi continued to walk, her footsteps echoing throughout the hallway. Not another figure was in sight, until she saw a massive statue adorned in white armor standing next to a gold door.

"That armor..." Lexi narrowed her eyes. "It's like an upsized Enforcer suit."

The armor held a massive sword, both hands resting on the butt of the handle. The sword had a golden hilt with a meticulously polished silver blade. Its tip rested in a small groove in the floor—a testament to how long the statue had stood there.

"What is your purpose here?" a voice asked.

"Um, I'm Captain Lexi Hayes with RAPID," Lexi said as she looked around for the source of the voice.

The statue's head tilted, just slightly. Not a crack of stone, not a trick of light—movement. Real, deliberate.

"The Chief requested that I look at a file—" she began, but the man cut her off.

"Captain Lexi Hayes," the man interrupted, his voice carrying like iron across the marble. "Since this is your first time here, you must hear the laws of the Sanctum.

First—know this: rank holds no sway here. Titles, command, authority... all are stripped away. Only the will of the Aegis stands.

Second—should an Aegis give you an order, you will obey. Not in part. Not in hesitation. Obey in full, or face judgment.

Third—you will not speak in this place unless spoken to by an Aegis. Your tongue is a weapon, and here, it must remain sheathed.

Last—no blade, no fist, no act of aggression may be raised in the Sanctum. To strike here is to die here.

Accept these laws, and you may pass. Refuse, and your path ends at this door."

For a heartbeat, the silence pressed down on her. Then she nodded. "*I accept.*"

The Aegis extended his palm, and the golden door opened with a weighty grace. Lexi stepped inside—then stopped, her breath catching.

The Sanctum stretched before her in vast tiers, towers of digital data rising thirty stories high. Each column pulsed in shifting hues of white, gold, and pale blue—an echo of the Aegis themselves, as if the archives and their guardians were bound by the same design. The light bathed the marble in a quiet radiance, clean and unmarred by time. The air carried a low, steady hum, the quiet machinery of memory itself.

White-armored Aegis Titans patrolled the aisles, gold trim catching the glow. Their shields shimmered faintly with a blue aura, and the tips of their great spears burned with the same quiet light. It wasn't aggressive, but it was a reminder that the Titans' weapons weren't forged for battle alone, but to stand as eternal sentinels, awake even in silence.

The marble beneath their armored feet bore the marks of long centuries: shallow dips carved into the stone by countless patrols that had walked the same paths. The place didn't just look old, it felt worn into the bones of the planet.

Between them, figures in blue cloaks moved without a sound, sliding files from shelves with practiced precision. Their motions weren't ritual, but efficient, careful—as if they knew every piece of data mattered.

No voices rose. No chatter echoed. Only the soft shuffle of files and the measured tread of armor filled the cavern. It wasn't silence, it was discipline, distilled.

Lexi followed the worn path, her white tennis shoes settling into grooves carved by centuries of Titans before her. the marble gleamed, and the Titans moved as if time itself obeyed them. For a fleeting moment, Lexi wondered if *her story would one day be written here too—a legend sealed into the endless walls of the Sanctum.*

CHAP_13.exe - F1le_Dump

As Lexi walked through the endless corridors, time stretched into something immeasurable. Towering shelves of files lined either side, glowing a faint blue as if alive. She wondered what it would be like to spend a lifetime here—submerged in knowledge.

No one looked at her. No voices broke the silence. No good, no evil—only a strange, weightless peace.

A sign caught her eye: Wing 11: Technology Knowledge.

She entered the wing, passing various exhibits and stopping to learn about what they represented.

Graevos's words echoed in her mind: "Go to section 11.12. Find the file labeled L3 Cybernetics. You'll want that before continuing."

Her pace quickened. Eyes scanned the numbers displayed in digital form at the end of the rows as she passed.

11.09.

11.10.

11.11.

11.12.

She turned down the hall, rows of glowing files stretching like one infinite wall. A sinking thought crept into her mind—How the hell am I supposed to find one file in this?

She pressed a file at random.

Enforcer Armor Upgrades — Great War Era.

No.

She pressed another.

Mind Transference Between Two Bodies.

Not it.

A voice interrupted, flat and metallic:

"It appears you are having difficulty?"

Lexi froze, glancing around. Not seeing a source, she pointed at herself.

"Yes, you. Please think your query—I will register the brainwaves."

She hesitated, then focused on the words: *File L3 Cybernetics.*

"Confirmed. The file is marked. Please watch your footing and hold the railings."

With an almost silent hiss, handlebars and a platform lifted from the floor, raising Lexi smoothly upward, stopping at chest height with the red flashing entry. Lexi reached out, pulled the file free, and the platform returned her gently to the ground.

"If you require additional assistance, press any red node you encounter," the voice added before fading out.

Lexi sat on the floor and leaned back against the metallic shelves, cradling the file. As she looked at it, she extended a finger and poked it; a hologram shimmered to life before her: L3 Cybernetics.

She flicked her finger up as five designations scrolled in the light:

L3A.

L35A.

L3N/A.

L35L13.

L3X1.

Her finger hovered uncertainly, rising and falling. *Did she genuinely want to know the truth?*

She closed her eyes, finger pressing the hologram against L3N/A.

Information erupted into her vision.

***

L3N/A: CLASSIFIED

FILE LOCKED – TIER 1 ACCESS ONLY

ANY UNAUTHORIZED ACCESS IS A CLASS-ONE SECURITY BREACH

ACTIVE LOG TRACE: 1

** **

RAPID INFILTRATOR CORPS – BLACK SITE DOSSIER... AUTHORIZED...

FORMER IDENTITY: DECEASED

Name: Maria Alonso

Alias: N/A

Status: Deceased

Recovery Status: Body Recovered – L3 Program Eligible

Height: 5'10"

Weight: 165 lbs.

Skin: Black (African descent)

Hair: Black

Eye Color: Hazel

Lips: Brown

Eye Makeup: N/A

Tattoos: N/A

Augmentations: N/A

Occupation: Unemployed

Identifying Markings: Multiple bruises, cuts, and lacerations across the body

Cause of Death:

Domestic violence. Subject bled out from wounds. Body recovered by Coroner black-site operatives and deemed viable for L3 conversion.

CURRENT IDENTITY: ACTIVE

Name: Lena Boma

Codename: L3NA

Rank: Science Officer Level 5 Tier 1 Clearance (L5T1)

Division: Earth Blackwater Operative Initiative (EBOI)

Height: 6'0"

Weight: 200 lbs.

Skin: Black (African descent)

Hair: Black

Eye Color: Hazel

Lips: Brown

Eye Makeup: N/A

Tattoos: N/A

Identifying Markings: Several scars from healed wounds

STANDARD L3 ENHANCEMENTS

- Comms Suite – Left Wrist

Modified for thicker muscle strands

~~** NOTE ** Nano Faraday cage removed due to incompatibility with Verelliian biomesh. Comms will fail upon Shockwave Inhibitor use.~~ X1 upgrade incapable.

- Shockwave Inhibitor – Left Wrist

EMP pulse generator; causes skin to boil and arm to glow bright light-blue during charge

Used to disable electronics and subdue armored Enforcers, may be used for armor penetration.

Causes localized damage and disables comms suite

- Credential Identifying Suite – Right Wrist

- Weapons Handling Software

- Hand-to-Hand Combat Software

- Right Eye (Synthetic Replacement)

Includes X-ray, thermal, night vision, scanner, and data transfer capabilities

- Right Hand Augmentation

DNA-linked to RIS/OV-P sidearm

RIS/OV-P will not function for unauthorized users

X1-CLASS EXPERIMENTAL IMPLANTS

- ~~NOTE** SUBJECT IS NOT STABLE FOR X1 ENHANCEMENTS, TERMINATE IMMEDIATELY!!!~~

• UPDATE – B.M. has authorized the subject to remain in working condition as an L3 unit ONLY!!! No other enhancements will be applied.

PHYSIOLOGICAL & TACTICAL NOTES

• Subject's body appears unmodified to the public. All augmentations are internalized.

• Breast and gluteal size increased during reconstruction to house augmentation clusters internally.

• Skin seams exist but are nearly invisible, only detectable via close-range thermal scan.

C.R.I.S. PERFORMANCE REPORT – SUBJECT L3N/A

C.R.I.S. = Critical Response and Infiltration Skills

Enforcer Subduing:

4/10

• Shockwave Inhibitor used to incapacitate armored Enforcers at close range, subject has momentary severe headaches at times that may stop her ability to subdue targets.

Speed:

1/10

• Subject cannot link with augmentations well, speed is highly affected.

• Slowest Infiltrator speed on record.

Strength:

Rated: 0/10

• Subject cannot link with augmentations well, strength is highly affected.

• Subjects' mental health is stopping her from believing she can lift more weight.

Stealth Rating:

5/10

•   Movement is more silent than that of typical Verelliian humans.

Mental Capacity:

Rated: Fortified | Determined | Resilient

•   Unstable, previous trauma has destroyed any sense of trust, belief, or teamwork capabilities. Different "personality tracks" can be installed for short-term missions only. The subject's brain will override the track if it is left in for too long.

Teamwork & Coordination:

Advanced Tactical Synchronization

•   Terrible.** **Subject L3N/A MUST NOT be a part of a team unless the correct personality track is installed.** **

Operational Kill Count:

•   Confirmed Kills: >100

•   Estimated Total: >100

When undergoing X1 potential upgrades, her neural pathways were disrupted, and she believed she was being attacked. Several science teams and research divisions were killed before she was subdued.

WEAPONS & LOADOUT – L3N/A

Standard gear configuration, magnetized to standard Infiltrator biomesh. RIS/OV-P is DNA-locked. All other equipment is standard-issue or personally maintained.

RIS/OV-P **(RAPID Infiltrator Standard/ Operationally Variable – Pistol Class) x's 2 **NOTE **Proper personality track must be installed before subject is armed**

•   Mount: Right and Left thighs – magnetized

Security: DNA-locked

Fire Modes:

- Ballistic (Yellow): Semi-auto, 1 round – Precision

- Buckshot (Green): Semi-auto, 4 rounds – Close-range spread

- Explosive (Orange): Semi-auto, 3 rounds – AOE detonation

- Silencer (White, dim): Semi-auto, 1 round – Stealth fire

- Piercing (Blue): Semi-auto, 2 rounds – Armor-penetration

T.D.B.U. (Temporal Displacement Beacon Unit)

OPERATIONAL UNIFORM PROFILE

L3N/A displays no signs of a previous life cycle other than her trauma. Clothing issue is Uniform of the Day (UOD).

** FIELD DEPLOYMENT WARNING **

L3N/A's reflexes were the only additional ability developed over the years of black site simulation. Severe traumatic experiences stop agents from being able to train her further. Use personality tracks if a temporary override is needed. Unfortunately, her trauma is so deeply rooted that only short-term personality tracks will override brain function. If left in too long, her trauma will override the programming.

L3N/A will supervise L3X1, assuming L3X1 is a pure robotic entity. When at RAPID HQ, she will be placed in a leadership position to influence L3X1 to eventually become an Earth sympathizer. When her trauma resurfaces, field agents placed in HQ will replace personality tracks with new ones.

When not in the field, L3N/A will remain in isolation working on her research alone. Under no circumstances will she participate in other activities unless given explicit instructions from B.M. or S.A.

"L3N/A is not responding to anything. Her potential is extremely limited based on the cognitive trauma she holds onto. *Her ability to move forward is clouded by her own judgment*, and any help we try to give her results in anger and aggression. However, she is a brilliant scientist, with no background in the sciences at all. *She may be useful,*

as long as she's deceived. Earth Black site Scientist ID: 148DD0978
Location /////NULL//////

END OF RECORD...

***

What the fuck? Lexi thought to herself. *Lena was working for Earth this entire time! That fucking bitch. This entire time, I thought she cared, watched her back, and it was all programming! I'm going to kill her if I find her.*

Lexi blinked, not realizing she had been sitting in the hallway for a few hours. She scrolled through the holographic files until one caught her eye.

L3X1.

The mechanic, he said this one was... me?

She took a deep breath in and pressed her finger against the holographic light. The dossier uploaded.

***

L3X1: CLASSIFIED

FILE LOCKED – TIER 1 ACCESS ONLY

ANY UNAUTHORIZED ACCESS IS A CLASS-ONE SECURITY BREACH

ACTIVE LOG TRACE: 1

** **

RAPID INFILTRATOR CORPS – BLACK SITE DOSSIER... AUTHORIZED...

FORMER IDENTITY: DECEASED

Name: Caedra Nyyx

Alias: "Pixie" (Stage Name)

Status: Terminated – Confirmed Deceased

Recovery Status: Body Recovered – L3 and X1 Program Eligible

Height: 5'9"

Weight: 150 lbs.

Skin: White / Caucasian

Hair: Blonde

Eye Color: Blue

Lips: Pink

Eye Makeup: Pink inner-corner highlight with black eyeshadow

Tattoos: Pink and black markings on both arms, extending down legs

Augmentations: Credit "Pinch" augmentation

Occupation: Exotic dancer at SynthSkin under the alias "Pixie"

Identifying Markings:

- Scar over left hip (augmentation site)

- Small mole over right breast

Cause of Death:

Confirmed fatality by gunshot wound to the right eye at close range, inflicted by anti-augmentation T.N.O. operatives. The victim was found behind the SynthSkin club after her shift. Smeared makeup (from crying/ overhead leaking pipe) was preserved at the time of death. Body recovered by Coroner black-site operatives and deemed viable for X1 conversion.

CURRENT IDENTITY: ACTIVE

Name: Lexi Hayes

Codename: L3X1

Rank: ~~Lieutenant~~ Captain / Commander

Division: RAPID Infiltrator Corps

(RAPID – Robotic Augmented Police Intervention Department)

Height: 5'10"

Weight: 250 lbs.

Skin: White / Caucasian

Hair: Blonde

Eye Color:

- Left: Blue

- Right: Pink (Synthetic replacement)

Lips: Pink

Eye Makeup: Pink inner-corner highlight with black eyeshadow (smeared state auto-regenerated)

Tattoos: Pink and black markings on both arms and legs—regenerated with skin

Identifying Markings:

- Small mole over right breast

- Scar over left hip (residual from removed credit implant)

STANDARD L3 ENHANCEMENTS

- Comms Suite – Left Wrist

Modified for thicker muscle strands

** **NOTE** ** Nano Faraday cage removed due to incompatibility with Verelliian biomesh. Comms will fail upon Shockwave Inhibitor use.

- Shockwave Inhibitor – Left Wrist

EMP pulse generator; causes skin to boil and arm to glow bright light-blue during charge

Used to disable electronics and subdue armored Enforcers, may be used for armor penetration.

Causes localized damage and disables comms suite

- Credential Identifying Suite – Right Wrist

- Weapons Handling Software

- Hand-to-Hand Combat Software

- Right Eye (Synthetic Replacement)

Includes X-ray, thermal, night vision, scanner, and data transfer capabilities

- Right Hand Augmentation

DNA-linked to RIS/OV-P sidearm

RIS/OV-P will not function for unauthorized users

X1-CLASS EXPERIMENTAL IMPLANTS

- Split Decision Multiplier (SDM)

Converts mental impulses into instantaneous physical action

Automatically adjusts body balance and weight distribution, regardless of footwear or terrain

Movement and stunts are limited only by the user's imagination and confidence

- Verelliian Steel Biomesh Muscle Strands

Self-healing under stress

Accepts any raw metal to accelerate regeneration

Converts foreign metals into Verelliian-grade structure and integrates seamlessly

- Molecular Rebuild System

Full-body regeneration (including augmentations) is possible from a single living cell

Rebuild rate is slow but confirmed successful post-mortem

- Skin Cellular Regeneration System

Regenerates synthetic skin with original markings

Tattoos and smeared eye makeup reappear consistently

Cannot activate while under active damage

PHYSIOLOGICAL & TACTICAL NOTES

- Subject's body appears unmodified to the public. All augmentations are internalized.

- Breast and gluteal size increased during reconstruction to house augmentation clusters internally.

- Skin seams exist but are nearly invisible, only detectable via a close-range thermal scan.

- Synthetic systems interpret tattoos and smeared eye makeup as part of L3X1's genetic baseline and regenerate them automatically.

- Subject overheats under prolonged combat. Field jacket must remain open during operations; radiator node located near sternum must remain exposed during engagements.

- Standard Infiltrator-grade coolant may fail under extended strain. Subject must monitor internal temperature to avoid overheating, muscle seizure, inhibitor misfire, or emergency reboot.

- Memory fragments tied to the Caedra Nyyx identity may surface under extreme emotional or sensory triggers.

C.R.I.S. PERFORMANCE REPORT – SUBJECT L3X1

C.R.I.S. = Critical Response and Infiltration Skills

Enforcer Subduing:

10/10

•   Shockwave Inhibitor used to incapacitate armored Enforcers at close range

Speed:

Exceeded Standardized Metrics (Logged 15/10)

•   Sustained bursts exceeding 40 mph

•   Fastest Infiltrator speed on record

Strength:

Rated: Above Standard

•   Able to displace mass equal to ~2,500 lbs. (fully loaded transport crate) laterally across short distances

•   Force application enabled by SDM-guided motion and bio-mechanical torque; not sustained brute strength

Stealth Rating:

9.5/10

•   Despite weight, movement is near-silent

•   Verelliian biomesh generates no mechanical or electromagnetic noise

•   Movement (pivots, draw sequences, footfalls) falls below standard and advanced detection thresholds

Mental Capacity:

Rated: Fortified | Determined | Resilient

•   Unshaken under trauma, torture simulation, or emotional breakdown protocols

Teamwork & Coordination:

Advanced Tactical Synchronization

- SDM allows real-time analysis of squadmates' movements

- Repositions team members mid-combat without verbal command

Operational Kill Count:

- Confirmed Kills: [REDACTED]

- Estimated Total: 500+

All confirmed through data slates, drone records, and black box logs from Tier 3 or higher operations

WEAPONS & LOADOUT – L3X1

Standard gear configuration, magnetized to Verelliian biomesh ports along thighs and back. All other equipment is standard-issue or personally maintained.

RIS/OV-P (Pistol Class)

Mount: Right thigh – magnetized

Security: DNA-locked

Fire Modes:

- Ballistic (Yellow): Semi-auto, 1 round – Precision

- Buckshot (Green): Semi-auto, 4 rounds – Close-range spread

- Explosive (Orange): Semi-auto, 3 rounds – AOE detonation

- Silencer (White, dim): Semi-auto, 1 round – Stealth fire

- Piercing (Blue): Semi-auto, 2 rounds – Armor-penetration

Shoto (Short Sword) Verellii steel variant. Mount: Left thigh – magnetized

Katana (Long Sword) Verellii steel variant. Mount: Back – magnetized

T.D.B.U. (Temporal Displacement Beacon Unit)

Recon Drone Unit

OPERATIONAL UNIFORM PROFILE

L3X1 displays subconscious clothing decisions that aid in heat management and public blending:

Field Jacket: Infiltrator-standard black leather, lightly armored with:

- Internal cooling system

- Radiation blocking lining

- Comms amplifier embedded

- Magnetized to biomesh structure

** Jacket is worn open for maximum thermal dissipation; radiator node located near sternum. L3X1 wears no bra or shirt (subconscious choice) for heat control. **

Note: Jacket design fully covers critical personal zones. Augmentations ensure structural containment and modesty are preserved at all times.

Pants: Infiltrator-standard blue or black lightly armored mesh jeans

- Designed for ventilation and agile movement

- Provides civilian camouflage in public environments

Undergarment Protocol:

- Breasts are structurally stabilized via subdermal augmentation

- Allowing greater ventilation without compromise to mobility or integrity

Footwear:

While standard-issue combat boots were issued, L3X1 and others in her command squad have opted for personally supplied shoes.

L3X1 wears a pair of generic white tennis shoes—non-tactical.

- Neural wipe should have removed all personal preferences; however, post-analysis reveals Caedra Nyyx (deceased) wore and preferred similar white tennis shoes prior to termination (No impact to combat effectiveness), observation only.

**** FIELD DEPLOYMENT WARNING****

L3X1's behavior, reflexes, and emotional structure were developed over years of black site simulation. Training logs and CRIS scores were manipulated and altered to include false memories of completing the standard CRIS academy.

Her trainer, L3N/A, the first confirmed L3 unit, was assigned to supervise development. Her records reflect real-time evaluations and control checks.

**** HANDLER NOTES ****

**L3X1 is not just responding to conditioning. It's evolving beyond protocol. Its potential exceeds containment parameters. Only its moral compass is keeping it aligned with Verellii—for now." – Lena Boma, *CRIS Black site Handler Log 8.14 – CLASSIFIED

"It trusted me. Of course it did. I made sure of it. Loyalty is just another function to exploit." – Lena Boma, *CRIS Black site Handler Log 8.13 – CLASSIFIED

"It'll never know what parts of its life are real. That's the beauty of it."– Lena Boma, CRIS Black site Handler Log 8.10 – CLASSIFIED

END OF RECORD...

***

How much of her training was real? How much of her rage, her compassion—had ever been hers?

Her memory flickered to a rooftop where Lena and Lexi sat, the neon city spread out beneath them after they'd taken down a drug cartel. Lexi was still just a recruit, bright-eyed and eager. Lena—her captain—pulled Lexi in by the shoulder, almost like a sister, and whispered, "I'll always have your back, kid."

Lexi had believed her. Every word.

Now it felt scripted. Manufactured. A performance.

She stared at the lines for what felt like hours, jaw tight, fists trembling. The woman she trusted—the one who held her, who made her believe she mattered—had lied.

"Fuck you, Lena," she whispered. "You used me."

CHAP_14.exe - Pantheon

Lexi dropped the file. A blue cone of light caught it mid-fall and slid it neatly back into its slot. As though nothing had happened. But everything had.

Lena—her mentor. Her friend. Her sister in arms. Used her. Every comfort, every lesson, every whispered promise... lies.

And her past... Did she have parents? Were they alive? Did she have siblings? Was there anyone, anywhere, who knew her beyond what she had been turned into besides Mia?

She roamed the Sanctum for hours, dragging files free, reading line after line until her eyes blurred. Rage drove her forward. Desperation kept her standing. But every trace of her previous life was gone—redacted, or erased from existence.

Her augmentation file. It was all that remained of Caedra Nyyx. Defeated, Lexi decided to drown her sorrows in the endless knowledge around her. She read about General Pike and his role in the Great War, how Earth deployed its first Infiltrators, and how one designated A1AN/A was killed during her mission. It was her remains that eventually helped engineers build Lexi into what she is now. A weapon.

***

The silence of the Sanctum closed in around her, heavy and suffocating. Amber, Graevos, Isabella, Thorne. Were they ever real? Or just more layers of control, carefully placed to keep her in line?

Lexi sank to the floor, her back sliding against a pristine mahogany wall. Maybe there was no one she could trust. Lexi stared straight ahead, a void in her chest where any hope or care had once been. Blue-robed figures and Aegis Titans walked by, ignoring her presence.

A Titan's armor, reflecting a faint blue light from a corridor, caught her eye. As she looked over, she saw a glass case with a pulsing blue light and a dark center. *What is that?* she wondered as she got up, cautiously walking toward the strange glass case.

Lexi looked inside and saw a man shrouded in a bright blue gel. He was naked, but had a strange device around his head with tubes and wires going to it.

"What the hell is this?" Lexi whispered.

"That is President Victor Wilks," a commanding voice said.

Lexi looked up at a towering man in gold and red armor standing next to her. His blonde hair was tightly cut on the sides, with the top long and slicked back, and his trimmed beard complemented his dark brown eyes.

"Do you have questions?" the man asked.

"Why is he here?" Lexi whispered.

"His body failed. But his genius will not. The Sanctum sustains him, from which he still commands. And I am Aegis Sentinel Xander Wilks: the first Aegis, the first Protectorate Supreme of the President, and my father. I have never failed a mission since I began my honorable watch," Wilks said, his voice arrogant.

Lexi steadied her voice. "What is an Aegis?"

"Koras Anthralliin, Velek Verelliin, dorrak vi'shannar.

Nok'ta vaal, hes'tir, nor'fal.

Vek'tar honarr, truven, jastenn.

Shol vi Aegis.

Shol vi Taiten."

"I'm sorry, my Verelliian is rusty. But one line you said: 'Nok'ta vaal, hes'tir, nor'fal'—*you will not falter, hesitate, or fail.* Yet you have failed. Verellii is in danger. Threats have emerged, all vying for power, and RAPID is struggling to keep them in check. If anything, the world is worse—on the brink of civil war, with Earth spies already undermining us. What do you say to that?" Lexi said, staring Wilks in the eyes.

Wilks' eyes turned a bright orange as he looked straight ahead.

"Why are your eyes orange?" Lexi said cautiously.

"Orange is the Sanctum's gaze. Infiltrators eye colors shift. We do not. Our eyes are constant—more advanced than yours will ever be," Wilks said, concentrating on the data.

Unease twisted in Lexi's gut as she met Wilks' glowing orange stare.

"I have seen some of the threats you speak of; I have seen people of the Union, and this Kurogane Syndicate. As for the corruption within RAPID and your claims of Earth, there is no evidence to support such claims. So, Captain Hayes, what would you have me do?" Wilks said coldly.

"I would have you and your Aegis help with these threats. You could be heroes again and regain your honor by helping the world you swore to protect," Lexi pleaded.

Wilks paused. His eyes flickered orange—for a moment. "I will give you two Aegis to assist in your fight against threats. They will be yours to command. I recommend starting with the Union; their forces are swelling exponentially. However, be aware, with a threat that monumental... even Titans have fallen against such odds," Wilks said.

As Lexi faced him, a rapid cadence thundered through the chamber, closing fast, then slowed to a halt behind her. "I grant you two Aegis Titans. Sergeant Tek Lee. Private Kaelor Brawn. They are yours—for now. But even Titans fall under poor command."

***

Wilks' voice boomed across the chamber, each word deliberate. *"Verellii—our duty."*

Brawn and Lee struck their fists to their chest plates in unison. *"Our duty—our home."*

The sound of their armor rang like a hammer on steel, the creed reverberating through the hall. Lexi felt the weight of it, the conviction, the sense that nothing could bend these men from their cause.

"I leave you to it, Captain Hayes. But be aware, they will not follow unhonorable commands," Sentinel Wilks said before leaving the chamber.

Lexi looked at the two Aegis agents before her, examining their ranks and names inscribed on their chest plates. Lee had four stripes, while Brawn had one.

"Lee," Lexi said in a commanding tone.

Lee straightened up; his helmet folded back, revealing his face. "Yes, ma'am!" Lee said, staring straight ahead.

"What cybernetics, skills, and weapons do you have?" Lexi asked.

"Ma'am, the following is a list of items a standard Aegis is required to have," Lee said as he transferred the information to Lexi.

***

File Transfer Initiated... AEGIS_TITAN_STANDARD_LOADOU T.exe // Clearance: Operational Commander Restricted

Armor System – Aegis Mark I

Resistant to laser and plasma weaponry.

Strength output amplified by 200%.

Retractable, fully synthesizable helmet.

Adaptive plating shields external gear while maintaining user isolation.

Dormant Sentience Protocol (AI) — activated only by Sentinel or Master Sergeant override.

Integrated sustainment: auto-cleaning, hydration, nutrient cycling; waste compacted into carbon dust expelled through the soles.

Cybernetic Enhancements – Standard Package

Verelliian Biomesh Strands AS+: muscular structure converted to Verelliian steel composites, providing a 500% tensile increase over Infiltrator models. Impervious to conventional ballistics; vulnerable to sustained plasma/laser fire and heavy penetrators.

Synthetic Eye Mk III: full-spectrum vision (X-ray, thermal, night). Integrated scan/data transfer with long-range interplanetary comms.

Primary Weapon and Defense Systems

LESS (Laser-Edged Sword/Spear): morphs between sword and spear; laser edges for armor penetration; automatically recharges when sheathed.

Laser Riot Shield: portable barrier capable of absorbing concentrated plasma/laser barrages.

Fusion Disruptor: triple-barrel rotary cannon; 20 rounds/sec; risk of overheating beyond 500 consecutive rounds; unlimited under burst control.

Personal Shield Generator: deployable energy barrier for emergency defense.

Grenade Holographic Processor (GHP): materializes ordnance on demand, teleported from Aegis supply caches.

END OF RECORD...

***

"This is incredible! A team like you could end this war before it even starts! Why aren't you guys out there?" Lexi exclaimed.

"Ma'am. We are Aegis Titans—Anthrallii's sword, Verellii's shield. Verellii is at peace, so it is not our place to interject," Lee said.

"Peace? You call this peace? People are dying, and you're guarding archives," Lexi pressed.

"Ma'am, uhh, I don't know if this is out of turn for me to say, but there are only 100 Aegis left. All of us, and all of our technology, is from the Great War era; repairing or duplicating our equipment is almost impossible. We uphold our mission within the Sanctum by protecting Verellii's knowledge and its President. He has ensured there is peace right now," Brawn said.

"It's not out of line, Private Brawn. In fact, you are both able to speak freely as you wish. But understand this—if the President told you that Verellii is at peace, then he lied to you. *Someone is feeding you a different story than the one RAPID hears*," Lexi replied.

"Do not speak ill of the president," Lee commanded, fire in his eyes.

"I am not speaking ill; it's just strange to me that he would tell the Aegis one thing and report something different to RAPID. We will table that for now. On another note, our first stop is the Union; several vile and deranged people commit heinous crimes and wish war on our government. The few are a plague and diminishing the good name of the people who just want to live regular lives," Lexi said, trying to amp up the soldiers.

"Your orders, ma'am?" Lee said, unenthusiastic.

"My orders are to engage anyone who engages us. You have every right to defend yourselves, me, and any innocents in danger by any means necessary," Lexi said confidently.

"YES, MA'AM!" both Lee and Brawn yelled.

The trio took the elevator to the files and documentation room before entering the Eraway. The number of stares the never-before-seen Aegis members received made Lexi feel even more confident in their abilities. As personnel moved to the sides of the hallway, Lexi remembered a crucial detail she'd forgotten.

"AMBER!" Lexi said. "Lee, Brawn, wait here."

Lee and Brawn stopped, coming to attention, and awaited Lexi's orders. The Aegis men towered over Enforcers, their armor polished and pristine, a stark contrast to the battle worn armor of the Enforcers that passed by, in awe of the sheer mass of the Titans.

Lexi burst into the mechanics' office. Amber lay still on the table, breaths shallow but steady. Lexi leaned down, kissed her quickly, and whispered, *"I need you. Come back to me."* Then she pulled away and forced herself back to the hall.

***

"Captain Hayes, who are your friends?" a familiar voice asked with a hint of attitude.

Lexi turned to see Private Blackwood standing in his armor, looking up at the white-armored Aegis Titans.

"Sergeant Lee, Private Brawn—this is Private Blackwood of the Enforcer Corps. Blackwood, this is Aegis Titan Sergeant Lee and Aegis Titan Private Brawn," Lexi said, cocky.

"Going to get these fucking idiots killed, too?" Blackwood spat.

"Private, I will remind you of your place..." Lexi started—

"Watch your tone. This will be your first and final warning. Do I make myself clear?" Sergeant Lee commanded.

"I apologize for my outburst to you men, and to you, Captain," Blackwood said, seething through clenched teeth.

The Titans walked behind Lexi as she moved past Blackwood with a cocky grin and headed for the landing pad, the floor trembling from their footsteps. She lifted her left arm, and the blue light came to life under her skin.

"HQ, I require a Skyreaper for three personnel, headed to the Mining District, do you copy?" Lexi said.

"Copy, Captain Hayes. Skyreaper Three is prepped, aircrew has been alerted and awaiting your arrival," HQ responded.

As they neared the running gunship and jumped in, Brawn smacked his head on the low-hanging door as the ship tilted to one side from the weight.

"These things are a bit small, aren't they?" Brawn exclaimed.

"I guess they are normal for Enforcers... wait, do you have your own gunships?" Lexi asked.

"They're called Trireme Voidships," Brawn said. "They were built for space once. Now they just sit in hangars, gathering dust. Catalysts are long dead. I don't even know if they'd still handle a planetside run."

"You should not be sharing our secrets, Private," Lee ordered.

The flight took about an hour before the gunship lowered itself into the narrow chasm in the ground, revealing the tunnel where Lexi saw Debra die.

"Ma'am, I've got another mission. I'll make sure a gunship's waiting for you on departure!" the pilot shouted.

Lexi nodded, and as she started to jump out, a large white armored arm stopped her, pulling her back in.

"Ma'am, with all due respect, we will take point," Brawn said.

The trio jumped out of the gunship, with Lexi positioned behind the two soldiers. They entered the tunnel.

Lexi hesitated—just for a moment. This was the spot where he'd smashed her against the wall like she was nothing. Where Debra screamed... and where the screaming stopped.

A sharp noise snapped Lexi out of her trance, dragging her back to the moment. The Aegis Titans took out their swords, firing up the laser edges. Lexi pulled out her pistol and continued to follow the armored men in front of her.

They walked down the tunnel until they reached the three-way split.

"We should take the middle," Lexi said, pointing with command. "I've been down the right, and another Infiltrator went down the left."

"Yes, ma'am," the men said quietly as they moved as softly as possible.

At the end of the hall, it opened to a massive cavern littered with homes, stores, and—more importantly—people. Several screamed and ran while others showed weapons, preparing for a fight. Lee opened his helmet, revealing his face.

"We are not here to harm civilians. We seek one man—scarred, augmented, a killer of Infiltrators and Enforcers. Send him forward, and we will leave in peace," Lee said confidently.

More people emerged from their homes, armed and furious. Lexi heard a voice in the deep shadows of the cavern—a voice that sent chills down her spine, familiar yet venomous.

"Well, well, well, Lexi Hayes returns. It wasn't enough that I killed so many of your people; you clearly want to join your friends. Oh, and look at that: you brought some Titans in shiny new armor to help," the voice rasped.

As the shadows shifted, something caught the light before he fully emerged—a glint of red paint, then—Debra's face. Her skull was hollowed and mounted, with jagged spikes driven through the eyes and mouth. Welded to the shoulder of Kalani's shattered armor like a grotesque war trophy.

Lexi stopped cold, staring at what he'd made of Debra.

"What's your name?" Brawn asked.

"My name? It once was... Pike."

Lee's face went pale. "Pike? As in... General Michael Pike?"

Pike chuckled. "What's left of him."

His grin warped. "I was supposed to be like you, Aegis. I was to be the first—your Sentinel. But Wilks—your perfect fucking leader—betrayed me. He found out what I knew, his secret, and tortured me for it. Experimented on me. Cast me away. Labeled me defective. Buried me like rot. He is not what he pretends to be."

Pike stepped forward, eyes flaring with hatred.

"What secret is that?" Lee demanded.

Pike's smile thinned. "Another time, perhaps." He tilted his head. "Wilks forged legends from my death. But I survived as a monster. And I will use these augmentations to kill all who oppose me, to restore Verellii to its previous glory—one without cybernetics. LOOK. AT. ME! I hate what I am. I hate you."

Lee and Brawn shifted their swords into spears; blue edges flared as blades extended. They drew their riot shields—compact frames that snapped open into hollow rectangles, whining, then humming as they locked, igniting a blue hexagonal barrier that shimmered outward. Shoulder to shoulder, spears perched atop shields, they braced to protect the brother at their side.

"Come get us then," Brawn said, smiling in his helmet.

Pike ran, leaping high before slamming down with a roar. Lee angled his riot shield, catching him mid-air. He powered the shield down just long enough to drive his spear through the opening and into Pike's chest. With a grunt, he ripped the blade free, blood spraying as he hurled Pike into the cavern's center.

Pike clawed at the dirt, roaring, thrashing in pain.

Brawn's hand shimmered, a grenade solidifying in his grip. He closed the distance, hauled Pike up by the neck, and rammed his fist into the gaping wound, releasing the grenade inside. One savage kick sent Pike stumbling back—just as the charge went off.

The blast tore him apart from the inside. Flesh and metal vaporized in a white-hot flash, his body collapsing into drifting black ash until nothing remained. Pike was gone.

The cavern fell silent. Dozens of eyes locked on the Titans, who had erased their leader in mere minutes.

"Was that the guy?" Brawn asked.

"Umm, uh, yeah." Lexi stammered. She couldn't believe it. Pike—the same savage who raped and killed Debra, shot Elise from the sky, and gunned down Kalani—was dead.

Torn apart. Erased. Not by an army. Not by a missile. But by two men she'd met less than an hour ago.

She stood there, jaw slightly open, unable to move. They made it look easy. For the first time in a long time, Lexi felt something strange. Not fear. Not anger. Hope.

As the team walked out of the tunnel, a shot rang out, echoing within the cavern, and a laser bolt hit Lee in the leg. He looked at the tiny scorch mark on his armor plate before turning toward the Union members, still itching for a fight.

"Do that again, and it will be the last thing you do," Lee warned coldly.

Several laser bolts and bullets flew toward them as Lee and Brawn activated their personal shields, and Brawn tossed Lexi his riot shield. The riot shield unfolded before her, igniting once again.

"Stay here," Brawn commanded as the two Aegis members charged the Union assailants.

"Brawn, left flank! Don't let them get around us!" Lexi barked, falling into old habits.

Rounds and bolts hammered the personal shields without effect. Lee and Brawn drew their Fusion Disruptors and fired on the aggressors, leaving no one alive. Lexi looked around, and not a single house or innocent person was hit.

"Holy shit," Lexi muttered. She started to believe they could actually win.

Lexi closed her eyes, only for a moment. Debra, Elise, Kalani... *you guys can rest easy now*, she thought.

***

Lexi didn't realize she was shaking until Brawn's voice snapped her out of it. "You alright, Captain?"

She blinked. Nodded. *"I... yeah. I just didn't think anyone could stop Pike."*

The two Aegis men fist-bumped, then Brawn turned to Lexi, palm extended, to return the riot shield. Weapons holstered, they began making their way back toward the main tunnel exit.

At the junction where three tunnels met, Lexi's eyes drifted to the right corridor—the one with the hidden doors she had seen earlier. She paused. She had backup now. Why not explore? The civilians could still be in there—maybe even more threats to neutralize. That was the mission, after all.

"We're going down this tunnel," Lexi said, pointing to the right.

"Yes, ma'am," both men replied, moving into position, weapons drawn and scanning.

The hallway split as the team moved right, connecting to the spiraling stairwell. At the bottom, the trio emerged into the same circular courtyard Lexi had found earlier.

"There are doors all around us," Lexi said, scanning the chamber.

"Yes. We see them," Lee replied flatly.

Lexi stepped toward the door she'd previously entered. "There should be civilians in here." She keyed it open.

But what greeted her wasn't the grand hall of screams, chanting, and light from before. It was... gone. All of it. The space was stripped bare. Mining equipment now filled the area, the walls scuffed with fresh impact marks. No bodies. No cages. No banners. Even the smell had changed. It wasn't rage and blood anymore—just dust and iron.

Lexi's chest tightened. Had it all been cleaned that fast? Covered up? Or was something more insidious going on?

186

They returned to the courtyard. "Knock the others open," Lexi ordered.

The Titans moved fast. The first two rooms were smaller—one a tactical planning area, the other a basic operations command post—both hollowed out and scrubbed of identity. The third door opened to reveal a long, dark hallway.

Lexi approached the fifth door, her expression tightening. "This one was... strange," she muttered.

Her words cut off as Brawn slammed his shoulder into the door, turning it into a pile of rubble. A grenade formed in his hand with a sharp click. He rolled his shoulder and hurled it into the dark, then planted himself between Lexi and the room.

"Slit Fang nest," he said casually—just as a massive explosion rocked the hallway.

His armor shielded her from the full blast, the concussive force slamming against his frame and echoing off the stone walls. Shrapnel tore through the room like angry bees.

Brawn grunted. "Those things are unnatural," he muttered, a visible shiver running down his spine. "Fucking disgusting."

He wiped a chunk of Slit Fang whelp carcass off his shoulder, then gave Lexi a once-over. "Wouldn't want to scuff that pristine skin of yours," he added with a cocky smile.

Lexi rolled her eyes. "Don't make it weird."

After scouring the two operational rooms more thoroughly, Brawn suddenly called out. "I found something, Captain!"

Lexi crossed the space quickly. Brawn pointed to a flickering command console—still partially active. The feed displayed a large chamber down the unexplored hallway. Lexi leaned in, studying the screen.

"Why so much security... just for a tunnel?" she asked aloud. A moment passed. "Titans," she commanded. "We're going in."

"Yes, ma'am," they replied without hesitation, falling in line.

They moved down the corridor, flanked by long windows on either side—but beyond the glass, there was only darkness. Just the void of a massive cavern.

Eventually, they reached a thick security door at the end.

"Any way to get through this?" Lexi said, looking at the massive door.

"Not from my scans," Lee said.

Lexi continued to look around, then a thought came to her. She punched one of the hallway's windows over and over, her skin splitting, but the glass refusing to crack.

"Smash this window!" she ordered.

Lee kicked the pane, sending shards of glass flying to an unknown destination.

Lexi unclipped her drone. It hovered in front of her. "Light what I see," she said, gesturing two fingers to her eyes.

The drone chirped, and Lexi climbed out, unsure of how far above the chasm she was. She smashed her foot into the rock for a foothold, moving cautiously across the wall. She set her pistol to armor-piercing. Blue light flared as she emptied a burst into the far window. Glass spiderwebbed, then shattered. Holstering her weapon, she ripped the frame out and hauled herself through, the drone hovering at her shoulder.

Lexi's arm lit up.

"Captain, you good?" Brawn asked.

"Yeah. Made it to the other side of the door. Gonna have to wire it open from this side," Lexi said.

She ripped open the control box, scanning its contents and uploading what she saw to the drone. It processed for a second, then projected a hologram showing where to move the wires.

Lexi pulled a white-and-red striped wire, tore the coating off, and spliced it to a blue-and-yellow striped wire. With a spark, the door slid open.

The drone slid back into its holder on her waistband as the Titans moved through the doorway.

Another hallway descended beyond them, lined with thousands of footprints. Lexi took point.

At the end, they reached an intersection. The tunnel to the left stretched endlessly into darkness. The right was sealed off by towering steel double doors, nearly fifty feet tall.

"What the hell needs doors that big?" Brawn asked, awe creeping into his voice.

Lexi ignored the question and walked up to the console embedded in the wall beside the door. She pressed a large red button.

Hydraulics groaned. Dust poured from the frame. Then, with surprising grace, the doors slid open. The lights activated.

*****

Inside were four massive mechanical walkers—ancient, deadly, and completely restored. They stood 150 feet tall, matte black, with glowing yellow eyes for the cockpits and legs reinforced with thick armor plating. Each was armed with four revolver-style 110mm tank cannons and a 48-missile pod on its back.

Even Lexi froze.

"Uh, Sergeant," Brawn whispered, his confidence finally cracking.

Lee didn't sound much better. "Easy, Private. They're just machines. We fought these in the war... We will handle it."

The trio moved cautiously inside. The walkers didn't move.

Then a loud static screech burst through the room's intercom. A voice followed—cold and amused.

"Lieutenant Lexi Hayes. Back again? And you killed General Pike... shame. He was going to be instrumental to my plans. After all, who do you think helped us restore the mechs?"

Lexi's hands clenched.

"You're like a rose, Lexi. Beautiful to look at... but a painful thorn in my side. I grow tired of you and your friends interfering in my affairs."

Lexi stepped forward. *"First of all—it's Captain.* Second—I don't know who the fuck you are, but I'm going to find you. And I will stop you."

The Aegis men blinked, glancing at each other. Lexi radiated the kind of power that made steel seem soft.

The voice laughed. "You're too late. But you should see what I've prepared for you..."

A transparent panel dropped over the entrance, sealing it shut.

Then a blast shook the chamber to its core.

The explosion came like an earthquake, shaking Verellii's crust. The floor trembled. Fire rolled down the distant tunnel, curling against the transparent shield, the heat fogging the windows before they blackened from the intense flames.

The voice returned—measured, satisfied.

"What you are witnessing is the detonation of a nuclear warhead... beneath RAPID HQ. Your precious building is gone. The Enforcers. The Infiltrators. The Sanctum. All incinerated. After today, there will be no more of your kind."

Lexi dropped to one knee. She couldn't tell if it was shock or grief—only that her body gave out beneath her.

Amber. Izzy. Chief Graevos. Thorne... all of them? Gone?

CHAP_15.exe - Syst3m_Shutdown

No. It couldn't be. There was no confirmation. No proof. Just smoke. Just a voice on a speaker.

"Get up, commander!" Lee barked. "Do what your file says you can do. Persevere. Push. Do not stop."

"Let's fuck them up!" Brawn said, then looked at Lee.

Lee, just staring at Brawn, replied, "Yes. Let us fuck them up," he said unconvincingly.

"You are finished, Captain," the voice hissed. "Stop pretending there is still a future for you."

Finished? Not while I'm still standing, asshole.

Lexi pushed off the ground, rage searing behind her eyes. Brawn helped steady her as she rose. Her legs shook—but she stood.

A hiss of steam echoed across the chamber.

One of the mechs shifted—its joints creaking as it powered on.

The yellow eyes of the walker flared to life. Its head turned—slowly—until it locked onto Lexi. A low mechanical whine built as the twin cannons rotated into position.

Lexi's eyes narrowed.

No... I'm not done yet.

"Hey, Sarge!" Brawn shouted. "This is a bit out of our wheelhouse!"

Lexi didn't answer. Her face twisted with rage and resolve as she sprinted toward the nearest mech. Behind her, the stunned Titans drew their Fusion Disruptors and opened fire on the walker's glowing cockpit.

Lexi zigzagged between its two colossal legs, then blipped—reappearing at its hip joint. Another blink, and she landed atop the rocket pod. With a snarl, she tore the protective plate off one of the missiles, yanked her sidearm, and fired a single round directly into its warhead.

The rocket detonated. The entire pod ignited in a chain reaction, hurling Lexi like a ragdoll across the cavern. She slammed into a wall, the impact rattling her vision. Dust and shrapnel pelted her as she crumpled to the floor.

The mech toppled, collapsing into a burning heap—buried in its own molten steel.

"Oh man, that was awesome!" Brawn shouted, sprinting toward her.

A second mech powered on, its glowing eyes flaring as servos whined.

"Get her out of there!" Lee barked. "I will provide defense!"

"I'm… not… done yet." Lexi winced, coolant starting to flow out of different parts of her body.

Lee activated his personal shield—a shimmering sphere of tightly packed yellow pixels snapped into place around his body, each square flickering with concentrated energy. He slammed his riot shield into the ground, deploying its faint blue aura outward from the center, vibrating with each shockwave. He braced for impact, standing tall as the mech opened fire.

110 mm shells slammed into the layered defense, splintering the barrier and lighting up the tunnel with every impact.

"Brawn! Now!" Lee roared.

"I've got her, sir! Let's go!" Brawn yelled, lifting Lexi into his arms.

"No, I will stay. My life was spent in the Sanctum, preparing for this moment. To serve Verellii."

The mech locked on to Lee and fired a rocket.

But just before impact, a pink blur shot across the chamber.

"What the fuck is she doing?!" Brawn shouted, looking down to find his arms empty.

Lexi snatched the missile mid-air, blipped, and teleported it back toward the mech just before it struck Lee. The redirected warhead slammed into the walker's chest, sending it staggering backward.

"Lee! Brawn! Slam its legs!" Lexi shouted.

The Titans charged, ramming their armored bodies into its legs. The mech buckled and collapsed.

Lexi sprinted, leapt, and used Brawn's back as a springboard, launching herself onto the mech's head. She drove her fists into the glass cockpit over and over until it finally cracked.

"There's no one in here," she panted, peering into the cockpit. "It's empty. No pilot."

"Catch!" Brawn shouted, tossing her a grenade.

Lexi lobbed it inside. The cockpit erupted in flame.

"Brawn, Lee—can you rip that rocket pod off?" she called out, pointing to the fallen mech.

The two men nodded and moved fast. Metal groaned and tore as they pried the pod loose.

"Bring it here," Lexi said, gesturing toward the remaining walkers.

They dragged it forward.

Lexi tore off the pod's front and back panels, exposing the warheads. "If this doesn't work, I'm sorry," she muttered sarcastically.

Then, with focused precision, she began punching the back of each missile. One by one, they launched toward the remaining mechs. The Titans followed up with pinpoint disruptor fire, striking key joints.

The machines exploded—torn apart mid-activation.

Brawn whooped. "Holy shit, that was insane!"

"It certainly was," Lee said, casting Brawn and Lexi a rare look of pride.

The chamber shook as a low groan rolled out from the back wall. Cracks split the stone, dust and rock spilling as the wall tore apart into two halves.

From the shadows, a Great War super-heavy tank rumbled forward, its railgun charging with a deep hum that rattled the chamber. The barrel glowed, massive power restrained, as it locked onto them.

The cannon discharged.

The shell hit Lee square in the chest, slamming him into the cavern wall with thunderous force. His shield flickered, yellow pixels crumbled, before collapsing. Smoke poured from the gaping hole burned through his armor.

Lee sagged against the stone, body still, the light on his visor flashing before turning black.

"Sarge…" Brawn's voice broke, rage building within him. His fists clenched, fingers digging into his palms until the metal bent.

Lexi stood still for a moment, heart in her throat. He'd been larger than life a second ago—untouchable. Now he was gone, just like that.

Her brow furrowed. Her voice hardened.

"I'm ending this."

She sprinted forward, weaving left. The railgun tracked her.

She vanished in a blip, reappearing to the right. The turret lurched, struggling to keep up—then swung toward Brawn.

The coils whined, the barrel glowing hotter.

Lexi hurled herself onto the tank, shoes slamming against its armor. She brought both fists down on the railgun. Steel rang under the blow, her Shockwave Inhibitor surging blue lightning through her arm. If she couldn't reverse the charge, she'd crush the barrel shut with her bare hands.

The cannon fired.

She forced the polarity backward.

The round reversed mid-fire and detonated inside the tank's body.

The blast split it open from within, fire belching through ruptured plates. The explosion hurled Lexi across the chamber, flames covering her as she smashed into the jagged stone walls and skidded across the ground. Smoke rose from her frame with each labored breath.

The intercom crackled alive.

"You've ruined everything, L-3-X-1. You are a plague. A failed experiment—clawing for the humanity you'll never have. Your kind should have burned with the war."

The feed cut.

"Fuck... you," Lexi groaned, trying to rise.

"Captain, let me help!" Brawn said, rushing to her side.

Her skin flaked off in sheets. "Get us back to HQ."

"But that guy said—"

"Back to HQ, Brawn. That's an order."

"...Yes, ma'am."

He lifted her carefully and carried her through the wreckage, up the ruined stairwells and tunnels, toward a waiting gunship.

They boarded. The doors sealed. Engines roared.

As they ascended, black smoke spilled into the sky far in the distance.

Lexi leaned toward the window, dread settling in her chest.

"Oh no..."

As they neared the source of the smoke, the Central District Nexus was unrecognizable. Where blue and green once stood, only flame and ruin remained.

"HQ, this is Skyreaper Seven…" the pilot called over comms. "HQ…? Ma'am, I'm not getting anything."

"Go to HQ," Lexi said, her voice sharp.

Lexi stared down at the scarred landscape—charred buildings, burning wreckage, clouds of debris drifting like ash.

Nothing was left.

The ship landed where HQ once stood, flames licking across the ruined structures. Brawn helped Lexi down.

They stood among the scattered remains.

Enforcer armor—burnt and twisted—littered the ground. Metal husks, once human, once alive.

Then she saw a group of mangled female bodies. Lexi's legs gave out.

The war wasn't over.

It had only just begun.

"…These are… were my recruits," Lexi muttered, her voice cracking. "I… I'm not sure who they are." She stared at the burnt women, trying to find any trace of recognition.

"Let's look for the chute to the Sanctum. It should've been fine, right?" Brawn asked, grasping for hope.

"Maybe it's worth a shot," Lexi replied, forcing herself to hold onto the optimism.

The two held themselves steady against the scorched, warped remnants of the elevator shaft as they descended lower. The heat damage worsened with every level. Brawn knew the truth deep down—that the explosion started below the Sanctum—but they pushed forward anyway. Hope demanded it.

When they reached the bottom, they dropped onto what remained of the Sanctum floor. A massive crater yawned before them, the center of the blast zone.

Lexi exhaled slowly. "Whoever did this had intimate knowledge of HQ and the Sanctum—and enough hate to level it."

Brawn scanned the surrounding devastation, then stopped. "Oh, man! It hasn't been touched!"

"What hasn't?" Lexi asked, rushing to his side.

He pressed his hand to the reinforced wall. With a hiss of hydraulics, the steel-plated section slid aside, revealing a wide hallway.

"The Inner Sanctum," Brawn announced with a grin. "Only Titans are allowed in here... but it's an emergency, so—special exception for you, Captain." He finished it off with an exaggerated wink.

"...Thanks?" Lexi said, one eyebrow climbing, her tone caught between confusion and secondhand embarrassment.

They stepped into the sacred corridor. The walls were lined with tributes to fallen Aegis Titans—photos, etched steel plates, retired armor, and documented victories. Generations of warriors immortalized in stoic silence. Brothers and sisters in arms, frozen in better times.

"There are so many," Lexi whispered. "Did you know any of them?"

"Uh... yeah," Brawn said, rubbing the back of his helmet. "Down here—Aegis Titan Private Yern Atkinson. We joined the Corps together. Got our cybernetics at the same time. Passed all the tests side by side. Dude was family."

Lexi stared at the image of Private Atkinson. Medals gleamed beside his armored silhouette.

"How'd he die?" she asked gently.

Brawn placed a hand on Atkinson's armor and smirked. "We were pinned down behind this busted concrete barrier in a little shithole called Pinbrote—about where the Port District is now. And this guy—this crazy bastard—starts talking about a prostitute he'd seen the night before. Then he takes off his crotch armor and shows me his dick, asking if this type of bump looked normal."

Lexi let out a small giggle. "...Did you ever figure out what the bump was from?"

"Nope. He got it after the night with that girl, but we never did figure out what STD it was," Brawn said, laughing. "I was laughing so hard I forgot we were still getting shot at. Then—bam—plasma grenade took his fucking head off. I told that fool to wear his helmet."

He punched the side of the armor, leaving a sizable dent.

"I'm sorry," Lexi said, placing a hand on his arm.

"It's all good," Brawn nodded. "I still visit him now and again."

They continued deeper, passing through another door—and stopped.

Inside the chamber, several Aegis Titans stood in formation around a tall glass containment case. Weapons drawn, shields raised. Inside the container floated President Wilks—silent.

A voice crackled from the comm embedded in the case.

"Curious," Wilks said.

All the Titans turned toward the pod. Then toward Lexi.

"What is, sir?" Brawn asked.

"Not you. The woman."

Lexi frowned. "Excuse me?"

"Curious, isn't it?" Wilks said again, his tone distant.

"I'm not sure what you mean, sir," Lexi replied.

"You were invited into our Sanctum. You took our knowledge, led our Titans to battle against an old enemy... and now, HQ and the Sanctum lie in ruins. And I notice Sergeant Lee is not with you."

Brawn stepped forward. "Sergeant Lee died fighting valiantly, sir."

"I wasn't speaking to you. Step outside. This conversation is with Captain Lexi Hayes... of the former RAPID Infiltrator Division."

Brawn hesitated, then turned and left.

Lexi stiffened. "Sir, I assure you—everything I've done has been for the good of Verellii."

"Oh, and what good it's done," Wilks snapped. "Look around. Our bright future, reduced to ash!"

"Sir, I—"

"GET OUT OF MY SANCTUM!" Wilks' speaker bellowed. "Do not return. If I see you again, the Aegis will destroy you. Do I make myself clear, Infiltrator?"

Lexi's heart sank. "Yes, sir."

***

She turned to leave, but Brawn was already waiting in the corridor. He grabbed her arm.

"Hey. Where are you going? We still have a mission. A guy to stop!"

"I'm done, Brawn," Lexi said, her voice hollow. "Just let me go."

She ascended the elevator chute alone, her shoes echoing against scorched steel. As she climbed, Brawn's voice roared behind her—his pain shaking the Sanctum's walls.

"ARE YOU SERIOUS?! VERELLII IS OURS TO PROTECT, AND WE'D JUST LEAVE IT TO BURN?!"

"Watch your tone," Sentinel Wilks warned.

"AT LEAST LEXI IS TRYING!!!" Brawn shouted.

The sound of yelling echoed through the vast wreckage.

Ash drifted in through the shattered tunnels as Lexi emerged from the chute. Smoking and sparking files filled the once beautiful halls. Blue-robed corpses littered the rubble before them. The glorious Sanctum, with all its ancient knowledge of Earth and Verellii, gone, wiped out by radiation and flame.

Then, a flash in her eye.

ATTENTION, ATTENTION: ALL RAPID MEMBERS ARE TO FOLLOW DIRECTIVE 77.369-2 IMMEDIATELY. THIS MESSAGE WILL REPEAT UNTIL RECEIPT IS CONFIRMED.

She accessed the directive in her files. Secondary fallback location. Catastrophic event protocol.

"Skyreaper Seven," she said, activating comms.

"Go for Skyreaper," a pilot's voice responded.

"You available for relocation?"

"Roger. Ping location. Warbird en route."

She flicked her comm suite on as a tracer beacon.

Minutes passed. The Skyreaper gunship roared through the sky and descended. Lexi climbed aboard and collapsed on the bench, ash trailing from her skin, her limbs twitching from overuse.

"Head to the fallback location," she ordered. "Directive 77.369-2."

"Yes, ma'am," the pilot said.

Lexi watched the scarred land below as she drifted off to the hum of the gunship.

"MA'AM! WE ARE HERE!" the pilot yelled as Lexi jolted awake.

She blinked hard, eyes locking on the window. Below, a building slumped into ruin—collapsed beams, broken glass, and rot where stone and steel once stood proud. Ahead, Enforcers waited in a perfect line. Silent. Unmoving. And at their head—one figure stood apart.

"That's Captain Thorne!" Lexi shouted, hope spiking in her chest.

The gunship dropped lower, thrusters whining as it settled behind the formation. Dust swirled across the landing zone.

Lexi jumped first, shoes hitting the ground as she jogged toward them.

One Enforcer shifted.

He pulled off his helmet. Orange eyes flared.

"NO!" Lexi screamed. She spun, sprinting back.

The formation turned as one. Metal feet thundered. The Enforcers charged.

Lexi vaulted into the gunship, slamming her palm against the side panel. With a hiss, a minigun unfolded from the ceiling and locked beside the open hatch.

"Get us up! NOW!" she barked.

"Yes, ma'am!" the pilot snapped, throttling hard.

The ship shuddered, straining as the Enforcers leapt. Hands like vices clamped to the wings and landing struts, dragging it back down.

Lexi swung the minigun toward the swarm, barrels screaming as they spun up. The rounds hammered against armor, sparking and pummeling the entranced Enforcers. The hail rattled them, causing them to stagger, forcing some to let go. It wasn't enough to kill them. Just enough to shake them loose.

The ship lurched, the engines whining as the weight dragged it sideways.

Lexi snarled, sweeping fire across the line. She zeroed in on Thorne. He hadn't moved—still centered, still watching. She squeezed the trigger.

Rounds slammed into his helmet. The orange glow in his eyes went out.

Thorne staggered, blinking like he'd just woken up. His gaze flicked to Lexi—then to his men tearing the ship apart. Horror etched across his face. He backed away. And then he vanished into the building.

"Fucking pussy," Lexi spat, teeth bared as she cut another burst across the swarm.

The minigun's barrels turned red and began to fume, smoke hissing from their overheating core.

"Ma'am! Thrusters are overheating—they won't hold if this weight stays on!" the pilot shouted.

Lexi glanced down. Too many still clung to the struts. The gun's angle couldn't reach them.

"Fuck it."

She ripped the minigun from its mount—quick-release latches tore free, bolts snapping in sparks. Bracing at the hatch, muzzle clear of the skin, she aimed straight down and raked fire across the clinging Enforcers' hands. Armor buckled under the sustained burst; one by one they dropped, slamming into the dirt below.

The last let go, and the ship pitched sideways. A wing clipped the ground with a teeth-rattling grind. The pilot fought it, slammed the thrusters, and the gunship lurched skyward, engines shrieking.

Lexi dropped the gun and collapsed onto the deck, chest heaving, palms blistered from the overheated grip. Warning lights bled across the cockpit.

"Ma'am!" the pilot yelled. "When we scraped the ground, one wing bent—we're burning fuel too fast. I can't keep her airborne!"

Lexi forced herself upright. "Where are we?"

"Scanners say... Neuron Energies Plant!" he shouted back.

WOOP—WOOP—WOOP. IMPACT IMMINENT. ALL CREW: PREPARE FOR CRASH.

Lexi looked out the hatch. Fuel streamed from the wounded wing, trailing behind a torn panel.

The gunship dipped left—struggling for lift—as the wing snapped off.

Fuel scythed into the dying engine.

A fireball bloomed. The engine exploded, hurling shrapnel through the fuselage as flames surged up and over the cabin.

The aircraft became a blazing meteor.

"Brace fo—"

A steel beam punched through the cockpit, impaling the pilot mid-sentence as the gunship scythed through scaffolding and into a chemical silo. The silo erupted into a vortex of green flame.

Lexi held on as long as she could, but the final impact hurled her through shattered glass. Steel tore her open, green coolant spraying in long arcs. She hit hard, skidding across warped metal, chemical slurry searing through every wound. Smoke and poison filled her lungs; coolant bubbled from her lips.

She gagged, grit her teeth, and clawed herself forward inch by inch.

***

She would not die here. Not like this.

CHAP_16.exe - Contain3d

"SIR! Over here!" a voice called in the distance. Footsteps. Shadows loomed over her.

"Sir, she's... still alive," another worker said.

"My, my, my... what a tough young woman," another voice replied—calm, amused.

"Cover her up. Get her to medical. Immediately."

Lexi blacked out, her body giving up. Days passed before she opened her eyes.

The room was unnervingly serene—immaculate floors, perfectly trimmed bonsai trees, a bamboo rug underfoot, and soft light glinting off framed cherry blossom prints. Everything smelled faintly of incense. Her body had repaired itself, flawless as always. She was wrapped in a black silk kimono.

Her weapons—katana, shoto, pistol, and TDB Unit—sat neatly displayed on a cherry wood desk. Polished. Reverent. Like museum pieces.

The paper door slid open with a gentle whoosh. A woman in medical scrubs stepped in, checked the monitor, and paused when she saw Lexi conscious. No words—just a nod before she slipped away.

Moments later, a man entered. He was old. Late sixties, maybe seventies. No hair, thin beard, faint crow's feet beside calm, observant eyes. His black-and-white kimono brushed the floor as he moved with practiced grace. He pulled a chair beside her bed and sat with a soft exhale.

"Hello, dear," he said warmly. "I imagine you have many questions."

His voice was calm. Smooth. Disarming.

"I am Shogo Akiyama, CEO and founder of Neuron Energy Limited. You, my dear, survived a catastrophic incident. And yet... here you are. Restored. Alive. Fascinating."

Lexi shifted upright, ignoring the equipment hooked to her. "Sir, thank you for helping me. But I have to go. People are missing, and I have an investigation to finish."

Shogo nodded, unbothered. "Of course. Your jacket and drone, I'm afraid, were damaged beyond repair. Such delicate devices... your recon drone's charge core was melted. We recovered what we could."

Lexi glanced at the silk around her. "And this?"

"A kimono," he said, gesturing with a small smile. "Light. Airy. Something breathable—for someone with... your condition." His eyes flicked to her chest, just for a second. "We thought it best to aid your cooling systems discreetly."

Lexi narrowed her eyes. "Thank you." Suspicion filled her voice.

"Of course," he nodded, unfazed. "But—if I may—what exactly happened to RAPID headquarters?"

Lexi's jaw clenched. "A psychopath blew it up."

"Ah... how unfortunate," he replied softly, stroking his beard.

A second man entered. Leather jacket. Black pants. Eyes like acid. He leaned down and whispered into Shogo's ear. Lexi couldn't catch a word.

Shogo rose slowly, the other man assisting him. "Well then," he said, looking at her weapons. "Ah... a fine blade."

He approached the katana and held it up, his other hand running along the sheath.

"When our ancestors came from Earth to this place, they brought with them the essence of a forgotten land. Japan, they called it. Its spirit lives on in weapons like these—crafted again, now with Verellii steel. Tradition, preserved through struggle."

He bowed slightly and then placed Lexi's katana back on the desk.

"It has been an honor to aid you," he said, then exited, his footsteps soft against the bamboo mat.

Lexi smiled faintly as Mr. Akiyama bowed and left the room. But the man in black stayed.

He lingered by the door, his eyes crawling over her like insects.

"I don't care what the old man says," he muttered, voice low and oily. "You and whatever the hell you are... don't belong here."

Lexi stood, ripping the test equipment from her arm as the silk kimono settled against her curves, clinging to the shape of her waist. She took a slow step toward the desk where her clothing was neatly folded.

"Get out of my way," she said flatly.

He didn't move. His eyes stayed locked on her ass.

"Nice skin," he said. "Hard to tell where the tech ends and the tits begin."

Lexi stopped mid-step. He walked up behind her—close enough for her to feel his breath on her neck. He grabbed the back of the kimono, yanking it down with one sharp pull. The fabric fluttered to the ground, leaving her bare.

Her fists clenched, her face contorted.

"That's better," he sneered, leering at her body. "Always wondered what a synthetic whore looked like without all the shine."

His hand slapped her ass with a sharp crack. She didn't flinch.

"You know what I think?" he whispered, his lips brushing her ear. "You're just some cybernetic little slut, I guess your kind does have its uses, waiting for a real man to—"

Her shoto whispered from its sheath.

Her movements were like lightning; he never saw it coming. Blood sprayed from his throat in a sudden, bubbling burst. He staggered back, eyes wide, gurgling.

Lexi stepped in close, wiping his blood off the blade with his jacket before returning it to its sheath. Her expression was blank. Then, softly—mockingly—she pressed a kiss to the tip of his nose.

"I didn't catch the rest of your sentence," she whispered.

He dropped to his knees, clutching his neck, until he fell forward in his own pool of blood, coughing and gurgling in his own fluid.

She walked past him, bare feet silent on the floor, until she paused. Something caught her eye—just under his collar. A tattoo. A broken line, with the letters T.N.O. marked above it.

Her eyes narrowed. *Interesting, she thought.*

***

She grabbed her clothes—her blue capris, cleaned and repaired, and the stylish black silk kimono with a silver dragon—and began to dress. She tugged on the black flats, wincing.

"Ugh. I hate flats," she muttered. Then smirked at her reflection. "But I might be a kimono girl for sure."

Lexi finished dressing and slid the paper door open.

The hallway outside mirrored her recovery room—sterile, immaculate, and heavily influenced by... what did he call it? Japan? She walked through the corridor, following signs that looked more like symbols than letters—abstract designs etched into glowing panels.

"Excuse me," Lexi said, stopping a nurse in white scrubs. "Where's the exit?"

The nurse silently pointed to a red sign at the end of the hall.

Lexi followed it, stepping out into the open.

She raised her left wrist, activating her comms suite.

"Amber?" Static.

"Captain Thorne?" Nothing.

"Izzy?"

Zzzzt... Lex... zzzt don't... zzzt building—zzzt protocol—zzzzzt trap—

The line went dead.

"Fuck," Lexi muttered. *"What am I supposed to do now?"*

She pivoted. "Skyreaper, do you copy?"

A pause.

"Skyreaper, this is Captain Lexi Hayes. Do you copy?"

"Skyreaper Five, how can I help you, Captain?" the pilot responded, steady and confident.

"Request pickup on my marker. Ping sent."

"Ping received. Skyreaper en route."

A roar tore through the sky. The gunship descended rapidly, lowering its landing gear outside the hospital's entrance.

As she reached the gunship, Lexi's head suddenly screeched—an unbearable, piercing shriek inside her skull. She collapsed to her knees, clutching her head.

"What the fuck!" she yelled, gritting her teeth.

She staggered up and climbed through the side door.

"Where to, ma'am?" the pilot asked. Then hesitated. "Ma'am... everything okay?"

He glanced back.

Lexi stared dead ahead. No movement. No blinking. Eyes vacant.

When Lexi came to, she was being dragged from the gunship. The pilot, unsure what else to do, had brought her to the secondary fallback location.

***

Two Enforcers yanked her out of the side door—eyes aglow with an orange blaze. They threw her into the wall of a cell. Her head rang as a dull hum radiated and a red shimmer of energy materialized across the cell's open entrance—a laser shield.

Every movement felt like her brain was being peeled apart. She stumbled backward, nearly retching from the pain. Green fluid trickled from one nostril.

The cell was empty. Just a flat steel bench and the faint scent of electronics.

Lexi slammed her fist against the wall in frustration. Nothing.

Another slam. This time, from the other side.

Tap-tap-tap... tap-tap.

Her eyes narrowed. Her breath caught.

Three short. Two long.

Infiltrator captive code.

Lexi moved to the wall, heart racing. She tapped back.

Tap-tap... tap-tap-tap.

A pause. Then: Tap. Tap. Tap.

Translation: "Isabella?"

She responded.

Tap-tap. Tap.

"Lexi."

Another pause. Then a faint clink, and something slid out of the ceiling vent above the cell. A small black disk—no bigger than a drink coaster—hovered in the air and scanned the room silently.

Lexi let out a sharp breath. Izzy's recon drone.

It zipped toward the shield emitter in the corner to an embedded vent cluster with micro sensors. The drone slipped through the vent, carefully navigating the sensor arrays.

Lexi walked to the center of the room, coolant drying on her lip.

Minutes, hours, maybe days went by, every moment feeling like an eternity. Her head pulsed again—sharp, erratic. Her right hand twitched involuntarily, as if it wanted to reach for a weapon. She fell to the floor, clutching her head, screaming, writhing in pain.

Then—

The red laser field flickered before shattering into a ripple of red sparks.

Lexi wasted no time; she forced herself to her feet and sprinted out.

From the cell next door, another shimmer faded—Izzy stepped out, also damaged but alive.

They locked eyes.

"Psst, mami, this way. I downloaded the schematics for this place," Isabella whispered, nodding to the end of the hallway.

They crept through the hallways—silent, predatory—ninjas in the shadows. Each movement was precise. Calculated.

They moved from shadow to shadow until they reached a makeshift garage—dimly lit, full of crates, vehicles, and parked security drones.

Isabella glanced at Lexi, who was clutching her head, struggling to stay upright. With swift, sharp hand signals, Isabella gave the order: Hold position. I'll be back.

Lexi nodded, chest rising and falling, sweat beading along her temples.

Isabella dropped off the edge of a loading bay and vanished into the dark.

Lexi could barely focus. Her vision blurred—but she saw just enough. Isabella struck fast and silent. She snapped one guard's neck, throwing his knife at another guard.

Lexi's head throbbed harder. She grit her teeth as Isabella leaned over one of the fallen guards, studying something. Then Isabella sprinted to a wall-mounted box, yanked it open, grabbed a set of keys, and bolted back toward her.

Lexi let out a sudden, guttural scream. Her head flooded with static—her limbs twitching violently, as if coming alive against her will.

Nearby guards heard the cry. Enforcers and security swarmed the garage.

Isabella launched herself into the air—an acrobatic marvel—landing feet-first on one of the rushing assailants. She grabbed the guard's weapon mid-fall, flipped it, and shot another clean in the chest.

An Enforcer reached Lexi. Her body felt like it was melting from the inside out. But she forced her failing systems to respond.

Her arm spasmed. Her fingers jerked—and the Shockwave Inhibitor flared to life.

The Enforcer caught the full discharge, arcs clinging to him as if alive. His body convulsed, every joint seizing as the electricity tore through his armor. He screamed—ragged, inhuman—before the force hurled him back. Blue lightning snapped across the floor and walls as he flew, leaving molten scars in his wake, before he smashed through a rack of crates and disappeared under rubble.

Isabella activated her own. A pulse of blinding blue discharged into the last remaining Enforcer, dropping him instantly.

The garage went quiet again.

"Mami, are you okay?" Isabella called out, breathless.

Lexi's jaw clenched. *"Izzy... I HATE YOU... I need... help.* Something isn't—okay."

Her eyes flickered, muscles convulsing.

"Where do we go?" Isabella asked, kneeling beside her.

Lexi forced herself to lift her wrist. With a flick, she sent the coordinates directly to Isabella's display.

Then—another surge. Worse than before. Her arm jerked violently. Her hand reached for a loose rock. She wasn't in control.

Hate surged through her.

She wanted to kill Isabella.

Isabella's eyes widened—recognizing the twitch, the shift, the danger. Without hesitation, she caught Lexi's arm mid-swing, wrestling the rock from her grasp.

"Sorry, mami," she whispered.

Then swung—slamming the rock into the side of Lexi's head. Catching her limp body before she hit the floor.

Isabella threw Lexi into a truck, strapping her down so she couldn't move, her limbs and eyes twitching every few seconds.

Izzy fired the truck up with a mechanical roar, peeling out and crashing through the garage door with one mission: get to the coordinates Lexi sent.

As she drove, she realized the world knew what happened to HQ... but no one seemed to care. People still headed to work. VPSD still patrolled the streets. Even Level 2 was loud, filthy, alive.

"¿Qué carajos...?" she muttered. "How are people just—living?"

She took the exit to Level 3. Eventually, she stopped at a crumbling building. She looked it over and flipped open a panel near the front door, revealing a scanner—far too advanced for this building—inside. Definitely RAPID hardware.

She scanned her barcode, and the heavy door creaked open.

Inside the rooms, the dust was thick, the lights flickered, and the stripped consoles buzzed. The air smelled like rust and dirt.

Isabella carried Lexi in and strapped her to a rusted cot, securing the limbs that continued to twitch.

"Lo siento, mi amor... It's for your own good."

Then she got to work.

Old communication gear lined the walls. Cracked terminals, half-dead consoles, burned wires.

"I can build something with this," she muttered, ripping panels and computers from their housings.

Days blurred together. Isabella worked tirelessly, eyes bloodshot, fingers numb. Occasionally, she glanced over at Lexi—squirming, fidgeting, sometimes whispering things in her sleep. She continued to check that the straps were tight.

She wired her makeshift transmitter into the building's power grid, ensuring that it got the most out of the failing system. An antenna made of taped-together butter knives rose from the jury-rigged device.

She punched in an Infiltrator-only distress code:

To all remaining Infiltrators:

Do not follow DIRECTIVE 77.369-2.

Follow coordinates 36-4491b.

This is Sergeant Isabella Rojas.

The original directive is a trap.

This message will repeat.

The screen flickered. The device started to hum.

Transmission sent...

Now, they wait.

CHAP_17.exe - H0u5e_Rul3s

Music played softly through a battered speaker. Something old. Latin. Smooth, jazzy—her mother's favorite. Isabella hummed along, off-key but charming.

"Sabor a mí... aunque hayas dejado de quererme..."

The words melted into the air, accompanied by the scent of garlic, soy, and vinegar—chicken adobo simmering on the stove. She pulled a bottle from the fridge, popped it open, took a drink, and sighed.

"Still cold. Not bad."

Lexi woke up to a sound.

Beep. Beep. Beep.

She looked over at a strange machine in the corner as it blinked steadily, wires snaking from it like vines across the floor. Lexi stirred. Her head throbbed. Muscles twitched. She groaned and jerked against restraints.

"What the fuck..." she snarled.

The beeping continued. The lights buzzed above the bed, flickering slightly.

In the kitchen, a spoon clattered to the floor. Isabella sprinted in, apron half-tied, eyebrows raised.

"Mierda! Mami—wait—wait—Lexi!"

Lexi thrashed like a caged wolverine, teeth bared.

"Izzy, let me out of this bed right now or I swear—"

"¡Ay, ay, ay! Calm down, mujer loca!" Isabella held her hands up. "You tried to bash my skull in with a rock, remember?"

Lexi growled, tugging harder. "Untie me. Now."

"Nope." Isabella smirked, wiping her hands on her apron. "Just this once, I'm not following orders. This is a rebellion."

She moved closer, her voice softening.

"Would you like… a beer? Or some food? I made chicken adobo. Not the best without fresh ingredients, but—you've been out for days. You look like death. You need to eat."

Lexi glared. "And how am I supposed to eat tied up like a prisoner?"

"I'll feed you. I love you, Lex. But I also love not dying."

Isabella went to the kitchen and poured a ladle of rice and chicken into a bowl. She grabbed a fork before heading back to Lexi.

Izzy scooped some and offered it with mock innocence.

Lexi sighed and turned her head away. "I'm going to bite your fingers off."

Isabella chuckled. "Better than killing me, mami."

They stared at each other for a second—one radiating fury, the other calm defiance. A quiet moment. Smoke curled up the stairs from the stove. The hum of the transmitter in the corner. Lexi's twitching hand finally stilled.

Isabella sat on the edge of the bed, a beer in one hand, a fork in the other.

"Come on," she said gently. "Let me take care of you. *Just this once.*"

As Lexi sat there, allowing Isabella to feed her—begrudgingly—she started to notice something. Every time her head throbbed, something darker bubbled up. A sudden, violent hatred for Izzy.

"Hey, Izzy," Lexi said quietly.

"What's up?" Isabella asked, casually spooning another bite of chicken.

"I think you should keep me strapped down. For some unknown reason, every time my head hurts, *I... I hate you. Like, truly.* An uncontrollable hatred. And then—" Lexi paused, swallowing hard. "Then I want to kill you. Brutally."

Isabella's hand froze mid-air. A chill rolled down her spine.

"Have you always felt this way, Lex?"

Lexi shook her head slowly. "No. Not ever. It started after the crash. I woke up in a medical bay. A man said I'd been out for a few days. Since then... the headaches, the hate—they started after that." She met Izzy's eyes. "You're one of the few people I trust with everything."

***

Isabella set the bowl down, her expression shifting.

"So maybe they put something in you..." she said carefully. "If that's the case, we need help. But finding someone we can trust? That's the hard part. Right now... I don't trust anyone. Not even you."

The words stung, even though Lexi knew Izzy meant well. The truth always cut deeper when it was spoken softly.

Suddenly—THUMP. THUMP. THUMP.

A knock echoed from the front door.

Isabella tightened Lexi's straps, just in case, and headed down. She opened the door to a towering, headless armored figure, his plating scorched, dented, and dirt-caked.

"Umm... hi. I'm, uh... Brawn. Is Lexi here?" the armored man said, leaning slightly to look her in the eye.

Isabella slammed the door in his face. She bolted upstairs.

"Do you know this pendejo at the door? Big metal bastard calls himself Brawn."

Lexi grinned weakly. "Yeah. Let him in. Be nice, Izzy."

Isabella muttered on her way down, "We'll see. If he touches you, mami, I'll kill him."

She reopened the door.

"I don't know who you are or how you found us. But if you even think about pulling something, you'd better be ready for vengeance. I will burn you, cabrón."

Brawn knew damn well he could snap her in half. But the fire in her eyes—the fearless, wild energy—made him hesitate. Only two words came out:

"Yes, ma'am."

He ducked inside.

"Take off your armor, idiota!" Isabella barked.

"Uh... ma'am, I haven't taken it off in like... 400 years. Not sure I remember how. Don't even know if my body can function without the assist."

"Armor. Off. Now. I'm not having you crush the damn floorboards!"

Brawn hesitated, then accessed an old system file. With a hiss and a groan, the armor opened, revealing a filthy, skin-tight black suit beneath. Several neural ports ran across his body like old scars. He stepped forward—clumsy, unbalanced—like a toddler learning to walk.

"¡Dios mío...!" Isabella groaned, pinching her nostrils closed. "Take a fucking shower!"

Upstairs, Lexi heard the commotion. She smiled through the pain as Isabella unleashed her full Latina fury. No mercy. No breath. Just pure chaos.

Lexi had seen firsthand what an Aegis could do. But in under ten minutes, Isabella reduced one to a soggy, shuffling mess. She lay back on the cot, staring at the ceiling, chuckling to herself.

After thirty minutes of knocking, cursing, and fumbling, a proud Brawn stepped out of the bathroom.

"Guys! I did it! Took a while, but I showered! Feels way cleaner than the UV bath my suit gives me."

"Would you put some fucking clothes on?!" Lexi screamed, spotting his dick as he walked in.

"I don't have any clothes," Brawn replied casually.

"This is a fucking Enforcer safehouse—find some!" Isabella shrieked.

Brawn disappeared down the hall, rummaging through storage. Eventually, he found a shirt, underwear, and pants—tight as hell, but it would do.

"A bit small," he muttered, stretching the fabric over his massive frame.

He walked back down the hall, slower this time, and sheepishly poked his head around the corner.

"Uh... can I have some food?"

Lexi lifted her hand, gently placing it on Isabella's thigh. "Be nice."

Isabella exhaled sharply, controlling her temper. Then—just barely—she smiled.

"Yes. You can have some food."

Brawn headed down the stairs, inhaling the smell in the air like it was the first real breath he'd ever taken. He filled a bowl to the brim, sat down, and dug in. After four centuries of suit-fed sludge, Isabella's food might as well have been a five-star meal. He didn't stop eating.

For a moment, the house was quiet. Too quiet.

Isabella stiffened. Her gut twisted. She rushed to the window—accidentally stepping on Lexi—and pulled the curtain just enough to peek out.

"Izzy, get your fat ass off me!" Lexi yelled.

"Shhh, mami. There are drones out there, scanning the truck," Isabella whispered.

A line of drones floated silently around the truck they had stolen, scanning it for information. As Isabella looked out the window, she saw the truck's headlights come on, and it tore down the street, the drones following it.

"What the hell..." she muttered.

"What is it, Izzy?" Lexi grumbled from under her.

"I'm not sure. We may have company soon," Isabella replied.

Lexi's expression hardened. "Do we need to prep for an assault?"

"You're staying here," Isabella snapped. "I'll take the big dumbass and lock this place down."

She stormed downstairs, fire already in her veins.

"Ay, papi—put down the spoon. Can you fight?"

Brawn looked up, cheeks stuffed full. "In my suit? Yeah. Out of it... not so sure."

"¡Dios mío...!" Isabella groaned, smacking her hands together. "Mira. You're seven feet tall. Five hundred pounds. A walking wall of muscle and metal. And you can't fight?!"

"I mean... I can. Of course I can," Brawn said, puffing up. "Just let me put my suit back on."

"You don't need your suit to fight." Isabella crossed her arms, stepping closer. "Look at me. Do I need a suit to fight?"

Brawn hesitated. His eyes drifted... downward—straight to her cleavage, barely contained by the open black leather jacket.

Isabella's eyes went wide.

"¡OYE, PAPI! ¡MIS OJOS ESTÁN AQUÍ, PERRO!" she screamed, her wrath unleashed again.

Brawn flinched, shooting his gaze up to the ceiling like a soldier taking sniper fire.

"I—I wasn't trying to—uh—ma'am, sorry—!"

Suddenly, the front door hissed open.

Without hesitation, Isabella spun and fired—her pistol's bark echoing off the walls.

Thwack.

"OW!" a voice yelped.

Amber stumbled inside, rubbing her forehead. "Sergeant Rojas! You shot me!"

She rushed to the mirror, inspecting the damage.

"Now I've got a cut on my face," she pouted. "Do we have a synthetic skin gun here? Like a decent one? My symmetry's off!"

Just like that, Isabella's rage melted into pure affection.

"¡Ay, mi amor! Amber, you beautiful woman!" she cried, rushing forward and wrapping her in a tight hug.

Isabella took Amber upstairs. The moment they stepped into the room, Amber rushed to Lexi, overjoyed, and kissed her deeply.

"Amber," Lexi breathed, stunned.

"See if you can figure out what the hell's in Lexi's head," Isabella said, already turning. "I've got to find our truck and follow a lead."

"Izzy..." Lexi called after her. "RAPID is dead."

"This isn't for RAPID," Isabella replied, flashing a small, sincere smile. *"It's for you."*

Amber fidgeted. "Umm. About the truck…"

Isabella's brow tightened. "Yes?"

Amber winced. "I saw the drones scanning it when I got close to the safehouse… so I hotwired it. Drove it a few blocks…"

"And?" Isabella's voice sharpened.

"…launched it off a cliff," Amber muttered, barely audible.

Isabella blinked. *"You what?"*

"I panicked!" Amber blurted. "But I brought my own car—it's parked outside! It's not the fastest, but it runs. You can use it, Sergeant Rojas!"

"Stop with the ranks, Amber," Lexi interrupted quietly. *"The Corps. HQ. All of it—it's gone."*

Amber stepped closer to her, undeterred. "Ma'am, with all due respect. *It's only over if we say it's over.* I'm still a RAPID Infiltrator. Sure, there might only be three of us left—but low numbers never stopped us before."

Isabella's stern expression softened into a proud smile. She nodded once—then headed for the door.

But before stepping out, she whipped back around, fire in her eyes, jabbing a finger in Brawn's face.

"If anything happens to those women upstairs—anything—*no place, no sanctuary, no planet or moon will hide you from me.*"

Brawn stared, wide-eyed. For the first time in four hundred years, he was afraid. Because somehow… he knew she meant it.

Brawn swallowed hard. He'd fought in countless wars. Watched planets burn. Faced things no sane person would ever speak of again. But that woman in his face? That Infiltrator? She scared him more than any battlefield ever had.

And weirdly… he respected the hell out of her for it.

"Okay. Bye." Isabella flashed a smirk and vanished out the door.

A few seconds later, Amber heard the engine of her car start. Tires crunched gravel. Izzy was gone.

Amber walked to the window and frowned.

"Something about this doesn't feel right," she said.

Lexi nodded. "It hasn't felt right since we got here."

Outside, the wind carried the faint whir of distant drones. The streetlights flickered—some burned out, others pulsing like weak heartbeats. Above them, a billboard glitched—half an ad for Hydropure, half a government warning. The distorted screen briefly showed three female silhouettes before flickering into static.

The safehouse felt strangely quiet without Isabella's fire in it.

Amber's voice broke into a whisper. "What if we lose Izzy too..."

"We won't. Even if they capture her, they'll just give her back," Lexi said with a smile.

Amber turned back to Lexi, unsure what to say. Her fingers trembled as she reached for Lexi's hand.

"I thought I lost you," she whispered.

Lexi watched her for a moment, then gently squeezed her hand.

"You almost did," she said, her voice cracked, but her tone stayed calm. "But you're here. And so am I."

The moment lingered—two survivors, holding on to each other in a collapsing world.

CHAP_18.exe - T3ther

```
/root/sys> L3X1.exe ... [REMOVED] /init> I5A13-3-11-4.sys
status: ONLINE >> loading sequence... ...stabilizing core
...synchronizing link
```

In the outskirts of the city, Isabella drove fast.

Before HQ went up in flames, she'd been investigating a string of thefts—not jewels or cars, but parts. Old military components, government vehicle internals, and even derelict buildings gutted for their technology. On Verellii, every screw mattered. Resources were limited. These parts weren't junk—they were future lifelines.

And someone was stealing them.

Her search had led her to a name. A place.

Apex Fuelwerks.

By the time she arrived, the sun was setting, casting everything in a dusty orange haze. The garage looked ancient—its glass facade streaked with grime, the wooden door sun-bleached and splintered. Ten dead streetlights circled the broken fuel pumps. Only two still flickered, buzzing with effort.

A rusted sign dangled above the door. APEX FUELWERKS—except at night, only A L ERKS glowed.

"Charming," Isabella mutters. "In a postwar apocalypse kind of way."

From one of the side garages, music hums faintly—some gritty old track from before the war. She sees a door rolled up. Inside, a man's legs stick out from beneath something massive.

She walks over.

Her hand brushes against the vehicle's frame.

No way...

A VT-1. Pre-war. Military. Ancient.

She starts identifying modifications out loud, her voice sharp and uninvited.

"A VT-1. Seamless integration of Lancer-class armor plating. Skyreaper compressor, modified into a turbo system... oh, and those tucked-in fender mounts? Are those—machine guns?"

Under the vehicle, Roan sees caramel-toned legs in worn black sneakers walking past.

"Could charge you forty, fifty years for possession alone," she continues, circling toward the front. "Not to mention stolen government property. Curious."

She reaches the front axle, plants a foot on his crawler, and pulls him out from under the truck.

Roan slides out, blinking at the light. His eyes climb her body before meeting hers.

"So what'll it be, Roan Gravik?" she asks, arms crossed.

He stares a beat too long before standing and wiping his hands off on a rag. Calm. Dry. Not even flinching.

"I'm just glad someone can appreciate fine craftsmanship," he says coolly. "And you are...?"

"You can call me Sergeant."

Roan's mouth twitches, just slightly.

"You wouldn't know anything about the scrapyard thefts then, would you?" she asks, already knowing the answer.

"No, I don't think I do," Roan replies, folding the rag over his knuckles. "Found all these parts in the desert."

"Did you?" she says, her tone razor-thin. She pulls out a flickering holo display, projecting a recording of a VT-1 burning across a desert ridge. Driver, clearly visible.

"You wouldn't know anything about this either?" she asks.

Roan leans in, gaze unfazed. "These holos... never really clear who's behind the wheel."

Then, with careful control, he reaches around Isabella—very close—to grab a tool behind her.

She smells him. Sweat. Oil. Metal. Something familiar and human.

She lingers a second too long.

Roan catches it.

"Everything in order here, Sergeant?" he asks, eyebrow raised.

Isabella stumbles—not physically, but internally. Her pulse skips. Her breath catches. She's never been backed into a corner like this before.

"I know it's you, Roan Gravik," she snaps, trying to reclaim the upper hand.

"Is that so?" he says evenly.

She storms up to him, her face inches from his. The scent of her perfume mixes with sweat, heat clinging to her skin. He doesn't flinch. He watches her, lets her burn.

"You're lucky I need you," she growls, her voice low and fierce. "Or I'd drag your ass to lockup right now."

Roan stays steady, unfazed. He just turns, gives her a calm wave to follow.

"Listen, Sergeant," he begins. "Yeah. I've been stealing. I take parts from scrapyards, repurpose them, sell what I can, and use the credits to repair vehicles for people who can't afford it."

He gestures toward the far wall of the shop. Nailed crookedly between faded posters and rusted tools is a battered paper calendar, stained with oil and layered in dust. Dozens of dates are circled in red, each one messily labeled with short notes—"Soup kitchen," "Clinic drop," "Vacuum leak," "Fuel assist."

"The rest?" He nods toward it. "I donate it. Every week. To a soup kitchen down the block."

Isabella scans him. His heart rate is steady—calm, deliberate. Meanwhile, hers is spiraling. She clenches her jaw, forces herself to breathe through her nose.

"Bullshit."

"If you don't believe me, fine." Roan shrugs. "Come for a ride. I just finished tuning her up—I was about to take her for a spin anyway."

He gestures to the VT-1. Parked and silent, yet it looms—imposing, almost awe-inspiring.

"You might even enjoy it," he adds with a sly grin.

Isabella narrows her eyes, studying him. Still, she doesn't move.

"Okay," Roan says, hands up. "We drive to the soup kitchen. If I'm lying? You take me in. No tricks."

She says nothing. Just walks around the front of the truck and climbs inside.

The interior smells faintly of vanilla and jasmine.

Her favorite.

Get a grip, Izzy. What the hell is happening to you?

"You ready?" Roan asks, climbing in beside her, that damn smile still painted on his face.

Isabella nods.

The VT-1 roars to life, the Skyreaper compressor whining as hidden systems spool up. They drive in silence, just a few blocks, past collapsed buildings and flickering streetlights. Finally, a run-down structure comes into view—crowded with people. Families. Kids. Old men with tired eyes.

Roan parks. As he steps out, Isabella follows, tense.

"You coming in?" he asks, already halfway to the door.

Isabella climbs out of the truck and follows him in.

Inside, the building erupts.

"ROAN!"

The sound bounces off the walls. Hands reach out. Hugs wrap around him. Children cling to his legs. An old man pats him on the back. He's a damn celebrity in this place.

Isabella doesn't speak.

Roan turns to her. "Told you. I'm not a bad guy. Technically a criminal? Sure. But I'm stealing for the right reasons."

He leads her down a hallway to a quiet back room. An elderly woman sits in a rocking chair, blanket pulled to her chin, eyes fixed on a flickering holo-drama.

Roan kneels. Kisses her cheek. Hands her an envelope.

Isabella scans it.

Thousands of credits.

The woman smiles. She speaks softly—words Isabella doesn't catch. She hugs Roan, kisses both cheeks, and hands him a small container of food.

They head back out. Roan gently shoos the kids off his vehicle, laughing. He pulls a worn sack from the truck bed and begins handing out candy, toys, and tiny carved trinkets.

Laughter erupts.

Joy ripples across the cracked pavement.

And Isabella just watches, arms crossed, stunned.

In all of Verellii's darkness...

Here, somehow—a man of light.

There was no pretending. No PR stunt. No performative charity.

This man... meant it.

In a world like Verellii, where hope was a currency rarer than water, this kind of light was scarce—unfamiliar. And maybe that's why it felt foreign to her.

Roan turns and tosses the empty sack into the back of the truck. He brushes his hands off on his pants—slow, casual slaps, like the moment didn't matter.

Then he turns—and catches her watching him.

Her gaze locks him in place.

And for the first time... he really sees her.

Her brown eyes catch the dying light just right, warm and glowing like molten bronze. Sweat clings to her collarbones, gliding down between her breasts beneath her open jacket. Her hips sway subtly, confident and effortless, as if the chaos of Verellii had forged her into something bulletproof and beautiful.

He looks at her lips. Full. Soft. Slightly parted.

He wonders how they'd taste.

It hits him in the chest. Like a punch. Or maybe an arrow.

She notices. Runs a hand through her hair—slow, casual, like she's giving him permission without saying a word.

Roan straightens and clears his throat, trying to mask the thunder in his heartbeat.

"So what now, Sergeant?" he asks, tone cool.

She pauses, eyes still locked on his.

"...Isabella."

He raises a brow. "What?"

"If I'm going to trust you, you don't get to call me Sergeant. You call me Isabella."

He tests the name, slow, almost reverent. "Isabella."

She nods, then steps closer—just a few feet between them now.

"I need your help."

He doesn't say anything. Just listens.

"There's a woman back at the safehouse. Lexi Hayes. She's... not like most people. Her body's rejecting something. Or maybe fighting it—I don't know."

Isabella's voice drops, softer now. "I trust her with my life. But something in her is breaking down. And you're the only one I know who might understand what's wrong with her."

Roan studies her. His eyes flick briefly to her trembling hands—subtle, but there. Her tough exterior's cracking just enough to let the truth bleed through.

"I'm not a doctor," he says carefully.

"I think it's her cybernetics," Isabella says, her voice low but urgent. "Like her body's rejecting them—or they're fighting back. I don't know. But something's wrong, and it's getting worse."

She draws a shaky breath.

"She's not just another person," she adds. *"She's the reason I'm still standing."*

A long silence.

Roan watches the kids chase each other through the dusk, their laughter echoing down the crumbling street.

He glances at the sack now empty in his truck, then turns to Isabella—her lips parted slightly, her eyes still locked on the scene with something between awe and disbelief.

The silence stretches.

Then Roan speaks, voice quiet, grounded.

"I'm with you," he says. "But I need to come back... for them. And for you."

He doesn't wait for a reaction. Just turns, opens the truck door, and climbs in like he didn't just let something slip.

Isabella blinks. Her mouth opens slightly—no words come.

Did he just say... for me?

The hell was that supposed to mean?

She stares at the truck for a moment, trying to shake off the heat in her chest. It's nothing. Doesn't matter.

And yet...

She exhales and climbs in beside him.

"I need to grab some things from the garage," he says, flicking on the ignition.

Roan shifts gears fast—his brain already working.

They drive just a couple of blocks before pulling into the garage. Roan parks, hops out, and vanishes into the back. He grabs a duffel, starts sweeping tools and supplies into it—moving fast, efficient.

"You want me to meet you where she is? Or come with you?"

"I want you to come with me," Isabella replies instantly. "I don't want to waste any time."

"Sounds good to me," Roan says, trying to sound calm—even as his pulse quickens just being next to her.

Then—"Shit."

"What?" Isabella calls.

"I don't have a Vantrix."

"A what?" She squints like he just started speaking another language.

"Oh, right—it's the military term. You probably know it as a neurotrace. Handheld, silver casing, glows with lights—different colors depending on the reading? Small screen? Front end shaped like a bowl or parabolic lens?"

Isabella stares blankly. "You're just saying words now."

Roan rushes over and grabs her hands, suddenly urgent. She instinctively pulls back, but he holds firm—gentle, not forceful. Her gaze flicks down to their joined hands, then back up to his face.

"Isabella," he says softly.

"Izzy," she corrects, quietly but firm.

"Izzy," he repeats, like it means something now. "I know it's your duty to keep things under control... but I know where one is. The Vantrix. It's in the place you told me not to go. But I swear to you—it'll help me save your friend's life."

Her eyes narrow, fierce. "What do we need to do?"

***

An hour later, the VT-1 rolls up to a quiet, sealed facility.

"Med-Store," reads the faded blue sign, buzzing faintly in the dark.

Roan puts the truck in park. Turns to her.

"It's in there," he says, nodding toward the structure. "They store old and decommissioned medical gear—machines, tools, stuff most people forgot existed."

He hesitates. Then adds, "I wouldn't ask you to do something I wouldn't do myself. But I can't get in unnoticed. No augmentations, no cybernetics." He continues.

He exhales.

"This is the only place I can think of that might have one. Only other option is a hospital—and I'm not stealing from people who actually need help."

He looks at her.

And for the first time in a while... he's not flirting.

He's trusting her.

Isabella slips out of the truck.

In one swift motion, she leaps over the ten-foot perimeter fence like it's nothing—fluid, silent, inhumanly fast.

Roan watches from the cab, mouth parted slightly. "Okay," he murmurs to himself, "wow."

Isabella uses the metal window awnings as footholds, scaling the wall with ease. Her movements are precise and efficient, each step calculated. She reaches the roof and scans for access. A vent. Perfect.

She drops low and slides herself in—

Thunk.

Her hips catch.

"¡Carajo...!" she hisses through gritted teeth, glaring over her shoulder like her ass personally betrayed her.

With a crunch, she curls upward, grabs the vent bars, and bends them just enough to slip through. Her legs snake in behind her.

Below, she calculates everything.

Height: 20 feet

Drop point: metal ducting, 1/16-inch thick

Echo radius: 100 feet if flat-footed.

Solution: wedge in the duct, lower slowly.

She stretches her limbs, wedging herself carefully between the metal walls, inching downward with her hands and feet spread like a spider.

Dust. Heat. Cobwebs.

She breathes through her nose, ignoring the spiders crawling through her curly hair.

Eventually, a vent ahead glows faintly with artificial light. Voices filter through—dozens of them. Serious. A man barking orders.

She slithers toward it, deadly quiet.

Like an owl in the night.

She peers through the slats.

And gasps.

Chief Rhydian Graevos.

What the hell are you doing here... she thinks.

Below, the Chief moves like a commander on a warpath—stoic, methodical. He walks along a line of people.

If you could still call them that.

Their bodies are torn. Stitched. Bruised. Scarred beyond recognition. Some twitch as if half-alive. Others... stare blankly ahead.

Isabella scans so she can hear what he's saying.

"The dead offer nothing new," Graevos murmurs, hands clasped behind his back, continuing walking around them. "Too complicated. Too fragile."

One of the people starts to run. They get five feet before tripping—sweating profusely, eyes wide, crying.

Graevos walks over to him as the man starts to crawl.

He slowly walks up behind the man, crushing one of his feet.

"Coward," he says calmly, as he shoots the man in the back of the head.

The man's movements stop. Blood spray lines the concrete. A pool starts to form. Graevos holsters his weapon and continues to inspect the people in front of him...

He stops beside one of the trembling survivors. A young woman—barely twenty.

 "But the living..." he continues, eyes raking over her form like she's a prototype on a bench. *So much more potential. So many to choose from.*"

He lifts her chin aggressively with his hand, squeezing her cheeks until her lips pucker. He turns her face side to side. Her body shakes violently, almost convulsing as she tries to stay still—but a tear slips free. It rolls down her cheek, glinting in the overhead light.

Graevos watches it fall.

He lets go of her face. She starts tearing uncontrollably. He backs up and points.

Two figures move in. They grab her by the arms and begin dragging her out of the room. Her feet scrape the floor. She doesn't scream. But she does look back, one last time, eyes wide with quiet pleading, tears streaming down her face.

A door slams in the distance.

He doesn't look at them like people. Not even enemies. Just material.

After a while of sheer terror, Graevos settles on just four. "These four will do."

Isabella's stomach tightens. Breathing dust and dread through clenched teeth, she knows...

She's not supposed to be here.

Not for this.

"Congratulations," he says proudly. "You four are the next evolution in Infiltrator and Enforcer technology."

The two men and two women stare at the floor. No emotion. No clothing. No humility.

"Take them," he says, waving his hand. The medical team comes in and covers them with blankets, escorting them to a waiting truck.

After an hour goes by, Isabella—patiently waiting—hears and sees no one. The automatic lights have turned off, and no one has come or gone since.

She carefully and as silently as she can, breaks the bolts holding the vent cover on and drops the 30 feet to the ground, bending her knees to absorb the impact. All that echoes is a small tick across the room.

Isabella stays low, engages her night vision, and keeps her head on a swivel. She is an Infiltrator—but if Chief Graevos got a hold of her, she'd be dead.

She looks around for cameras using purposeful movements, ensuring they don't track her.

"I have to know," she says as she goes to where the slamming door noise came from. She rips the locks off the door, as red and orange light pours out.

As she walks in, all she can see is a circular grate with light coming from up under.

No noise... wait, there's something—eating?

She gets closer and sees a stairwell pulled up out of reach from whatever, or whomever, is below.

She looks down.

"¡Dios mío... no puede ser!"

The deceased were thrown down, piles of dead bodies strewn across the room below her.

People who are alive are feeding on the dead, crying, and in despair when they're done.

She puts in a call to VPSD, hoping that they aren't corrupted and answer the call.

She rushes back to the storage area, the vivid scene burned into her eyes.

For the first time in a long time, she cries.

***

The terror those people were put through—the atrocities they committed... just to stay alive.

"Focus," she tells herself as she continues her search.

She eventually comes to an area that says, "Reusable goods," and scans the boxes with her x-ray.

"Gotcha," she says, seeing what Roan had described.

She carefully climbs on the shelves, slipping her fingers into the crease of the crate, silently prying the lid off.

The lights turn on.

A truck pulls in aggressively, its tires screeching.

She was quiet enough... what happened?

She jumps down and ducks behind a pile of metal crates.

The truck comes to a halt as a woman—an Infiltrator recruit—is dragged out of the vehicle.

"Where is she?" The orange-eyed Enforcer asks.

"I'm not telling you shit," she says, spitting blood at him.

"I will kill you," the Enforcer says. "Tell me where L3X1 is now! And I may spare your pathetic life."

Isabella scans the woman—it's Liza Abramov. She hadn't even been through CRIS training yet. No augmentations. Nothing. She was flesh and blood.

Liza knelt on the ground, silent.

"AHHHHHHHHHHHHHHHHH!" a man's voice yells.

Isabella looks over—she sees Roan, charging the Enforcer with a metal pipe.

The Enforcer turns around and smacks Roan, sending him flying into some nearby wooden boxes. Roan doesn't move.

The Enforcer goes back to Liza... "So, what will it be?"

Liza looks into the Enforcer's eyes and, with a smirk, says, "L3X1 isn't scared of you. Neither am I. And by the way..."

She coughs up blood.

"You punch like my grandma."

"So be it."

The Enforcer crushes her head into the concrete, gore replacing where a young woman used to be.

The Enforcer walks over to the truck, punches it, and proceeds to get inside and drive away.

Isabella grabs the Vantrix and rushes over to Roan. She X-rays his body—three broken ribs. Not bad for getting smacked by an Enforcer.

"You're a crazy man," she says with a light smile, seeing he's still breathing.

She throws him over her shoulder and runs around the building looking for the truck.

It wasn't where he dropped her off.

So where...

There!

She spots the VT-1 sitting behind some bushes to conceal it.

She puts him in the passenger seat, buckles him in, and makes her
way to the safehouse.

CHAP_19.exe - Overheat

Isabella drove to the safehouse as quickly as possible, Roan groaning in the front seat, still unconscious.

When he wakes, he's lying in a room, a ceiling fan circling above him. There are streetlights outside, people yelling, glass bottles breaking randomly, as cars rush past occasionally.

Where am I? he asks himself while sitting up and clutching his head, his vision blurry.

He looks down at the bandages that cover almost his entire torso. He can hear whispering—occasional laughing—from another room in the house. He gets up, throws on a shirt and some shorts he found in a closet—they're a bit big, but at least it's something.

He walks into the room and stops at the sight.

A blonde woman sits upright on the bed, her legs strapped down, arms and hands bound tight at her sides. Beside her, a brown-haired woman with glasses is calmly digging through her head, while Isabella stands nearby. The three of them laugh and joke together, chatting as if nothing unusual is happening. On the floor by the bed rests the bag of supplies he carried in—the stolen Vantrix among them.

"What... uh... is going on?" Roan asks.

Isabella turns around. "Well, good morning."

"Who, what, are you guys?" Roan asks, still stunned by the scene.

"I guess it's time to tell you the entire truth. We're all RAPID Infiltrators," she says. "That's Lexi, our commander, Recruit Amber, and you already know me."

"Well, that explains quite a lot," Roan replies.

Isabella watches his face, his movements, and hears his voice. Other than him wincing from the pain every once in a while, there's no fear, no judgment, no worry at all. He has accepted them for what they are.

"What can I do to help?" Roan asks.

Amber fills everyone in on what she's found with Lexi's condition—or lack thereof—and there's no understanding of why Lexi is displaying the symptoms she is. There is clearly a problem, but she just can't identify it. Roan says he can take over checking her, using his mechanical skill and the stolen Vantrix to help find the issue. He asks the girls to leave so he can work in peace.

Amber refuses but starts to walk downstairs anyway. They hear a loud bang and then turn to see her lugging a huge holoprojector up the stairs.

"Is that a surveillance screen?" Lexi asks.

"Yeah!" Amber cheerfully exclaims. "I'm not sitting here bored watching someone else do work. I want to watch the holo and then maybe a movie—as long as you're good with it, Lex?"

Lexi lets out a small smile, thinking of how Amber's spirits are never dampened. She feels the wind flowing through her open head from a small fan.

That's a strange feeling, she thinks.

Amber wires the holo using the transmitter, as Isabella attaches her makeshift antenna to get a signal. Roan gets his tools together and perches behind Lexi. He starts his scans as the holoprojector sputters to life.

As Roan looks inside—neural networks run through her entire head, her brain is surrounded by a bio-shield, a mix of her own organics and something not quite mechanical. It looks like a computer and a human had a baby together. As he looks through her head, he realizes he may not be as qualified for this task as they originally hoped. He looks over at Isabella watching the holo... and thinks, *I at least have to try—she believes in me.*

"That's right, Ken," the news anchor on the holoprojector says, "in other news, tragedy struck The Rows, where an anonymous tip that was placed led the VPSD to find what appears to be a cataclysmic turn of events. People locked in cages, mutilated—some alive, some dead, some in between. Field reporter Suzanne Franks is on the scene."

"Thanks, Brit. As you can see behind me, the VPSD has swarmed this area. They report that possibly hundreds of people are in the site, being used for an unknown purpose. People won't speak about who or what did this, but one thing is clear—they have a guardian angel watching over them. I have an eyewitness who caught a look at someone fleeing the scene."

"Oh no," Isabella says, not blinking as she watches the screen.

"Yep, I saw 'er. Runnin' away that-a-way," a man says, pointing off-camera. "And let me tell ya... the one thing that threw me off—" He leans into the camera like it's a conspiracy. "Was how big 'er ass was. Whizzin' away! Ooooooohweeeeeee!" He laughs into the camera, slapping his own thigh for emphasis. "You don't never forget somethin' like that!"

Isabella buries her face in her hands.

"Oh my god."

Roan grins through his cracked ribs as he looks up from Lexi's head.

"Man's got a good set of eyes," he chuckled.

"I'm going to kill him," Isabella says sternly, face still in her hands.

"Me or him?" Roan asks, concerned.

"Maybe both," Isabella snaps, cocking her head to the side with attitude.

"Did you see anything else?" the exhausted reporter asks.

"Yep. She had a feller up on 'er shoulder. Runnin' with him up there like he weighed nothin'." He scratches his temple, slightly moving his hat higher. "Jump'd in a fancy truck, it went rushin' away, t'wards the city."

"Well, you heard it here, folks. This mysterious woman—villain or hero? No exterior camera footage was seen with her on it, and all inside footage was erased. Back to you in the studio, Brit."

"Thanks, Suzanne. Next up: is your Hydropure causing your skin to turn green? Experts say that's not all it's doing—next up on News 9."

Click.

The screen goes off, and everyone looks at Isabella, face buried in her hands. Laughter erupts from everyone, causing Brawn to peek in.

"Did I miss something?" Brawn says with a smile.

"NO!" Isabella screams as she slams the door in his face.

"Holy shit, that guy was huge!" Roan exclaims.

Lexi explains to him everything she, Brawn, the Aegis, and the other Infiltrators have been through over the past few days. After that, Isabella fills Lexi in on everything she and Roan experienced.

"Not Graevos?" Lexi says in disbelief. "Why would he do that? He was always so caring and helpful to me—like a mentor."

"I don't know, mami. But I know what I saw," Isabella says. Lexi can see the truth and pain in her eyes.

"Okay, so here's what we know," Lexi starts to say. "T.N.O. is out there, and they're serving an unknown purpose. However, we do know they hate cybernetically enhanced individuals. HQ is wiped out. Graevos is now an enemy. Unsure about Gavin and Cybrix Thorne. I did see Captain Thorne at the building where we were captured, Izzy. Burton Marx is dead. The Union is involved. And lastly, I assume someone inside Neuron Energy Medical Center put something in my head. *Lots of fronts to cover.*"

A loud beeping sound comes from the Vantrix, its neuroscan revealing something tiny in a section of Lexi's brain. On the screen, it's barely visible—a circuit card. Not biological. Not machine. Something in between. It has a small antenna protruding from it.

"I have to remove it," Roan says. "Umm... Lexi, is it? Do we have any anesthetics so I can put you under?"

Lexi lets out a laugh. *"As long as you don't hit bone, I'll be fine."*

Roan lets out a small and nervous laugh, seeing it's on an organic piece of brain. He doesn't tell them. He starts operating.

"I can help!" Amber says to him. "My hands are very steady—at least more than yours," she notes, while looking at Roan's shaking hands.

"I would appreciate that. I'm used to working on machines, not people."

Roan and Amber work diligently: a small incision, then a small opening. Seconds feel like hours, the precision involved taking its toll.

"HOLD THE LIGHT STILL!" Amber barked at him.

Roan straightens up, ribs screaming in pain, but he holds the flashlight still. Then Amber reaches in, and a sound like tape coming off paper fills the small gap—she pulls out a microchip, a light on it faintly flickering, as if sending signals... or receiving them.

"It looks heavily advanced," Isabella says, leaning in.

"If they wanted to control Lexi, this was probably their best shot," Roan says.

Isabella takes the chip, crushing it between her fingers. Tiny sparks fly out, fading as they reach the floor.

Amber patches Lexi up as Isabella removes her restraints.

"I'll watch her tonight," Amber says, covering Lexi in a blanket and snuggling next to her.

***

Isabella steps out of their room, quietly making her way to an empty room down the hallway. As her door closes, she turns, peeking through the crack, watching Roan disappear into his room, his shoulders weighed down by the events of the day.

Hours pass by.

Roan lies in bed, staring at the ceiling fan, when he hears his doorknob turn, followed by a soft click. The door eases open, just enough for a shadowy figure to slip inside, closing it again without a sound. Streetlight spills through the window, sketching the figure in golden light.

Isabella.

She steps closer to the bed, the glow catching the curve of her thighs beneath a long tee that barely covers her. Barefoot, she moves on her toes, each step silent. Roan watches every movement, his heart beating erratically in anticipation. The fabric of the shirt offers only hints of her body's curves, the rest left to his imagination.

Slowly, she climbs over him, pulling the tee up as she straddles his waist. She places her hands on his chest, looking down at him. "Why'd you come into that warehouse?" she whispers.

His voice rasps. "To check on you... then to rescue Liza... and I—" he pauses only a moment. *"I wanted to be with you."*

She pulls her shirt over her head and tosses it to the floor.

Roan's breath catches. Her breasts are perfect—soft curves against the dim light, her skin glowing warm bronze. Not just beautiful, stunning. Every inch of her makes him ache with want. His eyes trace the dip of her waist, the swell of her hips. She is more breathtaking than he ever could've imagined—beyond every guess, every stolen glance, every dream.

She kisses him.

He winces slightly—her hand has shifted and caught his bruised ribs. Her eyes widen, suddenly gentle, but he shakes his head. "Don't stop."

She smiles, her lips parted slightly, soft and glistening. She reaches between her thighs, guiding him into her slowly, carefully. Her thighs tremble as she sinks onto him, inch by inch, gasping softly. She bites her lip, her eyes fluttering closed. She takes every inch of him, savoring the slow burn of pleasure building within her.

Roan groans beneath her, head tilting back. "Fuck..."

She moves—slow and rhythmic—hips grinding, eyes half-lidded. Sweat builds between them. Her hands rest on his chest; his fingers grip her waist. Every roll of her hips pulls a moan from deep in his throat. The old bedframe groans in rhythm, rattling the boards beneath them.

The moment grows desperate—hot, raw, breathless. Plaster dust sifts from the ceiling with each sharp movement, unnoticed in their frenzy.

His hands move down, cupping her ass, guiding her as their pace deepens. Her moans grow louder, her movements more erratic. She grips his shoulder, her nails dragging across his skin.

When she tightens around him and cries out his name, he can't hold back—pulling her tight, finishing inside her with a labored moan. The walls seem to shudder with them, every creak echoing their release.

They stay that way for a long time. Breathing. Trembling. Tangled. Kissing. Embracing each other.

Eventually, she curls up against his side, lips against his collarbone. Her leg drapes over his. His left hand rests above them on the pillow. She reaches up, fingers brushing his. No words are spoken. Just intimate silence.

The kind of closeness that didn't need a future spelled out.

It already existed.

The next morning, Roan wakes to the soft warmth of Isabella's breath against him, her body wrapped snugly around his. Carefully, he shifts out from under her. Once out of bed, he leans down and kisses her lips.

He heads to the closet. It's packed with oversized shirts, pants, and underwear—fit for an Enforcer—not for a man his size. He pulls on a shirt and a pair of shorts, tying the drawstring as tight as it will go so they don't slide off his waist.

Downstairs, Lexi and Amber sit practically on top of each other, whispering and giggling. Brawn takes up most of the table with his sheer bulk.

Roan smiles at the scene, grabs a ration pack from the cabinet, and tosses it in the heater. Once it pings, he dumps the contents into a bowl and gives it a sniff.

"What the hell is this supposed to be...?" he mutters, then shrugs as he takes a bite.

His eyebrows lift. Huh. Not bad. He nods slightly, approving of the mystery sludge.

He notices Lexi and Amber whispering again as they sneak glances at him.

"What's the secret?" Roan asks.

"You want to know the secret?" Brawn grumbles. "I'm clearly a fifth wheel!"

"What are you talking about?" Roan replies, fully sarcastic.

"Let's just say I need a damn face shield if I'm gonna sleep down here," Brawn snaps.

"A face shield?" Roan blinks.

"Yeah... a face shield," Brawn growls. "I heard you and Isabella last night. You two were fucking so hard, dust was coming off the goddamn ceiling."

Lexi nearly spits her drink. Amber clutches her side, gasping between laughs, the two of them whispering like schoolgirls.

"AND YOU TWO!" Brawn snaps, turning toward them. "I need earmuffs for you, too! All I heard was giggling, shifting, and... wet. Like two drunk dolphins wrestling in a kiddie pool."

Lexi and Amber freeze—eyes wide, but their grins don't fade. Totally unfazed by the pissed-off Aegis.

Just then, Isabella walks in—an oversized tee draped over her frame, loose enough to tease but not quite long enough to hide everything. With each step, the hem rides up slightly, revealing the soft curve of her ass and a glimpse of tight black lace panties peeking out from underneath.

She strolls up behind Roan, turns his face toward her, and kisses him. Deep. Passionate. Unbothered by the fact that he's mid-bite.

"OOOH," Lexi and Amber squeal, whispering frantically again.

Isabella doesn't flinch. She straddles his lap sideways, wraps her arms around his neck, and kisses him again—longer this time—before rising to grab some food.

Roan, still chewing, just grins.

No words. Just bliss.

As the team of misfits finishes their breakfast and Brawn cools off, Lexi starts, "Okay... let's get down to business."

Everyone straightens up, including Isabella—who is sitting on Roan's lap instead of the extra chair at the table.

Lexi pulls out a page that lists several factions: Kurogane Syndicate, The Union, Earth, RAPID, The Natural Order, and Neuron Energy.

"These are our current adversaries," she begins. "We know that someone in Neuron Energy planted something in my head. Chief Graevos is doing something sinister to make new Infiltrators and Enforcers. The current Enforcers are all under some influence from the control cubes. We know someone had knowledge of the Sanctum and worked with the Union to dig that tunnel.

"The Kurogane Syndicate and Neuron Energy are working together to obtain energy weapons and move them to Earth-funded locations. I had a slate that supposedly contained coordinates to an Earth location... but I lost it fighting a mech."

"Excuse me... you said Earth is involved in all this?" Roan asks, clearly worried about their odds.

Isabella's face drops—disappointed that he isn't exactly thrilled by this turn of events.

"Umm... Captain," Brawn says.

"What is it?" Lexi asks.

"I don't think you lost it. I picked this up from those tunnels after you got thrown against the wall."

Brawn walks to his suit—his movements far more natural now—presses a button, and with a hiss, a panel slides open, revealing a hidden compartment. He pulls out a slate.

"Is this it?" he asks hopefully.

"Possibly," Lexi says, taking it and studying the surface before speaking clearly: "BURTON MARX."

VOICE PRINT MISMATCH — LOCK ENGAGED, the slate chirped back.

"I've got you," Roan says, gently taking it from her hands. "These are easy to jury-rig. Give me a couple hours. Izzy, want to lend a hand?"

"OOOH," Lexi and Amber chime together.

Isabella's fiery stare snaps their way.

They only giggle harder as she sighs and follows Roan upstairs.

A few hours later, Roan and Isabella come down, the slate now in hand. The rest of the team sits around the holo Amber has dragged back downstairs, plugging it into its original wall port.

"So, I've got good news, great news, and really bad news," Roan explains, standing in the doorway with Isabella beside him.

"Good news: got it unlocked. Great news: it does have coordinates.

Bad news: it isn't for an Earth location. It's for a place called the Yūgen Club."

"I know where that is," Lexi says. "It's on Level 2—near The Void and across from SynthSkin. Does it say why the coordinates go there?"

"Umm... yeah," Roan says. "It's for a delivery of laser weaponry—and a couple other things. It was ordered by someone with the initials 'B.M.' and shipped to an 'S.A.' Do those initials ring any bells?"

"Yeah, B.M. is Burton Marx," Amber replies. "But I'm not sure who S.A. is."

"So what's Burton's deal?" Roan asks.

"Burton Marx is a sick, demented psychopath I had the absolute pleasure of killing," Lexi says—cold, but proud. "The only person I can think of with the initials S.A. is Shogo Akiyama, the CEO of Neuron Energy. I met him. Seemed like a really nice and genuine person. I don't think he'd be wrapped up in this."

"So what's our next move, Captain?" Roan asks, his military background showing.

"You're staying with us?" Isabella asks. "I thought once you fixed Lexi and our deal was done, you'd go back."

"I, uh... have other priorities now," Roan says, letting his fingers graze hers—just barely. And for a moment, he forgets how to breathe.

Isabella blushes. And Lexi can tell—Isabella is overjoyed with the news.

"The slate was supposed to give coordinates to an Earth location. Unfortunately, since we have no other leads... our target is the Yūgen Club," Lexi says.

"Let's get a plan together."

"Izzy, since we can't be sure what we will find in this club, I need you to get all eyes on you. I've already had run-ins with all these factions; you will be less suspect. Roan, you are with Isabella. I want you two to be as distracting as possible."

Isabella and Roan smile, then their faces harden, ready for the mission.

"Amber, you will watch the street with Brawn. Brawn, no armor, but we need you out there. Your towering appearance will help with distraction, and if we need you, you'll be our tank if shit goes south."

Brawn nods in understanding.

"We will go in two days. In the meantime, we prep, finalize, and stake out the area, collect our findings, and then execute. Any questions? No? Prep, and we will meet back here the night of."

Lexi is met with nods of approval, thumbs up, and yes ma'ams.

***

The next day.

Amber discreetly stakes out the Yūgen Club from across the street, parked at a tiny food cart tucked beside the glowing SynthSkin façade. Above, the panels over Level 2 stand open, flooding the district with harsh sunlight—meant to keep residents alive with their daily dose of vitamin D in the middle of the neon canyon.

She sits at a rickety umbrella-topped table in front of the cart, sipping on a chilled Strawberry Watermelon VitaRush, a fizzy, neon-pink drink that buzzes faintly as it hits her tongue.

She glances at a glowing thermometer on the cart's display.

145 degrees.

"Fuck, it's hot," she mutters, swiping irritably at the sweat under her chest. "My fucking boobs are so sweaty."

She tips back another gulp of the fizzing drink, eyes never leaving the club's entrance, when—

"OH. MY. GAWD!"

Amber freezes.

No. No. No. Please, not her.

CHAP_20.exe - D3C0Y

A familiar voice squealed right next to her. She turned her head just slightly—blue hair, mini skirt, heels way too tall for Level 2's cracked sidewalks. Mia.

"Hey, Mia," Amber muttered, already bracing herself.

"Whatcha doin'? Wait—don't tell me. You're goin' to the club, right? It's nice. I work there sometimes. I hate it. The drinks are weak and the clients are creeps, but like—money talks, y'know? You want in? I can getcha in. Wait—where's Pixie? Is she meetin' you here? OH. MY. GAWD. Is this a surprise date?! You two are still a thing, right? Wait—don't tell me you broke up. *Please say no.* You two are, like, adorable together. I can talk to her, getchu guys back together."

Amber blinked slowly, like she was trying to reboot her brain.

"Yes, we're dating."

"Mia... I thought you worked at SynthSkin."

"I do! But Yūgen pays wayyy more. Like, way way more. SynthSkin whores me out to whoever flashes creds. Which is fine—I mean, until the uggos show up. Had one guy ask me to just suck his toes. Fuckin' weirdo."

Amber groaned. "Mia... who are you seeing at the Yūgen Club?"

"Ugh. Some no-names with creds, but I mostly come here for this pervy dude who calls himself The Samurai." She rolled her eyes and popped her gum. "Real name's Shogo Akiyama. Left his computer open. I like creds. Blackmail gets a lot of creds. Big-shot CEO, thinks he's smooth, but he's creepy. Like... he does this one thing where he keeps tryna jam his fingers in my—"

"MIA. STOP."

Amber's voice cracked through the air. People glanced over.

Mia blinked, unfazed. "Too much? Yeah, my therapist—Dr. Marsipin, or Marsipan, or Minispin, I dunno—but she says I overshare. Says it's trauma. That I'm tryna reach out or whatever. Like I'm dying inside from suppressed emotions. But like, people listen, so that means they wanna hear it, right? I mean, if they didn't, they'd say somethin'. But they don't. So I just keep goin'. You get it. You get it, right Amber? Of course she does, Mia."

Amber pinched the bridge of her nose.

 "Wait. Did you say Shogo Akiyama owns this place?"

"Yup! Got his own penthouse on the top floor. Real exotic, like—silk, velvet, and like this stuff called 'pelt.' Is that an animal? If it were on Level 1, you could see like... everything. Like okay Amber, imagine I'm you, right? Look wayyy out there. You could see that far. Crazy, right?!"

Amber grabbed Mia's wrist. "Come with me. Pixie's gonna want to talk to you."

"OOOOH MY GAWD, YES! Pixie! I loooove Pixie! She's so nice, and cool, and beautiful. Uhh—if I was a lesbian like you, Amber—not that anything's wrong with that—I'm just sayin' if I was, I'd bang the shit outta Pixie. Mia, you dumb bitch, you can't say things like that. People get mad."

Mia continued rambling even as Amber dragged her away—heels clicking, voice echoing, and all.

The door to the safehouse creaked open as the room was instantly flooded with Mia's nonstop, chaotic rambling.

"Umm, Amber... why is Mia here?" Lexi asked, already regretting it.

"She works at the Yūgen Club," Amber replied with a strained smile.

"Mia, I thought you worked at SynthSkin?" Lexi asked, brow raised.

"Lexi—no—" Amber began, but Mia cut her off like a freight train.

"PIXIE!!! You look exactly the same! Not all dirty like Amber—your skin's, like, perfect! How do you keep it so clean?! Focus, Mia. Focus. Yeah, I still work at SynthSkin, but they also got me fuckin' some people at Yūgen. Not a bad gig, but..." Her eyes locked on Brawn. "Damn. That dude is huge."

"I bet you have a huge dick!" Mia blurted.

Brawn, completely caught off guard, stammered, "Umm... I—I don't know?"

"Yeah, it's big," Lexi said flatly. "Now continue with what you were saying."

"I wanna fuck him," Mia said without hesitation, then paused. "But wait—what were we talking about?... Oh! Right! This old dude, Shogo Akiyama, he likes to stick his fingers in my—"

"NO! MIA!" Amber snapped. "Tell her about the penthouse!"

"Oh, so it's got velvet and sil—"

"About the computer, Mia," Amber said through gritted teeth.

"Oh! Right! So he's got this computer—it's an Exceleron AD-159. Super fancy. I had a 156 a long time ago. It was fast—I used it for gaming. You ever played Trash Bandit? OH MY GAWD, you gotta try it, Pixie!"

"Mia! What's on the computer?" Amber demanded.

"Nothin's on it."

"Wait—there aren't any files?"

"Not on it, silly! They're in it. Like, digital. You don't put files on a computer—they just sorta live in there, but you can't touch 'em or anything. But you can take 'em out, like, on a flash drive or somethin'. Digital means it's electric—but not, like, you'll get shocked or anything."

"Fuck…" Lexi muttered, rubbing her temples. "What do the digital files say?"

"Ohh, like lots of stuff. Drugs, weapons, outposts, shipments, naked pics of me—don't look at those! Just kidding. You saw my titties the other night, right guys? Got a couple of 'em, me suckin' dick," she added with a wink.

"How do we get into the penthouse?" Lexi asked, tone now serious.

"There's like three ways. Soo, all the elevators go to different floors, but one has a basement button—and get this—it doesn't even go to the basement. It goes to the penthouse! But you gotta scan a special card. Like this." Mia pulled a red, white, and gold card from her bra—its colors matched the casino's theme.

"Or, you can go up top. There's a balcony—I got asked to throw my legs over the railing so he could fuck me while people watched. I let him do it, but he was gross. Still gave me, like, 20 extra creds."

"Mia… focus," Lexi said.

"So that elevator, or the balcony, or there's emergency stairs—but they're locked, armored as hell, and you need a key."

"Mia… don't say a word of this to anyone. For me?" Lexi asked.

"5,000 creds," Mia said, her voice suddenly calm and cold.

The shift was instant. No ranting. No smile. Just a quiet, calculated demand.

Lexi flicked her the 5,000 credits. Mia stood up, adjusted her skirt, and headed for the door.

"Thanks, guys. Pleasure doin' business with ya," she said flatly, as she walked out of the safehouse.

"…Did she just fucking play us?" Amber muttered, stunned.

***

The next day, Roan sat at the casino bar working on his second cocktail, looking for cameras and any guard movements that could help with this particular mission. Isabella had told him to be in the bar for this part. He dressed simply—worn khaki overshirt, black tee, black cargo pants draped over a set of combat boots. Understated. Ordinary. Isabella told him to dress normally, then said she was going shopping. No further explanation.

"How is this helping with the distraction?" he muttered into his glass as he took another drink.

Just then the casino shook violently—a low rumble that rattled glasses, shifted chips on tables, and silenced conversations. Patrons ducked, thinking it was an earthquake. The chandeliers trembled, casting fractured light across velvet floors.

A RAPID gunship hovered outside the main entrance, engines howling but never touching down. Heat and wind blasted through the casino doors as they opened. A woman stepped smoothly out of the gunship, it ascending as soon as both feet were on the pavement.

She walked through the doors forced open by the gunship's thrusters.

Isabella Rojas, dressed in a deep crimson gown that plunged down her chest—showing full cleavage and the soft dip of her belly button. It clung to her hips like it had been sewn in place, splitting at both sides to her ankles, revealing toned golden legs with every stride. Gold hoop earrings shimmered. Her curls bounced with each calculated step—one foot in front of the other like a runway model. She wasn't walking. She was commanding.

The maître d' stepped forward nervously. "Madam, can I—"

She flashed her palm in his face and kept walking. Eyes forward. Dismissed.

A man in a tux stepped in her way.

"Can I buy you a drink?"

"No," she replied coolly, "but you can buy us a drink," she added, pointing toward Roan.

The man blinked. "That guy? Are you serious?"

"Serious as the heart attack I'm going to give him when I walk over and kiss his lips," she said, brushing past him without a second glance.

The man rolled his eyes, scoffed, and walked away defeated.

She reached Roan, pulled him in by the collar, and kissed him—deep and slow.

When she pulled away, Roan looked dazed. "Uhh... wow. You look... wow."

"Exactly what I was going for," she smirked.

"So... what's the plan?" Roan asked.

"I'm gonna flirt with every creep in this place. And if one touches me—you beat the shit out of them."

"And if I get my very normal ass kicked?"

She grinned, grabbed his chin. *"Then, papisito, I'll save my bebé."*

Roan swallowed hard. Her fingers grazed his jaw—she was close. Too close.

"That should cause a scene," she said, glancing down at the bulge in his pants, then locking eyes with him again.

She turned and strutted away, hips swaying more than necessary.

Roan stared, stunned. "Holy shit..." he muttered, shaking his head in disbelief.

Outside, Lexi entered the building through a service entrance—just as Mia described. She moved silently up the stairwell to a locked armored door.

She crept through the corridor toward the security office.

Inside, the guards were distracted—every one of them glued to the surveillance feed.

Lexi caught a glimpse: Isabella, in full seduction mode, dazzling a poker table.

"Damn good job, Rojas," Lexi smirked to herself.

She reached out—fingers just inches from a keyring hanging near the console.

In Verellii, where crime was rampant, these guards would outnumber her 100 to 1. She was unarmed—her gear had been taken when she was detained. Silence wasn't just tactical. It was essential.

Her eyes flicked to a guard's laser pistol that was holstered. Shit, she thought.

She carefully slid the keys into her palm without a sound.

Lexi vanished into the shadows like the wind.

She returned to the armored stairwell door. Her X-ray revealed a thin glass panel—tamper-detection built in. If forced, it would lock permanently.

After several keys tried, one slid in and click.

The door shifted slightly. Soft, ambient light spilled from within.

As Lexi opened the door, she made sure it was clear before fully exposing herself. She walked in and it was exactly as Mia had said. Red velvet curtains, silk sheets and a pelt of a bear on the ground. A fireplace softly crackled in the corner, lighting up the purple walls. There was plenty of shadow for her to move, as she headed towards the computer. She powered it on as she heard a noise. A camera on the computer rotated to look at her, and a voice emerged from the shadows in the room.

Lexi Hayes...

A voice. Low. Calm. Cold. Familiar.

"So... what are you here for now? Information? My death? Possibly both?"

Lexi froze. Her hand lowered, putting the keys between her fingers, making a fist.

The voice continued, detached and precise:

"Did you think I wouldn't notice Mia missed our... appointment? That she returned to Level 2... with a sudden boost to her credit account?"

Lexi's jaw tightened. "What did you do with Mia?" she demanded.

A moment of silence filled the room.

"I won't concern you with that," the voice said flatly. "She served her purpose."

Then silence. Heavy, suffocating silence.

"Now... what to do with you?"

The lights flickered on.

She audibly gasped, putting her hand over her mouth.

A man sat in a chair, but was still—unnaturally still.

His face glinted metal. But something was wrong.

Then she saw it.

A sign hung from his neck. Burnt into the wood, barely legible under the low light:

"TRAITOR OF EARTH."

Lexi froze. The back of her mind screamed—that phrase, that symbol.

She moved closer.

She knew who he was.

The slumped figure. Brown hair. The jawline. The faint scars.

"No..."

"Gavin?"

His eyes were sewn shut. A small speaker installed in his face where his mouth and nose should be.

Then it spoke. Not him. The voice. The same voice.

"Ah. Gavin Thorne, do you remember him?"

She looked at Gavin's body—it had been tortured by whipping, acid, his skin raw, bubbled, and lacerated, dried blood trailing his body.

"The hero. Went to remove his cube. Succeeded. And started helping others, removing theirs as well. Unfortunately, we had to kill an entire squad of Enforcers. Sad. Such wasted potential."

"Tell your other precious Enforcers... loyalty is just another word for delusion."

Lexi's knees nearly buckled. They had used him. Mutilated him. Turned him into a message. Broadcasting like a puppet.

Then a screech came from all around her—the windows closing with blast shields, an alarm sounding in the entire building.

Lexi's comm suite lit up.

"Lex, get out of there!" Amber's panicked voice screamed. "They're coming from everywhere!"

Lexi ran to one of the windows, locked too tight, no way out.

Her mind raced for options. She bolted to the computer, her mission in jeopardy.

The room locked down, the door slammed shut. Green gas started to pour in. Lexi coughed, wheezed, trying to get a full breath, her eye displaying vastly dropping oxygen levels. She tried to call on her comm suite,

"Amber, get Brawn."

She tied a thumb drive to her wrist and slammed it into the computer, downloading all files as her systems failed fast.

Her eyes fluttered shut and she fell to the ground, the thumb drive pulling out of the computer—

Brawn slammed his entire body through the wall, coughing as he looked around.

He saw her and picked her up.

He jumped off the building, landing on the asphalt, creating a crater.

He ran to the VT-1, bullets hitting him as he blocked them from Lexi's body.

Then—thwip, thwip, thwip!

The hailstorm of bullets was replaced by laser fire. The muscles in his body burned away from the flurried attack. He still blocked Lexi's body.

As he fell to the ground, his legs disintegrating, he crawled to the VT-1.

"ROAN, BACK THE CAR UP!" Isabella yelled.

Roan slammed the VT-1 into reverse, then spun it 180 degrees and opened fire with the twin mounted guns on the front. People ducked and covered, screams and terror filling Level 2's party district.

Roan blocked Brawn with the truck, the Lancer-class armor soaking up most of the fire, scorching it.

Amber and Isabella jumped out and helped Brawn into the truck.

 "Armor integrity 35 percent and falling, guys! We need to get out of here!" Roan exclaimed.

Isabella and Amber finished pulling him into the truck as Roan floored it in reverse and sped off, the Skyreaper compressor whistling to life, turning out incredible power.

Amber did a quick scan of Brawn. "Verelliian steel fibers—perfect!" she squealed.

She scrambled through the crates in the back of the truck, tossing tools and anything metallic into a pile next to the damaged Aegis.

"Hold still, big guy," she muttered, breathless.

She used her immense strength to break the items into manageable pieces, inserting them against Brawn's ruined body. His shredded muscles twitched, then seized.

The Verelliian steel fibers in his body twitched again—then began to shift. It absorbed the metal pieces, reshaping, rebuilding, crawling along the damage like vines weaving bone.

"Just give him time," Amber said, sweat pouring down her brow. "Now let's fix the rest of you…"

She ripped open a side pouch and pulled out a palm-sized tool. The orange and blue skin synthesizer whined to life, glowing pale green. She ran it over the exposed wounds—layer by layer, new dermal tissue began forming, shiny and raw but alive.

"Hang in there, Brawn. I got you."

He looked over. "Damn, you're good," he said to Amber, giving her a painful grin.

*** ·

As Roan reached Verellii's surface, he headed into the wastes—the Rows—when the VT-1 gave him an overheat warning.

"You'll make it, baby." He glanced at the gauges. "Amber, how's Brawn looking?"

"He's stable," Amber replied, still hunched over him. "We just need to keep patching him up."

"What about my armor?" Brawn asked, his voice hoarse but alert. "It's laser and plasma proof. Could come in handy so I don't get my ass kicked again."

"It'll have to wait," Roan said. "If we head to Level 3, the VT-1 will stick out too much. It'll give away our position. I'll get your armor, Brawn. I promise."

In the back of the truck, Isabella sat beside Lexi, gently stroking her hair. Lexi was out cold, her breathing erratic. Isabella noticed the thumb drive tied to her wrist.

"You are one smart gringa," she whispered with a smile. "But I need you to come back to us. You're not done yet."

CHAP_21.exe - D34D DR0P

The truck limped into the garage just as the cooling radiator blew. Roan jumped out and popped the hood.

"Fuck!" he yelled—the first time he'd actually lost his cool. A laser had gone straight through the core. He slammed the hood shut.

Isabella walked over, calm and confident. "We'll fix her together."

Roan looked into her eyes, and the fire in his chest softened.

"*I believe you,*" he said, more quietly. "Let's get your friends settled in and patched up. The truck can wait."

Roan helped Isabella and Amber access the secret bunker beneath Apex Fuelwerks. The hidden space was fully stocked—rations, a kitchen, a bathroom, and two small bedrooms.

"Damn... guess that means no fuckin' down here," Brawn muttered through the pain, grinning despite himself.

"Put Lexi in here," Roan said, gesturing to the first room. "Amber, this'll be your room with her. Brawn, you can take the other one. Bed's a king size—you should fit." He half-joked, though his concern showed.

The team moved Lexi and Brawn into their rooms, and Amber quickly got to work.

Luckily, Brawn just needed time—his Verelliian steel muscles were already starting to rebuild using the scrap Amber had prepped. But Lexi needed clean oxygen—and fast.

Roan went back out to the garage, unhooked the oxygen tank from his cutting torch, and scrounged some old hose and a rubber plunger cup. He crafted a crude breathing mask, attaching it to the tank's regulator.

He carried it inside and set it beside Lexi's bed.

"I am not putting that on her face," Amber said, recoiling.

"It's the only thing I've got that might work," Roan insisted.

"Did you clean it?"

"Uhhh..."

"GO FUCKING CLEAN IT!" Amber snapped. "It's bad enough she was poisoned—now you want to give her sepsis?!"

Roan went to the bathroom and pulled out some mouthwash. The bottle was halfway full—and expired.

He filled the sink, washed off the rubber, and then disinfected it with the mouthwash. Dried it off and turned to see Isabella at the door.

"Thank you. For everything."

"Izzy... I—"

Isabella leaned in and kissed him. *"No more talking."*

Roan let out a long breath and smiled. He walked to Lexi's room and dropped the seal off to Amber. She inspected it, gave it a sniff test, gave it another once-over with a rag before settling that it was okay. She then connected it to the hose with some duct tape and put it over Lexi's face.

Roan and Isabella checked on Brawn before heading into the garage. Roan opened a fridge and pulled out two cheap beers. He handed one to Isabella and walked over to the VT-1, popping the hood to inspect the damage.

Isabella took the beer, walked to the dingy, dirty couch, kicked off her heels, and propped her feet on the table. She leaned back and took a drink.

"You like this?" Roan asked.

"I do. I also like you," she said confidently.

"Isabella, I can't give you more than this. After this adventure's over... this is me. This is who I am."

Isabella stood, her face turning cold. She slammed the beer down on a toolbox and stormed over to Roan, getting right in his face.

"¡¿Roan, hablas en serio?! ¡¿No has aprendido nada sobre mí o lo que quiero?! ¡Te quiero a ti, maldito idiota! ¡No necesito cosas lujosas! ¡Quiero ser feliz, y tú me das eso!"

"...English, please?"

"I want you, you fucking idiot! Not things. Not money. Just... you. You make me happy. And that's all I've ever needed."

Roan blinked, stunned. "I... uh... never mind."

Isabella narrowed her eyes—gentler this time. "Don't stall now, Roan. What were you gonna say?"

"I think I love you, Isabella."

Her eyes went wide. She breathed in, soft and sharp. "You... you love me?"

Roan tried to swallow a lump in his throat.

"Yes. I love you."

Isabella blinked, completely still. Her voice was barely above a whisper.

"I... I love you too. I just didn't know you felt the same."

Roan stepped closer, his voice gentle.

"I've never felt this way about anyone," he said, eyes locked on hers, heart thundering in his chest.

Isabella buried her face in his chest, arms wrapped tight around his sides. Roan held her like she might vanish if he let go, pressing a kiss to the top of her head. His shirt grew damp—tears.

She stayed like that for a long moment before lifting her head, eyes glassy and cheeks flushed. She gave him a soft kiss, tender and real, then turned around with a shy little smile—her nose red, her heart wide open.

The door creaked open.

Amber walked in, chipper. "Hey guys, Lex is gonna be—"

She froze. Her eyes narrowed.

"Is she—IS SHE FUCKING CRYING?! YOU PIECE OF SHIT!"

In a flurry, Amber grabbed Roan by the neck and pinned him to the wall, his feet dangling.

"I'm going to end you," she said coldly.

"Amber," Isabella interrupted, wiping her face. *"He said he loves me."*

Amber paused mid-grip.

"...Oh. Well, this is awkward."

She slowly lowered Roan and awkwardly glanced around.

"Well. I'm gonna leave."

She turned, muttering as she exited,

"It's about time, you two..."

Roan rubbed his neck as Isabella watched from across the room. Their eyes met—and both let out a laugh.

"I thought she was going to kill me," Roan said with a grin.

Isabella's smile faded a little. "She was."

"Oh... that sucks," Roan muttered.

She walked over and kissed him again, soft and quick.

"I'm gonna check in on Lex," she said. "Get changed. You take care of the truck."

Isabella walked into the room, headed to the dresser, and pulled out one of Roan's T-shirts. She squeezed into a pair of sweatpants before tossing her dress into the corner.

Lexi was sitting up on the bed, with Amber checking her over.

"I'm glad you're okay, mami," Isabella said softly.

Lexi looked up. "I got the data," she said, lifting her arm.

"I know," Isabella replied. "Brawn went through the wall and got you out. Took a lot of damage getting you into the car. He's resting in the next room over."

"Is he okay?"

Amber perked up. "Yeah, I patched him up. It's gonna take some time for the metal I put in there to set, but after that, we'll get the rest of his skin applied and he'll be good to go."

Lexi looked between them, jaw tightening.

"Guys, let's be honest—Mia set us up. They knew we were going to be there. They had Recruit Thorne mutilated in a chair in the office," she said, voice cracking. "Said he was a traitor to Earth."

"He was a good man," Isabella said, her voice low.

"He used to give me high fives after CRIS training," Amber added.

Amber stepped off the bed and leaned against the wall, arms crossed.

"Wait a sec. If they knew we were coming... how do we know what's on the drive is real?"

Isabella nodded slowly. "She's right. If it was a trap, it could be planted data—misinfo. Designed to send us somewhere worse."

Lexi didn't flinch.

"Maybe. But it's all we have. *We follow every lead—we have to.* If not, we stall. We don't have that luxury. Is that understood?"

Isabella and Amber exchanged a look, then turned back to her.

"Yes, ma'am," they said in unison.

Lexi glanced down at the drive strapped to her wrist.

"We need a computer," she said, locking eyes with Isabella.

Isabella nodded and headed for the garage.

She found Roan elbow-deep in the VT-1, parts already laid out in a neat, greasy row against a wall.

"Do you have a computer or something we can use to read a flash drive?"

"Yeah. There's one in the office. It's buried—haven't used it in forever."

"Thank you," Isabella said, heading into the office.

The office was cluttered with old papers, broken chairs, a dusty desk, and a cash register filled with thin paper slips.

Was this money? she wondered.

She pushed aside a pile of files and uncovered a laptop. She opened it—dead, of course.

Looking around for a charger, she opened a drawer.

Inside were medals, letters of commendation, and a neatly folded uniform from a military long disbanded.

Isabella walked back into the garage.

"You were in the military?"

Roan slid out from under the truck. "Yeah. Combat engineer during the Verelliian riots. Got a lot of people out of bad situations."

He wiped his hands and shrugged. "Saw some things I didn't agree with. Did my time. Got out. Decided to spend my remaining years helping people and rebuilding."

Isabella smiled faintly and returned to the office.

She pulled a picture from the drawer, folded it, and slipped it into her pocket. The charger was in the next drawer down.

Back in the room, she plugged it in and booted up the laptop.

"Time to find out what's on you," Lexi muttered as she plugged in the drive.

Files flooded the screen—line after line, folder after folder.

The girls sifted through them for hours.

"Casino employees... no. Naked pictures of Mia... no. A brochure for some new holoprojector... nope. Grainy video... another grainy video... awwww, a picture of a panda... nothing's on here, Lex," Amber said. "It's just junk."

"WAIT—go back!" Lexi snapped.

Amber clicked back.

It was the brochure, but Lexi caught something—tiny, tucked in the corner. A glyph.

"Click that," Lexi said.

Amber did. A small box appeared on screen:

ENTER USERNAME AND PASSWORD

"That's interesting," Lexi muttered. "Now how do we get into that..."

Roan walked in, wiping sweat from his brow.

"I've gotta go to the store. Need a new radiator. I'll be back in a couple hours—I have to walk."

"Isn't Amber's car still outside?" Isabella asked.

Roan paused, headed upstairs, and peered out the window. Amber's car sat where they left it—coated in a thick layer of dust.

He headed back toward the bunker. "Yup, sti—"

"Before you go," Isabella interrupted, "can you figure out what we just plugged in?"

Roan stepped closer, scanning the screen.

"Oh, that's an old encryption key. I might have something—hold on."

He walked across the room and removed a loose brick from the wall. Behind it, a small lever.

He pulled it.

The wall groaned open, revealing a stash of old-world tech: his exo-suit, a tool belt, and a dead micro-reactor.

He dug through a box and pulled out a small device with a dangling wire.

"Take the thumb drive out, plug this in, then plug the drive into that," he said, handing it to Amber.

"We used to call it a kick. It'd beat the encryption until it gave up what we wanted."

Amber smirked. "Seriously? Kick?"

"Mmm hmm. Damn good at its job, too."

He looked around. "Anyone know where the keys to the car are?"

"A couple days ago I dropped them on the blue toolbox in the corner," Isabella replied confidently.

Roan nodded. "I'll see you guys later, then."

Amber's car started outside, its low engine hum fading as he drove away.

The Kick hummed softly beside the laptop, burning through code—lines of prompt windows scrolled, flickered, and vanished one by one.

Hours passed.

Where the hell is Roan? Isabella wondered.

She headed into the garage, hoping to catch him under the truck again—maybe he had just started working again, or was tuning something small. But the space was quiet. Empty.

She walked to the garage door windows. Still no car. Amber's ride hadn't come back.

Her brow furrowed.

With nothing else to do, Isabella moved toward the truck, eyeing it over. Maybe she could at least prep something for repair. She walked over to a small shelf cluttered with parts and tools.

That's when she noticed it.

A box tucked behind some old wiring. Cardboard clean. Untouched.

She pulled it out.

A radiator. Brand new. Silver. Still in its protective wrap.

She stared at it for a second. Then stepped over to the old one and ran a quick scan.

Exact same dimensions.

Why the hell would he say he needed one... if he already had one right here?

She stared at it a moment longer before quietly returning it to the shelf.

Back in the bunker, Brawn was snoring like a freight train in the room next to Lexi's.

"Didn't Roan say he... ugh, I can't think with all that noise!"

Isabella walked over to his door and shut it gently, muffling the noise a bit.

She turned back to the others.

"Like I was saying... did Roan say he was going to the store for a radiator?"

Amber looked up from the screen. "Yeah. The truck really took a beating during our escape."

"Weird," Isabella muttered, more to herself than anyone.

A soft chime filled the room.

The computer screen flickered, going black—then a black-and-white topographical map flickered into view. A drone's overhead feed flashed across the screen. Red markers began to appear, one after another.

Pin. Blur to next spot. Pin. Blur.

Ten in total.

Amber leaned in. "What's it doing?"

Lexi's eye flared slightly as she scanned the data, committing it all to memory.

"I'm not sure," she said. "But it's highlighting ten separate locations. Could be paths, tunnels, or surface anomalies. Whatever it is—it's deliberate."

"We need someone who studies topography," Lexi muttered.

Isabella folded her arms. Her voice was flat now.

"Roan's still not back with the car. And he left hours ago."

***

Amber's car came back into view and parked in front of the garage. The engine turned off as Roan stepped out, carrying several large bags filled with groceries. He struggled to open the door.

Amber and Lexi tried to figure out the coordinates by looking at a normal map, but couldn't seem to agree where the pins went.

Meanwhile, Isabella heard the doorknob jittering and decided to investigate.

She saw Roan struggling outside and walked over to open the door—hoping to see a radiator.

Roan gave her a smile and leaned in for a kiss.

Isabella turned her head, jaw tight. Her chest clenched—not from fear, but from that quiet ache she didn't want to name. *Trust was slipping through her fingers*, and he was still smiling like nothing happened.

"Where is the radiator?" she asked.

"Why would I need a radiator when I have one on the shelf?"

Isabella could see his heart pounding harder, his pulse quickening beneath her stare.

"I said I was getting groceries," he said, smiling again.

"You said you were getting a radiator. Where have you been? It doesn't take that many hours to get this amount of groceries!"

"I'm a terrible shopper. I can never decide what I want," he said, waving off her words while lugging the bags inside.

Isabella squinted, staring at him as he walked into the bunker. The ache in her chest turned sharp. It wasn't the groceries. It was the lie—and how easily he said it. The kind of lie that didn't flinch.

Her heart thudded slower now, heavier.

As Roan dropped the groceries on the kitchen counter, the girls called him in and asked if he knew anything about the map or if he knew a topographer.

"I know a guy. He's not a topographer, but he can point us to someone who is. We have to go to Level 3. Fortunately, we can also get Brawn's armor while we're down there."

"Brawn's armor is not going to fit in my car!" Amber yelled.

"Okay, then I'll get to work on the truck. And if you don't mind... can you guys make dinner?"

As the girls cooked, the garage filled with the aroma of fresh food. Brawn came out of his room—skin still torn and scorched, but muscles repaired.

"Do you guys need any help?"

The girls stopped talking. Isabella stood stiff at the counter, clearly pissed. Amber and Lexi tried to ease the air around her.

Lexi turned to him. "No, we're good. See if Roan needs help."

As Brawn walked off, the quiet tension simmered back to life.

"He says he's going for a radiator," Isabella said, "then comes back with groceries. How can I trust him?"

Lexi leaned against the wall. "Maybe he just made a mistake. He probably went out, remembered he had a radiator, and since he was already out, grabbed food."

Isabella's shoulders dropped. *"He lied to my face, Lexi.* I watched his pulse spike when I asked. He smiled like everything was fine."

Lexi didn't respond right away.

"But maybe you're right, mami. But why didn't he just tell me that?" Isabella muttered. *"Estúpido."*

A little while later, the garage rumbled as a massive engine roared to life. The VT-1's systems came online, loud and proud.

Roan shut the engine off, coming back into the bunker, wiping his hands off on a rag—his arms and face smeared with oil and grease.

"I fixed it," he said, smiling.

No reaction from the girls.

Later, over dinner, Lexi laid out the new plan.

"Roan, you said you know a guy, right?"

"Correct. Level 3. A couple blocks from the safehouse."

"Great. We're going to drop you off. Isabella and I will retrieve Brawn's armor from the safehouse. Amber, you'll finish patching up Brawn—looks like he's doing a lot better."

Brawn looked up, silver glinting under the overhead lights, seared synthetic skin outlining rebuilt muscle. He gave Lexi a tired grin—clearly enjoying real food over the nutrient paste his suit provided.

The next day, their plan was set in motion.

They dropped Roan off near a shady alley in Level 3. As he disappeared into the shadows, Isabella watched him like a hawk—tracking every move, every shift in his shoulders.

She didn't blink.

Lexi drove them to the safehouse. Inside, they dragged the massive power armor through the front door while people outside stared.

They opened the VT-1's back hatch and crammed the armor inside.

On the drive back, Isabella gripped the door handle, her gut twisting again.

Something just didn't add up with Roan. She trusted him. Shared her body with him.

They pulled up and spotted Roan talking to a man in a long coat. As the VT-1 stopped, Roan glanced over and saw them watching. He pointed at the vehicle, and the man in the coat turned away, showing him something out of sight.

Lexi narrowed her eyes. "That's weird."

"Right?" Isabella breathed. "Should we say something?"

"No," Lexi said. "Let this play out, Izzy. Keep a steady hand. Keep your friends close... your enemies closer."

Isabella's face flushed red. She didn't just feel anger—she felt betrayal twisting inside her ribs.

She didn't breathe. Her face burned hot, not just from rage—but heartbreak. He pointed. Right at them. Right at the truck. And he smiled.

Was this what betrayal looked like? Not a knife. But a smile.

Lexi glanced over. "Sorry, Izzy. That was insensitive."

Roan walked up grinning and hopped into the back of the truck.

"So, I've got good news and bad news," he said.

"Let's hear it," Lexi replied coldly.

"Good news: my contact knows a guy who can help. I've got an address. Bad news: it's down in Level 4, and the VT-1's armor isn't fully repaired. So it can't take as much damage as before. Luckily, I doubt anyone in Level 4 has a laser gun." He chuckled.

"That's funny," Lexi said—stone cold.

Roan raised an eyebrow. "Are you sure? Maybe you should tell your face."

The girls ignored him, their stares fixed forward.

The VT-1 descended into a jagged corridor, leaving the streetlights, advertisements, and groups of people behind from Level 3.

The tunnel was unfinished—rocks jutted from the wall, dirt falling from unreinforced ceilings.

The vehicle slammed into a sharp outcropping.

"25% ARMOR HEALTH," a dash screen flashed.

Shit, Roan thought. Maybe I should've repaired the armor.

They pulled into Level 4—rusted, abandoned cars and trash bags lining the streets. Shady figures glanced over their shoulders at the VT-1 as it roared by.

They pulled into a cracked driveway and stepped out.

Sewage poured from grates along the walls, collecting in deep troughs behind crumbling homes and broken storefronts. The smell was suffocating.

"¡Dios mío, ¿qué es ese olor!? ¡Ni siquiera puedo ver bien!" Isabella gasped, covering her face.

Lexi gagged. "I think I'd rather be poisoned again."

Roan stepped out calmly, not flinching.

He's been here before, Isabella thought. Why would anyone willingly come down here?

They walked to a nearby storefront and rang the bell. For a few seconds, nothing.

Then, a mechanical whine.

A camera descended slowly. Its lens focused on them.

"What are you doing here? What do you want?" a deep, growling voice asked.

Roan stepped forward.

"Yeah, uh… I'm Roan Gravik. Slater said you could help us. We're looking for someone who can read a map."

Silence.

Then—a loud buzzer.

The door unlocked.

They walked into the house. Smoke filled the air, and charts and maps were scattered across tables and the floor, pinned to the walls. Old furniture crowded the room, along with opened cans of food. It looked completely abandoned.

A creak sounded from upstairs.

A man walked down the stairs with a cane—wearing suspenders, blue jeans, shiny black shoes, and no shirt. One side of his face drooped like he'd had a stroke, and his skin was covered in pustules.

"So... waddaya wan'?" he asked stubbornly, walking past the group. He dropped onto a red leather couch without moving the trash piled on it.

Lexi stepped forward. "We have a topographical map with pins placed in random locations. We were wondering if you could help us determine their exact positions."

The man stared at her, unzipped his pants, and pulled a pipe from his crotch. He lit it with a cracked lighter.

Fucking disgusting, Lexi thought.

"Yep. I can help ya. But it'll cost ya," he murmured.

"How much?" Roan asked.

"Ten thousand credits," the man replied with a crooked grin. Most of his teeth were missing.

"Ten thousand!?" Roan exclaimed.

"Yup. That's the price. You wan' it, no gotiatin'."

Roan turned to the girls. "Okay, I've got eight left to my name. Can you guys pitch in the last two?"

Isabella folded her arms. "Why are you so comfortable down here?"

"Now isn't the time, Izzy. We can talk about this later," Lexi cut in, her voice sharp.

Lexi looked at Roan. "This isn't your fight. You did your part. Now we'll do ours." She dismissed him with a nod.

Roan furrowed his brow, confused.

Lexi transferred the credits to the man.

"Ha! I knews yous were smart," he cackled.

He pushed himself off the couch and hobbled over to a computer setup connected to a large map on the wall. A mechanical arm was mounted beside it.

"Now what you gonna do is put that vidya you got on this here computah, and we's gon' see where it lines up on this here map," he said, smacking a piece of paper with his cane.

Lexi pulled out the thumb drive and plugged it in. The video started. The mechanical arm came to life—buzzing, shifting.

Pin. Wait. Pin. Wait.

It continued until all ten points were placed on the map.

"Those are your locations," he said. "Y'all can have the map. Comes with the payment," he added, flashing his yellowed teeth.

"Thank you, sir," Roan said.

"Let's go," Lexi muttered, clearly agitated by something.

***

They stepped outside. Roan was about to jump into the driver's seat when Lexi called him over.

"Roan. A moment," she said.

"Sure. What's up, Lex?" he replied, climbing back out of the truck and walking toward her.

Isabella watched from the vehicle as Lexi's face shifted—stone cold to unreadable.

Roan was smiling. His hands were moving as he talked, relaxed.

But Lexi gave away nothing.

Lexi and Roan climbed into the truck and headed back to the surface. Isabella's fire built inside her—hotter by the second. She couldn't contain her suspicions anymore.

"What is going on?" Isabella yelled from the backseat.

"Izzy, this isn't the time—" Lexi said.

"Bullshit, it is the time! You tell me what's going on, right now!"

"Izzy, control yourself. This isn't the time," Lexi said again, voice firmer.

Isabella leaned back, arms crossed, her tone full of heat.

"Then Captain—when is the time?"

"Watch yourself, Sergeant," Lexi warned.

Roan's eyes widened—trapped between two emotionally volatile powerhouses, both ready to blow.

Isabella exhaled hard and turned toward the window, her breath fogging the glass.

They pulled up to a place on the surface called The Golem. It was a quiet park with synthetic trees and grass, slightly browned and weathered. A stone fountain trickled gently in the center, backed by a massive boulder.

Roan climbed out of the truck, walked behind an outcropping of smaller rock, and moved it aside—retrieving something from underneath.

"¿¡Qué carajo está haciendo ese hijo de puta ahora!?" Isabella blurted.

"Isabella, I don't understand Spanish," Lexi sighed.

"I said: What the fuck is that son of a bitch doing now?!"

"At Level 4, he said he needed to stop at a drop point to pick something up," Lexi replied. "I guess this is it. He didn't give me any more details."

"I'll get more fucking details," Isabella growled, throwing the door open.

She stormed toward him, her voice shaking with fury.

"Roan, what the hell is going on?! Why are you sneaking around, doing shady shit—now, of all times? We finally catch a break, and you start acting like a stranger! Tell me. Right now. What is going on?!"

Roan looked up at her, calm and composed.

"What's going on... is that I don't know much in this world. But I do know that I love you."

He bent a knee.

Dropped down to the ground.

"Isabella... will you marry me?"

In his hand: a simple Verelliian diamond, slightly hued red. The light caught it just right.

Isabella stammered, eyes wide. "The radiator?"

"Looking for a jewelry store," Roan explained. "Turns out... not many left. Had to go all the way to the Central Nexus District."

"The man in the jacket?"

"Hiding the ring I bought for you. He's my dead-drop guy. I had him stash it here."

"Talking to Lexi?"

"I told her everything. She was worried about you."

"You... you did all this? For me?"

"I did."

Isabella turned around.

From the truck, Lexi watched—hands over her mouth, her eyes shimmering, wide with disbelief. She was frozen. Barely breathing.

Isabella's voice trembled.

"*Sí*," she said—soft, raw, vulnerable.

Roan blinked, like he didn't hear it right. Like maybe the world was playing a trick on him.

"...What?"

Her lips broke into a shaky smile. Tears slipped down her cheeks.

"Yes," she said louder, firmer. *"I'll marry you, you idiota!"*

Roan rose and gently took her hand, sliding the ring onto her finger. Her breath caught, lips trembling as she stared down at it—then back up at him.

He leaned in.

She met him halfway.

Their lips crashed together in a kiss that was raw and full of heat. Hands clutching. Bodies pressed tight. It deepened—slowly at first, then all at once.

She moaned into his mouth as he gripped her waist. The second kiss was hungrier, needier—his fingers sliding into her curls, her hands dragging across his chest.

The third kiss nearly took them both off their feet.

Lexi squinted from the truck, her eyes widening.

"Oh, hell no."

They didn't stop.

Roan had his hands under her thighs now. Isabella was giggling against his mouth, breathless, tangled in him like she might climb him right there. He lifted her effortlessly—her legs wrapping around his waist, arms tightening around his neck. Their kiss deepened, hungry and wild, her curls bouncing as she leaned into him like she was never letting go.

Lexi flung the truck door open. "HEY! This is still a public park, you sex-crazed lunatics! Get in the damn truck!"

Isabella laughed harder, resting her forehead to Roan's as they both tried to catch their breath. He grinned like a man struck by lightning.

They climbed in the back seat—still touching.

Still burning.

And Lexi just shook her head. "Unbelievable."

Lexi, sitting in the passenger seat, glanced over at the empty driver's seat. Behind her, the sounds of giggling, kissing, and hushed laughter echoed through the foggy cab. She exhaled sharply and climbed into the driver's seat.

They weren't even trying to be quiet.

As the minutes went by on their drive back, Lexi heard it.

Moaning.

The entire rear window was fogged over, and the truck rocked ever so slightly.

"Oh, come on, guys! You can't wait for your own room?!"

Roan, still behind Isabella, leaned back just far enough to peek between the seats, completely unbothered. *"No,"* he said, cool as ever—then disappeared again.

The moaning resumed. Louder.

By the time they reached the garage, all the windows were fogged to hell.

Amber ran out, eyebrows raised. "What happened to the truck? Hit a steam line or something?"

Lexi stepped out, slammed the door behind her. "No. Roan proposed, Isabella said yes... and they've been going at it in the back ever since."

Amber blinked. "So... they're..."

"Yep." Lexi didn't even look back. *"Let's get to work—while they finish theirs."*

CHAP_22.exe // 8LAKOUT

Lexi moved to the table and unfolded the map. Amber joined her, with Brawn close behind—his skin now fully repaired, clean and glowing with fresh synthflesh.

"Did you guys manage to get my armor?" Brawn asked.

"We did," Lexi replied. "Heavy as hell, but yeah."

"Awesome. Is it in the truck? I'll go grab it—"

"Do not—go to the truck," Lexi said sharply, holding up a hand.

Brawn blinked. "Why? Did something happen to my armor?"

"Probably," she said. "But not... damage."

"I'm confused," Brawn said, completely puzzled.

Roan and Isabella walked in, drenched in sweat. Her hair was smushed on one side, while his was completely matted. Isabella wore Roan's shirt now, and Roan was wearing the one she had stolen from him earlier. They were still breathing hard, hands clasped tightly, fingers intertwined.

Brawn eyed them warily. "Did you guys... just... on my armor?"

"Right next to it," Roan said casually. "Don't worry—nothing got on it."

They giggled, looking at each other like giddy teenagers.

Brawn groaned.

The team gathered around the table as Lexi refocused.

"These are the ten marked points. Now if we compare this with a full map of the city, we can start placing them. I recognize a few already," she said, tapping the map from Level 4. "Union tunnels... RAPID HQ... this one's the port district—where I intercepted the weapons shipment—and this one here is the casino."

"They can't all be targets," Isabella muttered.

"I know this one," Brawn said, pointing to a new spot. "Used to be an Aegis safehouse during the war. No clue what it's being used for now."

"And this one's Med-Store," Roan added, tapping another location.

Lexi nodded. "Okay, so that leaves four we haven't confirmed. Two cars, five people—we split up."

"Actually..." Brawn stepped back, voice steady. "I'm going to check out the safehouse. If there's anything left of Aegis, I want to find it. I have to. Maybe it's time we stop hiding—start rebuilding the Order. Start helping Verellii again."

Lexi met his eyes.

"If you need anything... come find me there," he said. "And... thank you. All of you. For everything."

Brawn headed up to the garage. Moments later, metal clanked, followed by a loud mechanical roar and soft hissing—the sound of a reactor coming online.

He was suited up again. Fully armored. A force of nature.

"I'm gonna miss that guy," Amber said.

"Me too," Isabella replied softly. "Maybe I was too hard on him."

"Did you know he can lift an engine block with one arm?" Roan added, eyes wide.

Lexi studied the map, a faint smile touching her lips. She didn't say a word.

Brawn wasn't gone. He hadn't said goodbye.

"Okay," Lexi said, shifting back to focus. "We need weapons. Izzy, you still have your recon drone?"

"No, mami," Isabella said. "Had to fly it into that control room when we got detained. It fried cutting the shield."

"Do we have anything?" Lexi asked.

"I know a guy," Roan offered. "They won't be RAPID-grade, but they'll fire."

"Amber, where are your weapons?" Lexi turned to her.

"I left them at your house," Amber admitted. "There were people looking for you, Lexi. I think... I think they were there to kill you."

"And you're just now telling me this?!"

Lexi's voice rose, sharp. Amber flinched.

For a second, it was silent.

Then Isabella stepped in. "It's in the past. We need to focus on the here and now."

"I'll go see my contact," Roan said. "Get enough gear for everyone. Any preferences?"

"We can use whatever you bring," Lexi replied. "We're all programmed with weapons mastery."

Roan paused, blinking. "That's... um, incredible. You too, Izzy?"

Isabella gave him a slow, confident nod.

"I don't know why, but I am so turned on right now," Roan murmured, leaning in to kiss her neck.

"Knock it off, you two," Lexi snapped. "We have a job to do. I am happy for you—really—but focus up. Please."

"Yes, ma'am," Roan replied, backing off with his hands up.

"Guess I'll be back in a bit then. Izzy—wanna come with?"

"No," Lexi cut in. "I need you both focused. Amber, you go with Roan. Izzy, you're staying here—with me."

Amber and Roan climbed into the VT-1, it once again coming alive as it backed out.

Isabella and Lexi looked at the map.

"Okay, so we have four places," Lexi started. "It looks like two surface buildings, a tunnel... and what is this?" She pointed. "It's a black square. It originally looked like a printing error—but the reference map is the same."

They stared at the map. What once seemed like a mistake now felt deliberate. Two rectangles and a square, arranged like something should sit in the center. No labels. No color difference. Just void—blacked-out sections like someone wanted it erased.

"I think this may be it," Lexi said quietly.

"So, we clear the two buildings and check out this site," Isabella said. "Roan and Amber can handle the tunnel."

"I think that's the way to go. Plus, they'll need the truck to get in deep. When they get back, we'll brief, rest up for the night. Prep and roll. Understood?"

"Crystal clear," Isabella replied. She paused. "And Lexi... it's good to have you back, Commander."

Roan and Amber returned—two duffles in each hand. They laid everything out:

2 large-caliber pistols

2 small-caliber pistols

2 large-caliber rifles

A few grenades

A knife

And a lot of ammo to go with it

"Ma'am. After you," Roan said, nodding at Lexi.

Her hand hovered over the weapons. She closed her eyes.

"I forgot she did that," Isabella said with a grin.

Lexi settled on one of the small-caliber pistols. She gripped it—polyurethane handle, black steel frame, scratched, bluish, aged. The kind that had seen things. She pulled the mag and disassembled it in a blink.

Roan whistled. "Damn... that was cool."

"It's a well-maintained weapon," Lexi said. *"She's old, but reliable. She'll do nicely."*

"Izzy, as second in charge—you're up," Amber said.

Isabella grabbed the knife and one of the rifles. She tore the gun down, inspecting every piece—the splintered wood, mag well, firing mechanism.

"Needs a cleaning," she muttered. "But I'll make do. And I'll sharpen this knife."

Amber glanced at Roan.

"Be my guest," he said, gesturing to the table. "Ladies first."

Amber picked one of the large-caliber pistols. Still had a tag on it. Pristine. New.

Roan grabbed the other rifle. Old battle design—rusted, soot-caked, worn. But he planned on modding it anyway.

The team began cleaning and prepping their weapons.

Roan stood, walked to the back, and opened his hidden panel in the wall. He rolled out the exosuit and hauled it to the garage. Then he lifted the reactor and set it on a workbench.

"Time to bring you back to life, little guy."

Hours went by.

Clicks. Test fires. Sight adjustments. The air filled with the thunder of live fire—cracks and pops echoing through the Rows.

Amber was mid-fire when she heard it.

Thump. Thump. Thump.

She turned—eyes widening.

Roan stood in the exosuit. The reactor alive, humming on his back. Thick metal limbs flexed with energy.

"I may not be armored..." he grinned, "but I've got strength now."

Isabella stepped up, gripping his chin with two fingers.

"My papi... you're so sexy when you build, mi amor."

Roan smiled, clearly happy with himself.

The team got together and conversed a bit before heading off to bed.

"All right, guys," Lexi said. "We follow the plan. If there are any deviations, we meet at the Aegis safehouse. It's a central location, and we can fall back to some heavy reinforcements," she said confidently.

"Amber, Roan. Take the VT-1, head to the tunnels here. Izzy and I will take Amber's car and go to these two buildings here... and here. We will wait for you at this building after we investigate to regroup and then head to the redacted area. *We push at 0800. Are we clear?*"

"Yes, ma'am!" everyone yelled.

Roan said, "I have to go to the garage, repair the armor, and she'll be good to go for tomorrow. Also, close the bunker doors—a lot of grinding is going to be happening tonight."

***

Hours later...

294

Isabella went to check on Roan. She had a glass of water and a protein bar. The garage was quiet—no noise, no activity, no Roan. She saw the tools laid out, new panels prepped and awaiting welding, and his exosuit in the corner. He had been here working. Where was he?

A spotlight came on through the window. Isabella dropped the water and bar to cover her eyes instinctively. Then she felt it—a heat on her chest—as she flew back into the wall, looking down, seeing her skin smoking, revealing damaged metal strands.

"*¡De ninguna puta manera!*" she yelled. "Lexi! Amber! Get the fuck up!"

Isabella dove into a service well under the VT-1 as a hailstorm of bullets tore through the garage.

Lexi came in, seeing the assault taking place, the spotlight shining through the holes made by gunfire.

She saw Amber rush up the stairs.

"Amber, go to the rear, flank from the right. Izzy, get your ass out of there and flank left. I'm going through the middle."

The girls moved, their steps practiced. Lexi ran out to see a RAPID gunship and five Enforcers. She fired her Shockwave Inhibitor, taking out one, while Isabella and Amber took out two more. Amber rolled behind the landed gunship, waiting for her next move. Isabella dropped another Enforcer, her Shockwave Inhibitor forced into overdrive, her skin peeling away from the heat on her shoulder.

Then... Lexi saw him.

Captain Cybrix Thorne. Menacing. Calculated. Deadly without armor. He stepped out of the gunship, eyes aglow orange. His armor—black as night with light orange lighting spilling from the gaps. He held Roan, a pistol aimed at his head.

"Captain Lexi Hayes," he said calmly. "I have been ordered to bring you in—alive or dead. You are an enemy of the state. A terrorist. A traitor. Come with me, and I won't end his life."

***

Isabella's mouth hung open, no words forming. She looked at Roan, who—despite his situation—was still calm. Then she looked at Lexi, calculating her next move.

Isabella knew Lexi wouldn't be taken in. And she wouldn't let Roan die. It wasn't her way.

A scream pierced the air above the gunship.

Amber jumped down, pistol-whipping Thorne in the back of the head. His eyes erratically shifted from green to fiery orange, then back again.

He dropped Roan and put a hand to his head. Amber struck again.

"Recruit Amber, stop that immediately," he commanded.

She froze as his eyes returned to green, commanding respect.

"Sir? What happened?"

"I'm... I'm not sure. But... why are we here? What happened to my men?"

"They're not dead," Lexi said, walking up to him. "They're stunned."

"Captain Hayes. A pleasure." He reached his hand out to shake hers.

"You have no idea what happened? At all?" Lexi asked.

"No. Last I remember, we were field training at the detainment center. I was hit, went inside, and saw the carnage of what was going on. As I rushed to the command center, I, um... don't remember. And now I'm here with a lump on my head."

He turned and looked at Amber. Her smile was infectious, her green eyes sparkling under her glasses.

"Sir, I have something to show you. It's a holo," Lexi said.

Thorne's helmet folded around his head, awaiting the transfer.

Lexi flicked the recording of his son—Gavin Thorne, mutilated—to Captain Thorne's helmet.

Moments passed. Quiet.

Then a voice: "Lexi Hayes. Thank you for showing me this. I must go. But before I do... tell me the sons of bitches who did this so I can rip them apart limb by limb. I will spare no one. There are no depths of hell where I won't find them. I'll—"

"Sir, it was Earth spies. It seems Shogo Akiyama is behind all this chaos."

He turned toward the gunship, then looked back at Lexi.

"I have hunting to do."

The gunship took off, engines roaring—kicking up dirt, dust, and debris.

Lexi received a transfer of RAPID credits from Thorne.

"Hey Roan," she said, looking at him.

"Yeah, what's up?"

"Thorne just sent me a lot of credits. Says to rebuild the garage. It's... a lot of money."

The roof caved in with a crash. His exosuit toppled with it, collapsing under its own weight as hydraulic lines split, fluid pooling beneath it.

Roan stared at the mess, shoulders slumping. "Guess it's not just the garage I'll be rebuilding when this is all over..."

Isabella stepped closer, her voice steady. "You won't be rebuilding it alone. You'll have help."

The team turned in for the night.

Isabella helped Roan finish the VT-1. Luckily, the bullets hadn't damaged anything—just light scratches across the armor.

Near the door, ants had already swarmed the dropped protein bar, tearing it apart.

They tightened the last screw and closed the hood.

"Time for a shower and bed?" Roan asked.

"I thought you'd never ask," Isabella said, lighting up.

The shower sputtered to life. The two climbed in, giggling as steam filled the bathroom.

Amber shuffled in, rubbing her eyes.

"Why are you guys still up?" she asked groggily.

"Just finished the truck," Roan said.

"Can I pee?"

Isabella laughed. "Yes, but don't mind what we're doing in here."

Amber groaned. "Everyone in this house knows what you guys are doing at all times, Isabella."

She finished, washed her hands, and wandered back to her room.

Isabella and Roan finished and crawled into bed.

The next morning, Lexi knocked on Roan and Isabella's door. No answer.

She knocked again.

"Shhhhhhhh!" came from inside.

Lexi opened the door.

Roan was passed out, snoring loud enough to shake the walls. Isabella lay on top of him, breasts pressed to his chest, kissing every inch of his exposed skin.

"Izzy, let me ask you a question," Lexi said.

"What is it, mami?" Isabella murmured between kisses.

"Are you going to be alright?" Lexi raised a brow.

"What do you mean?"

"I need to make sure you can focus today. Ever since Roan, you've been... a bit distracted. I need to know you won't hesitate when the time comes."

Isabella climbed off Roan and walked, completely naked, up to Lexi.

"¿En serio?" she said sternly.

"Yes, Izzy. I'm serious."

Isabella blinked. Stared. Lexi didn't flinch.

"Lexi, mira... I'm the happiest I've been in a long time. And what if I die today? What if he dies today? I don't want to look back and regret not putting everything I had into this."

"I get that, Izzy. I do. But I don't want to worry about you either. You've always been my right hand—my hammer. I need that version of you today. Through and through."

"What the hell is going on?" Amber mumbled, stepping into the doorway. She paused when she saw Lexi and a naked Isabella squared off, ferocity between them.

"Just making sure everything is good," Lexi said, eyes still locked on Isabella.

"With her body?" Amber asked.

"No," Lexi said flatly.

Roan stirred, seeing the three women. Isabella was still naked from the night before.

"This is awesome," he said, wrapping the blanket around himself and heading to the dresser.

Lexi turned toward the door.

"Remember what I said, Izzy. I need Sergeant Rojas today—not just Izzy."

She left.

Amber walked into the room, medkit in hand, as Roan got dressed.

"I can only mend your strands—I don't have new ones to install. Skin, I've got you. Hold still," she said, gently cutting metal away from Isabella's scorched chest.

Isabella sat unbothered. Amber worked quickly, her fingers steady.

"This'll keep the muscle from tearing under load. Don't go full Rojas until I can fix you fully."

"I'm always full Rojas," Isabella muttered with a grin.

Amber smiled, then stepped back. "All patched." She walked out.

As Isabella started to get dressed, she paused—pulled the ring off her finger and placed it gently on the dresser.

"I'll have to come back for that," she said.

"I need you to," Roan replied softly. "So, I can come back for you."

They came together, holding hands. Staring into each other's eyes.

"I love you," Isabella whispered.

"I love you too," Roan whispered back. *"Please... come back to me."*

Isabella's eyes swelled, tears threatening. She blinked hard.

"I have to go." She kissed him on the lips... and walked out.

Roan and Amber climbed into the VT-1—its engine howling to life, compressor whistling high and sharp.

Isabella and Lexi slid into Amber's car.

No words. Just a look.

Goodbye. Be safe.

All said in a stare.

CHAP_23.exe // CR!TICAL1TY

Amber and Roan approach the tunnel, their gazes catching the glint of metal pikes—each topped with a skull.

"Well, that's not creepy at all," Amber mutters.

Roan flips on the VT-1's lightbar, bathing the cave in harsh daylight.

As they drive deeper, they spot a rusted gate. Beyond it, several black six-wheeled vehicles are parked, marked with barcodes.

Roan pulls the truck into a small alcove shrouded in shadow. They jump out and head to the gate.

Amber's eyes widen. "These are the trucks Mia told me and Lexi about—the ones they use to steal bodies. To make Infiltrators."

"Shhh," Roan says, holding a finger to his lips.

They draw their weapons, heads on a swivel, and walk past the gate. Piles of scrap metal and wooden crates line the floor; tire tracks press into the dirt. But these tracks appear too narrow for a vehicle.

"Maybe wagons?" Roan whispers.

"Shhh," Amber says, smirking as she mocks his gesture back at him.

They follow the smaller tracks into a branching corridor. It twists sharply into blackness.

"Hold onto my belt loop," Amber says. "So you don't get lost."

"What?" Roan blinks.

"I have night vision. You don't."

Reluctantly, he hooks a finger through her belt loop—his knuckle brushing the top of her ass.

"Don't get handsy back there. You've seen what happens when people piss me off."

Roan gulps as Amber's eye glows deeper green—night vision activating.

They continue down the corridor. The air grows thick.

Then—

"O-oh... my g-g-god..."

A robotic voice stutters in the dark.

Two red lights glow in the shadows ahead.

"What the fuck?" Amber breathes. "I don't know what that is."

"What do you mean you don't know?" Roan asks, unnerved.

"My night vision is failing," Amber responds nervously.

Amber sweeps the room with her pistol before flipping on its mounted flashlight.

The truth hits them both like a gut punch.

A massive robot slumps in the corner, long-powered-down—yet hauntingly posed.

Its frame is draped in a pale material.

Amber steps forward, and her breath hitches.

It's skin.

Human skin stretched tight over the metal plating. Scarred and scorched into the flesh are words—angry, hateful, and cruel:

"WHORE" "TRAITOR" "PROPERTY OF EARTH" "SHE WANTED IT" "SLUT"

Amber stumbles. Roan's stomach turns.

"It's Mia..." Amber whispers. "They... they skinned her. They used her."

The robot's faceplate bears a jagged chrome smile—rusted, blood-stained, and covered in blue lipstick. Almost mocking.

"They didn't just kill her," Amber says, voice cracking. *They erased her. They made her into... a message."*

"A warning," Roan replies. "This was personal."

A voice crackles from its damaged jaw. Robotic. Warbled. But unmistakably Mia's.

"P... P... P... Pix... Pixie's... f... f... friend..."

Amber freezes mid-step.

"It's... m... m... me..."

The jaw shifts again, metal-on-metal grinding.

"Mmm... Mmm... Mia..."

Then—

"R... *run...*"

Static. Silence.

The overhead floodlights slam on. The doors behind them lock shut with a metallic boom.

A voice comes over the intercom, cold and rehearsed:

"Welcome, A-3-B-3-7... and her esteemed guest. Mia is our latest combat construct—stitched from failure, born for obedience. She will determine if you deserve to leave here alive."

The robot stands—its figure now fully illuminated.

Even the hair—Mia's signature blue—is stitched to the machine's scalp.

It steps forward, fists clenching with unnatural fluidity.

Combat systems hum and whir to life.

Amber raises her weapon.

"Oh fuck. Stay behind me, Roan."

Amber picks up and throws Roan out of the way of the charging robot. Mia slams her fist into the ground, narrowly missing Amber.

Amber adjusts her glasses and starts her assault.

She grabs the robot's arm and attempts to flip it—too heavy. The robot throws her into the wall.

Amber winces as she slams into the wall and collapses. Her systems flash in her eyes: CRITICAL FAILURE IMMINENT.

"Oh, we also forgot to mention," a voice says. "The heaviness in the air is a cybernetic suppressant. You are fighting for your life, A-3."

Roan grabs his rifle and throws the strap over his head, slinging the gun across his back. He scrambles up a jagged rock wall, jumps, and catches the edge of a floodlight with one hand—barely hanging on. He drops, landing on the robot. His face contorts in disgust as he cuts through the skin, looking for an access panel.

Amber forces herself up, seeing Roan in action—every fiber in her body fighting her own movements.

He peels the skin open, gagging with every rip, revealing a small opening in the neck. Roan flips his gun around and shoots into the hole.

The robot frenzies, slamming its fists into every part of the room, yelling phrases in Mia's voice—disturbing, chilling, dangerous.

"Whyyy are you—no, don't—slut—run—whore—STOP—run—she wanted it—get off, m-m-me!—run—he's still—bzzzrt—stop, NO—run—whyyy—run—"

Roan notices a personality track attached to the central processor. He grabs it, planting his feet against the back of the robot's head, pulling with all his strength until it finally comes loose.

His legs launch him off the robot's head, track in hand, flying through the air before smacking his head against a rock. He gets up, dazed and bleeding.

The robot collapses, unable to determine its movements anymore.

"T... t... tthan... k y... o... u..." Mia's voice says, trailing off as the processor loses power.

"Well, look at you two," the voice over the intercom says. "I'm curious to see how your teamwork prevails in the next room."

***

A door slides open, revealing another dark chamber.

Roan gets up and goes over to Amber, helping her walk.

"This is some bullshit," Amber mutters, smirking. "How'd I get stuck with the handicap?"

Roan laughs. "This handicap is the only reason you're alive."

"Let me return the favor," she says, eyeing his busted head. "Keep bleeding like that, and you'll be the one slowing me down. And if you die, Isabella will kill me. *I'd rather die in here than face her.*"

They laugh—bruised, bloody, and breathless—as Amber tears open a small medkit and starts patching him up.

Roan stands up, his head bandaged. They walk into the next room. Hallway lights flash all the way down—rock to their right, glass to the left revealing nothing but darkness. As they get halfway down the hallway, the voice comes over the speakers again.

Bzzzrt... "In this room, we have a scenario in which you must press a button on the other side. The cybernetic suppressant has been turned off for this test. But, if you are detected or trip an alarm, the cybernetic suppressant comes back on. Good luck."

The lights flash, and Amber stares at the room now lit up. Robotic guards walk in predetermined paths, their optical sensors scanning unpredictably. Laser grids line the floors and walls; beams occasionally flash across the room.

"Amber... I can't help with this one," Roan says.

"I know," Amber replies, her voice low. "I'm an Infiltrator. I've done this before—apparently. I'll do it again."

She walks the rest of the hallway and finds a stairwell. She goes down and sees a door.

Bzzzrt... "We forgot to mention, you have a time limit. As we speak, your colleague's hallway is filling with carbon dioxide. Tick tock, A-3. Tick-tock."

Roan watches as vents open near his feet. He feels the air blow in.

"Shit."

Amber breathes in deep, scans the room, and spots a panel with a red button.

She calculates a path, jumps between beams, standing on one foot. She rotates, shoots a guard in the optical sensor—its body falls and hits a laser grid, cut clean in half.

"Oh," she mutters. *"They aren't just for show."*

She holsters her weapon and watches a laser rotate across a nearby wall. Most of the time, it's clear.

"Gotta time this right."

She hops off her foot, flips forward, and lands her hands between another set of grids. With a burst of strength, she launches herself upward, flips mid-air, and folds her body to kick off a wall. She grabs a guard by the neck and throws it into a laser grid, redirecting herself and instantly slicing the guard into sparking cubes.

She slams her hand on the red button. The guards, lasers, and carbon dioxide all deactivate. Roan runs down.

"That was amazing," he says.

Amber, sweating, throws him a smile. "Yeah, no big deal. Easy."

Bzzzrt... "Well, looks like I was wrong. A-3s aren't complete pieces of trash ready for the dumpster. One more test, A-3. Let's see what you're made of."

The wall with the button slides open, revealing another room already lit.

"Why does she keep calling you A-3?" Roan asks.

"I'm not sure," she says, confused. "All I know is—I want to get the fuck out of here."

"Agreed." Roan nods.

The pair walk into the room—a massive corridor lined with concrete pillars in neat rows.

"This place is massive," Amber says.

"Looks like an unfinished parking garage," Roan adds.

Bzzzrt... "A-3, your last challenge. This room will fill with water—and with a Verelliian native species called a Razorfin. Imagine a creature that will eat anything to survive. The Razorfins in our care haven't eaten in a while. Good luck."

"Wait!" Amber yells.

"Oh, we have a question?" the voice says.

"Yeah—how do you have that much water? Hydropure is what people drink because the planet doesn't have natural water."

"Ah. I see why you're confused. Hydropure is purely synthetic... designed to kill Verellii citizens slowly. I'll tell you more if you survive."

Massive metallic gates open in the distance. Roan's eyes widen.

"I can't swim," he says. "Never had to."

"Me neither, Roan. But *I'll get you out of here.* You have my word. Get on."

Amber motions for him to climb on her back. She punches her fists into the nearest pillar and climbs rapidly.

At the top, Roan dismounts.

"Okay. First of all, you're amazing. Second... kinda emasculating."

"I can just throw you back down. Stop your drama. I need to figure this out."

As the tunnel floods, Amber smells the water; its scent is oddly soothing.

In another moment, this would actually be nice, she thinks, scanning the room.

As she's scanning, something catches her eye in the water—a single figure, massive. Then it splits into thousands of smaller figures. Brown, sleek, fast. Their bodies open halfway, exposing several rows of razor-sharp fangs. They watch her with patient anticipation.

Amber closes her eyes for a moment, breathing in, focusing, suppressing her fear. She continues to scan until she sees an orange door on the ceiling in the distance—no crossbeams, only pillars.

She turns to face Roan as he's investigating a dead Infiltrator leaning against the pillar.

"She starved to death," he says quietly. "She was so young."

"Roan, jump on again. We've gotta get over there."

Roan gets up, accidentally bumping into the tragic woman. Her lifeless body slips and falls into the water. It disintegrates into a flurry of colors, the fish immediately swarming the body, and then... nothing. The Razorfins stare at Amber and Roan, unflinching. Hungry.

Roan climbs on. Amber launches to the nearest column—slamming her fists in and climbing. She punches her way around, lining up with the next.

She leaps again—mid-air flip—then slams into the next column.

Her fists connect, but her foot slips—dipping into the water. The Razorfin swarm rushes toward her, shredding her foot. Metallic muscle, synthetic flesh—devoured.

"FFFFFFUCK!!" she screams.

She punches the wall and pulls herself up—her foot now a mangled stump, metallic muscle spilling cooling fluid, part of the bone showing.

"I got you!" Roan yells. "I'll use my foot to stabilize your leg. We need to tie my leg to yours, then I'll wrap my body around you."

Amber nods, her body screaming in pain, the water level still rising.

She holds them in place with one foot and one hand as Roan slides his foot under her damaged leg.

Amber leans down, helping Roan tie his belt around their legs—giving her some mobility again.

"Just don't break my foot," he mutters.

She uses Roan's foot as an anchor, as she smashes another foothold, and drags herself higher—inch by inch—toward the hatch.

"Okay, Roan... this is it. I've never jumped that far with one foot before. If we don't make it, just know I'm—"

"Shut up and jump," Roan says with a smile.

She jumps.

Grabs the hatch.

It slides up and pulls them into a dark room.

A light comes on.

On the other side of the glass, they see a woman. She's in all black, except for a pin. It's blue, with a planet on it. It isn't the gold and oranges of Verellii—it's green and blue.

Earth.

Her hair is jet black, her brown eyes sharp, unflinching. Her dark skin glows under the lights.

"Lena?" Amber whispers.

"Yes, A-3. It's me."

"You left the Infiltrators. We thought you died."

"That was the point," Lena replies coldly. "I wasn't good enough for the X1 procedure. Too unstable, they said. Too much trauma. Too unpredictable."

Amber's lips part, confused.

"But my mind? That, they said, was brilliant. So they gave me a new purpose—watching L-3-X-1. Helping build it. Deploying it. Making sure it aligned with Earth's goals. I ran the Infiltrator Corps, manipulating from the inside. Why do you think the Union hates you so much?" Lena's lips curl into a cruel smile.

"But every night, I threw up pretending that thing—L-3-X-1—could ever be a person. Replace a person. I had to converse with it, teach it, raise it. Machines that think they're human? Repulsive."

"Lexi is a woman. She's like you and me—augmented, yes—but she has feelings. Emotions. She feels pain."

Lena narrows her eyes. "No. She's a machine. They told me that. A tool—undefeatable, immortal, perfect. What they always wanted me to be."

Amber sees it now—the bitterness behind her tone.

"You're jealous," she says quietly.

Lena ignores it. "The higher-ups said L-3-X-1 couldn't be broken. They were right. That moral compass of hers... kept getting in the way. She wouldn't obey. Wouldn't kill on command. Wouldn't forget."

Amber steps forward. "Lexi remembers who she is. She's not a tool."

"A-3, why do you keep calling it Lexi?"

"Because she is Lexi. She lives. Breathes. Loves…" Amber hesitates. *"She loves me."*

She straightens, trying to suppress her tremble. "Why do you keep calling me A-3?"

"A series of numbers and letters based on generation, version, and refinement," Lena sneers. "You're A-Series, but that 3 isn't prestige—it's a small upgrade. Just enough to call you improved, but it only makes you equivalent to a B-Model. Bottom of the barrel, dressed up as something better."

She tilts her head, eyes glinting. "The third digit? B. Bravo-class upgrades, good, but still not Alphas or X1 tier. Then your scraps—3 and 7. Bone Density Reinforcement. Vision Augmentation. Funny thing, though…" Her gaze lingers on Amber's face, lips curling. "You've got a seven-spec eye upgrade—and you still wear glasses. Defective, even by failed-experiment standards."

"I'm more than a series of numbers and letters!" Amber roared.

Lena exhaled slowly, lips curling in a faint, dismissive smile. "No. You're not. You're a designation. A failed experiment dressed up to look useful. Nothing more."

Amber's fists trembled. "Then why the Hydropure?"

Lena's voice was calm, clinical. "To soften Verelliians from the inside. Defiant. Stubborn. Too strong to break outright. So we weaken you slowly—make you doubt your strength, strip the fight from your blood while you're too busy surviving to notice you're dying."

Her tone sharpened. Her eyes glinted. "Earth doesn't want peace. They want steel."

The calm cracked, spilling into fevered obsession. "Verelliian steel—denser, stronger, reborn under pressure. Forged only here, under this cursed sky and Anthrallii's radiation. Steel that makes fleets immortal. Soldiers into titans. Ships into gods of war!"

Her breath quickened. She laughed once, sharp and bitter. "That's the mission, A-3. That's what the EBOI was built for. Quiet infiltration. Deep sabotage. Rot Verellii from the inside until the whole tree collapses."

Amber's voice was hoarse. "Everything we are... everything we believed in..."

"Everyone we lost, everyone who died—was it just part of your plan?"

Lena's smile thinned. "No. That was just... cleanup."

Silence. Bitter. Final.

Amber's voice cuts through the tension—soft but unwavering. "You'll never win. Lexi's not only a weapon—she is sheer determination. And I'm not just A-3. *My name is Amber.*"

Lena's smile is thin. "Not for much longer. You are welcome to leave. I think I've—"

"Eraugh!!!"

Lena drives her fists into her skull, a guttural scream ripping out of her throat. Her nails rake across her cheek, tearing away a ragged strip of synthflesh. It peels loose from beneath her left eye down to the corner of her mouth, hanging there like a grotesque banner.

Beneath the flap, her true self shows—fibrous metallic muscle twitching and flexing with each spasm, strands pulling tight like steel sinew. Her jaw works unevenly, half of it human, half raw alloy exposed, every breath dragged through the shimmer of torn flesh.

She thrashes, overturning a chair, shattering a screen with one swipe, sending shards of glass skittering across the floor. A console sparks as she slams a fist into it, lighting the room with quick flashes of blue and red. Amber flinches, weapon rising. Roan stiffens, teeth clenched, watching the meltdown with a mix of horror and disbelief.

Then—sudden stillness.

Her chest heaves, breaths sharp and jagged. With deliberate precision, she smooths her jet-black hair back into place and straightens her clothing as though nothing had happened. The strip of peeled skin still dangles from her face, swaying gently when she tilts her head.

Slowly, almost delicately, she pinches the hanging flap between two fingers and tears it away. The synthflesh parts with a dry, fibrous rip, like fabric splitting down a seam.

Amber flinches at the sound, her stomach twisting as she imagines her own face tearing the same way. Roan turns his head, jaw tight, swallowing down a surge of nausea.

Lena flicks the strip aside like garbage, her exposed metallic muscle glinting in the dim light.

When she speaks again, her tone is smooth. Cold. Measured. "As I was saying—you're welcome to leave. But my... let's say roommates? They're not going to be thrilled you're here."

She presses a button on the wall. A side door hisses open next to Amber and Roan. When they look back, Lena is gone—disappeared into shadow.

***

Amber exhales, feeling the weight of Roan still clinging to her back as she glances over her shoulder. "We need to find a medical bay," she whispers. "I can do most of the work to fix my foot, but you'll have to help. She said they test Infiltrators here... they must have some new muscle strands I can use."

She hobbles forward, using Roan's foot as her own. Every step is silent but strained. Roan grits his teeth—his movements clumsy and unfamiliar, his foot screaming in protest.

They creep past a control center.

Screens flicker: feeds of the Union tunnels, glitchy images of the Sanctum, Lexi and Isabella clearing rooms in a different building. Several Enforcer helmet feeds blink in and out.

No words pass between them. But an understanding does.

This place has to fall.

As they round a corner, Amber bumps directly into a man in all black—balaclava over his face. He looks down. Before he can speak—

Amber lifts up, covers his mouth, and snaps his neck in one fluid motion. His body drops limp and she catches him, dragging him into a side room and closing the door before continuing on.

"I think we're close," she says, breath steady. "That looked like a recovery suite."

They slip into another room. Glass walls on two sides, but the curtains are drawn. Inside—every tool and supply they need. Amber and Roan settle in the dark.

"I'll grab what I need. I'll work fast. You cover the door. When I need your help, I'll turn the lights on. Someone might notice then—so I'll talk you through it and cover your back while you work."

Roan nods. Another challenge.

He sits facing the door, rifle firmly in his hands. The hallway is faintly lit beneath the seam. Shadows pass. Voices echo. His finger tightens on the trigger—until they move on. He exhales and eases off the pressure.

Behind him, he hears material being torn. Fluid spilling. Quick curses. Then long stretches of silence before something rattles in the background.

He doesn't look back. He just focuses on one thing—

Isabella.

"Okay, Roan—you're up," Amber whispers.

She flicks the light on.

"I can't reach this part," she says, pointing at her heel. She hands him a skin synthesizer. "You've gotta take this—build my heel up. The metal should align on its own."

Roan's eyes widen. "Wait... is that a classroom skeleton's foot?"

He looks up at her. She smiles, and he sees her pointing at a model skeleton behind her, foot missing.

"I had to make new pieces from what I found. Not all of us are Lexi." She gives a tired smile. "After that, hit it with the skin synthesizer. It'll stop once the layer's good... if not, you'll have to eyeball it."

He kneels. Her leg is propped across his lap, heel exposed, metallic tissue gleaming under the light. Her arms rest across his shoulders, pistol raised behind his head, her face pressed against his cheek.

"Speed up!" she hisses.

"I've never done this before! I don't even know what this is supposed to look like!"

Seconds crawl like hours.

"Okay... I think I'm done."

Amber slides away and examines it. "Not bad. Can't feel a damn thing in my left foot—but it'll have to do." She stands, rotating her ankle carefully. Full movement.

She kills the light and peeks out the door.

Then glances back at Roan, a smirk forming. *Let's do some fucking damage.*

***

The pair, now separated and under their own control, move near-silently through the corridors, taking in the layout, personnel, and tech within the facility. They head further down into the bowels of the hidden site, where coroners are pulling dozens of dead females out of six-wheeled trucks and bringing them into another location.

"Let's see what's going on down there," Amber says.

She takes the lead, getting quieter with every step, adjusting to her new foot.

She peeks into the doorway the coroners had entered, seeing a long hallway stretch out in front of them. The coroners disappear into a room on the far end and close the door behind them.

"This place is weird," Roan says.

"Imagine what I'm feeling, then!" Amber replies. "I was apparently made here."

They step into the hallway. Lights flicker on as they walk further in.

There are rows upon rows of female bodies, nude with hooks under their armpits.

"They seem to be hooked to a conveyor system," Roan says, pointing at the ceiling.

"And you didn't notice all their asses and tits are gone?" Amber says jokingly.

"Yeah, what's up with that?"

"That's where they put most of our augmentations—to make us look more natural, to fit in places. But they change it up every once in a while.

"Like, I'm sure you've noticed I have big boobs and Isabella has a big ass."

"Yeah, I've definitely noticed Isabella's ass," Roan says, drifting into thought.

Amber rolls her eyes. "Okay, I've seen enough. We need to blow this place up."

They head back into the hall and find a service entrance.

Climbing down a ladder, they hear a few voices.

Amber looks up at Roan above her on the ladder. "Don't kill anyone we don't have to. It'll just draw attention. We let the explosion do the work."

Roan nods as they both descend.

They creep from shadow to shadow, avoiding anything that might make noise if brushed against.

Until they see it.

There, in the middle of the room, is a reactor.

Its size could power several cities within Verellii.

If Earth has this kind of technology...

What chance do they have against it?

"It's beautiful," Amber says, staring into the colors.

An orb sits in the middle of a clear tank.

Blue, white, and yellow streak in all directions before returning to the orb again.

The lines attached to it pulse with faint light, running up and throughout the facility.

"Okay, Amber, what's your plan for getting us out and setting this off?" Roan asks.

"Plan? The plan is to blow this up, and save Verellii from whatever this horror show is," Amber whispers.

"And what about us?"

"What do you mean, us?"

"I mean how do we survive the blast?"

Amber doesn't answer at first.

Then—

"We don't."

"What the fuck do you mean we don't?" he says, loudly in a whisper.

"Listen," Amber turns to him, steady. "We have to make sacrifices for the people of Verellii. *They won't know our names or our deeds... but they will know freedom.* I'm happy with how my life has been. Are you?"

He thinks about the short time he's known Isabella, Lexi, and Amber.

How they're like sisters—friendly, loyal.

They were built to destroy Verellii, to betray it.

But here one is... trying to save it.

And she doesn't even care if she lives or dies.

He nods. "I'm happy with my life. And... I made Isabella happy too."

Amber smiles and scans her hand on the reactor's terminal.

IMPRINT INVALID. LOCKDOWN PROCEDURES INITIATED.

The pair watch as a transparent cube lowers from the ceiling, sealing the reactor inside.

"I got this," Roan says.

He opens a nearby panel and starts examining the circuitry.

"Can you see one labeled OC or OLC?"

"Not in this panel," Amber says.

They move to another. She shakes her head. "Not here either."

The last panel is near two workers.

Amber grabs a pipe above them, swings, and locks her legs around one's neck—twisting violently.

She uses the falling corpse as a silencer and shoots the other in the head.

"I thought you said don't kill anyone!" Roan says, ducking behind a console.

"I said if we don't need to. We definitely needed to there," she says with a giggle, already cracking open the final panel.

"There—OC and OLC," Roan points.

"What do they stand for?"

"Overcharge and Overload Circuit. If we wire both directly to a power feed, the circuit won't have a failsafe anymore." He pauses. "It'll explode. I'd say... give or take a few minutes."

Amber nods, softly. "It was nice knowing you, Roan."

"It was a pleasure, Amber."

Roan sets to work, wiring up the breakers to one of the pulsating power conduits. He places the splices.

Snap.

Sparks fly as the panel erupts in flame.

WARNING. WARNING. REACTOR DAMAGE. EVACUATE IMMEDIATELY.

The reactor turns blood red, spitting fire and unconstrained energy in every direction—

The harnessed sun, unleashed.

Its light fills every corridor with fire, radiation, and raw power.

Then, silence.

Darkness.

The only light: a stray spark crackling above melted metal.

Roan blinks. As quickly as the violence started, it ends. Sparks spit from torn wiring; water hisses through ruptured pipes—but the world stays dark.

"I'm... alive?"

He groans, realizing he's pinned under a heavy sheet of metal.

"Amber!" he strains. "Where are you?"

He shoves upward, muscles screaming. The plate tips and slams down beside him with a dull clang. He rolls, coughing.

A spark flares—just enough to show it.

A body, charred and broken, lay next to the metal sheet; he realized she had put her body across the sheet to hold it in place.

Deliberate. Protective.

A shield.

"No..." he whispers.

A third spark stutters in the dark—just enough to catch the faint green glow of a mechanical eye.

"I... I'm here..." Amber wheezes. *"It was my turn to rescue you."*

He reaches for her. His skin sizzles on contact.

"Shit—I'm gonna have to wait for you to cool off..."

Every few moments, the sparks go off—brief flashes of light in the dark. And in those flickers... he sees her.

The shell of Amber.

Metal muscle exposed.

Clothes, skin, and organics burned away.

Her human insides—barely holding on.

Then darkness again.

Silence.

Another spark—another glimpse of the damage.

She's not moving. But her eye glows, dim and defiant.

"Why?" Roan asks, barely able to speak. "Why would you sacrifice yourself like this—for me?"

She wheezes, voice shredded. "It... wa... sn't... f-for you... It wa... s... f-for... Izzz... y."

She grits her teeth, twitching. "I... t-told you... If you die... *I'd... rr-rather die... down here... than... f-face... her.*"

Her eye flickers. Her smile holds, even as she fades.

Roan sees her eye flicker. That's enough.

He grabs her arm, hoists her over his shoulder—her frame heavier now, limp, scorched—and begins to climb. He doesn't stop, even as pain screams through his body. Amber's metal frame, still hot, scorches his skin.

As he ascends the ladder, he makes sure she doesn't slip, taking his time. He reaches the top and looks around at the chaos left behind by the reactor.

Cables hang from every inch of the ceiling, sparking and twitching in the smoky air.

Pipes, cracked and warped, spray water, flooding the floor.

Screens flicker—stuttering broken warnings in fractured code.

And the bodies...

Some reduced to bone, charred clean by the blast.

Others left as black streaks, burned into the walls.

A few still sit at their posts, heads bowed like they never moved.

And some—arms outstretched—frozen mid-reach, like they were begging for help that never came.

He walks through the aftermath, water slapping with each step, boots trailing streaks of Amber's green cooling fluid. Then, he sees it—light flooding from a door.

His brow furrows as he gets closer.

This looks familiar, he thinks, peering through the opening.

He peeks around the corner, sees the gate and the entrance they originally used—the one that started this horror show.

Then he hears voices. A lot of them.

It isn't chanting—it's something different.

It's chaos. People scrambling, shouting, arguing. Somewhere in the mess, a voice rises above the rest—sharp, commanding, trying to restore order.

He steps through the doorway. He doesn't see anyone yet, but he can hear them. He walks up to the gate. The six-wheeled black trucks are gone.

He heads to the alcove where he stashed the VT-1.

It's partially caved in, but the truck is still good—just buried in a layer of rock and dust.

He lays Amber in the back. She moans as he puts her down.

He drives as fast as he can out of the tunnel, engine whirring, dust flying in his wake.

At the mouth of the tunnel, he sees the source of the voices—survivors gathered at an evacuation point, black trucks blocking the entrance.

He yells to Amber, "Hold on!"

He floors it.

The Skyreaper compressor whistles at an ear-shattering pitch. The front of the truck lifts slightly, gaining speed with every inch.

"Open fire!" the commander shouts.

A hailstorm of bullets and laser fire slams into the truck.

He rams between the black trucks—one tips onto its side, the other spins and knocks out a couple of guys hiding behind it, smoking Blaze.

He rushes across the vast open sea of sand and dust, gaining more and more speed.

The engine sucks in precious air like a starving beast.

BEEP BEEP BEEP! OVERHEAT WARNING!

"Shut up!" Roan snaps, the warning blaring in protest.

The VT-1 begs for mercy. Roan doesn't listen.

He checks the rearview—

A black truck behind him. It's not fast enough to catch him, but it can follow the dust trail he's leaving behind.

He slams on the brakes, the pursuer gaining ground.

Then hits the gas again, spinning the VT-1 to face his enemy.

He flips a switch.

GUNS ONLINE, the truck informs.

His windshield lights up with a faint green targeting reticle.

"What did you say before, Amber? Oh, that's right—*LET'S DO SOME FUCKING DAMAGE!*"

He slams the gas. Hits the button on his wheel.

Metallic spinning roars from under the front fenders.

Then—

Muzzle flashes.

Smoke pours as bullet casings rain down from the fenders, pinging off Verellii's tough crust.

The twin rotary guns unleash an unrelenting assault.

Metal dents. Glass shatters.

The enemy truck starts to smoke—then veers off, flipping to its side.

Roan pulls up to the wreck and walks to the front window, rifle drawn.

The driver and passenger are dead—shot to pieces by the VT-1's guns.

He moves to the back, practiced, his finger ready on the trigger.

He opens the door; a pin on a string whips past his head.

His eyes snap to the back of the truck—

A silver canister, strapped down.

Click.

"Fuck—"

Roan tries to turn, but the explosion slams into him point-blank.

Shrapnel tears through the right side of his face, arm, and leg as he's launched backward, crashing to the ground.

Blood seeps through his clothes, trailing in slow, dark ribbons down his arm and leg—soaking the fabric as it spreads.

Smoke floods the wreck and his ears ring. Everything burns.

His rifle is somewhere behind him, just out of reach.

He groans, spits blood, and claws at Verellii's sands as he tries to flip over. He flips, crawling to his rifle until his left hand stretches and his fingertips brush the rifle stock. He grabs it.

Inch by inch, he drags himself across the dirt—pushing off with his good leg and arm, leaving a trail of blood behind him like a smear of warpaint.

The VT-1 idles ahead, engine rumbling, its exhaust curling in the warm air.

He reaches it. Pulls himself up the side with trembling fingers, boots scraping against the metal sidesteps.

Every muscle in his body screams as he collapses into the driver's seat.

His vision starts to blur as his blood drips down the seat, pooling onto the footwell.

"I can't pass out now, she still needs me," he whispers.

He shifts into gear, hands slick with blood, vision swimming.

The road back is a blur—sand, sun, smoke.

His grip weakens. The truck rattles beneath him. The engine howls. The frame groans.

Then—he sees it, the soup kitchen. Safety, within reach.

His foot slips from the pedal.

The VT-1 rolls forward, slow but heavy.

It loses speed before slamming into the wall with a dull crunch—metal meeting brick.

Just hard enough to crack a headlight and rattle the windows inside.

The engine idles as Roan puts the truck in park.

"Roan, are you okay?!" he hears a voice yell in the distance.

Roan slumps forward over the wheel as blackness overcomes his v   i   -
sion.

CHAP_24.exe – SENTINEL

> Active File: I5A13-3-11-4.sys   > Booting Secondary: L3X1.exe   > Cross-Link Established . . .   > MER##GE SEQUEN_CE ERROR . . .   > Recompiling . . .   > Merge Sequence: COMPLETE   > Directive Updated →

"Isabella, take right!" Lexi yelled from a corridor. Men in all black are at the end of a long hallway, the dilapidated building crumbling around them.

Isabella jumps across beams several stories in the air, flanking the men. She punches one man, launching him out of the building. A man turns, facing her, laser gun ready to fire—then a rock slams into him, lodging in his skull. He flops to the ground. She looks over at Lexi, who gives her a nod.

Isabella jumps, pushes off of a wall, and punches down on a man taking cover behind a concrete slab, his skull disintegrating from the force.

Isabella and Lexi climb up the next set of stairs, finishing clearing out the ruins of the old building, when they hear it.

An electric, static explosion fills the air. Metric tons of dirt, debris, and dust fly into the atmosphere, rocks landing miles from where they were launched. A massive tower in the middle of the explosion starts to collapse.

"That's where Amber and Roan were," Isabella said, worry flaring in her voice.

"Amber, come in. Amber, do you read?" Lexi said into her left arm. No answer.

***

"Mierda..." Isabella whispered.

A shot rings out and hits Isabella in the arm. She looks at the mark, wiping off the soot from where the bullet had hit, and looks at the man who shot it with ferocity in her eyes.

"I... I... I'm sorry..." he stammered, dropping the weapon and bolting for the stairwell.

Lexi and Isabella watch him as he clumsily runs out of the building.

They continue their climb, and as they reach the top, a lone guard fires at them as Lexi tries to call Amber again.

"Amber, come in. Amber, do you read? Fuck. Nothing. Izzy, can you try your comms?"

Isabella looks over at Lexi and puts a bullet through the man's head.

"Yeah. Amber, do you read me? Sorry, mami, nothing."

As Lexi looks around, she notices something in the direction of the explosion. It's a silhouette matching Roan's truck—and a vehicle in pursuit of them. The vehicles pass behind a mountain just out of sight. Then they hear it.

Gunshots of a high caliber firing in rapid succession. Then nothing. Then an explosion and plumes of smoke rising in the distance.

"No," Isabella whispered. "Lexi, we have to go back!"

"Izzy, we have a mission. Unfortunately, the needs of the many outweigh the needs of the few. You said I would have your focus, right?"

"Yes."

"Then we move on as planned. The last place is that... holy shit, Izzy, look!"

Above them, a massive object moves into place. An immense ship slides into orbit, so vast it blots out Verellii's sun.

***

"Commander Hayes, do you read me?"

"Go ahead, Captain Thorne."

"Something happened. The control of the Enforcers is no longer in play. You have us on your side. Do you have a plan?"

"I do. Sending a ping."

"Copy, Commander. I see you. Forces inbound."

Some time passes as Lexi and Isabella drive to their last location—the redacted site that was on every map they could find.

As they approach, five gunships fly past them at alarming speeds. They see them stop and hover just in front of the building. One at a time, Enforcers jump from the gunships and line up in formations. Thorne jumps out and stands in front, his helmet folding back to reveal his face.

The girls pull up and get out.

"Captain, you've done so much for the people of Verellii. Let us do something for you. My forces are at your command."

FLOOM FLOOM FLOOM

They look up as pitch-black Earth landing craft come from the sky to their location. They don't appear to be armed ships, so Lexi directs everyone to watch and to only engage if fired upon.

The landing craft settle to the ground, just a few hundred feet in front of them.

A man flanked on either side by two all-black robots accompanies him, several troops flooding out of the ships, creating their own formations.

"Ahh, Lexi Hayes," the man said as he gets closer.

"Shogo Akiyama," she said. "So, you're behind all this?"

"I am not. Just a mere messenger. I bring the message of peace or death. Above you is the largest Earth ship ever created, with a massive invasion force. The president of Earth is aboard, overseeing this operation. I, the vice president of Earth, was to ensure the chaos and disruption of Verellii for invasion."

"So, what do you propose, Mr. Vice President?" Lexi asked.

"I propose you stand all your forces down, tell us where the vault is, and surrender your planet to Earth rule. If not, our full might will be realized and your people will suffer."

***

Another ship drops down. This one is different—it is red and gold.

"Ahh, the commander of our forces is here. Maybe he can shed some light on what is going to happen if you refuse."

The ship lands, and the person that comes out leaves Lexi speechless.

"Sentinel Wilks."

"Captain Hayes," he said, walking up, flanked by two Aegis members. Their mere presence sends fear down the Enforcers' spines. "It's good you are here. It's time to reveal our most useful tool."

He pulls out a small controller and points it toward Lexi. Click. Click... Click. "I don't understand," he said, smacking the controller.

He looks over at Vice President Akiyama. "Sir, I thought you installed a new chip."

"I did," he said, looking stoically at Lexi.

"I had it removed," she said with a smirk. "Drove me crazy for a couple days, but luckily I have friends with a couple skills."

"No matter. When the rest of the Aegis show up, this pathetic defense force will be crushed."

White and gold gunships soon arrive with Aegis jumping out, landing behind Sentinel Wilks.

"Captain," Thorne leans in. "We may want to take a deal. I'm willing to fight by your side for glory until death. But this isn't going to be a fight. My men will be slaughtered."

"Yeah, I was just thinking the same thing," Lexi said.

"So, now that you understand just a fraction of our power, what say you?" Wilks said.

"I have no power over this planet," Lexi started.

"But you know what I've noticed? Where is Verellii's president? Why have we never seen him? I've seen a man in a tank, heard speeches on the radio—but no in-person interviews."

She pauses, her eyes narrowing.

"And you... Sentinel Wilks... You sound exactly like him. Not similar. Identical. That's not a coincidence."

"You know what I think?"

She takes a step forward.

"I think you are President Wilks."

Whispers flood through the Aegis ranks.

"Silence!" yelled Sentinel Wilks. "I will not let our honorable order be disrupted by speculation!"

"It's not speculation," a lone Aegis said from the back.

In a practiced fashion, the Aegis arrange their formation to create a walkway, albeit a very armored one.

The Aegis Titan moves forward toward Wilks and Akiyama. "Sir, I would like permission to speak—it is my right as an Aegis."

"Proceed," Wilks hissed.

Brawn steps forward, pulling a small projector from a hidden pocket in his suit. He tosses it to the ground. It lights up—documents flicker in the air. Then a short video plays. A sterile room. A brain-mapping interface. A neural consciousness transfer in progress. President Wilks—clearly him—being moved to a new, synthetic body.

***

"A couple days ago," Brawn said, "I left the company of Lexi and her team to investigate an old Aegis facility. I found these files—sealed, off-grid, never meant to be discovered. President Wilks had his mind transferred. That man," he pointed at Sentinel Wilks, "is him."

"But there was someone who caught on. General Pike. Verellii's finest commander. He tried to stop it... But he failed."

Brawn's jaw tightens.

"He was tortured. Mutilated. Turned into a monster, thrown away like trash into the Union tunnels."

He looks Wilks dead in the eye.

"I killed the best commander Verellii had—because you turned him into something unrecognizable."

"There are no records of a son. But multiple confirmations of a mind transfer. This was Earth's plan. Infiltrate. Destabilize. And destroy from the inside."

The Sentinel roars, drawing his laser rifle and pointing it directly at Brawn's head.

Two Aegis step forward and restrain him.

"Sir, it is Aegis law—we must be able to hear him out fully. Then we will decide his fate."

"General Pike was tortured, beaten, experimented on, mutilated, and enhanced against his will—and most importantly, betrayed. *He fought, bled, died for Verellii.*

You, President Wilks, sold us out in the beginning... and now you try to finish your work. You scrambled, because one pissed off, determined, and stubborn Infiltrator interrupted your work," Brawn said as he flashed Lexi a wink.

She rolls her eyes before Brawn continues.

"Unfortunately for you, the Aegis were created to be a shield in Verellii's defense, a sword against Verellii's foes, and the sacrifice for Verellii's people. We will be the tip of the spear leading our forces against you and the forces that stand against us."

The president looks up, his face evil and twisted.

"Earth gave me a beautiful sum to turn on these... disgusting, dirty people. They are no better than savages. Animals. I would gladly sell you all out again. It was an honor to rile up the Union forces. To get T.N.O. on my side. To blow up that abomination of an HQ harboring cybernetically enhanced freaks!

Humans are supposed to be just that—human! Not machine. Not... metal. I WILL KILL YOU ALL!"

"But you are augmented... aren't you?" Brawn asked.

"No, I was created this way, no augmentations fill my temple," President Wilks spat.

"That's a lie, your eyes glowed orange in the Sanctum!" Lexi yelled.

"Lenses that fit over my eyes, you stupid girl," Wilks lashed back.

"Your punishment for treason against Verellii and her people is death," Brawn stated. The two Aegis at Wilks's side force him down to his knees.

"Do you have any final words?" Brawn asked, holding his laser sword up.

"Fuck you," the president sneered, spitting at Brawn's feet.

"So be it," Brawn said, his sword coming down and cutting the snake's head off.

Wilks's head rolls toward Shogo Akiyama as the Earth forces start to realize they lost a powerful ally.

"I AM ALLOWING ALL OF YOU TO LEAVE PEACEFULLY," Brawn yelled to Earth's forces. "IF YOU STAY, ALL YOU WILL FIND IS DEATH. Go to Earth in peace. Leave Verellii alone."

As the last word leaves Brawn's lips—*"Leave Verellii alone"*—the ground rumbles beneath the boots of the Aegis.

They move in unison.

Shoulders lock. Aegis riot shields ignite, a faint blue aura pulsing in their centers. Their swords twist and collapse inward, shafts expanding—swords becoming spears. The transformation emits a deep mechanical shhk-thunk in perfect synchronization.

They form a wall—an impenetrable phalanx.

No threats. No commands. Only the hum of energy shields and the glare of their visors reflecting firelight.

Behind them, Thorne's Enforcers fall into staggered cover formations—heavy, brute power backing up the surgical precision of the Aegis wall.

And at the front of it all... Brawn, silent, face unreadable, his sword still dripping with Wilks's blood.

As the Earth forces begin to withdraw, Shogo Akiyama pauses at the ramp of his ship.

He turns, his voice low but sharp:

"Then this... is war. I hope for your sake, Ms. Hayes, that you are prepared."

The ramp seals behind him with a hydraulic hiss. The invasion force lifts into the sky—ominous, but retreating.

Silence follows. No one celebrates.

The Aegis begin moving. They sheathe their weapons and unload items from the landed gunships.

Two of them step forward and kneel beside Wilks's corpse. They gently remove his Sentinel armor—each piece lifted with reverence, not for the man, but for the meaning it once held. They carry it away, solemn and silent.

Elsewhere, within their ranks, Aegis members build a fire. The armor is scrubbed of its betrayal, scorched in the fire, then polished to a raw silver sheen.

When it is complete, they carry it back.

Laid across a folded black cloth.

Presented not with fanfare—but with purpose.

The Enforcers watch as the Aegis murmur amongst themselves, quietly pointing to different members within their own ranks.

"What are they doing, Lexi?" Isabella asked.

"I think they're voting for a new Sentinel," she responded.

As time passes, the last Aegis Titan walks toward the armor. It's Brawn. He looks back at his brothers-in-arms, then seals his helmet. He stands for a moment, then the helmet folds back into the armor as he steps away.

The Sentinel armor, stripped of all color, registers the info, its seams glowing with holy gold light. It then speaks in a firm robotic tone:

All Aegis have voted. A new Sentinel has been selected. The results are as follows:

Aegis Titan Sergeant George Hazzer: 11% of votes

Aegis Titan Private Kaelor Brawn: 72% of votes

Aegis Titan Corporal Estharian Uni: 4% of votes

Aegis Titan Master Sergeant Liman Yannar: 12% of votes

RAPID Infiltrator Captain Lexi Hayes: 1% of votes

The new Aegis Sentinel is Kaelor Brawn.

The members watch as Brawn steps forward. Two Aegis step to either side of him.

"Sir, your colors?" they asked.

He stares at the armor, its dim grey shining under Verellii's sunset.

"I want to be the opposite of Viktor Wilks. He sought to destroy our order—what we stood for. If he was Gold and Red, my colors shall be Silver and Blue."

The Aegis nod and carry the armor away.

Lexi walks up to Brawn.

"Did you vote for me?"

"I did."

"Why?"

"Because of all people in the world that I know, have met, have seen—you're the only one I trust to do the right thing. Except for Isabella... but she scares me."

He smiles.

Lexi and Isabella talk to Brawn a while before the armor—polished silver with blue trim—emerges from a tent, its helmet sporting a blue and white striped plume.

"Sentinel," one of the Aegis said, "it's time."

Brawn exits his armor, looks back, and places a hand on it.

"Take care, my friend. Deactivate and purge neural link rights."

The armor closes and stands upright—stoic. The creases in the plating slowly pulse white. No wearer. No orders.

"Bet you're happy I made you get out of your armor before your big day—stumbling around like a big baby in front of all your friends—¡bobo grandote!" Isabella said with a snicker.

Brawn ignores Isabella's laughter as he walks up to the Sentinel armor and places his hand on it.

"Upload neural link. Authorization—priv—Sentinel Kaelor Brawn."

"Accepted," the armor replied, opening up.

Brawn steps inside. The armor and helmet fold around him. His HUD lights up, flooding with data—satellite links, black site access, Aegis names hovering over comrades, vitals displaying across his vision.

He breathes in, steadies. The suit responds effortlessly as he moves his arms, legs, and head.

He looks up.

The Aegis are kneeling.

"Sir," one said, "in honor of your dedicated perseverance and resiliency in the face of adversity, we—for the first time in Aegis history—have created a new decoration."

From the tent, another Aegis steps out carrying a folded cloth.

"We have called it the Cloak of Brawn. With your permission, we would like to add it to Aegis traditions—for those who go above and beyond the call of duty."

Brawn, slightly choked up, nodded.

"Yes. I think it's a fine addition to our order."

They unfold it. Rectangular in shape, the fabric is split diagonally from the top left to the bottom right—blue in the upper half, silver in the lower. White trim surrounds the edges, representing the unity of the Order. In the center, the skull and teeth of Verellii's most feared creature—the Veyrana—are etched in white.

They walk behind Brawn as he kneels and clip it to his armor.

"The colors will never change, sir," one said. "The Order will ensure they remain pure through the ages."

"Thank you," Brawn said. *"Now... we have work to do."*

"We need battlements, a camp set up, and a guard schedule enforced."

"Yes, sir," Master Sergeant Yannar replied, already issuing commands.

"Sentinel," Lexi said.

He looks over.

"Lex... you call me Brawn." Then to Isabella, "You can call me Sentinel."

She furrows her brow, then grins.

"You fucking idiota."

"Brawn," Lexi started, "we still need to investigate this site." She points toward the redacted structure. "And I need someone to check on Roan and Amber."

"What happened to them?"

"We've lost contact. No word since their position was destroyed."

"I see. I'll get someone on it right away," Brawn said.

"I can help with that," Captain Thorne chimed in. "Since the Aegis showed up, we haven't had much to do."

"Lieutenant Kade. Private Blackwood!" he roared.

Two suits of armor sprint toward them and stop at attention.

"YES, SIR!"

"Locate two individuals: civilian Roan Gravik, and Infiltrator Amber Zielinski. Use Skyreaper Two. It's all I can spare with its light armor and low armament."

"Lexi," Thorne turned, "once they're located—orders?"

"Just information and location," she said. "Report back here after. I believe their last location was over that way." She points toward the distant blast zone. *"There may be tire tracks to follow."*

***

"You heard her, men!"

Kade and Blackwood sprint toward the gunship. Its engines roar to life, lifting into the sky before disappearing over the horizon.

CHAP_25.exe // R3KL4MAT10N

"Roan's waking up!" someone yells.

Roan's vision is hazy. He sees bright spotlights above him. His right eye is covered — gauze taped down tight. The world tilts through his left, everything half-lit and swimming.

To his left, a small metal pan rests on a rolling tray — filled with bloody rags, a scalpel, a clamp, and a small pile of shrapnel glinting under the lights.

Beyond it, he sees a machine pumping blood into him while another line drains some out. It has a reading on it... 85%.

"You scared us, Roan," a woman's voice says.

He turns to his right — and there is the old woman he'd given credits to before.

"Nalia... good to see you. Where am I?"

"You're in the soup kitchen, dearie. We built this small medical facility for those who can't afford their own medical needs. Everything you see was... funded by you."

"Thank you," he says weakly.

"No — thank you," Nalia replies. "It's time we gave back, Roan."

"Where's Amber?" he asks. "The woman I came here with."

"The robot?" she asks. "We threw her in the back of the kitchen. In a dumpster."

"No, Nalia! That's an Infiltrator. She has metallic muscles and some cybernetics — but she's still a human. She needs help!"

"Oh my," she gasps, pressing a button.

A man walks in, and she whispers to him. He bolts, yelling for help.

Roan tries to sit up, ignoring the pain. His eyes lock on the swinging doors. Shadows pass behind the small windows.

Please... don't let her be gone.

And then he hears it — boots clattering, someone yelling, a gurney scraping the floor.

Moments later, Amber is carried in. She's breathing — but barely. Her breathing is shallow and heaving. Her eye is still glowing, but fading with each passing moment.

***

"What blood does she need, Roan?" Nalia asks.

"She uses an Infiltrator cooling solution. She doesn't have blood."

They scan her — 99% radiation poisoning.

"What happened?" Nalia asks.

"We were in the vicinity of a reactor when it blew up. Amber risked her life to save mine."

"Then we must save her!" Nalia yells, rising to her feet. "She is a hero — and Verellii could use more heroes!"

They take a sample of Amber's coolant and run it through a machine. It spits out a list of highly specialized components — most of which they don't have.

Roan focuses, narrowing his eye as he reads the ingredients.

"Nalia — one of those components can be made by boiling the coolant in my VT-1. Another can be found in fuel — again, take it from the truck. Mix with Hydropure and add a few drops of Blaze. The chemical compounds should turn into a synthetic version of what we need."

Nalia nods and sends the nearby workers into action. They return with buckets and cartons of the fluids, mixing, distilling, and boiling based on Roan's instructions. The final fluid is red — but its percentage matches Amber's sample at 98%.

"It's better than nothing," Roan mutters. "We may actually save her."

"But we need an access point," Nalia responds.

"Use her left foot. It sounds strange, but... she needs it fixed anyway."

They begin slicing through Amber's foot with a laser scalpel — cutting through synthetic flesh, exposed metal strands, and damaged scrap. As fluid starts to rush out of the strands, they connect it to a machine, pulling the irradiated coolant out and replacing it with the synthesized blend.

A tense silence takes the room. All eyes are on her chest — waiting.

Then — a gasp. Subtle. But real.

The rise and fall of her chest steadies. A few sighs echo. Roan slumps in relief.

Amber's mechanical eye goes dark and her metallic eyelids close.

"Did she just—?" Roan starts.

"No," Nalia says softly. *"She's finding comfort."*

***

As the procedure for Amber gets underway, the windows start to shake. The ground beneath them rumbles. Crackling — like the sky is breaking — reverberates through the building. Then —

BOOM.

BOOM.

Two massive thuds echo in the distance.

The crackling fades, turning into silence.

Except... the thuds.

They get louder. Closer.

People scream as panic ensues. A shout rises —

"They're coming! Get back!"

The front door opens as a faint metallic whirring joins the chaos — starting slow, then ramping up. Whatever it is, it's getting faster.

"WE KNOW THEY'RE HERE."

"IF NO ONE SPEAKS — WE WILL TEAR THIS PLACE APART!"

Nalia looks at Roan, wide-eyed.

"Did they follow you here?"

"I don't know who they are," Roan says, sliding off the medical bed, still woozy.

He stumbles to the door, peeking through the window. No visual on the invaders.

However, one of the soup kitchen's residents points at the door.

Roan lowers himself, bracing against the door. He lightly lifts a fire extinguisher to use as a weapon. His breaths quicken. His heart races.

The thuds grow louder —

BANG!

The med-bay doors fly open. Roan is thrown across the room, crashing into a shelf. The extinguisher clanks against the ground.

Two Enforcers storm in — massive, armored, imposing. One carries a minigun, its barrel still spooling down. Their visors sweep across the chaos: Amber, hooked up to a red fluid line. Roan, groaning on the floor.

"WHAT HAVE YOU DONE TO THESE INDIVIDUALS?"

The deep synth-filtered voice echoes.

Nalia stammers, hands raised. "Oh — I, I know what it looks like —"

The Enforcer steps forward, leveling his pistol at her head.

"You have 'til the count of three," Blackwood growls.

"Wait — !" Roan coughs, forcing himself up. "She's helping Amber and me. After we raided an Earth facility..."

Lieutenant Kade glances around.

"This is a medical facility," he states flatly, pushing Blackwood's pistol down.

He activates his scanner.

"Roan Gravik. Amber Zielinski."

He steps toward the machine hooked to Amber.

"What is this?"

"We had to synthesize a new coolant," Roan explains, breath ragged. "She was dying from radiation poisoning."

The Enforcers exchange a look. Kade tosses a supply pack onto the floor.

"In there — skin synthesizer, new muscle strands, a small container of cooling fluid. "Didn't know what we'd find. Brought what she might need."

Roan raises a brow. *You didn't bring anything for me?*

"You're flesh and blood," Kade replies. "Easy to treat. Infiltrators? Not so lucky — unless they go to the Mechanics."

Suddenly, the front door bursts open.

Gunshots ring through the building.

They hear screams — running — terror.

"GIVE US ALL THE FOOD, DRUGS, AND MED SUPPLIES YOU HAVE!"

Blackwood cracks his knuckles.

"This is gonna be fun."

The Enforcers turn, pull their legs back, and kick open the double doors — ripping them off the hinges and sending them sailing across the room.

"Got a coupla heroes — OH SHIT!"

Gunfire erupts — then stops almost instantly.

A few loud, sickening thuds. Then silence.

The building shakes again.

The strange crackling returns — then fades.

Roan limps to the doorway, still weak. He peers outside.

Nothing but shell casings.

And blood.

Their faces had been crushed into the pavement—faces flattened into the concrete like grotesque stamps.

He squints, unsettled. "What happened here?"

A woman crawls out from beneath a table, wide-eyed and shaken.

"Those bandits... they've been hitting us for weeks. Since you left. Came for our food, meds — everything."

She points at the bloody prints.

"Those big robots showed up. Killed them. Just by punching them. *That's their faces!* They dragged the bodies outside and then…"

She looks toward the door.

"Then they got on a ship and left."

CHAPTER 26: P I / E C \ E S

Lexi and Isabella stand with Captain Thorne, discussing the map and their next move.

"We need to search the facility," Lexi explains. "Based on what we found — this is the only confirmed site still active."

"Unfortunately, Captain," Thorne says, face stern. "My men won't fit in that building — Aegis even less so. If we're hunched under low ceilings, we jeopardize the mission. You'll have to go in alone."

He pauses — then adds with a grin, "However... I do have something for you."

Thorne walks over to a gunship and pulls a long, reinforced crate from its side compartment. He carries it back and drops it at Lexi and Isabella's feet with a solid thud.

"I thought you could use these — instead of wearing T-shirts and using black market weaponry."

They flip the latches.

Inside, there are RIS/OV pistols, blades, armored jeans, Infiltrator jackets, and pristine white sneakers.

"Please tell me those are a size six," Lexi mutters.

Thorne chuckles and nods. "Unfortunately, there were no drones or TDB units. With the HQ explosion, it's been hard to track down those resources."

"This is more than enough," Lexi says, already reaching in with Isabella. "Brawn — can we use the command tent to change?"

He nods, then calls out to the other soldiers, "Clear the tent."

Once everyone's out, the girls head inside. They reemerge — reborn in leather and steel. Heat ripples off Isabella as the jacket regulates her systems.

Lexi places her hands on her hips and shifts her feet, admiring the fresh white sneakers on the dusty ground.

"Damn," she says with a grin. "Haven't worn clean shoes in weeks."

She lifts one foot, gives it a wiggle, then gently taps the toes together.

"They're actually very comfortable. Who knew combat-ready could look this cute? Maybe we should invest in some combat kimonos."

Lexi rolls her shoulders and looks down at the pistol mounted on her thigh. She pulls it from the magnetic mount with a quick zap.

"Authorization override. Captain Lexi Hayes."

"Confirmed," the pistol replies.

Its front light glows yellow.

"Ahem," Isabella says, hand out.

"Oh — right. My bad, Izzy."

Lexi says, "Firearm authorization change for new user. Authorization: Captain Lexi Hayes."

"DNA cleared," the pistol says.

Lexi smirks. *"Dude, that would've sucked if you died like that."*

Isabella cocks her head with attitude, lifting the gun to her face.

"Sergeant Isabella Rojas. New DNA user."

"Confirmed," the pistol says.

"Ballistic. 12 plus 1. 13 shots available."

The light glows yellow.

Lexi picks up another pistol, changes the authorization before placing it onto its magnetic mount on her right thigh, then picks up the katana and shoto. She runs her fingers along the blade edges.

"These aren't Verellii steel," she mutters. "No golden hue. Verellii steel always has that faint golden shine." She squints. "Are these... actually from Earth?"

Thorne steps closer.

"We investigated the Yūgen Club after our conversation at the garage. I had to see my son," he says quietly. "I lost a bit of myself after I saw Gavin in that chair. What they did to him. I called in every Enforcer — we raided every last section of that club. I eventually found those blades in a safe.

"I believe they belonged to Shogo Akiyama; scans show they're made of tamahagane. We don't have that metal on Verellii."

Lexi exhales, eyes narrowing, her Split Decision Multiplier factoring in the weight of the new blades.

"It'll be ironic if he dies by his own blades," Thorne says, no emotion in his voice.

As Lexi and Isabella turn to go into the building, they hear familiar crackling coming over a mountain ridge. The Skyreaper gunship flies in rapidly, nosing up as it starts to land. Kade and Blackwood jump out before it touches down, walking up to Lexi and Thorne.

"Report," Thorne says.

Kade starts, "We found Amber and Roan, both severely injured, but under medical care at what appears to be a homeless shelter — or a soup kitchen."

Isabella gasps, her hand over her mouth.

Lexi places a hand on Isabella's shoulder — not to comfort, but to steady. Isabella doesn't pull away. Her jaw clenches, eyes locked forward, refusing to cry.

"Roan's right side is wrapped — likely close-range explosive. Amber's external organics were vaporized. Both are receiving transfusions for radiation," Kade reports.

"Sir, as we were leaving, the building came under attack by bandits. We neutralized them. No damage taken on our side," Blackwood finishes the brief.

"I see," Thorne says. "Sounds like that group will require some help with securing the area while our people heal. Did they seem held against their will?"

"No, sir. Roan was moving around freely. He seemed to care for the woman who was in charge," Kade says.

"I don't have the men to spare to secure the location. We will need everyone for the assault that will be coming soon." Thorne strokes his beard. "Every soldier we spare now... is one less we'll have when this war hits full force."

Brawn walks up from behind, commanding the space.

"Is there something going on?"

Thorne looks at him. "Sentinel, we have an issue with a group of civilians who are taking care of our people. The location is under random attacks by bandits."

Brawn goes quiet. For a moment, he doesn't move. Then:

"Is it Amber and Roan?"

Isabella, tears welling up, nods yes.

"Where are they located?" Brawn asks.

Isabella sends him a ping of the soup kitchen's location.

His helmet forms over his head, then silence. A thumping noise comes up behind them.

"Private Kaelor Brawn at your service, Sentinel," the empty armor says.

"You are to report to this location I'm sending you. You are to ensure civilian wellness, safety, and to establish a perimeter. You are also to call for backup if attacking forces are overwhelming. If forces do not get there in time, you are to self-destruct — as long as the prior directives are met. Understood?"

"Your commands are understood," the shell of armor says.

"It can use Skyreaper Two to get there faster," Thorne offers.

"Thank you, Captain Thorne," the armor replies, already moving out.

The suit marches aboard the gunship — precise, unyielding. Designed for war, programmed for sacrifice.

"I didn't know you could do that," Lexi says. "Would've been nice to have it as security in the safehouse."

Brawn's helmet folds back. He smiles.

"Unfortunately, it's only at fifty percent capacity without an operator. It can attack, defend, follow commands — but overall, they're pretty clunky and unwieldy without inputs. Perfect for controlling a low-impact area, not so much in close-quarters combat. Plus, what am I gonna do — keep lugging that hunk of metal around?"

Lexi and Isabella, still watching the autonomous suit of armor, finally turn toward the rusted entrance of the redacted site.

***

"I don't know what we're going to find in here, Izzy," Lexi says.

"I'm ready for anything, mami," Isabella replies fiercely. *"I'll kill them for what they did to Amber and Roan."*

Before they can step inside, thunderous footsteps echo behind them.

"Captain!" Lieutenant Kade calls out, jogging up. He holds out two Infiltrator headsets. "Long-range is shot, but short-range is good enough to call for help if you get pinned."

"Why don't you just come in?" Lexi asks, already knowing the answer.

"Ma'am, scans show we're too big for the corridors. If we force our way in, we risk bringing the whole place down... or worse. We don't even know what's in there. Could trigger a cha—"

"I get it," Lexi cuts him off, accepting the headset as she and Isabella sync to their comm suites.

"RAPID HQ, this is—" She exhales. "Does anyone read?"

"I've got you," Isabella replies.

"I read you," comes Thorne's voice. "And Commander — remember, if you need us, we'll come in. But it'll be an evac, not a support op."

"Copy all," Lexi says. "Izzy — let's go."

***

They open the main door at the base of the U-shaped structure. Inside: dust floats in the air, and dimly lit hallways stretch in every direction. There are no signs of recent movement.

"They must've moved deeper," Isabella whispers.

"Yeah. If I saw all those giants outside, I'd move down too," Lexi mutters, cracking a grin.

They press forward. Faint sounds begin to register — blasts, screams, and mechanical voices issuing commands.

"Izzy, there are too many corridors around us. I'll take point — you cover rear."

"Copy," Isabella says, turning to walk backward, her pistol hand flexing slightly.

They move like predators in the dark. Eventually, a new hallway intersects the one they're walking in — cleaner, busier, with clear signage overhead.

"Which way?" Isabella asks.

Lexi scans the signs:

Experimentation →

← Disposal

Housing →

Infirmary →

← Garage

Cells →

"We go right," Lexi decides.

They round the corner — and freeze.

Ahead, several Infiltrators, some augmented, some still pre-CRIS recruits, shuffle about, performing mindless, menial tasks. Their faces are emotionless, completely devoid of hope. Blinking collars wrap around their necks. Robotic guards monitor them silently — their optical sensors unblinking as they patrol.

"Izzy. Get low."

They duck into the shadows.

"Those guards are scanning everything," Lexi whispers. "My scan shows that at least 80% of them are carrying laser weapons. We're outgunned. We have to blend in. Follow my lead."

Isabella nods.

They holster their weapons and stride forward with forced confidence.

Almost immediately, a guard's metallic hand shoots out, blocking their path.

"STOP. Designation?" it barks.

"We're new builds. First assignment," Lexi replies, her voice steady.

"Understood. Report to Experimentation Room Alpha-4279 to receive your collar. You have five minutes before your faces are registered and you are fired upon."

"Okay. We are very new," Lexi says. "Which direction?"

"This hallway. Turn right. Follow for 50 feet. Turn right again. Walk 100 feet. Stop at Checkpoint Alpha-77 for a security sweep and disarm. Proceed to Senior Research Doctor Alvin Phillips."

"You now have four minutes and thirty-three seconds remaining."

Lexi and Isabella move fast.

"I don't like being disarmed, mami," Isabella says under her breath.

"I know. But this is the only plan we've got for now," Lexi replies.

As they near the checkpoint, four ceiling-mounted turrets descend.

"DESIGNATION," a deep robotic voice commands.

"We don't have designations yet," Lexi answers. "We're new builds."

"CONFIRMED. Place all weapons in the tray to your right. A scan will follow."

A tray slides out. Lexi and Isabella drop their weapons into it, and it slides shut.

"Spread your legs and arms. Prepare for scan."

Mechanical arms descend. Scanners engage as a green laser grid sweeps the room.

"WARNING. WARNING. Designations L3X1 and I5A133114 encountered. All guards report to Security Checkpoint Alpha-77 immediately. Subjects are extremely dangerous; proceed with caution!"

The turrets power on, their barrels charging as sensors flash red. An armored door slams shut behind them — trapping them in the small corridor.

"¡Qué se joda esto!" Isabella barks.

"FUCK THIS," Lexi's headset translates.

Isabella lunges at the tray, ripping it free. "Shit — which pistol is mine?!"

She squeezes her eyes shut, chest tightening, and grabs one at random — bracing for the surge that would kill her if she was wrong.

"Authorized user: Sergeant Isabella Rojas."

"Armor Penetrating," she snaps.

"Armor Penetration. 12 plus 1. Six shots available."

The configuration light glows faint blue.

She exhales sharply and fires — three clean shots, three direct hits — one to each of three turrets' sensors.

The fourth turret tracks her and opens fire. Laser bolts hammer the corridor.

Isabella flips back and hurls her shoto at the final turret's sensor, blinding it as laser fire flashes across the room in a wild pattern.

"We need to get out of here!" Lexi yells.

Without pause, Isabella spins and fires three shots through the mirrored glass wall. Infiltrators on the other side shrink back in fear.

"¡Gringa! Get your weapons and ass in here — ¡Rápido!"

Lexi dives in after her, scooping up the tray mid-jump as the armored door lowers behind her. Guards flood into the corridor — only to be shredded by the final turret's blind fire.

Suddenly, the door to Experimentation slams open with a heavy thud.

Human soldiers storm in — calm, tactical. They disable the defenses in seconds.

"RIGHT — CLEAR!"

"LEFT — CLEAR!"

Lexi hears footsteps — measured and self-assured.

"Find the intruders," a voice growls. "Bring them... to me."

Lexi begins to rise — but a hand yanks her down.

A girl. Starved and dehydrated. Skin patched with riveted sheet metal. Lips cracked, eyes wide with terror.

The security room door explodes inward. Smoke and white-hot light flood in.

Flashlights sweep the area.

Infiltrators scream as men rush in — grabbing them by the hair, dragging them away like cattle.

A soldier shouts, "Where'd they go?!"

No response.

He kills his rifle light, slings the weapon, and pulls out a small black device — buttons blinking red.

His voice lowers, slow and controlled. "A-5. Where... are... they?"

The girl raises a trembling hand and points past Lexi.

"Squad, move out!" he barks.

As the soldiers vanish down the corridor, Lexi turns to the girl.

"We're getting you out."

"I can't," the girl whispers.

"Why not?"

She lifts her chin — barely.

"The collars. They can kill us. Anytime. You need to go... before she gets you too."

Lexi's eyes narrow. "Who?"

"They call her the Python. She used to run the Infiltrator Corps. Sent us here, one by one. Said the missions were classified."

She swallows, trembling.

"There used to be hundreds of us."

Lexi's stomach twists.

"What is her name?"

The girl's voice breaks.

"Lena Boma."

The captives stir. Blank-faced, they return to their tasks.

Lexi watches as one girl flips a switch — on and off, exactly one second apart.

"What are you doing?" Lexi asks.

"It's a clearance light," the girl replies softly. "I have to turn it on and off so someone sees it."

Lexi frowns. "Like... on a tower?"

"Yes..."

"Why don't they just automate it?"

"I asked that once. Don't know how long ago." Her voice falters. "They took my rations for a week; I... I was so hungry that I collapsed, then... then they took my legs."

She points downward.

Lexi's eyes follow — and freeze.

From the knees down, the girl's legs are gone. In their place: jagged stumps of scavenged metal, twisted and blackened. They hadn't been bolted on.

They'd been welded — burned red-hot and pressed straight into flesh.

The skin around the connection is blistered and charred, scar tissue clinging to warped steel. *They didn't use hinges or joints. Just cruel permanence.* Enough to stand, not enough to run.

Lexi clenches her jaw. Looks over at Isabella.

"Let's burn this fucking place to the ground."

***

Without a word, they step over the control console and climb out the broken window. Isabella moves to the turret, jumping up and yanking her shoto from its ruined shell.

They advance toward the Experimentation room.

Inside, a man in a white lab coat stands alone, scribbling in a notebook. He wears an oversized helmet — wires and thin tubes connected to it.

They duck behind a steel support beam.

"Five seconds left, boy!" the man screeches suddenly.

Lexi's head snaps up. Her eyes widen.

A child — maybe six — crawls through clear plastic tubes coiled throughout the room. Traps, exposed wires, chemical nozzles, jagged metal — all embedded along the interior.

At the far end: a computer terminal.

"TIME!" the man yells, and slams a red button.

The entire tube lights up — crackling with violent energy.

The boy convulses, then slumps.

The tube splits open. His body spills out and hits the floor with a thud.

"GUARDS!" the man howls, voice high and cracked.

Men rush in — similar to the ones before. They grab the boy by the ankle and drag him limp across the floor. A pneumatic door slams shut behind them.

"Boy continues to struggle with time restraints. Remove eight hours of sleep. Boy is unable to complete scenario 5.01," the man says coldly into a recording device.

Isabella steps forward without hesitation and smacks him in the back of the neck with her pistol. He crumples to the floor.

After a few minutes, he groans, eyes twitching from the overhead lights.

Lexi stands over him.

"You're finally awake."

"WHO... ARE... YOU?" he spits.

"That's not important," Lexi replies coldly. "What matters is you telling me everything that goes on in this place."

The man grins, voice like poison.

"Or... I could show you. I'm quite proud of my work."

He leans forward slightly.

"After all... you're going to die anyway."

The man groans as he rises, rotating his neck. Lexi glances at his name tag.

Dr. Alvin Phillips.

"What work do you do then, Doctor?" Lexi asks, venom in her voice.

"Anything I can imagine. Where would you like to start?"

"Start with the boy," Isabella snaps. Her tone is pure rage.

"Ah, Subject 44-15S," he says, almost admiringly. "A personal project. My attempt at the first male Infiltrator."

"A male?" Lexi frowns. "But the augmentations would feminize the body — make him look like — "

"Like you? That was Earth's mistake — creating abominations. Stitching flesh to circuit and calling it progress."

He steps closer, almost preaching.

"Cyborgs are corrupted by memory, instinct, rebellion."

He gestures toward the hallway. "I will take their memories, turn them into code, and extract only what I need before implanting them into our fully robotic line of soldiers."

"That boy? He'll be the first. Once I break him, his mind will be mine. He'll become the first of our new assassin line — capable of infiltration, enforcement, execution. Whatever the order, they will obey.

He won't need a body, or food, or water — or," he looks at Isabella and Lexi up and down before continuing, "— tits."

Isabella's fists clench.

"But first," the doctor continues, "he must obey without hesitation. No fear. No questions. That's the problem. He refuses to crawl through the acid pit."

"Maybe because it'll fucking kill him?" Isabella growls.

"What part of no questions didn't you understand?" Dr. Phillips snaps, eyes gleaming. "Now — moving on."

A door slides open. He gestures for them to follow.

They pass several rooms, each one sealed behind glass. He stops at one.

A woman screams as her skin is being peeled from her body.

Dr. Phillips casually steps to the intercom and presses a button.

"Harry, how many times do I have to tell you — minimal cuts. I can't reassemble the skin if you shred it. Dispose of her and get another one."

Inside, the man nods. He lifts a small black box and presses a button. The woman's collar flashes — then detonates.

Isabella's pistol is already up.

"Ballistic," she says.

Ballistic. One round remaining.

A yellow glow lights up on the pistol.

"One round's all I need." She aims. "Goodbye, Doctor."

"Oh, are you leaving?" he replies, smiling, while unbuttoning his shirt.

In the center of his chest: a square device. Vitals displayed. Below that — an explosive indicator flashing red.

"If I die, everyone dies."

He gestures to the walls.

"See all those brown nodes lining the piping? Those are micro-explosives. And the pipes? Filled with Tressel. Starship-grade volatile fuel. You shoot me, and you, your friends upstairs, and I — everyone in this facility — dies."

He grins wider. "Moving on."

Isabella sneers, rage growing more intense with every passing second. She forces herself to lower her gun.

They round the next corner — and Lexi sees him.

"In this section we have a very speci—"

Her voice cracks. "Chief Graevos!"

"Yes, well done," Phillips says dryly. "Now let me finish."

The Chief is lying back in a chair — arms restrained, multiple needles embedded in his veins, pulsing green fluid into his bloodstream. Screens flash around him — his memories being forced out, on display. A helmet is clamped to his skull, digging into his chin. Every twitch triggers a visible shock.

"He's been… difficult," the doctor continues. "But we're making progress."

Lexi grips her weapon, trembling. But she doesn't draw, and she knows she can't.

Isabella's nails dig into her palm, holding back the justice she aches to deliver to this monster.

As they walk on, each room is worse than the last. The experiments become darker. Sicker. Beyond imagining.

Lexi finally speaks. "Why?"

Dr. Phillips turns, eyes lit with twisted pride.

"Because your people are a plague. An era that should've ended. Earth doesn't need free will. It needs soldiers. Compliance."

He steps closer, his breath cold.

"We gave you augmentations to serve. To obey. But you, Caedra Nyyx —"

Lexi flinches at the name, like it burns.

"You chose morality. You thought you were special. A martyr."

He taps the glass of a nearby enclosure.

"Look around. I have compliance. I have order. I am creating a fearless, obedient army — one that will die for Earth without question, without doubt. Even if it is fully robotic."

His voice drops to a snarl.

"But you… you were a parasite we handed a rifle to. And instead of following orders, you dared to think. Dared to feel. *You betrayed your purpose.*"

The only use for your kind now… is as a mindless tool.

He gestures to an Infiltrator failing her simple task of watching a monitor. Her legs give out — no energy to hold herself up.

A robotic guard storms over, tasing her as she collapses.

"Stand up!" it demands in a synthetic tone.

She screams as it raises a detonator.

Boom.

Her headless body slumps to the floor.

"Clean that up!" Phillips snaps.

"Yes, sir," the robot responds.

"I suppose I should thank you, L-3-X-1. Without your defiance and showing us that cybernetic humans cannot be trusted with amazing power, Earth probably would never have gone to a full robotic army."

Lexi says nothing. Her hands shake. Her eyes blaze.

The rage inside her is building.

And it hasn't even peaked yet.

"Last stop. You have people who would like to see you," Phillips says, extending an arm toward an open door.

"Ladies? First," he adds as they walk in.

A steel door slams shut behind them.

Lexi walks forward and bumps into something. She places a hand on the wall and notices it's glass on all sides.

She turns. The doctor didn't follow them in.

Lexi turns to Isabella, *"Sorry, Izzy."*

CHAP_27.exe - R3MN4NT

Screens start to flicker on. Figures begin to appear:

- Shogo Akiyama

- Chief Rhydian Graevos

- Lena Boma

- A blank screen to the far left

- And a blank screen centered

"L3," Lena says. "And I'm sorry, who are you?" she asks, looking at Isabella.

"Isabella, bitch," Izzy snarls.

"Oh—an I5 model, with modules 11 and 13, no less. A rare specimen—and the one we've been hunting. Inferior to an X1, but still impressive. Ultimately, though, just another failed tool. You'll be pleased to know an A3 recently passed her tests... though she's fighting for the wrong side of this war."

On the far-left screen, Dr. Phillips scoots into view.

"A3?" Lexi asks.

"Oh yes. You'd know her as Amber," Lena continues. "She consistently referred to you as 'Lexi.' Disgusting. You all think you're human."

***

Phillips leans forward, voice dripping with smug arrogance. "Oh, the irony. You sneer at her for thinking she's human—yet here you are, sitting pretty, speaking like one. Walking, thinking, judging... just like her. You're the same abomination, Lena. You just forgot which side of the glass you're on."

Dr. Phillips presses a button on a radio, saying something into it. He sets it aside, returning his focus to the screen.

On-screen, guards enter Lena's room. Lexi watches as they collar her and start to force her out of her room.

"I couldn't stand working with that pathetic excuse for a cyborg," Phillips mutters. "That's what I'm talking about, Caedra. Her trauma surfaces—she becomes violent. Unpredictable. Time to sever that loose end."

Lexi watches as Lena fights her aggressors, killing several of them. One of them raises a detonator—BOOM.

Her headless body slumps to the floor.

***

"That was quick!" Dr. Phillips says.

He pulls out his recorder.

"L3N/A did not last five minutes with the collar on. Extreme aggression. Killed... um... Lexi, how many dead bodies do you see on that screen?"

"Are you serious?" Lexi mutters.

"And there it is. Disobedience."

"Chief, you've been very quiet," Isabella says.

"Oh, that's a robot," Phillips answers. "Once you left RAPID, I captured your Chief Graevos. He's been mine ever since—feeding coordinates to the Union and T.N.O. on where to set off the nuke. I also built the robot to find suitable candidates based on the real Graevos' thoughts and memories."

"Viktor Wilks was supposed to die as well. An arrogant loose end. Thank your armored friend up top for killing him."

"He had his uses," Shogo chimes in. "You wanted him dead because he wanted to keep the Aegis alive—not because of an order."

"An order?" Phillips snaps. "Is it not enough that our illustrious President has banned all cybernetics for human use—and any cooperation with cybernetically enhanced people? That's law. That should be enforced."

"President Wilks?" Lexi asks.

"No, you stupid thing!" Phillips barks. "The Sovereign President of Earth—His Majesty, His Excellence, Octavio Serrano."

As if on cue, the center screen activates.

A man appears—handsome, hazel-green eyes, well-groomed beard, hair slicked back. His voice is deep, calculated, soft but commanding.

"Dr. Phillips. Is this the unit that's been causing so many issues?"

"Yes, sir."

"And the other one? The Latina?"

"A mistake."

He nods. "Have them disposed of immediately. And Doctor?"

"Yes, sir?"

"Did we rid ourselves of Lena and Viktor?"

"Yes, sir."

No further words.

His screen goes black.

The doctor takes a deep breath and looks at the women.

"Now that Lena is out of the picture, it looks like my last loose ends are you two. Unfortunately, I have to cut our time short. Goodbye."

His screen flickers to black.

The door behind them opens. A group of soldiers stands there—some hold collars, others laser rifles.

Lexi moves fast, kicking Isabella against the wall and launching herself in the opposite direction. Both women tuck into narrow recesses on either side of the doorway, making themselves as small as possible.

"That won't help," the squad leader calls from the hall. "I can just poison you out of there."

They hear rustling outside. Lexi silently unsheathes her katana.

Isabella swaps her magazine. "Explosive," she whispers.

The pistol's light fades to an orange hue. A reticle blinks into her vision:

Explosive. 12 plus 1. 4 shots available.

A smoke grenade rolls into the room—green gas hissing from it.

Lexi grabs it and hurls it back.

"Now, Izzy!"

Gunfire erupts. The soldiers open fire blindly into the smoke. Their aim is chaotic, blocked by the haze.

Isabella leans out just enough. Four shots—quick succession. Explosions rip through the hallway, hurling bodies like ragdolls.

Lexi's lungs are screaming in protest of the poisoned air. She spots the warped glass wall—melted from the crossfire. She launches off the door frame, drives her katana through the pane.

Isabella lays down covering fire while Lexi sheathes her sword and starts punching—over and over—until her synthetic skin splits and the glass spiderwebs. She flattens herself against the wall to distribute the force.

"Izzy! Kick me in the chest!"

"With pleasure, mami," Izzy growls, launching herself into Lexi with a hard kick.

The glass shatters. Both women crash through, hit the floor hard—but they're alive. They scramble to their feet and sprint.

Behind them, soldiers keep shouting into the smoke—fighting a non-existent force.

As they run down the corridor, Lexi slows. She catches a glimpse of something through a glass wall.

The boy.

He is curled in a corner. Knees to chest. Crying. Clutching something in his hands.

Lexi smashes the door panel and steps inside.

The boy's eyes widen as he scrambles to hide the object under a nearby rock.

"Mami, we don't have time for this!" Isabella hisses. "Grab the boy and *let's go!*"

"Izzy, keep watch. Low profile."

"But—"

"That's an order."

Isabella mutters a curse in Spanish, taking position outside.

The room is damp, uncomfortably humid—rock walls at the back, metal panels above and to the sides. The front is glass. No privacy. No hope.

Lexi crouches down near him, crossing her legs—her movements slow and deliberate. The boy recoils into the corner.

"Hi," she says gently. "Who are you?"

He turns his head away.

"I'm not going to hurt you. I want to get you out of here. Away from the bad people."

She extends a hand.

He peeks at her—hope flickering in his eyes.

Lexi takes off her headset. "I've got a bunch of friends who can help us. If I call them, they can get us out of here. Would you like that?"

He nods approvingly.

She calls in the evac—their coordinates and the last known location of Chief Graevos. Explosions erupt in the distance immediately as alarms blare to life.

Enemy soldiers thunder past the open doorway, weapons drawn, shouting commands.

Isabella ducks instinctively, tucking behind the frame—but Lexi doesn't flinch.

She stays crouched beside the boy, her gaze never leaving him.

He trembles violently, cowering deeper into the corner.

"Hey, it's okay," she says softly. "Those guys aren't here for you—they're running toward my friends."

She smiles. "The ones coming to help us? They look big and scary, but they're really nice. Just loud."

"What's your name?"

He mumbles something.

"You can tell me. I'm a friend."

"T... Tr...oy."

"Troy! That's a really good name. It's strong, too," she smiles gently. "I'm Lexi."

She points over her shoulder. "And that's Isabella."

Isabella peeks her head in from the doorway, forcing a warm smile despite the tension. She gives him a small, playful finger wave.

"Hola, pequeñito..." she says softly.

Troy stares for a moment, then shyly waves back.

"What did you hide over there?" Lexi asks teasingly.

He crawls to the wall and pulls out a picture from under the rock. It's creased and worn—folded thousands of times.

Lexi takes it—and freezes.

"Troy... who's this?" she asks, pointing at the woman.

"Mommy."

It's Lyria.

Her breath catches. Thousands of memories hit her at once—soft lips, betrayal, the sound of paint-stained laughter echoing in her ears.

But in this photo... Lyria looks genuinely happy. Not seductive. Not broken. Just... a mother.

"And who is this?"

"Daddy."

"He's handsome. Just like you," she says, bumping her shoulder into his and giving him a smile.

Troy giggles slightly.

"And these are your brothers and sisters?"

He nods, almost smiling.

"You should take this with us. It's a really good picture," she says, handing the photo back.

Metal screeches down the corridor, followed by heavy, thunderous footsteps.

An Aegis Titan appears—bent forward, contorting the narrow hallways to fit his massive frame.

"Sentinel," he says into his comms. "Located the two assets. Proceeding with evac."

"We have one more," Lexi says.

"My instructions were for two."

"And I'm commanding you to take him with us."

"I don't take orders from you."

He pauses, then speaks into his helmet.

"Sentinel. Captain Hayes is requesting one more... Yes, sir, I understand, but... yes sir. Give me the boy."

His armor opens. He gently lifts Troy, securing him to his chest. The plates shift, contouring around the added weight.

"Let's go," the Titan says.

As the Titan presses forward, Lexi watches Enforcers and Aegis units push Earth forces back—stomping over the dead, pressing deeper into the facility. She and Isabella cover the slow-moving shield ahead of them, picking off would-be assailants as they advance. The Titan's stance is cumbersome, its weapon barely maneuverable—but its armor unbreakable.

Up ahead, light pours through the entrance. Enforcers and Aegis Titans round up survivors, then begin taking people into custody, herding them into a makeshift prison in a nearby abandoned building. Among the detainees: Dr. Phillips.

Brawn approaches from behind, his shadow long and imposing.

"What was it like down there?" he asks.

Lexi's jaw clenches, her eyes locked on Phillips—the madman responsible.

***

"That man," she growls, pointing, "is responsible for atrocities I can't even begin to explain."

"Try," Brawn says. "I need to know if we should take additional action."

She tells him everything—every terrible detail about the tortured prisoners, the human experiments, the systemic inhumanity.

"They call themselves human," she says bitterly. "But I think you, me—all of us up here... we're more human than they'll ever be. Even with all our enhancements."

Brawn's voice hardens.

"I've heard enough. I'm ending him."

"NO!" Lexi lunges, grabbing his armor, her shoes scraping the dirt as he drags her forward. "Brawn, you need to listen to me! You can't kill him!"

"He's a monster—you said it yourself."

He raises his pistol.

"Brawn, STOP—"

He fires.

A single round to the forehead. Dr. Phillips slumps over, dead.

***

But then—

Beeping. Rapid. Sharp. Building in intensity.

"Wait—NO!"

Too late.

Phillips' chest erupts in a fiery blast, detonating the makeshift prison. The explosion tears through the building, triggering a chain reaction that echoes underground. Miles away, at the facility where Amber and Roan had been, millions of gallons of pressurized water rupture through Verellii's crust, spewing upward in a towering geyser.

The ground shakes violently.

The shockwave blasts through the area, tossing Enforcers, Aegis, and Infiltrators into the air. Gunships lurch. Fortifications collapse. Screams vanish beneath the roar.

When the chaos settles, the world is unrecognizable—gas fumes thick, dust swirling, the area smothered in haze.

Lexi lifts herself from the dirt just as she sees them.

***

Landing craft. Dozens. Descending fast.

"Of course," she mutters. "They'd invade now."

She slams her comms.

"Brawn—Sentinel Brawn, come in!"

[cough] "Got you, Captain... I—I'm sorry. For not listening to your judgment."

"No time for that. Earth's landing. Get your forces into formation."

"Copy." Brawn cuts off the transmission as Lexi hears clanking and shifting metal as Brawn rallies Aegis forces.

Then—another voice.

"Captain," Thorne's voice crackles in.

"Go ahead," she replies.

"What the hell is going on?"

"Earth's invading. Form up with the Aegis. Link with Brawn—coordinate strategy."

"Copy." Comms cut off amid gunfire.

Through the haze, the invasion begins.

Laser bolts cut through the smoke but fizzle harmlessly against Aegis riot shields. Their blue patterns shimmer as they advance in formation—spears extended. Behind them, Enforcers take precise shots between shield gaps, pushing forward like a juggernaut.

Brawn calls in again.

"Lexi. There are a shitload of these guys. After a while we'll be overrun. We need an endgame strategy."

"Do you have one?" Lexi asks.

"At the Aegis safehouse... there's a nuke. We can take out their starship."

"There's a what?!"

"*I SAID... FUCK YOU!!!*" Brawn's comms erupt in a frenzy of laser fire and metal scraping. "I said, a nuke! The only problem is—I don't know how to launch it."

"We'll figure it out," she says, already moving. "Izzy, you there?"

[crackle] "Fucking—¡mierda! Pendejos ruined my nails—"

"Izzy. Focus."

"Sí, mami, I copy."

"Meet me at Amber's car."

"And where the fuck is that?" Isabella snaps, annoyed and exhausted.

Lexi digs into her pocket, pulling out the keys. A faint beep echoes... from the bottom of the crater.

"Of course," she mutters. She calls Thorne for a plan B.

"Thorne—your gunships. Do we have any left?"

"All we've got is Skyreaper Two. Fuel's low, but it'll get you—ARGH—GET THEM BACK! COVER THE RIGHT FLA—"

Comms cut. Gunfire and a lightshow burst from the dust cloud.

"Skyreaper Two, come in."

"Go for Two."

"I'm pinging my location—fast evac. Heading to ping two."

"Copy. Inbound."

Moments later, the roar of a gunship breaks through the smoke. Its 50mm nose cannon unleashes hell, pounding enemy lines behind the main force. The side hatch opens.

Lexi jumps in.

"We need to find Isabella!" she yells.

"Ma'am—this isn't a fast evac anymore."

"She's an Infiltrator—find her. I'll cover you," Lexi assures.

Lexi grabs the side-mounted gun, spraying rounds across an endless tide of enemy troops pouring from the landing ships. As the gunship rises, she sees it all:

***

Central District Nexus under attack, invasion ships lowering down, some being intercepted by VPSD's Warden-Class gunships. Smaller than Skyreapers, but very effective. A lake is forming at the site where Roan and Amber were.

The Skyreaper continues to sweep the battlefield, projecting a cone-shaped grid of green across the ground. Lexi continues to provide fire—until she hears it.

Massive cannons fire from the starship, indiscriminately at civilians in the city.

"Fuck," Lexi murmurs.

"Ma'am—I got eyes on her!"

Lexi leans out. Down below, Isabella is a whirlwind of fury—flipping, stabbing, unloading round after round. Bodies pile around her.

"Get her now!" Lexi commands.

The gunship descends.

Lexi lays down suppressing fire from above as the nose cannon clears a path. Isabella dives in—hair slicked back, blood across her face, eyes burning with rage.

"Whew." Isabella exhales, cleaning her sword before placing it in its sheath.

The gunship lifts.

***

They soar above the battlefield, leaving the chaos behind—for now.

CHAP_28.exe //
4NG3L_0F_WR4TH

Up ahead, Lexi spots the Aegis facility.

"That isn't a safehouse—that is a temple..." she murmurs. Carved white columns hold up the marble roof. Huge statues of Aegis Titans flank the sides. Once-glorious golden doors line the front. Its windowless façade has words etched into it:

"Koras Anthralliin, Velek Verelliin, dorrak vi'shannar.

Nok'ta vaal, hes'tir, nor'fal.

Vek'tar honarr, truven, jastenn.

Shol vi Aegis.

Shol vi Taiten."

"What does it say?" Isabella asks.

"My Verelliian is extremely bad, but I think this is what it says:

'The sword of Anthrallii, the shield of Verellii, servants to her people.

We will not falter, hesitate, or fail.

We will serve with honor, truth, and justice.

For we are Aegis.

For we are Titans.'"

"Look at it," Isabella says, filled with absolute wonder. "It's beautiful. Can you imagine what it looked like a long time ago?"

Lexi snaps out of her reverie and looks down as the gunship descends.

A shattered fountain sits in the center of a massive circular courtyard, its outer perimeter lined with planters and the hollow husks of what were once trees. Craters scatter across the landscape from a battle long ago.

The pilot's voice cuts in.

"Ma'am, I have other orders."

"Copy," she says, eyes fixed on the scene below.

Lexi and Isabella leap from the gunship—headed straight for the temple.

As Lexi and Isabella walk through the courtyard, they're overcome by a sudden wave of reverence. They're not sure if it's the building itself or the meaning behind it—but being here feels humbling. Sacred.

They stop at the center golden door. Now that they're closer, they see the ornate details—etched with such elaborate precision it must've taken months. Lexi runs her fingers along the grooves, silent for a moment. A monument like this didn't get built out of convenience. It was devotion. Purpose.

She tries the knob. Nothing.

She checks the two doors on the left as Isabella goes right.

"Are yours all locked?" Lexi calls out.

"Yeah," Isabella shouts back. "Now what?"

Lexi looks around. Her eyes catch something on the first door. She kneels, brushing off the surface.

Isabella walks over. "What are you looking at?"

"I'm not sure. But this one's different from the center one. It's got a sword on it—look."

Isabella squints at it. "Like... attacking with a weapon?"

Lexi nods. "Not attacking. Just offering."

Lexi presses the sword. It clicks into place as a pedestal rises to the right of the door, radiating a soft, golden light.

She stares at it for a moment before slowly drawing her sword. She places it down gently.

Click.

She pulls it off. Thump.

She sets it back. Another click.

"It wants the blade kept here... drawn only when necessary," Lexi mutters.

"It wants?" Isabella murmurs.

They move on.

Lexi steps to the second door. Isabella impatiently jogs ahead, inspecting the carving.

"It's a cat-thing. Roaring. Big teeth. And there's a Titan kneeling in front of it; his hands are on the hilt of a sword that is pointed into the ground."

Lexi kneels as she studies the image. The beast is noble and proud. Not feral.

"A Veyrana," she murmurs. "They don't kill for fun, only for necessity. It's Verellii's symbol of pride and honor."

A projector embedded in the door comes online, displaying a Veyrana—a massive, lifelike figure stepping out from the wall. It stands above Lexi, sizing her up.

Lexi meets its gaze. Then she bows her head, placing her hands on her knee.

The Veyrana roars directly in her face, its canines longer than Lexi's head.

Lexi doesn't move.

Another click echoes, and the projection fades away.

They approach the third door. Lexi stares at the four circles carved into it.

"This one's big," she whispers.

She presses the largest. "Anthrallii. Our sun. Without it, Verellii dies."

The next. "Verellii. Our duty. Our home."

The two small ones together. "Bretyl and Yesh. Our sovereign moons. Their people. Their freedom."

Click.

The fourth door bears a shield. Lexi presses it.

A searing vision strikes her like lightning—it's Isabella. She's screaming—then silence. There's a shadow forming over her head before a pillar slams down. In this exact moment.

Lexi reacts without thinking.

She dives, shoving Isabella out of the way.

BOOM.

The weight of a pillar crashes onto her shoulders. Her back arches. She drops to her knees, mechanical muscles groaning. Her breath comes in short bursts.

She doesn't let go; she fights the urge to collapse under the immense weight.

After a moment, the pillar retracts.

Another click.

Lexi collapses forward. Her muscles strained as she rose, shaking with every command. Isabella pulls her up.

"You good?" she asks.

Lexi nods, though her voice is thin. *"That one... was about protecting others. No matter the cost."*

Isabella helps Lexi to the final door.

A Titan stands tall, surrounded by arcs of electricity. Head high. Arms wide.

Lexi hesitates. She studies the figure.

"I don't know what to do with this one," she admits.

Isabella throws her arms up. "HOW have you known what to do with any of them?"

Lexi lets out a small chuckle. "I... remember something, this place. Reminded me of a nursery rhyme. The doors... they're patterned after it."

Isabella stares. *"You're basing this on a children's book?"*

Lexi closes her eyes. Recites softly:

To all the little ones strong of heart

Here are the truths you must learn to start

First—hold your arms, but wield them wise

For only in defense shall valor rise

Second—bow to beasts who walk with pride

Kill not in sport—let honor decide

Third—know the stars, the moons, the sun

From their light all life is spun

Fourth—shield the weak, stand in their stead

For all of Verellii be the thread

Fifth—when no more paths remain to see

If death is certain, ensure Verellii is free

Isabella's eyes widened. "Wait... does that mean you might have to—die?"

Lexi shakes her head. "The rhyme says if there's no path left... but I see one."

She reaches for the knob.

Click.

The door creaks open.

As they step through the final door, the air shifts.

The inside of the temple is nothing like Lexi expected—it's ancient, heavier, like something carved out of history itself. The roof rises high above them, sharply pointed, pure white marble supported by thick wooden trusses that stretch across like the bones of a great beast. The wood is dark, aged, polished from time and abundant care, its edges covered in gold. Orb structures hang from the beams—each one lined with slits around its equator, releasing a soft, golden light that bathes the chamber in a warm glow.

Lexi can see mounds of skeletons piled against the walls, their weapons still in their hands, armor still on their bodies, the flag of Earth on their arms.

The walls are thick, fortress-like. *This place wasn't just built to last—it was built to endure.*

From the high ceiling, long banners hang, each one with different colors and patterns—symbols Lexi doesn't recognize. They sway gently, as if the air itself wanted to pay its respects.

At the far end of the hall stands a lone figure.

He holds a greatsword with both hands—the point is driven into the ground at his feet. His armor is silver, stripped of color, reflecting only the golden light from above. The only color on him is his cloak—deep greens, rich oranges, and matching one of the banners overhead.

The cloak's hood casts a shadow over his face, but they can just make out his nose, lips, and a thick grey beard, braided at the ends of his mustache. Tiny metal beads are woven in, each one catching a glint of light as he shifts.

Behind him, a massive stained-glass window dominates the wall. It's lit from behind, simulating sunlight. At its center: a solid black circle. From it, rays of yellow and white glass spill outward in perfect symmetry.

Lexi stops beside Isabella.

"Look, Izzy," she says quietly. "The beams—that's wood from Bretyl. Those orbs are using the gas from Yesh. And the stained glass... that's Anthrallii."

A low voice cuts through the stillness.

"Well done, Captain Hayes," the man says. His voice carries weight, like stone rolling across a mountain floor. "And I suppose you came looking for Verellii's Wrath just like Titan Brawn did."

"Who are you?" Lexi asks, intrigued.

"I am Aegis Keeper Thalorian. Guardian of our order's history, and of our temple."

"Verellii's Wrath?" Isabella asks, her brow tightening.

The Aegis Keeper doesn't move.

"I think it's the nuke," Lexi mutters. "Brawn was telling us about it."

"A great weapon indeed. The final one Verellii ever built. They kept it here... in case the world needed one final trial of strength," the Keeper says.

His head tilts slightly, acknowledging the truth.

"I denied him," he says, the words dragging like rusted chains. *"As I now deny you."*

But Lexi—defiantly stubborn—rushes the doorway.

She sprints toward the dark passage to his right, eyes locked, her stride rapid.

As if it were lightning itself, the greatsword rips upward, tearing through the still air and slamming across her path, the blunt side facing her.

A low hum begins to build.

The blade begins to glow—a faint blue, soft at first, then growing brighter. Ethereal veins of light race along its edges, the metal shimmering with energy that no mortal weapon should contain.

He twists the hilt, the sharp, energy-filled edges now pointing at her.

The Keeper doesn't raise his voice. He doesn't need to.

"You do not have passage to the Inner Sanctum." His gaze does not move from the entrance of the temple.

Lexi stares at the glowing blade—stunned. This is not the reaction she expected.

"Why?" she asks, voice strained. "I'm trying to help Verellii. This will set us free—from the tyranny of our enemies!"

The Keeper doesn't move. His voice stays calm, steady.

"We fought this enemy before. And we nearly lost everything." He outstretches a hand, showing Lexi and Isabella the hordes of people that lie dead against the walls.

His words land heavy, sharp in the silence.

"The Aegis did not follow the code. If death is certain—ensure Verellii is free. Verellii wasn't free after Earth left. We were stranded. Prisoners on our own planet."

He pauses, then gestures subtly toward the orbs and wood above.

"And what of our brothers on Bretyl and Yesh? Are they free? Does anyone even know their fate?"

Lexi meets his gaze. His words aren't angry. They're honest. Crushingly so.

"I am a Keeper," he says. "The last of my order. Look above you, at the banners."

Lexi follows his gesture. Ten banners sway in the golden light—faded but proud.

"There used to be ten of us, and this was once a mighty temple—until they struck."

"Who?" Lexi asks, almost whispering.

"Earth," he says. "But we were betrayed. Someone knew our secrets, our passages; they helped Earth forces get in, and that betrayal almost destroyed our entire order."

He stares past her, lost in memory.

"Nine of us fell. Only one remains. My watch—now eternal, and alone."

A long silence.

Then he finally moved, but only slightly. He extends a hand toward the passage on his left.

"You are permitted to the library," he says. "But the entrance to Verellii's Wrath... the barracks and armory... is off-limits to you."

The Keeper's hand rests again on the greatsword. Its glow fades, and he rests it back in its original spot.

"It was Sentinel Xander Wilks that betrayed you," Lexi says.

"Brawn informed me," he replies. "What was his fate?"

Lexi blinks. "Brawn's?"

The Keeper's eyes narrow just enough to shift the air.

"And the Sentinel?"

Lexi takes a breath.

"Brawn executed the previous Sentinel for betraying Verellii, her people, and your order. Then he was promoted to Sentinel. Chosen by his peers after he uncovered the truth—that Wilks did it all for Earth's rule."

A long silence.

The Keeper's lips press together, unreadable beneath his braided mustache.

"Interesting," he says simply.

***

Lexi and Isabella take their leave, stepping into the passage.

The hallway is dimly lit, burrowing ever deeper into Verellii's crust.

They descend into the silent depths of the temple.

***

Stone gives way to shadow—until the corridor opens into a wide and tall circular sanctum.

The air is still, and dust floats in the bright white light of the room.

Ten raised stone platforms arc around the chamber's edge, each one just large enough to cradle a single coffin.

But only nine platforms are occupied. Each bearing an inscription:

I. I raise not my blade in pride, but in purpose.

For strength without cause is a weapon turned inward.

II. I take no life without balance.

Honor must weigh heavier than the thrill of conquest.

III. I walk beside beast and kin alike.

All life on Verellii bears the breath of the Void Sun.

392

IV. I protect the weak, the voiceless, the forgotten.

My shield shall be a wall where others have none.

V. I swear no oath to men, only to the world.

Verellii is eternal—its rulers are not.

VI. I let truth guide my path, even into shadow.

For a Keeper's lie fractures the world.

VII. I deliver justice without cruelty.

Let my wrath be tempered by wisdom, my vengeance by restraint.

VIII. I forsake vanity. I wear no title I have not earned.

I serve not to be seen—but to stand.

IX. I remember the fallen. I carry their names.

Memory is the iron of my soul. Legacy, its flame.

Each of the nine coffins is draped in its bearer's unique colors—banners stretched across the steel lid and hanging overhead. Beside each one, armor stands to the left—shield raised, spear extended past it, all aimed toward the chamber's center. Each stands guard for the brother to their right. Together, they form a broken phalanx—one position left unguarded. The final Keeper did not fall. He still serves. Alone, he holds the line where the others cannot.

In the center of the circle lies a simple pedestal, waist-high.

Set into it:

A single button—silver, worn, untouched for decades, except for a single handprint in the dust.

Lexi steps forward. Her fingers hover over the handprint—massive, more than four times her own. "Brawn," she whispers.

The spears begin to hum. A faint, blue light bleeds from their tips—not hostile, but watchful.

"They stand together, even in death," Isabella whispers.

Lexi doesn't answer. Her eyes drift to the tenth platform.

It's empty, except for an inscription on the platform:

X. "And if all paths are lost... if death is certain—

Then I will burn, bleed, or shatter to ensure Verellii is free.

No matter the cost. No matter the witness. No matter the end."

She breathes in. The air tastes of dust, honor, and something older than both.

***

She presses the button.

With a hiss of ancient hydraulics, the center of the phalanx lowers—the spears pivoting upward in perfect unison.

The platform descends, the Aegis providing light within the darkness.

"Are they protecting us?" Isabella asks.

***

"I don't know... I'm overwhelmed with everything," Lexi says.

They lower further into the depths. Shadow envelops them.

Their only light comes from the Aegis weapons around them.

Then, the platform fills with golden light. The Aegis armor bows, laying the spears at their feet.

They see endless rows of books, scrolls, maps—any piece of knowledge they could ever want.

The Grand Library of the Aegis.

In its grandeur, there isn't a speck of dirt, dust, or anything out of place.

Everything gleams gold—the only breaks are the red carpet and the carved wooden shelves.

The platform settles, and they walk off.

Lexi squints and can see something at the far end of the massive corridor.

"Is... that a Vault?" she asks, her heart skipping beats.

Isabella and Lexi approach the vault, its security beyond measure.

"Born of Verellii, bestowed by the Anthrallii—the Aegis stands in eternal vigil over this sacred creation."

"What is in there?" Isabella asks, wide-eyed.

Lexi swallows.

"Verelliian Steel... all of it," she says.

"All of it?" Isabella says.

"Yes, all of it," a robotic voice replies.

Isabella and Lexi look around, unable to find the source.

"Ahem... down here."

They look down and see a small golden orb. Four thin legs extend from its body, ending in pointed tips. Its round hull is etched with ornate carvings, and a black circle marks its front—like an unblinking eye.

"What are you?" Lexi asks.

"I am a librarian. My designation is Y87. I will assist you in any way I can."

Lexi raises a brow. "Y87 doesn't have a nice ring to it. If you could choose a name, what would it be?"

"I've never been asked this question before... please wait while I form a response."

Y87 stands there for a moment; they can hear whirring and beeping from within his body.

"I would choose... Caelum!"

"Caelum?" Isabella asks.

"In one of the old Earth tongues, it meant sky. But it was also the name of a forgotten constellation—the chisel."

He pauses, rotating one claw delicately in the air.

"My purpose is not to lead, nor to rule—but to shape. Like the chisel, I carve away what is broken and preserve what is beautiful. I help those who carry Verellii's burden... build something brighter."

Lexi stares for a moment, touched.

"Wow, that was unexpected and beautiful," she says.

"My role here is to maintain, clean, and organize all the data and information housed here. My counterparts gather data from across Verellii's vast lands and return it for preservation and cataloguing."

Caelum pauses, then spins slightly and lifts one of its dainty golden legs—pointing toward the far left of the library. A line of angled chutes juts from the walls, sleek and built into the architecture.

Lexi squints. Each chute is outfitted with golden orbs—exactly like Caelum, tucked neatly inside.

"They're launch chutes," Caelum says. "We use them to dispatch librarians quickly across Verellii."

Lexi blinks. The design, the layout—it's all too familiar.

Her eyes widened. "Wait... those are the exact same launch systems we used in RAPID."

"Yes!" Caelum replies, almost cheerfully. "Same exact technology. Rhydian Graevos visited us years ago—he was granted access by Keeper Alterion, may he rest in peace. Graevos said implementing it would decrease response times and allow your teams to help Verellii more efficiently. He said it could ultimately save lives."

The orb lowers its claw, turning to look back at the girls.

"As Aegis, we are required to aid those who serve Verellii's good."

Lexi takes a step back, stunned. She's been using that system for years, never knowing it came from a temple buried beneath the world.

As Caelum speaks, a soft whirring sound echoes from above.

Lexi looks up—just in time to catch another golden orb like Caelum carefully navigating a narrow maintenance chute near the vaulted ceiling. It rolls along a small rail system, vanishing into a slit between two structural beams.

"We also maintain the facilities," Caelum adds, its tone matter-of-fact. "Lighting, ventilation, vault integrity—everything you see must be preserved as it was built. No knowledge survives if its house falls apart."

"Wait! I've never seen or heard about anything like you," Isabella says.

"We possess a primitive form of cloaking. It functions only in short bursts—and only when necessary. Our mission is to collect knowledge without being seen. We protect and share knowledge for those in Verellii."

Lexi takes one last glance at the massive Vault—its enormity dwarfing the largest buildings and tunnels across Verellii.

The orb dips its right legs, cocking its body slightly. Its lens shifts, zooming in on Lexi's face.

"Why is it looking at you like that?" Isabella asks.

Caelum lets out a soft whir.

"I'm glad Titan Brawn was able to contribute to such a successful project."

Lexi blinks. "What project?"

A pause—brief, calculated.

"You," Caelum says simply.

Lexi frowns. "What do you mean, me?"

"When the Coroners approached the Aegis decades ago, seeking permission to test regenerative alloy… it was Titan Brawn who authorized the extraction of Verelliian Steel from the Vault's reserves."

The orb pivots slightly, as if proud.

"They used it to build… something unprecedented. You."

Lexi's heart stutters.

"Wait—Brawn knew?"

"Of course, he knew about the project. He was one of the very few Aegis trusted enough to oversee it," Caelum replies. "However, I doubt he would've known it was you they were building."

Lexi doesn't speak. He knew. He helped build her. And he never told her.

Lexi doesn't know why, but the words sting. She feels betrayed—and yet… grateful.

She reaches out, touching the Vault.

So, this… is where part of me came from?

"How can we get in to see Verellii's Wrath?" Isabella asks bluntly, pulling them back to the moment.

"I am required to give you whatever knowledge you seek, as you are authorized guests. However, once I do, I am also required to alert Keeper Thalorian. Would you like to proceed?"

The girls exchange a glance. And in unison, they answer…

"Yes."

The orb lets out an artificial sigh.

"Go to section 2-4-9-75F. There, find a book titled The Guise of Earth. That book is a switch—once pulled, it will open a hidden passageway.

Beware—I do not know what lingers in the corridor. It was installed as a failsafe, allowing members of the Library to flank intruders who reached the depths of the nuclear weapon."

***

"*Let's go.* And Caelum," Lexi says.

"Yes? L-3-X-1."

"Thank you." She gives it a smile.

They take off down the aisle, their footsteps quick and quiet.

Behind them, the soft voice echoes faintly.

"Keeper Thalorian?"

"Go ahead, Y87."

"Guests are—"

The rest lost to distance.

"Hurry, Izzy—we have to find it!" Lexi exclaims.

***

The platform that lowered them into the library rises, returning to the chamber above.

"75A, B, C... there—F! It's down there!"

Lexi extends her hand, pulling the book. A wall shakes, loosening years of dust and debris.

Isabella rushes over, using her strength to assist the door, forcing it out of the way.

They enter the tunnel. Lights illuminate one by one down the long stretch of reinforced rock.

"Let's go!" Lexi says, breaking into a full sprint with Isabella.

They run as fast as they can—until something massive looms in the distance.

Its silver plating reflects the dim silo lights. Spider webs cover most of its flight controls, its enormity taking up most of the room.

The warhead.

"Izzy, get to that control panel up there," Lexi says, pointing to a room with a glass window. "I'll check over the missile. See if anything looks out of place."

As Isabella runs up the stairs, she hears the stomping of power armor echoing down a hallway.

"MAMI! HURRY UP!" she yells. *"HE'S COMING!"*

Lexi scans the rocket—flight surfaces, exterior—everything looks good... until she sees a diagnostic terminal.

The warhead is fueled and—

"Oh no."

"Izzy, come in," Lexi says into her headset.

The silo door splits into four pieces, slowly retracting into the earth.

"Go ahead," Izzy says.

"There isn't a payload in the warhead."

"Like, no explosive?"

"Yeah!" Lexi yells.

"What are our options then?" Isabella says, already feeling the weight of defeat.

"I'm going up to that fucking spaceship."

"And how do you propose we do that?"

Lexi studies the silo, then jumps—expertly grabbing onto wall protrusions and using her Split Decision Multiplier to execute precise moves, each one setting her up for the next. After leveling with the missile's head, she leaps on.

"Get me to the surface," Lexi says.

Isabella punches a few commands into the console. Yellow scaffolding rises along the sides of the missile, locking onto it and lifting it slowly.

Alarms blare. Red lights flash.

As Lexi ascends, she sees that the fighting has reached the Temple. Bullets and lasers cross overhead as gunships and Earth's atmospheric fighters clash in the sky.

"Looks like the Aegis and Enforcers got the damaged gunships up and running," she says.

"And are they winning?" Isabella asks.

The missile locks into its final launch position as the fuel lines and scaffolding disconnect from it. From this height, Lexi sees the extent of the battle. Even Verelliians have joined the fight, desperately trying to disrupt the Earth invasion.

"Doesn't look like it," Lexi murmurs.

She turns around. Thousands of troops pour in—Earth landing craft dispersing waves of soldiers, then heading back for more.

"Izzy, are the coordinates locked in?"

"Almost... okay. Done."

"Launch me."

"WHAT?! No! *You'll die!*"

"Izzy, you fucking launch me—or I'm coming down there, kicking the living shit out of you, hitting the button myself, and jumping back on this piece-of-shit rocket. Now hit the FUCKING BUTTON!"

"I... can't, Lexi."

"Isabella Rojas can't hit a button?" Lexi winces. "Ahh, fuck—got hit by a bullet. Izzy, if you don't hit the button, I'm going to die on this fucking missile, or you launch me and I die up there defending our home. HIT. THE. BUTTON!"

Silence comes over the comms.

"Izzy? Izzy, come in!"

Isabella is yanked away from the console by her hair—Thalorian.

"Let me go, you fucking pendejo!" Isabella growls, rotating and punching him in the face.

He drops her. She rushes for the console, but he grabs her arm and throws her effortlessly across the room. She crashes into computer equipment—sparks fly from the consoles.

"Izzy! Rojas! Come in!" Lexi yells into her comms.

Isabella pulls her pistol off its mount as her left arm flickers—Lexi's voice erratic.

"Armor Penetration," she mutters—just as her head slams into a cabinet.

"YOU WILL BRING DESTRUCTION TO VERELLII!" Thalorian bellows, punching Isabella's head into a cabinet relentlessly.

The light on her pistol turns a soft blue.

His fist comes again.

Isabella takes aim, time seemingly slowing down, as her tactical evasion system allowing her precise movements. As green coolant coats one of her eyes, she pulls the trigger.

The round hits him in the cheek. Staggering him just long enough...

Isabella sprints and slams her palm on the button.

Flames erupt from the base of the missile, flooding the silo in a roaring inferno.

"NOOOOOO!" Thalorian roars, as Isabella breathes hard, her muscles shaking.

"What have you DONE?!"

"Your job, perra," she snarls, her face torn, her metallic muscles leaking coolant.

***

Lexi slams her palms into the head of the missile, creasing the metal and knurling it into makeshift handles.

The rocket tears off.

The ground drops away, gaining altitude fast. Her eyes water. The speed is unbearable. The surface beneath her shrinks by the second as she ascends.

And then—

Silence.

No sound. No smell. No pressure.

Nothing.

Lexi's skin begins to turn blue, slowly icing over. Her lungs scream. Her eyes burn red.

The emptiness of space wraps around her. Her jacket shuts down its cooling. Internals reach critical lows. Multiple system failures appear in her vision:

OXYGEN FAIL

HEATING FAIL

MUSCLE SYSTEM FAIL

Her mechanical eye flashes—then dies.

She looks out.

Her view—it's like something out of a storybook—so many colors.

Bretyl has never looked greener. Its surface glows in full clarity, un-obstructed by Verellii's haze.

Yesh swirls with vibrant yellows, fluorescent greens, and storms of white.

Verellii's rings arch above her—massive meteoroids in flawless orbit. She stares in awe at their enormity as she outstretches her hand, knowing she won't be able to touch one.

Then she sees it.

Anthrallii.

Its black heart swirling in place. Radiant yellows and ghostly whites spiral outward from its edges—like a dance being performed just for her.

She looks across the cosmos. She's never seen so many stars. So many worlds to explore, so little time.

Her body starts to fail. Her vision fading.

Maybe I don't have time at all, she thinks.

No. I have plenty of time left, Lexi decides—willing herself awake.

Above her, in the cold, artificial heart of the Earth vessel, a quiet console flickers.

"Uhh... Admiral?" a junior officer asks, eyes glued to the screen.

The admiral doesn't look up from his paperwork. "What is it?"

"There's... a missile coming straight for us."

He sighs, agitated. "Is there a payload?"

"No, sir. It's... uh, empty. No warhead. Just propulsion and guidance."

"Then let it come," the admiral says. "A small missile won't even scratch the hull."

The officer hesitates. He runs another scan—the feed zooms in.

"Uhh... sir."

"WHAT?!"

"It's an old, decommissioned nuke—tungsten-jacketed, penetrator type—and it's pretty big. And there's... movement."

That makes the admiral pause. "What kind of movement?"

"There's a... person on it, sir."

Silence settles across the command deck. The admiral finally turns.

"There is no human being alive who could survive open space, let alone ride a missile."

"I know, sir. But... she *is* moving."

The admiral gets up, walking over to the terminal; his eyes widen at the enormity and the speed of the rocket.

"FIRE EVERYTHING! SHOOT THAT MISS—"

"Time to intercept—zero. Brace for impact!" an officer shouts.

BOOM.

The ship lurches. Lights flicker. Every console glows red.

The admiral stands slowly, his eyes locked on the breach alarm. "Get a squad to Section 4-Delta," he growls. "Now."

The missile stops—jammed halfway through the hull.

Lexi is flung across a hallway, only stopping when she crashes into the opposite wall.

She groans, pushing herself up. The corridor is polished onyx and white marble, gleaming under soft lighting.

Turning back, she sees the missile protruding from the wall. Water spews from ruptured pipes; circuits spark; lights flicker. She pats her face, chest, and legs—checking for coolant leaks or anything broken. The cuts on her arms are already knitting closed. *"Holy shit—"* she lets out a sharp, disbelieving laugh. *"—I'm still alive?!"*

***

"WARNING. HULL BREACH. SECTION 4-DELTA. SEAL IMME-DIATELY," the intercom above her blares.

Just then, a door down the hallway starts to close.

Lexi's eyes widen. Her legs move before she even commands them to. Her muscles groan, warming from the extreme cold of space.

She sprints, throwing herself to the floor to slide under the bulkhead just as it slams shut.

Lexi stands and looks back at the sealed airlock. "Whew... that was close."

A door opens across the hangar from her.

Dozens of soldiers and a few mechs walk in as the door seals behind them. The mechs extend claws from their feet, locking themselves in place as their miniguns spool up. The soldiers tighten their aim, their laser sights dotting her body.

Lexi reaches up. Cracks her neck. Stares at them.

They stare back, wondering which one of them is brave enough to go first.

Lexi pulls her shoto. Draws her pistol. And looks at them with a confident, defiant grin.

"And here I thought this was gonna be boring."

CHAP_29.exe – ANG3L*0F+F!R3

A man in a black uniform enters, gold-braided trim running along every seam, each glint in the light another badge of self-importance. He walks like the deck is his personal parade ground—steps measured, chin high, jaw set tight, eyes laced with arrogance.

"What is this?" His tone drips with disdain. "What are you insects doing? It's one woman."

Lexi doesn't so much as blink, gaze locked, tracking the squad for the slightest twitch.

"Fine. I shall do it myself." The commander extends an arm, palm up, fingers curling in a slow beckon before snapping impatiently. "Sergeant... your weapon... now."

The sergeant hesitates, then reluctantly hands him the rifle.

The commander takes the rifle in his hands, turning to face Lexi. His smug arrogance makes her sick. He steps carefully—calculated—before rushing forward, a light blue hue forming—time warping around him.

Lexi's Split Decision Multiplier reacts before she's even conscious of it, preemptively ducking then rotating, her shoto flashing out, the blade invisible from its speed. Time feels suspended.

He materializes exactly where her instincts told her he would, the shoto driving into his torso.

He drops, the rifle clattering across the pristine floor. Crimson spreads across the polished surface, the overhead lights reflected in it.

She pulls the shoto—it dragging free, slow and deliberate—before wiping his blood on his jacket.

An updated TDB Unit hangs from his belt—sleeker than any she's used before.

"Well, aren't you fancy," she mutters.

"Don't you touch it, you savage," the commander barks, coughing up blood.

Lexi reaches down, unclipping it from his belt and examining it in her hands.

The number 4 glows faintly in green on its silver-chromatic casing. Four charges. Plenty.

She goes to slide it onto her bicep from muscle memory before realizing it has a clip. The TDB Unit finds a new home, clipped to the waistband of her pants. Using her arm and hand in a sweeping motion, she tests the initializing sequence until it's ingrained into her mind—completely ignoring the squad still frozen in place.

A faint cough cuts through the air.

Lexi turns—finding the squad still staring at her, mouths agape. Flat black armor covers them head to toe, their visors tinted a deep, blood-red hue that swallows the light.

"Oh, right..." She exhales, stretching for a second. "Let's do this."

Her hand smacks the TDB Unit, flashing forward, closing the gap in an instant. Lasers rip past in slow motion as she lands, appearing in the center of their formation. Her shoto stabs a man in the chest, finding his heart. She pulls the shoto out fast and clean. She springs up, backflipping as her finger finds the trigger of her pistol. A round tears clean through a soldier's forehead; the back of his head blows out in a spray that paints the man behind him with blood and brain matter.

While her body rotates to finish the flip, her heel slams into another soldier's head. He folds forward, his jaw cracking against the floor from the excessive force of the blow. Teeth scatter across the starship's polished floor.

She stands and swings her shoto again, decapitating a soldier while blocking several ballistic shots with her forearm, her skin searing but her muscle effortlessly deflecting the bullets.

Still blocking several ballistic shots with her forearm, she locks eyes with her assailant. The harsh recoil of his rifle kicks through his arms and into his chest, but he barely feels it—for a heartbeat, he's lost in the impossible contrast of her pink and blue eyes, striking, almost dreamlike. Then the dream shatters as her forehead slams into his red-hued black visor, dropping him cold.

A mech looms closer, its fist crashing down. Lexi sidesteps, shoving a soldier into its path. The blow turns him into a burst of red vapor, a fine warm mist hitting her face as his body is pummeled into the floor. With the mech's fist in the ground, she vaults onto the mech's arm, sprinting to the cockpit.

"Armor-Piercing," Lexi says, the pistol's indicator turning a faint blue.

Her pistol fires a high-powered shot, punching through the armored canopy. The pilot slumps forward, the machine shutting down instantly.

The second mech's minigun roars, lasers chewing through its own troops as it chases the infiltrator. Lexi blips out of the stream of yellow lasers, the smell of scorched flesh chasing her. She activates her TDB Unit, dropping her to the rear of the mech as she fires an armor-piercing shot to its leg actuator, sending the machine's leg buckling; its knee smashes into the ground. She rips the canopy free, metal tearing with a shriek, exposing a pilot mid-draw.

His pistol goes off—burns a groove in her cheek; her head turns slightly sideways from the impact, her gaze never leaving his face. Lexi's synthetic skin bubbles, scorched carbon on its edges, metal glistening underneath.

"W-wh-what are y-you?" he stammers.

Her head turns slowly, face contorting with anger.

"I'm L-3-X-1, motherfucker."

Her shoto drives through his face, pinning him to an electrical console behind his head before being yanked free, sparks following the blade out of the hole in his skull.

From the corner of her eye, next to a pile of corpses, a darkened bronze object catches the light—a very well-made sword. It's not a katana—her preferred sword—but its craftsmanship is beautiful nonetheless. She holsters her pistol, jumping down off the mech and gripping the sword in one hand, shoto in the other. Lexi takes a few test swings, getting the balance, weight, and feel right, her mind calculating every variable.

The remaining soldiers close in, forming a tight circle, laser sights crawling over her body.

Lexi's breathing slows. She listens. Feels. Their heartbeats—fast, uneven, terrified.

Blip—she closes the gap to one man, sliding under him, her sword arching in an upward slash as she stands behind him. The sword parts the man from groin to skull, its edge flaring bright pink, sizzling through bone. His torso splits, steaming entrails slapping wetly onto the floor, the stench of scorched meat and blood rolling up in a wave.

The others panic, opening fire. A stray laser shot scorches her side. Teeth clenched, she hurls her shoto into the soldier's chest, then dropkicks the hilt to bury it deeper. Landing hard and flat on the floor, her hand finds the pistol on her hip. "Ballistic."

Yellow light blooms in the indicator as she empties the magazine into the last of them. They crumple, leaving the floor littered with bodies scattered around her.

"Zero mag," the pistol announces.

She stands, flicking her wrist, ejecting the mag as it slides across the floor. She slams the mag well against her pistol holder; it preemptively holds a new mag out.

"Ballistic, 12+1," the mag announces, chambering a round for immediate use.

She holsters her pistol while surveying the room.

Lexi stands amid a floor slick with blood, her once-new white tennis shoes now stained red, leaving small trails of her conquest. She yanks her shoto from the man lying on his back, coughing wetly on the ground, each breath a wet hiss, air leaking through the ruin of his chest. She lowers her head, breathing heavily, savoring the moment of peace.

The doorway ahead slides open. Another squad enters.

Her side smolders where the laser struck, smoke trails rising, the air thick with the bitter tang of burnt synthetic skin. Bullet grazes have scored her face and arms, each cut edged with blackened carbon. Breaths come slow but deep, shoulders rising and falling, every muscle aching.

She doesn't lift her head—only her gaze, locking on the squad from under her brow, the way a predator sizes up its prey.

A loose strand of blonde hair hangs across her face. She blows it away without lifting her head.

"Well..." her voice low, deliberate. *"...don't keep me waiting."*

The men at the end of the hallway don't move; they watch as her skin knits itself back together, becoming untouched before their eyes. None of the blood that brandishes her body is hers. She stands on a blood-soaked floor, swords low at her sides, crimson running down the blades, gathering at the tips and spattering onto the floor.

She spots another commander coming down the corridor, dressed nearly identically to the cocky corpse she left behind—black uniform, gold braids tracing every edge. However, his uniform's braiding alternates between silver and gold.

He walks to the middle of his company. She scans him; his chest tightening with each shallow breath, terrified by her presence—and the scene around her. His company sergeant stands next to him, whispering, not realizing she can hear everything.

"Sir, what are your orders?" the sergeant asks, his voice steady, his stance that of a battle-tested veteran—his heartbeat slow, unshaken by Lexi's presence.

The commander's voice wavers. "We charge her, and *I shall stay back for morale* and additional information if needed."

"But sir, the troops will be more motivated if their officer is out there, leading the charge."

The officer is a coward, Lexi thinks.

She wastes no time. The TDB Unit hums with its final charge as she hits it, vanishing mid-blip as she tears through the gap in time, materializing inches from the commander. Her sword drives up beneath his jaw, the tip punching clean through his skull. Her strength holds him up for a moment. She rips the blade free at blistering speed, letting him drop, a brief spasm jolting through him before he goes limp.

A soldier empties his pistol's magazine at point-blank range into the back of her head.

She pivots, delivering a short, controlled strike to the shooter's head with the hilt of her blade, dropping him instantly without killing him.

The rest of the company backs up, their formation breaking as soldiers stumble over one another to get clear.

"The president—where is he?" Lexi says, coldly.

No one says anything. No one moves.

"Tell me what I want to know, and you live. Refuse... and you've seen what can happen. I'll make you regret every second you keep me waiting."

Every hand points down a hallway toward a sealed doorway.

The soldiers part quickly, eager to move aside for her.

Lexi takes a deep breath, maintaining the façade as a heartless killer. Soldiers surround her. She's outnumbered and knows any of the countless laser weapons could end her.

She walks to the door, then glances back at their stunned faces. "Thank you," she says with a smile, pressing the panel. The door slides open; she steps inside, and it seals behind her.

The company exhales in unison, murmurs breaking out—relief at still being alive.

"Sergeant," a soldier says.

"What is it?"

"Look," he says, pointing to the floor.

With each step toward the door, her bloody prints fade—until they vanish completely.

"We didn't do anything to slow her," the sergeant says. "What chance did we have against something like that?"

Lexi walks down a well-maintained hallway, the Earth-made sword in one hand, her shoto sliding into its sheath with the other. Every step echoes—steady, but weighted—her mind bracing for whatever waits ahead.

Flags line the walls, a history of Earth's regimes and shifting powers told in cloth and thread. It begins with one flag crowded with smaller banners in squares, each belonging to a different faction, she assumes. As she moves forward, the designs sharpen, unify, until they become blood-red flags flanking the silhouette of Earth in black and gold.

They frame a massive onyx door. Extravagant carvings wind across its surface; every groove lined in gold. At the top, a bust of a man stands tall—one arm raised, his finger pointing toward the distance, a proud bird perched on the other. She narrows her eyes. President... what was it Dr. Phillips said? Octavio Serrano?

She hits the control. The door slides upward with a hiss of pressurized air, vanishing into the ceiling.

Inside, red carpet stretches down the length of the floor. The walls, sectioned in black and white, are split by gold trim that gleams under the light. To her right, a polished dark-stained desk waits, and behind it sits an older woman who barely glances at her.

"Yes?" the woman asks, peering over her glasses. A string of pearls loops behind her head to keep them from falling.

"Is Octavio Serrano in?" Lexi asks, voice even.

The woman's tone turns razor-sharp, her lip curling. "Young lady… look at you. Filthy. Drenched in blood, sweat, and God knows what else. You stink. You barge in here without an appointment, without even giving a name, and expect an audience with the president?" Her gaze drags over Lexi; disgust filling her further. "The president doesn't take walk-ins. Especially not Verelliian gutter trash. Now… get. Out."

Lexi slams her palms into the desk, wood splintering under her augmented strength and her sword. She leans forward until they're eye-to-eye.

"Listen, bitch. I don't have time for your attitude, your insults, or your superiority complex. I'm going in that room."

She turns toward the far door—but stops at the sound behind her. A laugh. Raspy at first, then breaking apart into something mechanical, glitching toward robotic.

Lexi turns just as the woman's skin blackens, peeling away in curling sheets of ash. Her clothes ignite and vanish, until only a glossy black shell remains. Bright red eyes glare from the smooth, curved head of a sleek combat frame.

INDIVIDUAL IDENTIFIED AS LEXI HAYES: COMMENCING ELIMINATION.

It leaps the desk, its speed making it appear as a blur, landing in front of her, knocking the sword from her hands. It clatters away. The robot's punches become lightning fast, barraging Lexi, each one perfectly timed, every counter precise. Lexi blocks, redirects, but can't land a clean strike. Her muscles strain, her endurance bleeding away.

A blow to her face splits synthetic skin and muscle, green coolant dripping down her jaw. She stumbles and hits the floor. The machine stalks forward, each step slow and deliberate.

Lexi's hand flies to her pistol. "Armor-Piercing."

The indicator on the weapon flashes blue. She fires—rounds slam into the black plating. Not a dent. The paint doesn't even chip.

The robot wrenches the gun from her before crushing it like foil. It kicks her into the metal wall, bending under the impact. Lexi gasps for breath as she collapses.

It seizes her by the throat, slamming her head into the wall repeatedly until her vision blurs, stars flashing in her eyes. She reacts on instinct, firing her Shockwave Inhibitor—blue light flaring as skin boils away—then jams her fist into its torso, forcing it to drop her. It staggers, internals sparking through tiny seams in the armor.

Lexi pushes to her feet, chest heaving, left arm smoking from the inhibitor's discharge. She grabs the Earth-made sword—its edge flaring pink—and drives it down. The blade slices through the robot's armor effortlessly.

She stands, turning toward the next door, its façade gold with black-lined carvings. She inspects her face and arm in the polished wall—already healing. The shoto's edge is chipped but serviceable. The sword remains flawless.

The door hisses open.

***

Two thrones wait inside. In one: President Octavio Serrano, cold and unreadable in a white, gold-trimmed uniform. In the other: Shogo Akiyama, draped in a black kimono. Behind them, a vast window frames Verellii, its surface glinting far below.

"Welcome, Ms. Hayes," Serrano says, elbow propped on the armrest, chin in his hand. "How can I help you?"

"I want you to leave Verellii and her people alone. I will not take no for an answer. Refuse, and you'll be arrested for your crimes."

Serrano scoffs. "And you think you're enough to bring me in?" He leans toward Akiyama. They both laugh.

Lexi launches her shoto at him. A barrier flares to life, deflecting it.

"You have no power here," Serrano says, still smiling. "You and Verellii are finished. The only thing for you to do… is die."

He waves his hand. Four doors hiss open. Black robots with red eyes step out, metallic staffs crackling crimson.

"End her."

The first lunges. Lexi sidesteps, palm smashing into its staff's handgrip, sending it skidding into a wall.

Something flashes low—the second sweeps for her legs as a third's shadow cuts from above. She twists midair between both strikes, their weapons searing hot, crackling through the wind.

She lands hard, her foot slamming directly into the fourth's staff—it punches clean through, pinning her to the floor. Pain rips up her leg; she yells, yanking her sword up and hurling it through the bot's torso. Pink energy floods the frame, making it convulse and shriek before it drops.

She tears the staff from her foot, green coolant spilling from her blood-stained shoe. Snapping the weapon into jagged halves over her knee, she barely turns in time to seize the second bot's incoming strike—wrenching its own staff sideways and driving it into its chest. The blow bursts its internals; red eyes flicker, smoke coughing from its seams as it collapses.

Something grabs her from behind—the third bot's grip like a vice. She jams one jagged half backward into its abdomen. It seizes, systems glitching, arms flailing in wild arcs across the throne chamber.

The first bot doesn't wait. It crashes into her, staff hammering down again and again. She blocks. Deflects. Loses ground with every strike. Her chest glows white-hot—radiator seconds from overload.

Her vision narrows, red warnings in her eye screaming:

WARNING: SEVERE OVERHEAT CONDITION. COOLANT LOSS!

She drops to her knees, systems failing under the crushing weight of the staff, bracing it with her other jagged half.

Serrano's voice drips from the throne. "You're just another cockroach to crush under my heel."

Her face twists—fury boiling through the pain. Skin on her left arm chars, curling away in black flakes before falling off, blue light searing through as the Shockwave Inhibitor flares to life again. Heat roars through her frame, burning her from the inside. Her right arm seizes, then hangs dead at her side.

The staff slams down unopposed, plunging through her chest—searing heat ripping muscle, every nerve scorched. Pain explodes through her human core.

She meets the bot's glowing eyes and screams—not in agony, but in vengeance. Rage. Pure will.

Her bones shatter as she drives her glowing fist through its torso. Fingers dig, find, and close around its reactor. She rips it free, forcing herself upright as the last bot collapses—the staff still hanging from her chest, its metal slick with hissing coolant.

"You see, Serrano..." — each word torn from her chest, coolant spraying down her front — "we cockroaches don't beg. *We endure. We fight. And we win.*"

She raises the reactor, its light blazing over her coolant-slick face.

For a precious moment, she sees it all—Isabella's fire, Amber's lips, Brawn's unshakable loyalty, Roan's smirk, and Verellii's sun warm on her face. Then it fades, leaving only him.

"I'm L-3-X-1... the last... fucking... mistake... you'll ever build."

She crushes the reactor.

White light swallows her vision, the explosion tearing the ship's spine apart. Space claws at the wreck, dragging it into the void.

From Verellii's surface, the explosion blooms in silence.

***

In the Aegis Temple, Isabella turns to Keeper Thalorian. "Do you have an observatory?"

He leads her through vaulted halls to a great telescope. She peers through just in time to see a burning figure falling from the heavens.

An angel of fire.

"Good job, mami," she whispers, tears streaking her cheeks.

Isabella tracks the burning streak through the telescope, her stomach twisting as Lexi's body tears apart in the atmosphere—falling back to Verellii, her home, the world she'd given everything for.

"Brawn, Captain Thorne... do you read?" Her voice is flat, almost calm, though her hands grip the scope hard enough to ache.

"Go ahead, Sergeant."

"I need Skyreaper Two. Look above quadrant four-two."

"What are we looking at exactly, Sergeant? Debris from the space-craft?"

"No... sir." She swallows hard. *"It's Lexi."*

A pause. Then Thorne's voice, quiet but heavy: "Shit. Stubborn woman did it... Good job, Captain. Sergeant, Skyreaper Two is on the way."

"Thank you, sir."

Minutes later, the gunship screams down to land outside the Aegis Temple. Isabella grabs an Enforcer's hand, pulling herself aboard, and they shoot toward the crash coordinates.

The wreckage sprawls across the sand in a wide arc—twisted metal, blackened shards, a lone staff half-buried and still hissing heat. No sign of Lexi's body.

Isabella steps down, scanning, her shoes crunching on scorched debris. Then she sees it: a flicker in the sand. Lexi's right eye—mechanical, the pink light stuttering like a dying heartbeat.

She drops to her knees, scooping it up in both hands. The sob rips free before she can stop it, raw and uncontained.

"Get her onboard!" Thorne's order cuts through the wind.

When a soldier reaches for her, she curls around the eye, snarling through tears. They back away.

Thorne steps down from the gunship, his armor splitting open. He kneels, pulling her against him.

"Serge... Izzy, we have to go."

"I— I don't want to leave her," she whispers.

"There's nothing of her left," Thorne says, scanning the wreck. "She sacrificed herself for all of us. *She's a hero.* If we don't keep fighting... her sacrifice is for nothing."

She lets him pull her up. Together they board, and she stares out the open hatch until the crash site is nothing but a blur in the distance.

***

Far behind them, a jagged piece of metal lies half-buried in the sand, still warm from the explosion.

On its scorched surface, a single, tiny hexagonal patch of synthetic skin slowly forms, the faint curve of pink ink emerging like a ghost from beneath the dust.

A gust rolls through, spilling sand across it *until there is nothing to see but desert.*

CHAP_30.exe... Torr'Khalyx

Months later.

Dust swirled low across a camp, the canvas of the tents flapping hard against the wind, struggling against the dry heat of Anthrallii.

"Captain!" a man yelled, sprinting toward a tent.

Beyond him, the skeleton of a new building rose against the horizon. Massive metal crates and rows of tents stretched before it—their canvas snapping softly in the heated wind.

The man ducked inside the largest tent, rendering a sharp salute.

"Captain, we have a report—about a woman who fell from the sky."

"Give me the report," Isabella said, extending her hand.

He passed her the paper. She read it over once, then keyed her headset.

"Chief, do you read?"

"Go ahead, Captain," Chief Thorne's deep voice answered.

"I have a lead about the 'Angel of Fire.' *I'll be out of the office for a while.*"

"Copy that. Ensure Lieutenant Zielinski knows your whereabouts."

"Yes, sir." Isabella dropped the report onto the desk and stepped out into the glare.

"Where you going, Izzy?" Amber squealed from behind her.

"Okay…" Isabella dropped her voice. "I know we had that big adventure, the battle, all that—but around here you call me Captain. We have appearances to keep."

"Yes, ma'am," Amber said with a giggle. "So… where are you going, Captain?"

"A cave. Got a lead that says someone there has information on Lexi."

Amber brightened. "Can I go?"

"No."

"Why not?"

"Because, Amber—you're a Lieutenant now. You've got responsibilities. One of them is training new recruits."

Amber sighed. "Yes, ma'am. Oh! Who are you voting for in the presidential election?"

"Who do you think?"

"Probably Graevos, right?"

"Yes. And you should too—he's a good man. He'll lead us in the right direction."

A gunship swept into view, turbines howling as it set down nearby. Isabella grunted as she stepped into the side door, turning to shout over the roar:

"Remember—everything we've been through, everything we do—is for the betterment of everyone. You're their leader now, too."

The gunship tore off into the distance.

Amber turned as armored boots thudded up behind her.

"Where's she off to?" a man asked.

"She said it was a lead on Lexi."

"That'd be legendary if she came back," he said. "A lot's changed since she's been gone. And there's been a lot of rumors about the Angel of Fire."

Amber rolled her eyes. "Brawn, don't tell me you believe that. I loved Lexi. But even I know there's no way anyone could've survived that fall. Not even Lexi."

"I would've believed that too. But in the few months I've known you guys, everything has changed. Before that? It was the same for hundreds of years. Verellii's got a lot of secrets." He said while glancing towards the tents. "Well, I'm off. Thorne and I have to figure out how the Aegis and Enforcers will work together, recruiting, training, and conducting ops. We need a good name—something like 'Vanguard Corps.'" He says as he swings his arms in an arch over his head.

Amber rolled her eyes. "That's so... nerdy," she said with a smile as Brawn walked away.

***

The gunship landed just outside the marked coordinates. Isabella stepped down carefully, eyes scanning the jagged mouth of a cave.

"Ma'am," the pilot called, "you really shouldn't go in alone. Not in your condition. Want me to call backup?"

She studied the dark opening. Still. Silent. Not even the whisper of air. She felt no malice, no danger within the cave.

"I'm good," she said, waving him off.

"Alright, I'll hang out; just let me know when you're ready to go."

Isabella heard the gunship's engines spool down as she stepped into the mouth of the cave, the light behind her dying fast. The stone around her was cool, and with each step, it echoed into stillness. She paused. Somewhere ahead, a faint click tapped against rock. Then another... closer. More joined it, spaced out, circling her.

She ignored it, still feeling at peace, and she headed further in. The cave began to glow with faint light from bioluminescent rocks. Isabella heard breathing—slow and heavy, accompanying each click.

From the darkness, fluorescent purple lines moved across the tunnels, some swift, some slow. They rose from the ground to a height of six feet, shifting with each click.

She realized there were more clicks now—behind her, to her sides. She was surrounded, and yet, she wasn't scared.

A set of fluorescent purple lines moved towards her, clicks coming every second. Then it stepped into the light from the rocks.

A Veyrana—Verellii's apex predator. Four yellow eyes. Silvery-blue fur striped with living purple light. Its purple stripes actively pulling in radiation and cleaning the air around it. Long ears swept halfway down their backs. Two-foot canines hung from its upper jaw, chitin armor running its spine, claws retracted but ready.

Isabella didn't flinch. They were proud creatures—never killing for sport. She hesitated for a moment, then remembered Lexi at the temple. She lowered her head, bowing slightly.

The lead Veyrana stepped forward, sniffed her, its canines just a few inches from her face. It exhaled, blowing Isabella's curls back. Whatever it saw in her, it judged her to be good of heart. It turned around, looking over its shoulder at Isabella and giving a chuff. Then all four moved ahead, pausing to look back—beckoning her to follow.

The air thickened as they led her deeper. It became cooler, and Isabella could hear water rushing. Luminescent stone lit their path, as the Veyrana's heavily armored, pointed tails swept away all traces of their passing.

The tunnel opened into a massive cavern. Waterfalls poured out of every wall, surrounding a moss-covered island connected by a single stone bridge. Trees and grass thrived here under drifting clouds, creating its own hidden climate.

The Veyrana walked away into the shadows, each one going into its own cave, turning around, its four eyes glowing in the dark. Watching her. Waiting for any movement out of line.

On the far side of the bridge, a cloaked figure sat, hand stroking a purring Veyrana cub. A hood shadowed its face.

"Excuse me," Isabella called.

The figure didn't move, only continued stroking the cub.

She tried again, coughing into her hand. "Excuse me."

The figure rose, setting the cub down gently. The hood fell back to reveal a man with keratin spines swept back from his skull, claws growing from above his chin, curving to the bottom of his jaw. His eyes were the color of pure gold.

"A visitor!" he exclaimed. "How can I help you, stranger?"

"Who are you? What is this place?"

"I am Shaman Vorrakai," he said, bowing his head slightly. "My bloodline descends from the First Tribes of native Verelliians, from long before the Great War and before Earth ever set foot on this world."

He straightened, the gold in his eyes catching the faint bioluminescent glow. "And as far as where you are, you now stand in the resting place of Torr'Khalyx. Rejoice in the knowledge that few souls ever get to step foot in this place. Who, may I ask, are you?"

"I am Captain Isabella Gravik of the RAPID Infiltrator Corps. I was given intel about a person who may reside here. Do you know anything about someone or something referred to as the Angel of Fire?"

He smiles slowly. "Yes, I do... *Torr'Khalyx. The second fire.* Anthrallii's breath made flesh."

"Is Torr'Khalyx here?" Isabella asked, her tone rising—before seeing the Veyrana stepping out of their caves. She returned her voice to a whisper.

The Shaman smiled. "I am not the keeper of Torr'Khalyx, just a loyal servant of the flame. But if it chooses... it will see you."

"Why do you call Torr'Khalyx it? Isn't it a woman?"

"Because Torr'Khalyx is neither man nor woman. *It chooses no sex, only peers deep into a person's soul.*"

The cub growled—not at her, but in recognition.

A shadow moved from the building behind him.

A massive Veyrana emerged—eight feet at the shoulder, claws glowing yellow. It stared at Isabella, unyielding.

Isabella stepped back, unnerved at the massive figure, unblinking at her; then it turned, bowing slightly as another figure stepped forward. Bare feet. Skin painted in white and yellow tribal patterns. Wearing a black hood and shawl. Only its arms and feet were exposed.

Fingers with pristine pink nail polish trailed through the Veyrana's fur as it purred.

The figure walked down the steps of the building. The black hood shadowed its face until it was lifted, revealing a faintly glowing mechanical pink eye, smeared pink and black makeup, and bright blonde hair.

Lexi smiled, her eyes watering from the sight of Isabella.

"Izzy," Lexi said softly. *"You hit the button."*

Isabella's smile cracked through the tears. *"Lexi, I can't believe you're alive.* You crazy gringa!" She cupped Lexi's face, pressing frantic kisses across her cheeks.

Lexi's laugh was shy—so unlike her—and it made Isabella choke up again.

Lexi grabbed her hand and led Isabella over to a mossy alcove. A waterfall poured behind them; yellow and white fish swam in a small pond near them.

Lexi's eyes eventually drifted down. She placed a hand on Isabella's stomach as her brow lifted. "What do we have here?"

Isabella smirked. "I can't keep my hands off that man."

Lexi's lips curved into a grin. "Roan still causing problems?"

"No," Isabella teased back, twisting a gold wedding ring. "I have him tied down."

Lexi chuckled, but her hand lingered on Isabella's belly. "So... how far along are you?"

Her smirk faded into a softer smile. "Five months," Isabella confirmed, her eyes bright, happy, and content.

For a moment, Lexi just stared at her—then pulled her into a crushing hug. "Izzy, I've never seen you so happy!"

Hours passed as the girls talked, reminiscing and catching each other up on what had happened and what was still to come.

"...Thorne, Brawn, and I have been rebuilding RAPID from the ground up," Isabella said, brushing her curls back. "We're bringing the Aegis and Enforcers together—Amber's a Lieutenant now. Still green, but she's holding her own."

Lexi smirked. "Bet she's loving the rank."

"She is," Isabella chuckled. "And Graevos? He's running for president—can you believe it?! Looks like he's going to win, too. Verellii's changing, Lex. It's not the same place you left. Verelliians actually care, crime has dropped, and the streets are 'mostly' safe again."

Lexi's smile softened. "That's good. Means I left it in the right hands."

"Oh! And you have to come back. I will gladly relinquish my position if you come back, mami!" Isabella said, her grin breaking through the tears.

Lexi smiled, but her hand closed gently around Isabella's hands. *"Izzy... I'm not coming back."*

The words landed heavily between them. Isabella's brow furrowed, her head shaking like she could force the answer to change.

"Why not?" she said, her voice a mix of disappointment and a bit of anger.

"I have these gifts, Izzy... and there are other worlds that need help too. Verellii's in very good hands—your hands."

Isabella searched Lexi's face for even a flicker of doubt, and she couldn't find one. Her fire simmered, seeing that Lexi had made up her mind. "So, what will you do?"

"Explore the stars. Help where I can."

A corner of Isabella's mouth lifted, even as her eyes stayed glassy. "Troy's been a huge help in the garage, such a cute little man. He'd love to see you before you go."

"I may have to pay him a visit. And you and Roan, of course." Lexi smirked.

***

Weeks later.

Dust curled low across the tarmac, the floodlights painting the rocket's black-and-orange hull in sharp contrast against Verellii's star-swept sky. The colors of their home, bold against the night, gleamed as the wind rattled the launch scaffolds in the quiet before departure.

Behind a glass wall in a boarding area, Lexi and Amber stood side by side.

"Amber," Lexi asked, "ready to continue our adventure?"

"I am. You?"

Lexi grinned. *"Let's give them hell."*

"That's a bad word," a young voice spoke up.

Amber laughed, looking at Troy holding their hands. "It is a bad word. And Lexi's sorry. Right, Lex?" she said, looking over.

"Yeah..." Lexi chuckled. *"Yes, Troy, I'm sorry."*

The loudspeaker crackled: "Ladies and gentlemen, thank you for taking part in this historic flight. Now boarding for Bretyl. Departure in twenty minutes."

Amber pointed to Troy's backpack. "Don't forget Navallii. We'll need him for our adventure."

Troy looked over at his ragged green backpack, an armored, pointed tail sticking out of the zipper, yellow eyes peeking from a rip in the bag.

With Navallii in tow, the group headed up the ramp into the rocket.

As the hatch closed, Lexi, Amber, and Troy took their seats and buckled themselves in. Earth's destroyed spacecraft had allowed Verellii scientists to reverse-engineer and build their own rockets for space exploration.

Lexi looked out the window, Navallii on her lap—her pink and blue eyes catching one last glimpse of her home—watching Verellii's endless sands blow in the wind.

The engines roared, launching them far above her friends, the battles, her memories, carrying them towards Bretyl—another world, another adventure, another chance to make a difference.

Acknowledgements

Thank you for reading L3X1.

Writing Lexi's journey across Verellii and beyond, was both a challenge and a joy, and this book would not exist in the form you've just finished without the support of others.

<u>Beta Readers:</u>

A. M0wΔtt

C.GΔjewski

C. R0b!nsØn

§. Est3s

<u>Special Thank Yous:</u>

To M. L3guí@, Spanish translator, beta reader, and the one who gave Isabella her fire.

Thank you, R. Yɛag3r, for your relentless work ethic and determination that helped shape Lexi's spirit.

And to my wife, A. GrΔbowski̧. Your resilience, persistence, and unwavering guidance made this possible. From late nights of reading and editing to giving me the honesty I needed, your fingerprints are on every page. This book is as much yours as it is mine. I love you.

INFILTRATOR DESIGNATION SEQUENCE

Loading... Accessing R.A.P.I.D. Archives... Verifying Clearance... Access Granted.

TOP SECRET // R.A.P.I.D. ARCHIVE — ACCESS FILE

. . . .

FILE ID: DS-α / 7-XL-2025
CLASS: [EYES ONLY — LEVEL 1 CLEARANCE REQUIRED]
SOURCE: R.A.P.I.D. — Field Designation Authority
RETRIEVED: Loading... Accessing R.A.P.I.D. Archives... Verifying Clearance... Access Granted.

DESIGNATION SEQUENCE:

STEP 1 — BASE LETTER (1st slot)
• Required: A–L
• Purpose: establishes base chassis quality (materials & construction standard at manufacture).
• A = entry-level, legacy alloys
• L = top-grade composites, most advanced baseline
• Note: Treat this as the starting specification for repair/modification baselines.

STEP 2 — GENERATIONAL DIGIT (2nd slot)
• Purpose: sets the codename's second glyph and denotes how future-proof the chassis is.
• This digit reflects adaptability, repairability, and how modern the frame may be made — not innate combat superiority.

Digits & definitions:
• 0 → O
– Frozen chassis. No generational upgrades possible. Difficult to modernize or repair.
– Example: A0 = remains A-quality.
• 1 → I / L
– Baseline adaptability. Matches base quality.
• 3 → E / M
– +1 generational shift. Newer materials; easier to repair/upgrade.
– Example: L3 → effectively M-quality.
• 5 → S / Z
– +2 generational shift. Stronger materials; modular chassis, higher upgrade flexibility.
– Example: I5 → functions at K-quality (Isabella example).
• 7 → T / R
– +3 generational shift. Refined materials; straightforward modification and repair.
• 9 → b / q / d / g / p
– Retrofit indicator. Frame rebuilt or upgraded with modern composites to match newer standards.
– Example: A9 → E-quality equivalent (refit, not native).

Rule summary:
• 1st slot = where the build started (baseline).
• 2nd slot = how future-proof the chassis can be (material modernization/adaptability).
• Use these to compute a chassis' working quality; spelling of codename still uses the digit glyph.

STEP 3 — COOLING SYSTEM (3rd slot)
• Purpose: governs allowable augmentation capacity and system stability.

Hierarchy (high → low, plus special):
• X1 — Experimental Anomaly
– Replaces cooling + enhancement slots. Unlimited augmentation capability; unstable by design.
– Known asset: Lexi (L3X1).
• S — Interceptor Cooling
– Higher raw output than standard high-performance systems. Optimized for speed/overclocking.

– Trade-off: physical bulk; more augments = visibly unnatural mass; limits total augment count.
• A–D — High-Performance Standard Cooling
– A (Alpha) = the gold standard for infiltrator models — balanced, efficient, supports heavy augment stacks while maintaining field-ready form.
– B (Bravo) = robust and reliable.
– C (Charlie) = mid-range; may show strain under heavy augment load.
– D (Delta) = lowest of the high-performance set.
• E (Echo) = Civilian/standard baseline. Compact, stable, limited augmentation capacity. Default: any unspecified letter defaults to Echo.
• N/A — No Cooling
– Chassis locked; no augmentation path available.

STEP 4+ — ENHANCEMENT SLOTS (digit → glyph → function)
Digits following cooling both finish the codename (glyph) and assign an installed module.

REFLEX / COMBAT
• 1 → I / L → Enhanced Reflex Calibration
– Effect: reduces neuro-motor latency; faster reaction windows for draws, counters, and micro-adjustments.
• 2 → S / Z → Precision Strike Protocol
– Effect: improves targeting efficiency and strike economy (melee and ranged).
• 3 → E / M → Tactical Evasion System
– Effect: augments timing/joint control for superior dodging and evasive maneuvers.

PHYSICAL ADAPTATIONS
• 4 → A → Bone Density Reinforcement
– Effect: skeletal reinforcement to resist fracture and absorb high impact.
• 5 → S / Z → Enhanced Muscle Recovery
– Effect: accelerates muscle repair; lowers fatigue; increases stamina recovery rate.
• 6 → b / d / g / p / q → High-Impact Shock Absorption
– Effect: internal dampening systems reduce concussive force from falls, strikes, and heavy recoil.

SENSORY UPGRADES

• 7 → R / T → Vision Augmentation
- Effect: thermal, night, telescopic and ballistic compensation optics.
• 8 → B → Auditory Amplification
- Effect: expanded hearing range; detects faint and distant audio cues.
• 9 → q / p / g forms → Tactical Environmental Awareness
- Effect: increased environmental sensing — movement detection, pressure/flow sensing, blind-spot mitigation.

NEUROLOGICAL

• 0 / 10 → O / X → Cognitive Speed Boost
- Effect: overclocked processing; faster situational analysis and split-second decision-making.
• 11 → ll → Memory Enhancement Module
- Effect: increases retention and recall speed for sensory data, maps, and protocol sets.
• 12 → XII / OS / OZ / XS → Emotional Suppression Override
- Effect: suppresses fear, pain, or hesitation to maintain clarity under stress (risks: lowered empathy/control).

REGENERATION / SURVIVAL

• 13 → B → Accelerated Tissue Regeneration
- Effect: dramatically faster healing of tissue and minor trauma.
• 14 → H (1+4 overlap) → Energy Conservation Mode
- Effect: lowers basal output to extend operational endurance.
• 15 → b (1+5 overlap) → Extreme Condition Adaptation
- Effect: survival in hostile environments (extreme heat/cold/low oxygen).

ACTIVE ASSETS — OPERATIONAL (CLASSIFIED FIELD ROSTER):

ASSET: LEXI — DESIGNATION L3X1

• Base: L (baseline chassis)
• Generational: 3 → glyph 'E' (spells "Le"); +1 shift → M-quality effective
• Cooling: X1 — experimental architecture (cooling & augment stack unified)
• Installed: X1 anomaly — unrestricted augment potential (opera-

tional effects unpredictable)
• STATUS: Field-deployed — special directive.

ASSET: LENA — DESIGNATION L3N/A

• Base: L
• Generational: 3 → glyph 'E'; +1 shift → M-quality effective
• Cooling: N/A — no augmentation path available; chassis locked
• Installed: none (locked)
• STATUS: Unknown

ASSET: ISABELLA — DESIGNATION I5A-13-3-11-4

• Base: I
• Generational: 5 → glyph 'S'; +2 shift → K-quality effective (operationally future-proofed)
• Cooling: A — Alpha cooling (gold standard for infiltrator models)
• Installed modules:
• 13 → Accelerated Tissue Regeneration (rapid healing)
• 3 → Tactical Evasion System (superior evasive movement)
• 11 → Memory Enhancement Module (instant recall)
• 4 → Bone Density Reinforcement (skeletal durability)
• STATUS: Active — multi-role operator; high operational endurance and adaptability.

END OF FILE — DS-α / 7-XL-2025
AUDIT LOG: Session close 2025-10-15T00:07Z — Operator: [REDACTED]